A PROPHECY OF UNDONE
THE BORNBANE SERIES
BOOK TWO

I.A. TAKERIAN

VEILED SECRETS. DEADLY SHADOWS.
THE LAST WHISPERS OF DESTINY.

A
PROPHECY
OF
UNDONE

THE BORNBANE SERIES

I.A. TAKERIAN

This is a work of fiction. The characters, incidents, and dialogues are products of the author's imagination and are not to be construed as real. Any resemblance to actual events or persons, living or dead, is entirely coincidental.

Copyright © 2023 by I.A. Takerian

All rights reserved. No part of this book may be reproduced in any form or by any electronic or mechanical means, including information storage and retrieval systems, without written permission from the author, except for the use of brief quotations in a book review.

Cover Art by Moonpress.com

Edited by Samantha Swart

Maps drawn by Rachael Ward

Chapter headings drawn by Etheric Tales

ISBN: 9798378329014

ACKNOWLEDGMENTS

To those who were consumed in the fires of life
To the shades of death that followed
To every new incarnation of yourself that stood from those
ashes
Hope can conquer all

PROLOGUE

Deep within Castle Delinval

Adrian had only gone this far into the inner sanctum once before. It had been to escort Mara on her thirteenth birthday; to stand before the nobles and take her official title as heir to the throne. She had been petrified to go, knowing how hated she was by much of her uncle's court. In her panic on the day of the ceremony, she had downright refused. Refused, unless Adrian, and Adrian alone, be there to walk by her side. His father had threatened him against the request, seeing as it was a break in tradition.

Adrian had done so willingly, happily. As one *should* do for someone they loved.

But now, here he stood, cold and alone. No princess with a shaking hand to hold for him to remind to walk with her head held high. It was only Adrian, heart pounding in fear and fury, standing in the candlelit shadows of the inner sanctum. He had burst in only a few short hours earlier, blind with wrath and bloodlust, demanding he be

I.A. TAKERIAN

released to save their princess, *his* princess. His sword was still clutched at his side, his fingers wringing across the metal anxiously as he waited.

He would never forget those final moments. The royal guard at the end of her hallway, standing amongst the discarded, groaning bodies of their comrades. Adrian rushed forward, forcing his way to the front to stare wide eyed into the room. Framed in the window, holding a terrified and bound Mara so close that Adrian wanted nothing more than to cleave his arms from his body, was a Dread. Magick runes across his skin gleaming a sinister shade of white; his eyes fueled by a blue glow that existed nowhere in nature. And beyond it all, he had locked eyes with Adrian.

And he had smiled before throwing himself and Adrian's heart from the window.

Adrian had screamed, rushing to the sill with arms outstretched. But it was too late. By magick, no doubt, the invaders had landed safely with their prize. A second man placed his hands on the untouched skin of Princess Mara. He threw her, kicking and screaming against her bindings, atop his dirty shoulder. They were off before Delinval knew what hit it.

Adrian had turned and rushed straight to the inner sanctum from there. When he burst through the doors it was to find Lord Lingrain and his battalion already knelt at the feet of King Grathiel.

They went silent, the guards on either side of the doors drawing their weapons on Adrian.

King Grathiel, clad in his night robes and looking eerily calm, raised his hand for them to lower their weapons.

He looked sadly at Adrian. "My dear boy. I knew you'd come."

A PROPHECY OF UNDONE

"They took her," Adrian choked out, forgoing all etiquette. "Mara. She's gone. You have to let me go after her."

King Grathiel took a very deep breath. "Allow me to finish issuing my first orders, Adrian. And then we shall speak. Lingrain…" He motioned for the man and his party to rise and follow him to an anti-chamber. The door clicked shut behind them, and Adrian was left to his thoughts in the desperate silence.

His mind was already racing with stratagem. He was arguably one of the most powerful swordsmen in all of Delinval. If it weren't for Mara, the title most certainly would have been his. His heart felt strangled, crippled at its own mention of her name. Even with all his strength, all his agility…magick was magick. He'd been too young to remember the war, but he'd heard every story from the elder knights. Every noble, every city maid and merchant of mid-age had a horror story from the battles that took place. What good would his silver and steel have against monsters who wielded the supernatural?

But these odds meant nothing to him. For Mara, he'd fight the Zenoths of old. For Mara, he'd fucking win.

The door to the anti-chamber finally opened, and King Grathiel strode into the room alone. Adrian knelt to the marble floor; head bowed in show of respect.

King Grathiel sighed. "Please. Stand. It is only you and I now, Adrian. Good as family."

Adrian rose slowly from the ground. "My King. I ask you again, release me on your orders. I will go alone, if I must. But let me go after her." Adrian was barely a knight, freshly appointed. He had no right to ask this. And if the King commanded he stay put…Well, then Adrian would give up every ounce of his nobility and take off after Mara anyway. It made his stomach clench painfully to think of

I.A. TAKERIAN

how terrified she must be. For she was surely waiting for him to be the one to do so.

King Grathiel was staring at him with an appraising look. "Do you know who attacked us, my boy?"

Adrian's jaw clenched as he remembered the smiling face of the bastard in the window. "Dreads, My King."

"And as such, you must also know they use the forbidden magicks."

"Yes, My King."

"Do you truly think you stand a chance against such atrocities, Adrian?" King Grathiel had asked it softly, sounding more like a father than Adrian's ever had.

He had spoken the very thing Adrian had just been contemplating. There was silence for a long moment. Then Adrian held his chin high, eyes flashing with promise. "I will save her. She's...Mara is everything to me." His voice broke. "And I would lay down my life if it meant her safe return."

King Grathiel was studying his face once more. "Hmm. I believe you. I've had that same look in my eyes, the same fire in my heart, for a woman once. It truly is an unstoppable force. Yes...Yes, I think I can give you what you need to fight these Dreads, Adrian." He pulled a small vial from the inside of his robes, hanging from his neck by a golden chain. The vial was made of black metal that seemed to be pulsing. Pulsing with magick.

Adrian took a step back on instinct. "What in the End of All is that?"

King Grathiel shook the bottle, and it emitted a strange jingling, like that of many bells. "This is something I keep very close to my heart. It helped us to win the Great War so many years ago. A gift to me, from a very dear friend." He looked up at Adrian, his eyes narrowed. "Sometimes, Adrian...Sometimes one must fight fire with fire."

"What are you saying?"

"You mean what am I *offering*." He held the vial out towards Adrian. "I am offering you a chance, my boy. By infusing yourself with magick, you could best those Dreads. They'll never see it coming."

Adrian stared at the softly pulsing vial but did not take it. "You are suggesting I corrupt myself…?" All Adrian knew of magick was evil. It was a destructive force that changed all it touched, for the worse.

But King Grathiel was shaking his head, offering Adrian a warm smile. "No. No, I think you possess exactly what you need to fight such a transformation. You are driven by *love*."

Adrian's heart hammered at this, taking the bottle gingerly from the king's hand.

King Grathiel held his arms wide. "Bring her home, Adrian. Bring her home, and I promise you, you will have her hand, just as you desire. You are the only one who could save her, and the only one meant to have her."

And this was the final words Adrian needed to hear. He saw Mara's smiling face in his mind, an image that was all but permanently engrained there. What better way to prove his true feelings for her than to prove how pure his love was for her. He could fight the darkness in the magick; could harness it and use it against his enemies. He popped the cork to the vial, ignoring the strange whispers that seemed to emit from it, and raising it slowly to his lips.

I'm coming, Mara. Just hold on. I'm coming.

CHAPTER 1
HOME

The sound of rustling leaves broke through the cloud of darkness. Mara scrunched her nose, smelling cinnamon and pine trees, fresh bread and salty air. The scents of the Hidden Village. Mara groaned, eyelids fluttering open. Everything on her body ached. It felt like she had been in a battle, one that she brutally lost. The sunlight, bright and unfiltered, was overwhelming. Mara squinted against it, blinking furiously to make out her surroundings.

She was lying in a small bed next to a window that took up most of the wall. The shutters had been pulled open, the wind brushing against her onyx curls. There were thousands of glittering potion bottles adorning the walls. Mara knew this place. She was in the healer's hut back home.

Home.

Her heart gave an anxious tremble at the word. Every event that had happened over the last month began to play back in her head. And with it came a renewed wave of exhaustion. It felt unreal, like something she had read

I.A. TAKERIAN

in a storybook rather than lived through. Footsteps resounded suddenly, and the door to Mara's room was thrown open.

Cyfrin filled the entrance, massive bags under his impossibly blue eyes. His skin looked paler than she remembered, his lips pulled into a tense line. They stared at each other in silence. Then Cyfrin's face split into a radiant smile.

"Welcome back, Dawnbringer." Relief ached in his voice, his rune tattoos pulsing bright.

"Move your ass. You're not the only one in the room, Cyfrin," Caerani's voice came in over his shoulder, commanding as she gave him a little shove. Cyfrin glared back at her, taking his place at the foot of Mara's bed.

The room was filled in an instant. Drake and Caerani entered first, looking as relieved as Cyfrin, and just as exhausted. El and Kain entered next, beaming at her. El had tear-stained trails running down her cheeks but gave Mara two thumbs up. Milios followed at the rear, squeezing into the room, and escorting a woman with them.

"Elise!" Mara cried as her friend hobbled into the room, supported by Milios.

She had bandages running down the length of her right leg. What looked like thick leaves had been stuffed into the wrappings. The wounds on her arms, head, and face had been bandaged as well. She flashed a dazzling smile at Mara. "I cannot believe you carried me for three entire days!" Tears welled in her eyes, the smile fading. "Even more so, I cannot believe you didn't tell me you got scratched by that Vikefo."

Mara had almost forgotten about her wound, swept up in the moment. Her hand drifted down to a large, bulging bandage at her side. She winced. "Ah, is that what it was

A PROPHECY OF UNDONE

called?" She returned Elise's cold stare with an apologetic smile.

Elise looked unamused. "Vikefos were created by failed Forest Dweller magicks. A combination of poisoned plant and magicked beast. Their venom is deadly, Mara. I don't want to think what would have happened if Cyfrin and Milios hadn't arrived when they did."

Mara cringed away from the bite in her tone. "There was nothing we could have done about it, even if I had told you! Filigro and his sheep took our flares when they raided our camp." Mara's eyes went wide as she said it. She took a sharp intake of breath, turning to Caerani. "He ambushed us, that bastard! Said he was going to kill me to open the way to the crown!"

"Ay, but you told him all about himself, didn't you?" Drake said, winking.

Caerani smirked at her. "Elise told us everything. From the sounds of it, you handled Filigro the way any of us would. A traitor to the crown is a traitor to us all."

Mara could see both Kain and Cyfrin looking at her with glowing pride. *Their little warrior, felling an enemy.* She smiled bashfully back at them, but the remaining fog around her memory was dimming. And the image of the One Who Sees All flashed across her mind.

Her eyebrows drew together in anger, fury wracking her voice. "There was something that happened while Elise was sleeping one night. Something I never told her."

The energy in the room shifted. Cyfrin, Caerani, and Drake all pulled away from her instinctively, Elise staring with her mouth slightly open. Mara fixed her burning gaze on Caerani. "Tell me about the Prophecy of Undone."

The room fell into petrified silence. Mara felt a pang of disappointment as every person in the room drew in a sharp breath. *So, they* all *knew then,* she thought, gritting her teeth and clenching down till her jaw throbbed from the pressure.

Caerani shook her head, looking down at her feet. "I suppose it was foolish of me to try and keep it from you. I just...we had already placed a lifetime upon your shoulders. You've had no time to even process. You were training every single day. You looked healthy, maybe even happy. I didn't want to disturb that peace."

Mara was on her feet, wobbling hard. Cyfrin was at her side in an instant, looking ashamed and avoiding her eyes as he steadied her. She allowed it, standing to the tallest extent she could while leaning on his arm. Drake looked uncomfortable, fidgeting absentmindedly with his rat skull necklace. Kain, El, and Milios were suddenly very interested in the labels of potion bottles on the walls.

"That was not your choice to make," Mara said, her voice cracking a little. "I lived in the dark my entire life. How could you all *lie* to me?"

Caerani gave her a sad look. "I'm sorry, Mara. There is no excuse. Please, let me make up for it now." She motioned for Mara to sit, eyeing her trembling legs.

Cyfrin lowered a begrudging Mara to sit on the edge of her bed. He remained standing by her side, head still bowed in shame.

Caerani sighed, rubbing the bridge of her nose, and thinking. "What I'm going to tell you...you mustn't let it weigh on your heart. No matter what, this is your home. These are your people. Nothing could ever change that." The silence was painfully heavy, Caerani meeting Mara's angry stare once more. "Long ago, centuries before the Great War or any of us were even a sliver in the universe's grand plan, there was the beginning of all magick. The Zenoth's adored what they had created here so much, that they gifted parts of themselves to the people who inhabited

A PROPHECY OF UNDONE

these lands. The ultimate gift. Each Zenoth shared the core of themselves twice, blessing us with the incredible magick we use today. When Mezilmoth was locked behind the Dark Gate, the spell that sealed him there took a heavy toll. The blood of a Zenoth so powerful that it's life force could keep him contained for what they hoped was forever. The only Zenoth to use celestial magicks."

Her eyes dropped back to Mara. "The Zenoth who gave power to the Dawnbringer bloodline. *Your* bloodline. And amidst the bloodshed of that final battle, an ancient seer divined a prophecy as old as the earth on which you stand."

Even the wind seemed to stop as she spoke with closed eyes, as if it knew the power behind her words.

> *"When time has passed, and earth lay black.*
> *When air chokes thick from corruption's crack.*
> *When darkness wins over sealed gate,*
> *And end of all is only fate.*
> *Only then can life be saved*
> *By starlit will and determined brave.*
> *Sealed back by dawn and light*
> *The blood of the one to end all plight."*

Mara stared at her, face void of emotion. The air felt heavy, her mouth suddenly very dry. She could feel Cyfrin looking down at her through his mess of hair, and she shook herself back to reality. "So, you're saying…You're saying that *I*…That the prophecy is talking about *me*?"

Caerani nodded slowly, eyes darkening. "We always thought it meant Alora. Our entire lives, we thought it was Alora. But I think she realized, towards the end…I think she realized that it was always meant for you." Mara saw the familiar flash of pain that lit deep within her eyes every time she spoke of Alora. "You are the last of the Dawn-bringer blood line, Mara. The only one with the power to seal the Dark Gate for good."

Mara's heart skipped a beat. The wind whipped back through the room. A small part of her couldn't help feeling that Caerani had been right to keep this from her. It was bad enough that she was training to fight in a war where they were vastly outnumbered. More than likely fighting against those she had once called her own. Now, she was suddenly the sole person responsible for the fate of the entirety of Zenafrost. She could feel the weight already beginning to crush her.

A hand patted down onto her head. Mara's wide eyes moved up slowly to Cyfrin's face as he tangled his fingers in her curls. He flashed her a glowing grin. "Don't think you get to take all the glory though," he said, his voice bright and warm. "We've been training for this battle our entire lives. You'll never be alone in this journey." His tone was light, but his eyes were hooded with resolute promise.

Kain had stopped perusing the potion labels, beaming as he stepped around Elise. "Oh, absolutely!" he said, jubilant. "You'll be lucky to get any action in with Cyf and I there. It'll be a blood bath."

"Not that we don't completely trust your ability to fight your own battles," El added, stepping forward with Milios to stand by her side.

"You proved you could do that by surviving on your own in the Forgotten Woods," Milios said, a serious expression on their perfect face. "And with Vikefo venom coursing through your veins, no less."

They were looking at her with such pride, such admiration. Mara felt tears well in her eyes. For the first time, perhaps in her whole life, she felt safe. Surrounded by her companions, she felt practically untouchable.

A PROPHECY OF UNDONE

Drake was smiling wide. "That's all something for a later day anyway," he said as Cyfrin ruffled her hair gently. "You passed the forests, by the skins of your teeth. But you've still got two challenges before you in the coming week, and a month aboard my ship following that."

Mara groaned. "A week?!" she asked, incredulous. "I just had my ass kicked by woodland creatures, was confronted by the One Who Sees All on my own and lived to tell the tale, *and* had a man with an axe and an unhealthy obsession try to *murder* me, and all I get is a week of rest?"

They all grew still, Caerani's face darkening. "The One Who Sees? Is that where you learned of the prophecy?"

Mara frowned, nodding. "What is she?"

Drake thrummed his fingers against the lid of the box at his hip, clearing his throat before he answered. "No one's quite sure. All that's known is she is more ancient than the forest itself. She has seen the world grow; evolve. And she speaks to it somehow. Not like how we do with magick. Truly *speaks* to it." He shivered. "She tolerates us walking the wood, but not without payment. She takes from each of us an earnest gift. Something that has meaning to us. And if you have no gift to give, then she will take something else in its stead."

"What will she take?" Mara asked, her voice very quiet.

Drake grimaced, Caerani's lip curled. "Whatever she sees worthy. Some say, even your soul itself."

Mara's eyes went wide, her hand fluttering to her chest as if to keep her soul protected within.

Drake went on. "I was with a soldier once, many years ago, who made the unhappy mistake of looking at her on our encounter." He looked grim. "She took both of his eyes to the very root as a reminder to never to do so again."

13

I.A. TAKERIAN

The room was suddenly cold, Mara shivering as everyone fidgeted uncomfortably. She gulped, trying to recenter herself before she spoke. "So...A week then?"

Drake chuckled. "Well, the new weeks in three days, deary. So really, you only have that long to rest." He was still smiling widely at her. "But that's part of the fun! You'll never know how strong you can be if you don't push yourself to the absolute limit!"

Mara was staring between him and Caerani, mouth agape. "But...But Elise's leg hasn't even healed yet!" she cried, motioning at Elise who stood propped against the wall.

Elise gave her a bashful look. "I'll have plenty of time for my leg to mend," she replied. "I technically didn't complete the first trial, as you had to carry me the rest of the way on your back." She looked almost relieved. "I'll just have to try again next go round! I won't give up that easily."

Mara gulped; her final excuse now gone. She looked back to Caerani slowly. "Three days?" she asked, face screwed up in displeasure.

Caerani flashed a crooked smile at her, eyebrow raised. "Three days."

CHAPTER 2
BREAKING DOWN THE WALLS

The healer had deemed that Mara needed to stay put in the cottage so she could keep an eye on the Vikefo's cut. She was rarely alone, her comrades keeping constant company by her bedside in shifts throughout the day. This afternoon it had been El's turn.

Mara had been insistent on learning as much of the Odelian culture, *her* culture, as possible while she was trapped in bed. El and Milios had been the utmost help in this task, bringing armfuls of tomes and texts each time they visited. Today's lot had been old folktales, some dating back to the very beginning of all things. And in a particularly ornate book, on pages glowing with dim golden light, was a tale about her father.

El was pointing to a beautiful, hand-painted picture on the first page. It depicted King Yvonar as a great beast, both man and wolf as one. "This was one of the reasons your father was so feared by our enemies."

Mara stared in awe. "What...what is he?" She traced her finger delicately across the glowing parchment, outlining her father's hulking form, talons and fangs.

I.A. TAKERIAN

"Really depends on who you ask," El replied, studying the pages of story that followed. "Some say he was born that way, destined to be our king in war. Others say he wasn't a man at all, but a monster sent by Zenafrost to counter the darkness that came." She rolled her eyes and chuckled. "Drake likes to tell tale that he watched Yvonar descend from the cosmos, on waves of moonbeams. No. No, I think Caerani's theory is the closest. She says he was bitten by a man with a curse. A curse of the moon that passed to your father in combat."

She flipped to the next page, a picture of Yvonar as a beautiful man holding an axe more magnificent than any Mara had ever seen. Behind him were creatures of the most ethereal, whose eyes reflected moon and stars within them. "It was this curse that led him to the Druids, beings that served the moon, and their God who ruled over it. They taught Yvonar to harness his curse; to turn it into a gift with which to protect his people." She winked, closing the book, and handing it to Mara. "I suppose that makes you touched by dawn *and* night then, doesn't it?"

It was Mara's turn to roll her eyes. "I've never once transformed into a great dog, El."

"Well, as far as *you* know."

Mara flicked El's knee, and she laughed in response. Then her face fell slightly, studying Mara's eyes with a sudden intensity. "You know I'm here, Mara. If you need to talk. If you're ready."

Mara's back stiffened, turning to face out the window and swallowing hard. She had taken great care to fill all her days, all her waking moments since discovering the truth of her origins. How was one to process even a sliver of what she'd been through these last months without crumbling entirely? She had too much she was responsible for. There was no time to pity herself.

Mara shrugged off El's words, choosing to ignore the offer rather than acknowledge it. "I'm a bit tired, El. It's getting late. Let's call it a night, yeah?"

El nodded, standing slowly with a sigh. "Of course. I understand."

IT WAS the evening before the next trial, the one that would send each Hopeful that survived the woods down into the Crystal Falls. Mara sat up in bed watching the sun set out the open window. The sounds of the village had lulled her reeling mind for the moment, a rare occurrence as she spent the last days lost in crushing thought. The Prophecy of Undone played over and over in her head.

"The blood of the one. The blood of the one."

She cringed as the words crashed around her. Doubts had plagued her mind even back in Delinval, where she knew all their history, peoples, and traditions. *How am I to be expected to lead those with more knowledge in their little finger than I possess in my entire body?* Mara felt like she couldn't take a deep breath anymore; like the weight of her duty was going to suffocate her entirely before destiny could be fulfilled.

What if I'm not powerful enough? What if all this training, the trials, their hard work...what if it was all wasted effort on my lacking body? If Grathiel already bested the mightiest of Odelian warriors once, if the magick of the Zenoths of old wasn't even enough to seal Mezilmoth in, if I can't even control when my magick works or not...

Mara was lost in "what ifs" when there was movement outside her door. It cracked open and Cyfrin slipped

I.A. TAKERIAN

silently into the darkening room. He closed the door behind him with a soft *click*, turning to face Mara.

The risen moon pooled light onto the floor, reflecting up to illuminate his face. *His beautiful face.* Mara pinched her leg, painfully aware of how thin her silk nightclothes were now that he was staring at her.

Cyfrin cocked his head, studying her flushed cheeks. "I thought I'd come to wish you luck. Before your trial tomorrow." He crossed the room and perched on the edge of her bed. "How are you feeling?"

Mara gulped and drew the blankets tight around her waist. She forced her heart to slow, lowering her hand to the bandage at her side. "I barely notice it now. Stopped burning sometime last night. The healer's been fantastic. A real miracle worker." It took concerted effort not to stumble over her words.

Cyfrin's eyes softened. "I'm glad to hear it. But I wasn't talking about your body." He reached out and tapped the side of her head. A small electric pulse sent a shiver down through Mara's cheek. "How do *you* feel?"

She wasn't sure how to answer. Just like with El, she feared that speaking it all into existence would be the final push to break her. Mara gave a little shrug. "I'm just trying to focus on one thing at a time. This trial, then the next, then the next. Sort of hard to think about being responsible for the lives of 'every and all' on top of that..." She breathed a humorless laugh, staring down at her hands.

"You're right. Shall we pack our bags and run then?"

Her gaze flew back to Cyfrin, taking in his mischievous smile and flashing blue eyes. She frowned. "It's not funny."

"It wasn't a joke."

They sat in silence, staring at one another. Cyfrin's stare was unfaltering, his expression suddenly serious.

A PROPHECY OF UNDONE

Mara fidgeted nervously beneath it. "That isn't an option, Cyfrin."

"It's always an option," he said, bemused. "Though I think it speaks volumes to your character that you don't consider it one." He was studying her face with such intensity. It was heady, all-encompassing. "You're not alone in this. In any of it."

His voice was soft as the honey smell from his skin. It engulfed her, her pulse quickening, fluttering. There was no way he didn't hear it. Mara pinched her thigh under the blanket, cursing herself. "I might not be alone, but it's my blood that is needed. And in that, I am bound in solitude."

"But it is not a burden you must face by yourself. We'll be right beside you, every step of the way, to help you carry it. And when you're stood there before the damned Dark Gate, I will be there to hold the line before you. I will keep you safe." He reached out and took her hand, silencing all thoughts in her head and narrowing them to just the spot where they joined. His eyes were crystalline flames; like the ones that danced in the hearth at the Grand Hall. "Let me help you. Let *us* help you," he said in a low voice.

Mara could not pull herself from his stare. She felt the truth fall from her lips before she could stop it. "I don't know how." It had come out as nearly a whisper, and the electrical pulse that constantly surrounded Cyfrin dropped to a gentle purr.

He was leaning in closer. "Neither do I. But I think it's time we both learned. Don't you?" His eyes were hooded, his soft words dancing around Mara on the night's breeze.

She gulped, her body growing very still. Her breath caught in her throat. Her brain was repeating one word, the same one it had shouted the night they had danced together.

I.A. TAKERIAN

Trouble.

Mara bit her lip to steady her nerves. But the motion backfired, Cyfrin's eyes dropping to watch the movement. "What are you thinking?" His voice broke through the deafening, pounding pulse in her ears.

Her eyes widened. *I'm thinking about how much of your body those runes must cover. I'm thinking about your voice saying my name, about your scent, about what you must taste like—*

Mara pinched her thigh again, shocked at how feral her inner voice had become in regard to this man. She forced herself to think about how annoying and cocky he could be; how sarcastic and snide. She frowned at his serious expression. "I'm thinking about your lack of respect for my personal space," she replied, lifting her chin slightly at him.

He blinked, mouth agape. Then he began to laugh, leaning back away from her. "Oh? Funny. I seem to recall someone saying something about how I was, what was it? Ah, yes. 'Far too handsome' to be irritating." He rubbed his chin in mock remembrance. "Mhm. Yes, I'm almost *positive* that's what it was. Now who was it that said that..."

Mara felt herself turn bright red, throwing her pillow at him with full force. It smacked into his cheek, shoving his head to the side as he cackled with laughter. "I didn't know what I was saying!" Mara cried; her voice much higher than usual. "I was tits up in deep wine and dizzy from dancing!"

Cyfrin nodded at her, the picture of sarcasm. "Of course, darling. And that's why you're positively glowing red at the thought, is it?" He drew a long finger down the side of her cheek. Her blood was hot, her heart beating hard enough to fly from her chest. She let out a huff of frustration, pushing him off the edge of the bed and to the floor. He stared up at her, eyes filled with a playful glow.

20

A PROPHECY OF UNDONE

Mara barred her teeth in response. "You're such a pig-headed, arrogant, egotistical…" Words were failing her, his handsome, amused face flustering her beyond measure. He stood slowly from the floor. He took a step forward, staring down into her red face with a look that could have thawed the Frost Falls. "You're a bastard sometimes, Cyfrin."

"And you may be the most magnificent creature I have ever encountered, my dear Dawnbringer."

The breath left her lungs. She felt sure in that moment that she would've done anything he asked of her. All reason had abandoned her, and Mara stared helplessly up at him.

His brilliant smile faltered, something unreadable passing across his face as he took in her heated expression. He looked like he was struggling with something, his tattoos gleaming a momentary blinding white.

Then he chuckled once more. He reached out to ruffle her black curls gently. "It's late. You need your rest." His hand dropped back to his side, and he turned on his heel to stride from the room. He glanced behind him as he reached the door, to the spot where Mara sat dumbfounded. "Dream sweetly." And then he was gone, leaving the faint scent of pine and honey.

Mara stared at the closed door; lips parted. *Magnificent creature. Magnificent creature.* She covered her face with her hands, feeling the heat from her cheeks. *Damn him,* she thought, taking deep, steadying breaths. *He's only said that to get a rise from you. He thinks it's funny to watch you squirm.* But she could still see his face in her mind, clear as if he was still sat at the foot of her bed. The way his eyes burned, the crook of his smile playing across his strong features. Mara groaned, throwing herself back on to her bed.

No one had ever made her so frustrated before, or so… so…*hungry.* She couldn't find a better word for it. Her heart

I.A. TAKERIAN

was finally beginning to slow as she brought her hand back to her face, dragging it slowly across the spot where Cyfrin's finger had traced.

She cursed herself for saying those things to him the night of the party. He was clearly going to hold it over her head. But the thought of that night brought back flashes of dancing with him; being led in his arms to the hypnotic pulse of the music. *And how it felt to be pressed so closely to him. Barely breathing. Electrified.*

"Magnificent creature," she breathed into the dark room, a small smile breaking across her face, betraying her. She laid there repeating the conversation in her head till she drifted into dreams filled with crystals, forests, and a man with lightning in his eyes.

CHAPTER 3
READING A SOUL

Mara had awoken the next morning with a start, the sound of people in the streets floating in through the open window. Her dreams had been deep but restless, and she would've been tired, were it not for the adrenaline now coursing through her. She dressed in the clothes El had brought for her the day before, a pair of black leggings and a flowing green bell-sleeved blouse. It was the first time she had gotten a good look at her reflection since returning from the woods, and she grimaced as she stared into the mirror.

There was a thin but deep cut healing on her cheek from where Filigro struck her. The wound from the Vikefo, though now healed, was still veined in green. The worst injury she had ever endured before this had been a few scraped knees as a child. It was strange, but perhaps fitting, that she was filled by a sense of pride looking at these new scars. These had been obtained through hard work and battle. These meant something.

For once, she had no weapon on her as she left the healer's cottage and stepped onto the cobblestone outside.

Drake had informed her that she would not be needing one for the coming challenge, a fact that Mara was more unsettled by than anything else. Kain, El, and Milios were waiting for her across the way from the cottage, Cyfrin leaned against a tree beside them with folded arms. The wicked smile was on his face as soon as their eyes met, and Mara sneered at him.

"Did you get enough sleep?" Milios asked as they started up the road with the crowd, towards the bridge that led across the narrow river.

"Did you have sweet dreams?" Cyfrin added in a pointed voice, glancing sideways at her.

Mara threw him a dirty look. "I slept *fine*, thank you. And no. I had no dreams," she lied through her teeth. From the way Cyfrin's smirk widened, she was sure he knew it.

The crowd was talking in hurried voices all around them, the excitement palpable as they started through the forest towards the falls. She could see the edge of the cliff ahead of them, Drake and Caerani already standing before the growing crowd.

Mara looked around, recognizing some of the faces from the previous challenge. "How many of us are left?" she asked, thinking back to the thirty of them standing before Caerani merely a month prior.

"Twenty-one," Kain replied, bobbing up and down on the balls of his feet in his excitement. "Four people managed to get their flares off and we made it in time to rescue them. Five never came out, including Filigro and his lackies."

Mara felt a thrill of terror chill her spine. Five warriors, trained by the best, didn't manage to escape the unforgiving wood. And four had failed, though left with their lives. She shivered, imagining what would have happened

A PROPHECY OF UNDONE

if the venom from her wound had spread any faster. *Would they have ever found us if I had fallen with Elise? Or would the forest have consumed us too?*

El took her hand, squeezing it and flashing a reassuring smile. "Don't worry. This trial involves nothing physically dangerous."

"*Physically?*" Mara repeated, emphasizing the word.

El gave her a sheepish look. "Well, there are some potential mental, spiritual threats. But I have the utmost faith in you!"

Mara groaned, throwing her head back to stare at the sky.

Cyfrin laughed beside her. "My offer from last night's starting to sound quite lovely, isn't it?" he murmured in his deep tone.

Mara threw him a cold look as El stared between them with curiosity. She opened her mouth with questioning eyes, but a silence was falling over the crowd.

Caerani had her hands raised to quiet them all, looking serious. "We gather here as we have many times before, to stand and bear witness to our hopeful warriors as they attempt to remove a crystal from the falls." She folded her hands neatly before her, staring around at their faces in the respectful silence. "This challenge has bested some of our finest over the centuries, dropping more trainees than any single trial. As reward, should you emerge victorious, your crystal will be yours to keep."

Drake drew his dagger from his hip, the one that matched Caerani and Alora's. He brandished it before him, on display for all. Caerani nodded toward the purple crystal glowing in its hilt. "Most imbue their weapons with the crystal's powers, helping to amplify your magick through the metal. It will be for you to decide." Her crooked smile flashed on her face. "But that is only if you

I.A. TAKERIAN

are successful in your task. Who amongst you shall enter the basin first?"

There was a ripple of anticipation that passed over the crowd. Mara shrunk slightly with panic, trying to make herself small. *Please, not me,* she thought. *I know there's got to be a catch. I won't be the first to make a fool of myself. Not today.* As if in response to this thought, Cyfrin raised up to his full height beside her, assisting to block her from view like a massive shield.

A man emerged from the center of the crowd. Mara recognized his blazing red hair from the training fields, his broad shoulders squaring up as he stepped before Caerani. He placed his hand over his heart, bowing low.

Drake smirked and Caerani inclined her head in response. The crowd cheered as he stepped onto the staircase that led to the bottom. His head disappeared as he descended, and they all rushed forward to gather on the edge of the cliffside to watch. Kain and Cyfrin elbowed their way through to the front. Mara, El, and Milios followed closely in their wake.

From their vantage point they could see the entirety of the basin. The sunlight gleamed off the water, throwing rippling rainbows of every color across the walls. The lake looked like thousands of tiny diamonds, liquified and moving. The man was at the bottom in moments, standing and staring about himself. The crowd was silent once more, the rush of the falls and the birds in the surrounding trees serving as the only sounds. Mara watched the warrior carefully, eager to understand what was expected.

He stood still, arms held wide, and head tilted. He looked like he was feeling something through the air. He turned suddenly to walk towards a gathering of clear crystals standing six feet tall on the wall behind him. He

26

A PROPHECY OF UNDONE

stopped before the tallest, studying it for a moment before reaching out a hand to touch its pristine surface.

The crystal instantly changed in color, blurring from red to orange, then yellow to green. It whizzed through every color of the rainbow, faster and faster. It made Mara dizzy to watch, and she instead settled her gaze on the man.

He had gone unnaturally still, akin to a marble statue. She could see even from here that the color was draining from his face. The crystal was twinkling, the sound of a hundred tiny bells on the wind. He stood this way for a long moment. And then the bell's sound vanished, replaced by an ominous hissing. El groaned; Cyfrin tutted disapprovingly. The crystal's color turned black.

Bang. The man was shot backwards through the air, slamming down hard on the ground by the lake's edge. He lay motionless as the crowd stared at him.

Kain shook his head. "Damn shame, that is."

The man's eyes opened, and he let out a scream. The sound rocked through Mara, chilling her to the bone as he grabbed the sides of his head and writhed on the ground. Caerani waved her hand, and the man vanished into thin air. Mara looked around, petrified.

Cyfrin leaned down to her ear, the closeness forcing Mara's mind clear for a moment. "She's just sent him to the healer is all," he whispered, his electrical field caressing against Mara's back.

"What happened to him," she hissed back, as another male hopeful stepped onto the staircase.

Cyfrin raised an eyebrow. "I suppose he saw something he didn't like."

She smacked his arm. "Saw *what*?!"

His eyes flashed as they turned to lock with hers. "Whatever it was that made him so upset!" he hissed back.

Mara growled in frustration. "Great lot of help *you* are."

He shrugged, eyes bright. "I'm not allowed to help. You've got to enter the tasks with the same air of mystery everyone else does."

Mara knew this but threw him a nasty look nonetheless before dropping her attention back to the basin.

The man now at the bottom was one of Kain's strongest students, one he had personally trained with the great sword. He was standing on the last step of the stairwell, hand extending to touch a different crystal cluster than the man previous. The colors began to swirl within it, the sound of bells surrounding them all. There was a moment of silence, the blonde-haired man standing stalk still, like his body was merely a shell where he stood. Then the tinkling bells became a harmonious 'hum'. It vibrated through Mara's core, sending waves of elation across her being. The crystal formation began to glow a bright green.

The man's hand sunk through the crystal's exterior like it was made of water, the surface rippling around his arm. He pulled it out slowly and raised his hand high above him. Held in his grip, almost invisible from this distance, was a small crystal the same shade of green the now clear formation had been just moments ago.

The crowd erupted, Mara cheering right along with them. The blonde-haired man beamed with pride up at them all, running up the staircase. He was met by celebration and open arms, people patting him on the back and shouting in excitement as he passed.

Mara still had no idea what the challenge entailed, or what happened when you touched the crystals below. But this at least granted her some hope. She wanted to ask the man what he had seen but knew she would receive the same sort of run around Cyfrin had given her. Her attention was pulled back to the stairway as the next hopeful began to descend.

They stood and watched eleven more hopefuls try to remove a crystal from below. Mara watched as all eleven failed, being thrown back across the ground from the stones they chose before erupting in similar reactions as the first man.

Mara felt sick, her stomach dropping further and further with every failed attempt of her comrades. Kain and Cyfrin were exchanging critical comments between each hopeful, as if this was some kind of sport.

It was hard to swallow, fear gripping her tight and threatening to never let go. Caerani waved her hand and vanished the current failed trainee from the basin, cutting their screams short and leaving them to echo around the walls.

Mara's feet were twitching, her brain sending signals to them to turn and run as fast as she could. At least in the woods, she had been able to clearly see her opponents. She had known what she was entering in to; prepared herself for the fight. But this was different. This was fear and mystery and madness. She felt her hands begin to tremble and clenched them into tight fists.

She couldn't stand here any longer. If she had to watch another warrior, strong and sure, collapse into a pathetic mess below the crowd of onlookers, she was positive her cowardly feet would win. She would turn and sprint right off the furthest cliffside. And her month of trials in the woods would have been for not.

As Caerani turned to face the crowd, awaiting the next volunteer, Mara took a steadying breath. She held her head a little higher, Cyfrin turning to her with wide eyes. She could tell from the look of quiet apprehension on his face that he knew what she was going to do. She willed her

I.A. TAKERIAN

feet to move her forward towards the stairs, the crowd falling into cold silence behind her. She didn't look back, too afraid of what she might see in their faces.

The walk to the bottom was torture, her heart beating from somewhere deep in her stomach. *Odd*, she thought, *I was sure I'd left my stomach back on the cliffs above.* She reached the bottom in what felt like no time, the basin blocking out all sounds aside from the running water. She gulped, her hand still gripping the railing of the stairwell as she stared at her surroundings.

"Whoo-hoo! Go Mara!" El's voice echoed down to her from above, Kain, Cyfrin, and Milios joining her cheers as they applauded.

Mara threw an awkward smile up to them and forced herself off the steps. She felt foolish, standing in the middle of the crystal obelisks. She still had no idea what to do, but she had to do *some*thing. She mimicked what the others had done, closing her eyes, and opening her hands at her sides. This only served to further how silly she felt.

Alright, she thought, focusing on her breathing and the sound of the lake. *We're here, and we're...standing? Listening? Feeling? What are we doing here? Damn Cyfrin. He could've at least given me a hint before I came down here to look like an idiot. Bastard. Stupid, beautiful, witty bastard---No!* She shook her head furiously, clearing her mind as it began to remember his face so close to her the night before; the feeling of his warm breath drifting over her lips. She refused to look up at the cliffside, not wanting to see the many eyes watching from above.

She took a purposeful breath, screwing up her face in concentration. *Zenoths, help me. What am I supposed to do?* Behind her lids, she could see a beam of light pointing straight at her. Her eyes flew open.

A glowing beacon was shooting into the air from the

30

A PROPHECY OF UNDONE

lake, the jutting crystals sticking up from underneath the water's surface. She blinked at it, mystified. Was this what the others had seen as well? The thing that had drawn them to a specific crystal? None of the others had gone to the lake for theirs, but she moved towards it nonetheless.

The cluster stood eight feet high, far enough into the lake that Mara had to enter to reach it. She hesitated on the shore before dipping a toe in, bracing for the cold. But it was the same temperature as her skin, giving the strangest sensation that there was no water at all. Like swimming through air. She stepped in, walking towards the crystal slowly. The water came up to her waist as she stood before the formation. Its glow was steady, inviting even, and Mara could hear it humming softly now that she was this close. She took one last deep breath before she raised her hand and rested it on the clear surface.

There was a sensation like a thousand pin pricks against her skin, and she was falling. Colors flew past her, twisting about her like shadows as she tumbled down. She had become so used to this sensation of being "traveled" that it barely bothered her now. She came to a halt, hovering in a vast white nothingness that now surrounded her. The tinkling bell noise was playing from somewhere far, far away.

"My. What wonderfully potent blood you have."

The voice was sultry and sweet, echoing from all around Mara as she spun about. Her eyes fell on a figure, floating at an incline on their stomach before her. His head was propped on his hands, tilted to one side as he observed her with a bored expression.

He had a slight, wispy frame; his hair flowing unnaturally like waves through water about him. It was morphing through every color imaginable with each passing wave.

I.A. TAKERIAN

His eyes looked like the lake's surface, sparkling like tiny diamonds with slit-like irises.

Mara blushed a little as she realized he was not wearing clothes, clearing her throat. "What do you mean, I have potent blood?" she asked, uncomfortable. "Do you make it a point to greet all your guests this way?"

He looked taken aback, floating to an upright position. A smile began to spread slowly on his face, and Mara felt a ripple of fear as she saw his finely pointed teeth. "Oh, I like you. Yes, I like you very much." He was floating around her in a circle, Mara remaining completely still as she watched him with cautious eyes. "It's been so long since someone actually spoke back to me, instead of just bowing and feeding me compliments."

Mara froze. "I wasn't told I needed to bow," she replied, nervous that she might have offended this being. She could feel immense power rippling from him as he came to stand before her.

"You don't need to. In fact, I much prefer if you didn't." He sat cross-legged in the air, hovering in the nothingness. "My name is Batair. I'm the spirit of the falls, and her protector therein."

Mara had never met a spirit before, and she had come dangerously close to offending this one with her flippant attitude. "I'm Mara," she replied, bowing her head ever so slightly in respect.

Batair laughed, the sound mimicking the bells around them. "No, you're not. You're Yvaine Dawnbringer. And you've come for me to read your soul."

CHAPTER 4
TIME WALKER

Mara was working desperately to keep her eyes focused on Batair's perfect face. She had seen his entire body as he came to an upright position, and her cheeks felt like they were on fire. She had barely ever seen a man shirtless before coming here and being exposed to Kain and Cyfrin, let alone being face-to-face with someone's whole manhood.

Batair tilted his head at her, sharp smile flashing. "And such dirty thoughts as well," he said, clicking his tongue at her in mock disapproval.

She blinked. "Can...you can hear my thoughts?"

He grinned wider, looking her up and down slowly. "I would make for a lousy guardian if I couldn't do something as mundane as that. Tell me: What do you know of this Trial, Yvaine?"

No one had used her true name to address her since she had learned of it. Mara shifted uncomfortably at the change. "Only that it's incredibly difficult. And that you've ruined quite a few days so far, from what I've seen." The

33

I.A. TAKERIAN

images of the screaming Hopefuls, blasted away from their crystals, flashed in her mind.

Batair waved a hand, looking bored. "I've ruined nothing. It is they who could not stand to look at the truth."

"I don't understand."

"They never do." Batair turned from her, raising his arms.

Mara had the sensation once more of being dragged along as if there was a string attached to her soul. They were suddenly surrounded by diamond-like walls. It reminded Mara of the inside of a kaleidoscope. She spun around slowly, mouth wide in awe as she studied the splendor. "What is this place?" she asked, breathless.

Batair hovered uncomfortably close to her for someone so starkly naked. "This is the Time Walk. A place where all come to be shown the truth; where one's being may be weighed and measured."

I don't like the sound of that. Once more, the images of screaming, thrashing Hopefuls by the lakeside played in her mind. She shivered.

Batair was staring at her with dark curiosity. "You are frightened."

"Should I not be?" Mara doubted very much if anyone who passed through this place did so with light heart. She frowned. "The other Hopefuls were already finished with their Trial by now, were they not?"

Batair smiled, reminding her irresistibly of a cat waiting to pounce. "Time works very differently inside this plane."

Mara froze. *Inside this plane. We're on an entirely different plane of existence?!* But she knew from watching the others that her body still stood in the crystal lake in the woods. The Hopeful's vacant eyes as they touched the crystals now made sense. "Is it only my soul that stands here with you?"

34

A PROPHECY OF UNDONE

Batair shrugged. "Your soul, your spirit, your life force…whatever it is you call it, yes. Yes, that is all you are at the moment." His pupils dilated. "I get the sense that you're stalling, Yvaine."

Mara shook her head, a little too quickly to be fully convincing. "No, just trying to get an understanding of what I'm stepping into." She let out a heavy sigh. *Not that there's another option at this point-*

"*It's always an option.*"

Mara gasped, her hands flying to her mouth in surprise. All along the diamond walls surrounding, Cyfrin's face had appeared. There were hundreds of the same moment playing the memory of Cyfrin from the night before again and again through his mischievous grin.

"*Always an option. Always an option.*" The sound grew more and more faint, echoing as the image of his face faded from the walls.

Batair was smiling wide, eyes glinting. "The Lightcleaver. Oh, how devoted your heart is, dancing to his voice."

Mara flushed harder, eyes narrowing in defensive anger. "Is this the challenge then? You pick apart my thoughts like the town gossip?" Mara hadn't meant to be so rough, but Batair seemed thoroughly amused by it.

"Such venom, Dawnbringer. I do hope you keep that spirit through the end of this. Your soul is quite beautiful; I would hate to see it damaged."

Mara shuddered. Batair laughed at the reaction. He was holding his hand out, hovering a good four feet above her. Her palms would have been slick with sweat and nerves, were she actually in her body. But not here. She hesitantly took his hand. He gripped it tight, still smiling as they began to rise at great speed.

They were rocketing towards the diamond ceiling,

35

I.A. TAKERIAN

black smoke swirling beneath its surface. Mara cried out as they collided with it, but Batair's body passed right through, pulling her behind him. Her eyes were still squished shut when she realized they were now standing on solid ground. She opened them slowly, and dread filled her. They were standing in the throne room of Castle Delinval, a crowd of people gathered around them. And sitting at the front, high upon a golden, wing-backed throne, was King Grathiel.

Mara felt her stomach plummet, her knees buckling. She made a move to reach for her dagger, but her fingers were met with empty air. Batair was entirely unbothered, staring around with a dull expression. It dawned on Mara that they were invisible here; two travelers watching a memory. One she knew too well.

Grathiel was addressing the court, discussing the coming month's taxes and tithes, when the doors behind them flew open. Mara didn't need to turn to know who it was. Her younger self rushing into the room, nearly tripping over her feet as she went. She was no older than seven here, dress torn and covered in dirt. There were scratch marks all over her chest and face, her unruly hair full of leaves and sticking out every which way. She slid to a halt as Grathiel raised a hand, the courtiers looking at her with mild disgust as they fell silent.

He was watching her with appraising eyes. "Mara," he purred, his voice rocking through her like an arrow. "Do remember your manners, my pet."

My pet. Mara grit her teeth, the vein in her head throbbing.

She watched her younger self bow low to him, a few leaves dislodging themselves from her hair with the motion. "I'm sorry, Uncle!" she cried, still bowing. Mara heard a few of the onlookers snickering. "It's just...I went

A PROPHECY OF UNDONE

to the s-stables to brush the horses. And Lingrain and Killian were there. And they p-pushed me down, Uncle! They kicked dirt and rocks in my face and called me a-all sorts of awful things!"

Mara could hear so much pain in the voice of her past. It broke her heart. She could vividly remember being this young and realizing how hated she was by the lords and ladies of the court; how despicable their children were to her because of it. She was the child who shouldn't have survived. Should have died alongside the princess in childbirth. Her existence meant the way to the throne was unobtainable. She wondered now if some of them subconsciously sensed that she never truly belonged there.

Grathiel was still admiring her with a cool expression. He gave a small smile. "Ah, well. Boys are boys, my Mara. They were having a bit of fun, that's all." He snapped his fingers, and Lady Lenorei appeared at his side; head bowed. "Lady Lenorei, take the princess to be cleaned. She'll need a new dress before dinner as well. This one looks thoroughly destroyed." And he waved his hand, dismissing them both as Lady Lenorei rushed to escort Mara from the room.

The world around them began to blur, and they were thrown into complete darkness. In the abyss around her, Mara could still clearly see Batair at her side.

He studied her expression intently. "Tell me what is in your heart," he said, eyes aglow.

Mara felt pained, unable to shake the image of her soft baby face covered in scratches from her mind. "Grathiel has no hold on me," she replied coldly. "That place was a prison. His lies were my shackles. That is all I have in my heart for Delinval."

But Batair's gaze had narrowed, raising his hands high once more. They were standing in her bedroom now,

I.A. TAKERIAN

moonlight pooling through her open window. Young Mara knelt before the sill, and she could hear small sniffles coming from her shaking form.

Her child eyes drew upward to the sky, tears falling down her cheeks. "Oh, Zenoths in the great Beyond," she was saying, her voice cracking with sorrow. "I beg you: Hear me. I'm so alone. Every moment of every day, I am alone and unwanted. Please. Please fix the part of me that makes me so...so *wrong*." A sob ripped from her, her head dropping into her hands.

Mara felt tears begin to well in her eyes, her hand floating up to reach for the child. To give her the comfort she needed.

But the room was already changing. They stood in a later memory now, though still in her bedroom. The floor was covered in broken paintings, torn bedsheets and destroyed pieces of glass. There were things still flying about, slamming into the walls as a teenaged Mara yelled in a rage.

Lady Lenorei stood amongst it all, her face screwed up in worry as she dodged the flying objects. "Mara! Please, you must stop this!" she cried over Mara's tantrum.

But she only roared louder, the noise mixed with the sobs shaking her body. "Why?!" she screamed, nothing left around her to throw. "Why does it matter?! Why does anything matter?! I am being raised like some prize pig to be sold at the most opportune time! To be given to a lord that will surely despise me, as I am despised by the entirety of this stupid place! And my uncle...my uncle will not hear me when I speak. He barely even looks at me. It is as if I do not exist!" She crumpled to the ground, renewed sobs ripping from her.

Lady Lenorei rushed to her side, falling to her knees, and wrapping her arms around Mara. She hushed her,

A PROPHECY OF UNDONE

rocking her gently from side to side as she continued to cry. They were swept into darkness once more.

Batair raided every corner of her memory, showing the most awful experiences of Mara's life.

When she had been left behind during a group game of "Shadows and Stones". She had stood in the forest for hours before a soldier had come to inform her the rest of the children had departed.

The time her uncle had openly critiqued her maturing body to a dining hall of grown men. How he had commented on her full, plump figure. She had been eleven at the time.

The time someone had slaughtered her favorite chicken, leaving its head for her to find outside the barn the following morning. No one was ever caught for the act. No one really cared to look.

The missed birthdays, the days spent alone in her bedroom, the "accidental" trips, pushes, shoves. Every glare, every glower of disgust, every rage filled fit and sleepless night spent sobbing in her bed—

"*Enough!*" Mara finally cried as they plunged back into darkness.

Batair looked at her with a merciless smile. "Oh? But I thought you said it held no hold on you."

Mara's own face flashed around them, repeating her words from before in a mocking echo. "*-has no hold on me. Has no hold on me. Has no hold on me.*"

She glared at Batair. "I lied. You know I did."

He tilted his head in agreement.

"I felt *everything*. I felt it all much too deeply, and it destroyed me every single day. I wanted family. I wanted to be loved. Every moment I spent alone killed a little part of me. And yet I still craved nothing but to be with them; to be a part of them. Even in my pain, all I wanted was to

39

I.A. TAKERIAN

make my uncle proud." Her eyes blurred with angry tears. "But my life there was nothing but agony. That is clear now. Looking back, none of it was ever real. Everything I ever knew to be, every bit of who I thought I was, was a lie."

Batair was staring at her with an odd expression. "And so, you are nothing then?" his voice whispered all around them.

Mara hesitated. The question felt loaded in some way, and she did not respond. There was silence for a few moments, Mara's heart aching. Then Batair raised his hands, and they were flying through the darkness once more.

They were back in her tower bedroom, the dark of night coming through her open window. Mara looked at herself in a flowing purple dress, hiding behind her door and staring past them with grim determination. She spun on the spot. There was Cyfrin, back to her past-self as she readied to pounce.

This was the night she had been taken. The night they had come to rescue her.

She watched herself attack Cyfrin, blushing as she saw how he studied her from head to toe. She grimaced at how poorly her fight against him had been, kicking herself as she watched her own surprise at his exposed face.

The world blurred, pulling her forward with Batair. They were in the tunnels below the Marred Lands, Mara spitting water at El with venom in her eyes. She winced, regret gripping her. She watched as Cyfrin reprimanded her for calling them Dreads, watched her rage grow with every moment. Another flash, and they were at the campsite beyond Ylastra, Mara practically dripping with malice as she sat amongst her rescuers.

She watched as flash after flash of memory whizzed

40

A PROPHECY OF UNDONE

past, Batair forcing her to relive every horrible remark she had made to her companions on their way to the Forgotten Woods. She flinched away from every word spat in hatred, every glare of absolute disgust she threw at them. It was an exact mirror of the way she had been treated by Grathiel's court. She watched each of their eye's flicker with hurt, something she had failed to notice back then.

They were standing in absolute nothingness again, Batair and her the only two things in existence. She felt hollow; disturbed at how angry her memories had been. *How angry I am.*

"You belong to nothing. A soul without a home. You don't even know who you are, blood of old." Batair's words rang around her like a thousand different voices at once, some yelling, others no more than a whisper.

Mara looked down and realized dimly that her hands had vanished. No. No, *she* was vanishing, her entire body disappearing before her eyes like smoke. She was sinking, Batair somewhere high above her now, his threatening smile lighting the shadows. The darkness was squeezing her tight, inviting her in with its cold grip. *At least the darkness is peaceful, void of the hatred and misery.* She was nothing. She was no one. Nothing she had ever felt had been truly real, save for the loneliness and desperation to belong. She was a plague, a curse. Would the end really be so bad?

"*Would that be so bad?*"

Mara stopped sinking, her eyes flying open. The voice whispered softly from somewhere high above her, a dim glow of light beginning to pulse in the beyond.

It was Adrian's voice.

She reached out towards the tiny light. The darkness fell away as her hand closed around it. She was standing on the edge of the river that ran through Delinval, small hands rubbing tears from her eyes as she shook. She was

41

I.A. TAKERIAN

no longer an outside observer in her memory, instead viewing it through her past-self's eyes. Batair, nowhere to be seen.

She was six years old. Some of the children of the court had thrown her favorite stuffed bear into the rushing waters, forcing her to watch it float away as they laughed. There was movement next to her, and she looked up to find a young Adrian smiling softly. In his hands, he held her waterlogged teddy bear.

"It's alright!" he said in a gentle voice. "Little did they know, Mr. Bear is an excellent swimmer!"

Mara felt a hesitant smile crack her face as she reached for it. Then the world blurred.

She was twelve, holding a sword with weak arms as she stood across from a grinning Adrian. "Don't be so hard on yourself. It's going to take practice before you're any good! That just means you'll have to be down here every day with me!"

Another flash. They were roaring with laughter, having dropped an entire bucket of fresh eggs onto an unsuspecting group of girls who had been bullying Mara all day as they passed below.

Flash. They laid on a hillside below a night sky speckled with glittering stars. One of them shot across the darkness. Mara made a wish, for love and belonging.

Flash. She was on horseback, arms wide and eyes closed as wind whipped through her hair.

Flash. Her first bullseye with a bow and arrow.

Flash. She had sliced clean through the training dummy with her sword as Adrian cheered.

Flash. Lady Lenorei sat at the foot of her bed, reading her favorite story as she lay sick in bed.

Flash. She sat at her window on a particularly beautiful

42

night, listening to the distant trill of music as she sipped her drink.

"*You'll never be alone in this journey.*"

Flash. It was three days before. She sat teary eyed between El, Kain, and Milios. Cyfrin's fingers halfway tangled in her black curls as they all smiled down at her. She felt warmth spread through her body.

Another flash. She was standing before Batair once more, his eyes wide with fascination.

Mara raised her head high. "I am not nothing." Her voice rang around them, powerful and calm. "The story I was told may have been lies, but my feelings never were. Who I am in my *soul* never was. And though it may have felt so, I was never truly alone. I have always had those that cared for me. I am not defined by my hardships. I am defined by what is in my heart, despite it all. By the few who have stood and loved me in the face of it all."

Batair was smiling at her, eyes glowing as the darkness faded from around them; a golden light taking its place in the vast nothingness. "Tell me then, oh Dawnbringer. Tell me what is in your heart."

The glow was heating Mara, filling her with a strange sense of peace. She smiled back at Batair. "Hope. I have hope in my heart."

There was harmonious humming beginning to rise about her as Batair beamed. "What a wonderful answer."

"*I have hope.*"

The words echoed around Mara, but it was not her voice that spoke them. In the diamond surfaces surrounding them, a young face appeared, nearly identical to Mara's. Queen Alora stood before Batair, with wistful eyes and stunning smile. "*If darkness comes, let it. I've not met a single day that cannot be brightened by the love surrounding me. And I will harness that light with a ferocity that will rival the sun. Above*

I.A. TAKERIAN

even my magick, that is the greatest power I wield. So, if destiny calls, I am ready. I have hope."

The image vanished, and Batair took Mara's hand in his. He leaned in close and kissed her forehead. The spot where his lips touched felt hot, the sensation spreading through her body as he squeezed her hand. The kaleidoscopic world was falling away, Mara's vision tunneling on Batair's grinning face. "I send you with hope, Yvaine Dawnbringer. Hope and love. And I wish you nothing but good luck along the way."

Mara was standing waist deep in the lake, eye's fluttering open. Her arm was shoulder deep in the crystal before her, it's surface rippling like the water, pulsing with brilliant golden light. The humming was vibrating through her, and she pulled her hand slowly from the crystal. She was met with no resistance, passing through it like air as she pulled her fist towards her. She opened her fingers, staring down at the hand that Batair had held just a moment before.

There, humming softly in the center of her palm, was a small crystal. It was rippling with every color imaginable, fading from one to the next seamlessly the way Batair's hair had. A smile started to spread across her cheeks, and she turned to face the cliffside, crystal held above her head in victory. There was a moment of stillness, where the sounds of the falls were the only noise.

Then the air erupted in overwhelming cheers.

CHAPTER 5
THE GENERAL OF FLAME AND VENGEANCE

They celebrated Mara's victory with near reckless abandon. The crystal she had pulled from Batair's plane of existence was like nothing any of them had seen before. Drake had asked to study the crystal after the trial, eager to understand it's mysteries before Mara attempted to fuse it with a weapon. And she had been more than happy to oblige.

Mara hadn't spoken of her experience during the challenge, and no one asked. It didn't seem worth the pain she was feeling to retrieve such a small stone, most especially when the price for failure was so steep. She wondered what sort of things her four comrades had seen during their trials but couldn't find it in herself to pry.

The Time Walk had shown her the lies hidden within her own memories, forcing her to see how mistreated she had been her entire life. It made her sick with anger to think about the injustices done to her as only a child.

The five sat in a tavern near the Grand Hall, reliving their respective challenges Cyfrin sat at her side, the orb lights shining down on his smiling face as he listened to

I.A. TAKERIAN

Kain tell his story. Mara took care not to look directly at him. She hated to admit it, but Batair had been right: Cyfrin made her feel things she had never had, set her heart racing, and left her mind feeling hopelessly lost.

Then again, he was also the single most aggravating person she had ever met. He knew exactly how to get under her skin, pestering her with near-gleeful vigor. She bit her lip, forcing herself to focus on the conversation instead of the way his jaw tensed with every smirk.

"Ay! I was trapped. Surrounded by Bulabores." Kain paused, turning to Mara with a serious look. "Bulabores are nasty little bastards. Ten feet tall- "

"Six, at most," Cyfrin interrupted, eyes glinting over the rim of his tankard.

Kain scoffed before continuing. "*As I was saying*. Ten feet tall, they were. Covered in bark to camouflage, but I saw them coming. Hard to miss so many sets of fangs." He wiggled his fingers before his mouth and set his face in a mask of grim remembrance. "They were coming for me. No less than seven of them. Talons nearly two feet long for fingers! And their eyes like cold pools of darkness. Had me with my back to the river, ready to wash it red with my blood." He flashed a dark, proud smile, reaching up to tap his great sword. "But they were never a *real* match for us. I made quick work of them and ate their corpses for dinner. They don't call me the Slash Master for nothing."

Cyfrin choked on his drink, sputtering. "The *Slash Master*?!" Cyfrin repeated, his voice full of laughter. "No one in your entire life has called you the Slash Master, you ass."

Kain pouted, folding his arms across his chest as they all jeered. "I've called myself the Slash Master loads of times, fucker. They'll sing songs of my exploits in taverns one day. You just have no respect for me."

A PROPHECY OF UNDONE

Cyfrin bowed dramatically to Kain, the face of mock apology. "My apologies, oh great lord slasher. I can only pray you find it in your heart to forgive me. You *massive* ass."

"It is a tad pretentious to give yourself a title," Mara added, granting her an amused look, and raised eyebrow from Cyfrin. "Are you the only one you've given a title to?"

"Of course not!" Kain replied, incredulous. "El's the Toxic Gas," El looked disgusted at this. "Milios is the Deadly Whisper. And Cyfrin is the Thorny Little Spark."

Cyfrin grimaced at him. "That's much worse than Slash Master. Never call me that."

Kain smiled. "I will never call you that. To your face." He turned to look at Mara, who was still laughing. "I've been trying to come up with a nickname for you. Lady Sunbeam? Sunspot? Sunny Smack?"

Mara nodded. "Sunny Smack is definitely the one," she replied, and they all nodded sarcastically in agreement.

Under the table, Cyfrin's leg rubbed against hers in their closeness. It sent an intense jolt through Mara's body, the strongest she had felt. It forced a small gasp from her mouth, and Cyfrin adjusted to pivot his body away from hers.

Mara frowned. He had called her a "magnificent creature" just a day before, but now this slightest of touch sent him all but running. She bit her lip. Perhaps that had been his way of distracting her from the trial, and she had merely read too far into it. It made no sense, in hindsight, for someone as irritatingly gorgeous as him to want anything to do with someone like her. There was just no competing with the long hair, the perfect bodies, the full lips of the Odelian women here in the village.

Mara stood up from her chair. "I'm going to go get

I.A. TAKERIAN

another drink!" she declared, a little more loudly than she intended in her frustration. She turned away to walk towards the bar, cursing herself.

Fate of the world in the balance, in the midst of trials that could very well be the death of me...And we choose now to get uncomfortable around a man? She paused her stream of thoughts for a moment. *Not uncomfortable. That's the wrong word for it. Too comfortable, maybe. Definitely flustered, annoyed, frustrated...but no. Never uncomfortable.*

As she approached the bar, mumbling angry swears to herself, she saw Caerani sitting alone. Her long white braid gave her away immediately. Mara took the seat beside her, and Caerani did not raise her head. Her beautiful green eyes were fixed on her drink, swirling it gently in her cup.

Mara raised a hand to the barkeep to bring her another. "You can join us, if you'd like. We have a table outside, and Kain was just regaling us with his, erm... *creative* nicknames for everyone."

Caerani chuckled into her cup. "Ah, I can't even imagine the sort of horrible things they'd call me behind my back."

Mara frowned at her. "Not behind your back. If there's one thing I know about Kain and Cyfrin, it's that they will gladly say anything they'd like to your face." *Magnificent creature.* Cyfrin's words filled her head and she grimaced. "No matter how unsettled it might make you."

Caerani lifted her head at this, raising her brows at Mara. Her eyes were soft, filled with distant thought. This was the closest she had ever been to Caerani, and in the dim orb light she could make out nearly invisible burns covering her arms. Her eyes widened as she took them in.

Caerani chuckled. "You should've seen them years ago. They were much worse back then." She rolled up her

A PROPHECY OF UNDONE

sleeves to reveal that the burns went all the way up her arms.

"How did it happen?" Mara asked, voice gentle for fear of crossing a line.

But Caerani just gave her a gentle look, sighing. She took a swig of her mead. "The day we lost you, I stood at the mouth of that damned mountain and gave every bit of myself to prevent it. I had made a promise to your mother. She was my best friend. Better than a sister…" She was smiling, but it was filled with such sadness. "I failed her that day. And you. I blew my soul in to a million pieces trying to keep them away from you. Cyfrin and I both. But, as you know, we were unsuccessful."

There was heavy silence between them. The music and laughing voices of the tavern seemed out of place for such talk. They both took sips of their drinks, Mara trying to keep the painful anger ebbing to life inside of her at bay.

Caerani continued. "Fire is one of the most untamable magicks. A lost art. It takes a lot of will and strength to bend it to your whim. I'm the only fire user left, in fact. It's incredibly powerful, but not without its consequences." She nodded down to the stretching burn marks. "You have to know your limits. And if you push the boundary, the fire will lash back. I've learned that the hard way a few times, but nothing like that day. I'm sure you saw the damage I did when you passed through Bardro's Gash."

Mara remembered the mouth of the mountain, crystallized with black; baptized in flames so hot that it changed the very composition of the earth around it. She nodded. "It was beautiful."

Caerani let out a little laugh. "Well, it nearly killed me. I still don't know how it didn't. When I came to, it was weeks later. We had lost you, the surviving Odelians were

49

I.A. TAKERIAN

in chaos, and Cyfrin had already slunk deep into the abyss of his own darkness."

Mara's heart ached, glancing out the open window to their table where the four sat howling in laughter and drink. *So much pain. There had been so much unnecessary pain in Grathiel's pursuit, so much death.*

Caerani finished her mead and pushed the empty tankard from her. "Cyfrin turned to drink to stem the guilt. We had to lock him in his room a few times and ward the door and windows because he drank three whole taverns out of everything they owned." She let out a cold laugh. "It was like he was trying to fill the void inside of him with wine. Or drown himself in it. Whichever came first." She looked out the window towards Cyfrin. "Kain, Milios, and El kept coming to ask me to intervene. But I never could. It felt wrong, telling him to move on from the pain, when I was drowning in it myself. Instead of drinking it away like Cyfrin, I swore to myself that I would never lose control again; would never let myself be bested by it. And I began to train anew. I worked my ass off, till I was bloody and burned and couldn't stand any longer. I did it for years. Twenty years of pushing past my limits every day."

She lifted her shirt a little for Mara to see the immense burns up her torso, smiling. "I don't think there's a single inch of me not covered in these. Drake calls them my battle kisses, the mad fool. But I can guarantee you: I will not be defeated again."

Mara was taking shallow, steadying breaths. The Odelians entire existence had been uprooted and torn apart. Caerani and Cyfrin had thrown themselves in the path of death trying to save her from Grathiel's grip. Her despise for him kept growing, beyond anything she thought herself capable of.

Mara cleared her throat, seeing the sad look in

A PROPHECY OF UNDONE

Caerani's eyes and trying to brighten her expression. "Do you usually drink alone? Because I was serious about you coming to sit with us. As long as you don't mind the crude humor—"

Caerani shook her head. "I'm just waiting for Drake. We're going to celebrate your success, and your good favor in the coming challenge." She raised her glass to Mara in cheers.

The mention of Drake's name reminded Mara of a question that had troubled her for weeks now. "Don't suppose you'll tell me about that box he's always carrying around?" she asked, brow furrowed. "You know, I swear I've seen him whispering to it before."

Caerani smirked, but her eyes flashed. "Ah. You'll have to ask Drake about that. It's not my business to share what strange goings-on happen with that man."

Mara glanced at her. "You've known each other a long time, have you?"

It was a simple question, but Caerani caught the implication in her words. She smiled warmly. "Yes. I've known Drake for eons. Him and I are bound, through better or worse, in this life and the next."

Mara smiled back at her, but it did not reach her eyes. It made her thoughts drift back to Cyfrin and the way her heart was falling so quickly. She stood from the bar and bowed her head to Caerani. "Enjoy your evening, general," she said, turning and marching back to her table.

Her four comrades seemed to still be mocking Kain for his made-up names, Cyfrin insisting that if anyone was "The Slash Master", it was surely him. They looked up with smiling faces as she approached.

Mara did her best to smile back, but her anger was burning brighter and brighter. "I'm just going to go do

I.A. TAKERIAN

some practice rounds in the fields. Just to shake off the excess energy from today. I'll see you all in the morning!"

El, Kain, and Milios beamed at her, not catching the hint of emotion in her voice.

But Cyfrin did.

His eyes narrowed, smile faltering. And Mara turned from them, slid out of the tavern in a flash, and was off into the night.

CHAPTER 6
FLUTTERS IN BURNED
SILENCE

Mara stood, bathed in the moonlight above the Brisenbane. She was shaking, face still hot after her conversation with Caerani. She felt herself verging on a tipping point, threatening to tumble into despair. After being forced to relive the cold, dark loneliness that her life had been, forced to see the damage that had been done to her as a child...listening to Caerani talk of the twenty-year purgatory she and Cyfrin had been through because of her... *Too much. It's too much.*

Mara felt herself cracking and raised her fists before her. She closed her eyes and began working through her fighting stances, just as she'd been taught. With every hit through the cool night air, she released a little piece of her anger. Her anger at Grathiel. Her hatred of everything he stood for, everything he was. The lies he had told, and the people who believed them.

She felt righteous fury on behalf of the broken child within her, and deep, agonizing sadness that she could never see Adrian again.

How could anyone be so cruel, so selfish, so evil? It was vile, everything Grathiel had done. It made her want to be sick. Made her want to set him ablaze in the square, as they did the effigy of Queen Alora. Of her mother.

Mara was roaring now, the volume increasing with each blow. Then, her fist collided hard with someone's palm. Their fingers closed around hand, jolting her as she opened her eyes.

Cyfrin stood before her, wincing, his tattoos glowing white. "That's enough," he said quietly, his voice gentle. His fingers were blackened, as if he had stuck his hand into flame.

Mara's eyes grew wide as she took in the training field around her. The earth had been completely leveled, a near perfect circle of crackling ash dug deep into the ground. The cracks in the gashes were still glowing with golden light as Cyfrin released her fist.

He studied her face intently as she gaped around. "I take it you weren't trying to renovate the landscape," he said jokingly, waving a hand around them. Grass began to sprout through the ash, the earth groaning like a mighty breath as it filled back to its normal level.

Mara made a rude gesture at him. "I'm not in the mood for your games, Cyfrin," she mumbled, glowering.

He smirked. "I wasn't aware we were playing any." He mimicked Mara's stance with a bemused expression on his face. But his eyes were shadowed with concern. "Do you want to tell me what's bothering you?"

Mara blinked at him, caught off guard. She was unsure how to answer. *Oh, I'm just in charge of saving the world, and have the guilt of hundreds of broken lives, including yours, on my shoulders and I can't even think of you without thinking of how much I want you—* Her inner dialogue was blaringly loud, and her eyes darted away from his in irrational fear that he might hear it. She stared out across the moonlit waters, Cyfrin still watching her. He waited patiently for Mara to speak.

"I just…I don't know how I'm going to do this. I have no control over the little magick I do have, obviously." She motioned all around them at the freshly grown grass where the ash had laid moments ago. "And if Grathiel was able to best all of *you* with the assistance of dark magick, then I just don't see what good I could ever do."

Cyfrin scoffed and she looked up at him. He had a strange look on his face, eyebrow raised. "You're afraid you're not powerful enough?" he asked, tilting his head to the side. "Weren't you the one who reduced Filigro to ash in the Forgotten Woods? From what Elise told us, there was barely even dust left after you were finished with him."

Mara blushed. "Yes, and that's exactly my point. I had no control over it. I was just trying to protect Elise. It was all I could think of."

Cyfrin's eyes flashed, and he took a step towards her, bending slightly to be closer to her face. Her breath caught as he flashed his wicked smile. "You have nothing to fear, Dawnbringer. I'll be there to protect you from all things dark and menacing."

Mara huffed, pushing roughly past him. "This isn't a joke," she said, angry.

"I wasn't laughing," Cyfrin replied in a low voice from behind her.

Mara couldn't bear to face him. "I've already ruined so many lives just by existing. I *must* atone by fulfilling the prophecy I just…I don't know how." Her voice was soft, barely a whisper as she spoke into the open air. They were silent, the sound of the waves against the rocks drifting about them on the wind.

I.A. TAKERIAN

"It's funny. I was just thinking of how many lives you've already improved by being here." Cyfrin's voice was much closer to her now, startling Mara who had not heard him move. Her heart skipped before doubling its prior pace.

She was surrounded by the smell of him; the warm, piney sweetness that she had begun to associate with her home. He was right behind her, reaching out a hand to pull her short, chopped curls behind her ear.

His breath was on her neck, sending a thrill through her body as she felt the electrical pulse that always surged off him filling the air. He let out a laugh that made goose-bumps rise on her skin.

"Tell me something, Mara," he purred her name, and she bit down hard on her tongue to prevent the noise that threatened to betray her from escaping. "Why is it that your heart races so when I'm near you? I can hear it, *feel it*. Especially when I touch you." He dragged a finger down her arm with a feather-light touch for emphasis.

Mara's head tilted back despite herself, coming to rest against his chest. She let out a soft sigh. She felt his breathing cease; heard his heartbeat speeding along practically in time with hers. "You make me nervous," she breathed. Her mind was fogging over with him, unable to offer anything but truth. Her worries, her doubts, her anxiety…It was all falling away.

She felt lips at her ear, heard a low noise escape him. "Is that what you call it?" His voice was husky, deep.

Oh, Zenoth's blood, she thought over the sound of her quickening breath. *I'm doomed.* It took great effort to spin around and face him.

Cyfrin's face was dark, eyes smoldering down at her. She watched them dart from her heated gaze to her lips and back again, nearly derailing her thoughts all together. "Stop taunting me, Lightcleaver," she growled.

A PROPHECY OF UNDONE

A thrill of excitement flashed across his grinning face. He stepped closer; his body achingly close to hers. She grit her teeth, forcing herself to ignore the way his jaw was set as he watched her.

"You've got it backwards," he purred. "It's *you* who taunts *me*. What I'm doing is *teasing* you, Dawnbringer."

Teasing you. The words filled Mara's head, her heart dropping. *Of course, he's teasing me. He knows it pulls me from the stress and the anger. It's just as he did last night. Distracting me.* She grimaced at Cyfrin, pushing him back. "I don't need you to distract me, dammit. This is exactly what I meant when I said I didn't want to play your games."

He was no longer smiling, his eyes haunted as he glowered down at her. "Is that what you think I'm doing, Mara?"

The sound of her name said in his threatening tone made the heat in Mara rise faster, her face flushing. His eyes glowed with dancing lightning, his runes bright across his skin. Sparks crackled around his hands as he stepped towards her once more. She glared up at him, refusing to show weakness.

He raised his hand, the sparks vanishing as it came to rest softly against her cheek. Her eyes widened, her heart now thrumming triumphantly in her throat. His eyes were filled with their bright, blinding intensity. Mara felt she might be swallowed by it. She wished to be.

He stroked his thumb across her cheek, lifting her face to his. They were inches apart, his stare burning into her soul. If she stretched up an inch higher on her toes, their lips would meet. Her eyes darted to his slightly parted mouth.

Something feral crossed his face. "So quick to assume the worst in me. Have you stopped to consider that I am, perhaps, entranced by you?"

57

I.A. TAKERIAN

Mara wasn't breathing, his scent washing over her as she fell speechless.

His eyes traced her lips, working slowly back to her flittering lashes. "Or maybe you're right. Maybe I'm just all sarcasm and distraction. Do I truly distract you, Dawnbringer?"

The jest partially cleared the fog in her brain, and she glared at him. "I never said I *was* distracted. Merely that you didn't need to put the effort in to doing so." She folded her arms, indignant.

The smirk fell from his face again, and his hands moved faster than her eyes could see. He had grabbed her fiercely by the waist, pulling her against him and leaning in close, too close. His mouth was so near to hers, his breath drifted through her lips. Mara let out a small gasp. She felt a low rumbling in his chest, like the roll of thunder before a great storm. She couldn't think, and she didn't want to. Here in his arms was the only time in her life Mara wanted to feel helpless.

Cyfrin laughed, the bass echoing through her. "You're a terrible liar, Mara." He drew his lips from hers, bringing them to rest against her forehead. Her skin tingled with electricity at the spot, and he released her from his grasp.

She stood where he left her, blinking at him as he took several steps back. His face was set in stone, his hands clenched. He flashed his evil little grin and bowed his head, starting to back away towards the forest path. "Rest well tonight. Try not to raise the entire field before the morning. You know how Drake gets about the circles being perfect." And with that, he left back towards the village, leaving her to stare after him.

Mara shook her head, trying to wrap her thoughts around what had just happened; wrap her thoughts around *him*. But it was impossible to sort through the tidal wave of

A PROPHECY OF UNDONE

emotion still flowing through her. And though she was furious with how care-free he had been while making her the absolute puddle she was now; she couldn't help feeling a little grateful. For he *had* successfully distracted her from toppling off into the darkness that waited within.

CHAPTER 7
THE HOLLOW WOMAN

Mara couldn't recall the last time she'd truly slept. The concept of drifting off to sleep was daunting, not to mention the nightmares that plagued her when it finally came. Not even the intensity of her training was enough to keep her mind at bay anymore. The emptiness that had perhaps always been within her had spread like a wildfire. Empty, save for the unshakeable anger. It sat on the edge of Mara's every thought, invaded her every moment. And she was beginning to fear what would happen when it all boiled over.

She had begun doubling down on her studies of the Odelian histories. For one thing, to be prepared for what was to come. For another, because Mara truly enjoyed the content she was consuming. Spell books, tomes, and rolled bits of parchment had taken up a permanent residence on Mara's bed. There was a single spot near the pillows that she had left clear for her to sit. El said it reminded her of a bird's nest. Kain said it reminded him of a cry for help. But Mara felt most at peace amongst the pages. It was the closest she could get to her parents and to her people.

61

I.A. TAKERIAN

She was stirring from her most recent nightmare, having fallen asleep curled around two open tomes. This was common practice for her nowadays, often waking up in the disarray of history and lore. Mara groaned, curling into a tighter ball, and trying to calm her heartbeat. This nightmare was one she had many times before. She stood on a great stage, with hundreds of faceless people pointing up to her in silence. Adrian ran at her across the platform, sword high and face screwed up in a hatred unlike Mara had ever known. She could not run, could not speak. All she could do was stand and wait for the inevitable wet gash of his blade through her torso. It felt so real. The smell of blood, the feeling of it pooling below her as Adrian gutted her with no remorse. And then she would awaken, drenched in cold sweat and panic.

This nightmare was perhaps the worst, even among the ones of monsters, simply because it was a very real possibility that they could someday come to fruition. She liked to think that Adrian would listen to the truth; that he would still stand beside her when he knew who she was. But her mind would quickly dash those hopes with thoughts of his sword, his loyalty to his kingdom, and his wrath.

She sat up slowly, pushing aside the story she had fallen asleep on, *The Cat and the Curse*. The sky outside was still black, overcast with the rainclouds that had rolled in during last night's practice. Her eyes lingered on the painting of her mother and father by the balcony, beaming at her. She was overcome by the sudden childlike want to be held. For her mother to rock her gently as her father told her it was alright, that it was just a bad dream. Her heart ached ever further at this.

It was comforting at times, to be in a room where her

62

A PROPHECY OF UNDONE

mother and father had lived. And equally as painful. Alora had carved her and Yvonar's initials into the doorframe of the balcony. She had pressed flowers of all kinds hidden in the assorted books on her desk. Her clothes, now Mara's, hung in the careworn armoire by the door. The faint smell of roses still clung to them. Mara had found a comical picture, drawn by her father's hand, that depicted Cyfrin's father as an overly inflated angry bear, yelling slurs at a dozen stick figures. It had been titled "The General of Horseshit". Notes exchanged between Alora and Yvonar, trinkets from their journeys, tokens of their love for one another. They all served as constant reminders of what once was. Of what Mara should have had.

A lump rose in her throat. The familiar feeling of anxious distress pushed tears to her eyes, and Mara could not stand it any longer. She swung her feet over the side of the bed, rushing from the room and closing the door with a soft *click* behind her. The hallway was dark, save for the sparce orb lights floating lazily about the ceiling. They cast odd shadows across the many decorations hanging from the walls. There was a creak of a floorboard to her right, drawing Mara's attention.

At the end of the hall, right before the turn-off to Cyfrin and El's bedrooms, stood the door to Kain's room. Mara could just make out his dirty boots by the entrance, and the shadow of a flower wreath tacked above it. El had worn it the night before Mara left to her first trial, and it had hung there ever since. It was thrown in sudden candlelit relief as the door cracked open, almost in tandem with Mara's. A short figure slipped out of the room, clearly trying to be silent as they closed the door behind them. The figure turned about to face the hallway, stopping cold at the sight of Mara.

I.A. TAKERIAN

El stood like a statue outside of Kain's door, eyes wide. "Oh, uh…oh…" She seemed at a loss, like a child caught in the act.

But Mara's face was splitting into a wide grin. "Why, Miss Stonerot. Alone in a man's room? The scandal of it all." She drew her hand dramatically to her forehead before dissolving into soft giggles.

El rushed towards her, making shushing motions with her hands. "Quiet! You'll wake the whole bloody hall!" She pushed the still-giggling Mara back into her room, closing the door behind them and breathing a sigh of relief. "Cyfrin would be at it for *weeks* if he'd caught me."

Mara perched on the end of her bed, the nightmares momentarily pushed from her mind. "Would he? I thought it was pretty obvious that you two were together."

El looked embarrassed at this, and a little hurt. "Well, we aren't. Not really."

Mara's smile dropped, reading the pain that crossed El's face. "I'm so sorry. I shouldn't have assumed…"

El waved her hand, shaking her head. "It's complicated, Kain and me. Really just me, if we're to be honest." She sat on the poof by Mara's bed, a faraway look in her eyes. "It's my magick. It's damned near impossible to contain at the best of times. Deadly, at the worst. Heady emotion just triggers it faster, and Kain…" She blushed furiously, dropping her face into her hands.

Mara understood without her needing to say so. "Kain gets your pulse racing."

"Aye, and my blood boiling." El breathed a laugh. "He loves me so much. Tells me every chance he gets. But I can't touch him. He's got all sorts of scars from the times we've tried. Horrible, nasty scars…" She trailed off, shutting her eyes from the memory.

64

A PROPHECY OF UNDONE

Mara's heart broke. This was agony in its purest form. To love and be loved, but never to lay a finger on the other. "I'm so sorry, El."

El took a steadying breath, offering a sad smile in return. "As am I. You'd think it'd deter him, a little. But not Kain. He just finds ways around my…situation." She leaned forward, dropping her voice as if they'd be overheard. "Take tonight, for instance. Nights like this one, we sit across the room from each other. Far enough so that my magick can't immediately get to him."

The night breeze seemed to stand still as she spoke, her gaze growing feverish. "We stand in the silent starlight and we just stare at one another. He studies my body with his eyes, and devours me with the sounds he makes…" She gulped, giving a hurried laugh. "And I'll spare you all the specifics."

Mara's face was flushed at the thought of Cyfrin staring at her in this way. Of the sound of her name on his tongue. "Zenoths be, Eleanora, I stand by what I said. Absolutely scandalous!"

El laughed, but her expression quickly shifted to one of inquisition. "And what were *you* doing up at all hours, your ladyship? Off to take a stroll through the lightning lit valleys, are we?"

Mara caught her meaning, throwing a pillow at her head. "No! I'm not sure where I was going. I just needed to get out the room for a moment." She glanced at the portrait of her parents. "Had another nightmare."

El nodded, solemn. "Ah, another sleepless comrade wandering the Great Halls at night then."

Mara raised an eyebrow. "Another?"

"There's not a single one of us that sleeps through the night anymore, I don't think. Caerani and Drake are up at all hours, doing Zenoths only know what." She shuddered at the thought. "We try to stay away from their wing. Milios has a room, but I don't think I've ever seen them use it. This hour, they'll either be out at the temple studying the stars, or perhaps down by the falls sharing secrets with the wind."

"So, it's true then," Mara interjected. "Milios really is speaking to the wind?"

"Oh, yes. Milios knows everyone's secrets." El smirked. "Makes for an excellent drinking companion, if you can keep up. Kain and I...Well, we're up a lot of nights as well." She blushed once more, biting her lip. "And Cyfrin barely ever sleeps. Just sits up in his room lying in wait for the next training or battle, and thinking of all sorts of shitty little things to say." Her eyes flashed. "Though, I've noticed those shitty little things seem to get quite the smile out of one little axe wielder."

Mara sneered at her. "I treat Cyfrin the same way I treat *any* of you."

"Oh, I should think not. Or else we might all have started kissing one another by now." El stood from her poof, making mock kissing faces at Mara.

"Back, you!" Mara yelped, rolling back onto the bed and launching another pillow at El.

"You know, if you're finding it hard to sleep without nightmares," she said, backing up towards the door as Mara readied another pillow to throw. "You can always imagine you came across our brooding Lightcleaver in the hallway instead of I. I'm sure he would have been more than happy to comfort you."

Mara growled, face hot as she threw the pillow at the closing door as El escaped. Alone once more, but in considerably better spirits now, Mara returned to her spot

A PROPHECY OF UNDONE

amidst the parchment and books. She picked up the story she had fallen asleep on, narrowing her gaze as she tried to force herself to focus. But it was impossible with the new thoughts floating around her head.

Have I really been so obvious?

CHAPTER 8
THE BEAST BELOW A LEGEND OF OLD

The third trial had approached must faster than Mara had hoped, though every one of them had seemed to. She awoke the day before to the great weight of anxiety resting on her chest. She had spent the last few days on the training fields with her comrades, working into the late hours of the night. Trying hard as she could to get control over her magick before descending into the catacombs below the temple.

Mara had trained mainly with Milios and El, Cyfrin and Kain watching from the sidelines as she failed again and again. Her frustrated roaring did nothing to alleviate her embarrassment under their watchful gaze. Mara had become very aware of how careful Cyfrin was being around her. Ever since that night on the training fields, it was like he was going out of his way to avoid being alone with her. She hated how much it bothered her.

Mara stood across from El and Milios in the blazing autumn sun, face red and screwed up in focus. They all stood motionless, watching as she shook with the force of her vigor. But nothing came from her extended hands, not even a

I.A. TAKERIAN

spark. Mara cried out in anger, throwing her head back and dropping her arms as birds shot from the treetops. "*Useless!*"

El gave her a gentle pat on the back. "Oh, don't be so hard on yourself! We just haven't found the key to unlocking your gifts yet."

Mara scowled. "What if there is no key? What if I'm doomed to being this loose cannon for all eternity? Ugh, *eternity*." She groaned, dropping her head in to her hands. It was a concept she had never had to confront before. One that made her headache, now that it was a reality.

Milios frowned at her. "If you look back on when you've used your magick without melding, each instance is marked by a big emotional moment. Perhaps your key is simply in figuring out how to tame that?"

Kain had stood a little straighter at Milios' words, an evil grin spreading wide as he leaned in to Cyfrin, whispering. A grin identical to Kain's twisted onto his face. Then they both turned their gaze to Mara.

Kain cleared his throat pointedly. "Let's give Cyfrin a chance to unlock that door, shall we? He seems to have a unique gift at getting under our Mara's skin. And we all know how much he loves a challenge."

Cyfrin's eyes were set solely on Mara as he approached her slowly. El and Milios joined Kain looking on from the outside of the circle. Mara gulped as Cyfrin walked closer and closer, stopping only inches away. He had been this close that night after the second trial, in this very spot. Right before he had grabbed her waist, placed his lips to her ear, breathed her name…

Her heart was thundering, and Cyfrin tilted his head at the sound. He folded his arms across his broad chest, leaning close. Mara held her breath, glaring at him. He smirked. "We're going to try a little game, Dawnbringer.

A PROPHECY OF UNDONE

Since I know how much you enjoy playing them with me." He raised his hand to the breast pocket of his leathers, patting it once. "There's a coin in my pocket here. I want you to take it from me. No weapons, just you, me and your magick. Sound easy enough?"

Mara frowned up at his glinting eyes. "What's the catch?" She bit the inside of her cheek as she sought for a double meaning in his words.

Cyfrin let out a wry laugh. "No catch. But you know how fast I can be."

She glowered at him, unable to shake the feeling of a trick behind his careful wording. She let out a heavy sigh and nodded curtly at him, raising her palms, and focusing her energy though them.

Cyfrin moved like a flash of light, his blue eyes leaving a glowing trail in their wake. He was behind her faster than her gaze could follow, his lips at her ear. "Quicker than that, Dawnbringer. I've seen children with better reaction time." He blew softly into her ear, and Mara felt his fingers graze across her leather clad ass.

She yelped, spinning in a rage. But he had moved again, just as quickly as before. He was behind her again, his hand around her ponytail as he gave it a firm tug. She cried out, butterflies taking off in her stomach. She flailed back to catch him as she spun. Another flit of glowing blue eyes and he was at her side. Mara could see the flash of his smile out of the corner of her wide eyes, and he leaned forward before she could stop him. His lips pressed against her cheek, the blood rushing instantly to her face as she gasped.

There was a soft electric shock that came from his mouth as he touched her, sending her mind reeling. Her heartbeat stuttered as she stumbled sideways away from

71

I.A. TAKERIAN

him. He grabbed her arm to steady her, chuckling with his merciless grin.

Everyone seemed to vanish, Mara completely forgetting their existence as her focus tunneled only on Cyfrin. Taunting her, waving her emotions before her in private was one thing. But to do it in broad daylight for all to see his childish game?

It was something Mara couldn't stand.

She roared, lunging for him with a speed she didn't know she had. His eyes gleamed with excitement. He moved out of the way, Mara stumbling through the space he had just been as he hoisted her arm above her to prevent a fall. Mara yelled out in frustration again, rising with fire in her eyes to grab at Cyfrin. He yanked her upright, her face dangerously close to his.

He was smirking, the dimples set deep in his cheeks and his eyes aglow. "Ah, see that?" he murmured in a low voice. "Milios was right. All it took was a little emotional *nudge*." He looked up, Mara's eyes following his gaze to the place where he held her arm in the air.

Glowing golden light was wrapping in and out of her fingers like the waves of the ocean beside them. It was warm like the sun on a hot summer's day, pulsing faintly. She gaped at it, a breathless laugh escaping her as the glow vanished.

Cyfrin pulled her completely to her feet, eyes apologetic. "Sorry. Kain and I thought it would be easier to illicit a reaction this way."

Mara's eyes narrowed to slits as she stared him down, Cyfrin shrinking slightly away from it. "Bastards. Both of you," she said, tossing something at Cyfrin's chest.

His hands flew up to catch it, staring down to where it sat. His eyes widened, mouth falling open. Then he let out a roaring laugh. "Fuck me!" he cried, jubilant. "When in

A PROPHECY OF UNDONE

the great gates did you snatch that? I didn't even feel it!" He tossed the coin at Kain, who looked shocked.

Mara gave him a vicious grin. "When you were busy breathing all over my face. It really wasn't that difficult. Your armors been looking a tad loose lately, and my fingers just slid right in. Have you been losing bulk, Lightcleaver?" Her eyes flashed with the playful wickedness she had learned from Cyfrin.

Cyfrin raised an eyebrow at her, sneering as Kain puffed out his chest. El looked thoughtfully between the two, nodding her head.

"No, she has a point, Cyf. You are looking a bit lean beside Kain. Have you been skipping your solo training sessions?"

Kain beamed. Cyfrin looked murderous. His face darkened, turning his head slowly to face Mara. She met the look with a harrowing glare, refusing to give up this small moment of gratification at his deflated ego. In a second, Cyfrin had pulled his leathers off over his head, golden skin glowing in the sunlight.

Mara felt lightheaded, breath coming in shallow spurts as she worked to keep her expression bored. Kain guffawed and pulled his armor off as well, much to El's unbridled delight, and they stood next to one another flexing. They compared every muscle on their bodies, from their broad shoulders to their chiseled chests. Their thick arms to their tree-trunk sized legs. Mara had to look away to stop staring in reverence at Cyfrin's gorgeous *everything*. There wasn't a single flaw she could find on him, not even the deep scarring through his face.

The image of his bare body, bathed in the light of the sun, was something she was sure would haunt her dreams for weeks to come.

They paused their training to eat a light lunch by the

I.A. TAKERIAN

hillside facing the crashing waves. Cyfrin and Kain were still shirtless, Kain looking highly amused while Cyfrin sat with brooding eyes. Mara's gaze traced the many tattooed runes that adorned Cyfrin's exposed skin. They twisted in spiraling patterns around his chest, across his arms, down his stomach and disappearing beneath the waist of his pants. Her stare slid down his sculpted stomach, across the tips of the V-shaped dip that led downwards.

Mara yanked her eyes up from his beltline and pinched herself. "Do those mean something?" she asked, motioning towards the markings.

Everyone looked suddenly uncomfortable, looking at anywhere but Cyfrin with feigned fascination.

He tilted his head at her. "They do." His fingers grazed across the runes on his right arm. He stretched it out towards her, allowing her a close look at his forearm. "They're part of an ancient warding spell. It was used to trap a good portion of my magick to prevent it escaping and destroying us all."

He said it in such a matter of fact tone, that Mara thought he was joking. Just another opportunity to flaunt his prowess.

Mara laughed, but Cyfrin's cool eyes were humorless as he stared back at her. The smile fell from her face. "You're serious?" she asked, remembering the sparks of blue lightning that sometimes surrounded his hands in moments of great emotion.

He nodded, face void of expression. "Wish I wasn't. The Lightcleaver's magick is very similar to fire in its difficulty to control. Mix that with the potency from my mother's earth magick and you've got a recipe for disaster. It's... I've hurt people before. Without intending to. It happened a lot when I was younger, and my father thought it best

74

A PROPHECY OF UNDONE

that we lock a portion of my magick away. For everyone's safety."

The group was quiet, the four of them staring out across the water with faraway looks. But Mara could not pull her eyes from Cyfrin. Of everyone here, he must understand best how terrifying it was to not be fully in control of one's ability. The image of Filigro exploding into golden dust before her in the woods haunted her nights; the thought of accidentally losing control and doing that to someone dear to her keeping her in constant fear. And *his* lack of control had been so extreme that his body had been bound, trapping his full potential within. She could see the ghost of painful memories in his eyes and bit her lip, the need to take away his hurt aching in her heart.

"At least they look good. Like something out of a painting," she said, voice soft.

He turned to look at her, surprised. A wry smile cracked his perfect face and his eyes glinted. Mara changed the subject before he could quip a witty remark.

"So, this monster in the catacombs, are you allowed to tell me about it? It's not *helping* me if all the other Hopefuls know what to expect, is it?"

Their expressions grew dark, exchanging looks of trepidation.

"It's a very old thing," El replied, fidgeting nervously at a rock on the ground. "No one can remember how it got there, or what exactly it is. Only that it was drawn here many centuries ago by the early Odelian ruler's treasure trove beneath the temple." She shivered, and Mara could see goosebumps rise on her arms. "The magick users of old could not kill it, could not figure out a way to remove it. So, they did the only thing left to keep it from causing any harm to our people. They sealed it within the catacombs, locked away with the treasure it so coveted."

"I'd say my prayers that you don't actually encounter it down there. That you find your treasure and leave without it finding *you*," Kain said in a low voice, his expression grimmer than Mara had ever seen it. "I caught a glimpse of it on my way out during my own trial. It was wearing bits of flesh. *Humanoid* flesh. From End's only knows how many failed Hopefuls and creatures unfortunate enough to get lost within the catacombs."

Mara felt the tight grip of anxiety around her heart. *A monster, then. I'll be expected to sneak past a monster and steal from its valued possessions, then escape with my life.* She could feel the color draining from her face at the prospect.

Cyfrin nudged her leg with his foot, smirking. "Don't worry," he said, eyes flashing. "If Kain here can get in and out with his ass intact, I have no doubt you'll get through with minimal effort."

Kain gasped dramatically, throwing a piece of bread at him as they all laughed. But Mara's smile did not quite reach her eyes as they rose to continue their training.

HOURS LATER, Mara walked slowly along the cobbled street towards the Grand Hall. She had left before the others, determined to bathe before they ate. She had spent the last few days covered in sweat, dirt, and exhaustion as they dined in the evenings, and she was beginning to feel more animal than woman.

Their conversation from the ocean side played over and over in her head, increasing her nervousness with every passing moment. Kain had tossed her a battle axe at the end of training, nearly identical to the one she had lost

A PROPHECY OF UNDONE

in the woods. She had been unsuccessful in her many attempts to replicate the magick Cyfrin had wrung from her earlier that day, and Kain had declared it a waste of time.

"We can continue her magick practice every day after the trials if she wants. But what she needs to focus on right now is *survival*." He had said it to the agreement of all.

Mara was frustrated, borderline enraged, by her lack of ability to control herself. But she knew Kain was right. Praying for her magick to work when faced with the beast below the temple would earn her nothing but slow death. Her best bet would be the battle axe now strapped to her back. She crossed the bridge to the Grand Hall, mind still racing. Her feet slowed to a halt, her eyes floating to the path that led to the temple in the woods. She paused for a moment, thinking, then turned to storm off into the tree line.

The Temple of the Zenoth's stood flush with the rock face behind it, vine covered stones showing centuries of time on their worn surfaces. The layout was entirely open, with great pillars holding the high ceiling in place. She had seen some devote priestesses wondering around inside before, but it lay empty this evening. She could hear running water in the distance and wondered if there was some underground water-source below her feet.

Hundreds of orb lights floated lazily about the arched ceiling above her; some birds singing from their homes atop the pillars all around. There were tapestries lining the walls, and all kinds of ancient artifacts propped on pedestals displayed about. Weather-worn statues of black and white smokey crystals lined the walls, their faces made flat with time. It was beautifully peaceful in here, and Mara found it hard to imagine a great monster hidden away somewhere below the sanctuary.

I.A. TAKERIAN

She stopped before a massive tapestry that stretched high towards the ceilings, disappearing into the distance above. Her eyes went wide, mouth open slightly. It was unreal in its glory, the thread woven into its surface sparkling in the multi-colored lights like it was made of their glow. The tapestry depicted a glittering winged being, standing with stunning arms wide before two figures. They were kneeling before it, embracing one another; practically intwined. A magnificent ring made of what looked like starlight surrounded the place where they were joined.

"What happened to showering before dinner?" El asked from beside her.

Mara jumped, too enthralled with the tapestry to hear her approach. El giggled at her surprise.

"I got distracted," Mara replied bashfully, looking over El's shoulder to the entrance of the temple. Cyfrin stood leaning against the furthest pillar, talking animatedly to Kain and Milios. "Are they not coming in?" she asked, nodding to the three of them.

El smirked, waving a hand dismissively towards the entrance. "Yeah, Cyfrin's not really allowed in the temple anymore. He had an altercation years ago with some of the priestesses that involved a rather nasty line of limerick." El's expression was dreamy, staring into the distance. "They locked themselves up in their quarters for two whole weeks to pray and cleanse themselves of their impurities. And then they forcefully 'requested' he never come back."

It sounded exactly like something Cyfrin would do, especially a younger version of him. Mara couldn't imagine how difficult he must have been back then, considering how ridiculous he was as an adult.

El turned her attention to the tapestry Mara had been admiring. "Ah," she said in a wispy, mystical voice. "You've found the Legend of the Tie."

A PROPHECY OF UNDONE

"The what?" Mara asked, her eyes returning to the sparkling string.

"I'm surprised you haven't come upon it in your tomes, with all the studying you do. It's one of the oldest Odelian tales, told to children mostly. The legend says that every form of magick was made by the Zenoths, as you already know. They gifted it to us so that we may live as they lived here. Each Zenoth gave of themselves twice, and the two that shared that magick were cosmically bound to one another. It linked them through a tie that was unbreakable; that transcended to the Beyonds and further."

Her eyes grew misty, letting out a helpless sigh. "Their souls were said to call out to one another, never fully complete without the other. Always searching for a way to become whole again. It's said that when Tied users acted in unison, they rivaled even the Zenoths powers. But, as the years passed on and magick became diluted more and more, muddling as it moved from generation to generation, the Tied casters eventually died out. It became impossible for magicks that were from the same source to recognize each other. And now it's nothing more than an old children's tale."

El finished her story, placing a hand over her heart. "Zenoths bless, though, can you imagine? Someone you're cosmically bound with. Tied to a soul, joining as one..." She trailed off, eyes sparkling with wonder.

"Are you ladies done staring at the wall?!" Kain called to them, groaning. "I'm *starving*."

"Oh, positively withering away, you are!" Cyfrin said mockingly, shoving him towards the path as he and Milios laughed.

El led Mara from the temple to catch up with them as they walked back towards the Grand Hall.

CHAPTER 9
IN DARKNESS DEEP

There was a much smaller crowd outside the temple the following day than there had been during the last trial. Most likely because this challenge took place underground. They stood before Caerani and Drake in the morning sun, waiting for the first Hopeful to emerge from the catacombs below. Caerani had informed them prior to his descent that they would have only four hours each to complete their task before they were considered failed.

"When you pass the magick barrier into the catacombs, you will be pulled to one of the treasures within," she had said to the silent crowd. "Which item calls to you will depend on how the barrier's magick reads you, and what it deems you worthy of retrieving."

There were only six Hopefuls left, including Mara. Most had been eliminated in Batair's time walk, some still being nursed to health in the healer's hut at that moment. They had been standing in wait for nearly four hours now, shifting uncomfortably as they held infrequent, muted conversation. Mara was dressed in her mother's

I.A. TAKERIAN

leathers, the green gemstones shaped like crawling vines glinting in the sun's light. Her axe was strapped against her back, and Alora's dagger sat in its usual hilt against her thigh.

She was reminded irresistibly of standing before the Forgotten Wood during her first trial, waiting nervously for what the month ahead held. That part of her journey felt like years ago, and just yesterday at the same time.

The crowd had fallen silent, staring at the mouth of the temple in expectance. Mara leaned towards Milios. "When the four hours are up, if he does not return, will one of you go to rescue him? Or will it be Drake? Or Caerani."

Milios looked at her with cold eyes. "If they have not emerged within four hours, then there is most likely nothing left to emerge. And the barrier will let none but the Hopeful past." Their words were gentle, but heavy with the darkness of which they spoke.

Mara gulped, turning with growing panic to look into the temple once more. A few minutes of weighted silence passed, the crowd seeming to hold their collective breath. Then Drake nodded gravely at Caerani.

She sighed, looking grim. She bowed her head for a moment, Drake following suit. "The four hours have passed," she said into the stillness, and Mara felt the sadness of everyone around her as they realized the first Hopeful would not be returning. The crowd folded their arms in prayer, a few of them gasping through tear-streaked faces. She had the realization that many of these Hopefuls still had families here in the hidden village. It made Mara sick to think about.

"Who will be next to retrieve their treasure?" Caerani asked.

Silence again. The river babbled in the distance and Mara focused on the sound, her breathing shallow. She

A PROPHECY OF UNDONE

could not stand here for another four-hour cycle, waiting to see what her fate would be. It was unbearable.

Standing a little taller, she stepped forward to bow to Caerani, who looked at her with steely eyes. Mara could have sworn she saw a flicker of fear in her beautiful face, and El made a small sound of panic from behind her.

"Dawnbringer," Caerani said, her voice reverberating through the clearing. "We send you in to the dark depths below with the blessing of safety. Safety and strength." She paused. When she spoke again, it was with a much softer, less commanding voice. "Go forth without fear, Mara. You are strong. Remember this."

Mara nodded, turning to her companions with cold determination on her face.

El looked terrified, eyes wide and hands covering her mouth. Kain nodded back to her, Milios gave her an encouraging smile. Cyfrin's expression was unreadable, but his eyes burned as he stared into hers. She held his gaze for a long moment before turning and striding into the temple.

She felt none of the calm, peaceful energy she had the evening before. Every sound, every trickle of water, every crackle of falling stone echoed around her menacingly as she descended the spiraling staircase to the catacombs. The deeper she went, the colder the air around her became. It smelled like stagnant water and something rotten down here, growing more pungent with each step.

The number of orb lights was growing less and less as she walked, her heart somewhere high in her throat. The dark, dank passageway began to widen, sloping down to a landing below her. Standing on its darkly slick surface, she squared her shoulders at what she beheld.

At the very end of the passage stood a narrow archway. The black wood framing it was carved with tiny runes, very similar to the ones adorning Cyfrin's body. A deep hum

83

I.A. TAKERIAN

vibrated around her, and the empty air inside the archway seemed to be moving slightly.

Standing before it now, she could feel heavy energy rolling towards her from within. Veiling the archway was some sort of spell, rippling like the surface of dark waters as she investigated it. It made the air look liquid, like something that might drown her if given the chance.

She took a deep breath, ignoring the goosebumps popping up in dire warning across her body. Every ounce of her being cried for her to turn back; to run up that spiral stairwell and return to her waiting companions. But she had not faced everything in the past months for nothing, and she refused to give up now. Gathering her courage, Mara held her breath and stepped through the archway.

A cold chill, like her blood had turned to ice, ran through her as she crossed the threshold. There was a great rush of wind down the dark passageway beyond. It whipped around her, throwing her curls about her face, and nearly knocking her down. In the whistling of the air, she could hear what sounded like whispers. Many voices, all speaking in a language she did not understand, passed through her.

"*Dawnbringer*," they all whispered at once, and Mara shivered at the eeriness.

The wind vanished as quickly as it appeared, and she suddenly felt something. It was thrumming in her very soul, like a string pulling her irresistibly onward. Caerani's words floated around her head. "*You will be pulled to one of the treasures within.*"

Mara grimaced, wondering what sort of item the ancient magicks here had decided she was 'worthy of'. "Hopefully something very small," she murmured to herself. "And preferably not trying to kill me." She squinted

A PROPHECY OF UNDONE

into the barely lit passage. The stone down here was black, slick with wet slime from the water source Mara felt sure ran under the temple. Her feet slid a little across the ground as she walked, the sound of dripping echoed about like hundreds of tiny footfalls.

The catacombs sprawled out in an unprecedented number of tunnels, weaving through the earth, and making it impossible for Mara to keep her bearings. She passed discarded weapons and bits of armor as she moved, trying to keep her steps as quiet as possible. Every couple hundred feet, she would stumble upon a pile of bones, teeth marks scratched across their clean surfaces. Fear panged in her gut as she stepped over them.

It was impossible to keep track of time down here. The orb lights were few and far between as she traveled mostly in darkness through the labyrinth of passageways. She allowed herself to be pulled along by the mysterious feeling in her core, her feet following where it led.

She was deep within the catacombs now, praying that whatever pulled her forward would also lead her back. Panic began to prod at her brain. *What if I can't find my way out? What if the magick stops as soon as I retrieve the treasure? What if the monster down here finds me first?*

Suddenly, a distant sound ripped through the damp tunnel towards her. An unmistakable scream. Mara froze as it bounced off the walls, rocketing through her like a knife as it made its way up the catacombs. Then all fell silent once more. Mara felt numb with fear at the sudden silence and bit down on her tongue. The pain recentered her focus and allowed her to proceed forward.

She focused deeply on the magnetic pull within her when she rounded a corner into a new hallway. Her feet halted instantly as she stared down beyond her, heart freezing in an icy chill as her breath ceased.

I.A. TAKERIAN

Crouched on the ground a few yards ahead was a massive figure. The sound of wet crunching, tearing, slurping reached her ears, and she realized with a thrill of terror that the monster was eating something.

Some*one*.

Illuminated by the dim light above it, Mara could see that it was covered in a patchwork body suit made of what was unmistakably flesh. They were all different skin tones, some covered in fur from whatever creature it had been ripped from. She had the sickening feeling that the rest of the patches covering it had come from human victims. Her eyes moved slowly downward to gaze in horror at what the beast feasted on. She had to stifle a gasp.

Laying in pieces on the ground, torn open to reveal his insides which the creature was slurping out of him, was the previous Hopeful. The one who had not emerged. Mara's hand flew over her mouth, feeling sick. The creature lifted its head suddenly, blood dripping to the stone floor from its mouth. Mara spun around in an instant, pushing her back against the wall around the corner to hide.

She needed to run. The magnetic pull was tugging inside of her, urging her against all reason to proceed down the passageway past the monster to retrieve her treasure. She cursed under her breath, closing her eyes, and trying to quiet her pulse.

The sounds from the monster's feasting had ceased, and she wondered with grim hope if it had perhaps moved on from its kill. She couldn't just stand here, wasting the time she had to complete her task. Her stomach clenched painfully, threatening to upchuck the entirety of her breakfast as she forced herself to steady her nerves. Moving with deliberate slowness, she peaked her head out around the corner to look down the passageway.

The desecrated body lay in the middle of the hall, but

A PROPHECY OF UNDONE

the monster had vanished from sight. Relief swept over her, but it was fleeting. She strained her ears, listening for any sounds of movement. Something wet dropped on her from the ceiling, much thicker than the droplets of water that had been raining down upon her as she walked. She reached up, making a face of disgust as her fingers touched the strange, warm liquid. She pulled her hand before her eyes slowly, rubbing the slime between her fingers. Her heart stopped.

They were red with blood.

Her eyes flew to the ceiling, and she cried out, stumbling backward into the tunnel. Poised on the stone above her, limbs stretched at odd angles, was the monster. Its eyes were round, black voids; glowing pinpricks of venomous green color staring down at her from within them.

It had blade-like talons for fingers, dug into the stone beneath it like a blade through cotton. Clumps of shaggy black hair hung down from its scabbed scalp, and she could see an impossible number of sharp teeth within its gaping maw. It cracked its head to an unnatural position, its mouth splitting wide till it opened from ear to ear. Then it let out a shriek.

Mara screamed in response, sliding on the stone floor as she turned to run back down the passageway. But she was much too slow. The monster launched from the ceiling, it's shrieks shooting through Mara's brain and rattling it within her skull. She screamed again as it slammed into her, throwing her across the slick ground. Mara slid to a halt, hands suddenly warm and sticky. She had been thrown straight into the opened corpse, her torso now covered in blood and bodily fluid.

Crying out in horror, she scrambled to her feet as the monster shrieked again. It slashed through the air as Mara fell back against the wall. The tip of one massive talon met

I.A. TAKERIAN

its target, tearing through the flesh on Mara's left arm like paper. She screamed as blood began to rush from the wound and down her arm.

Another shriek. Mara dove this time, narrowly avoiding what would have been a fatal gash across her throat. She unhooked the axe from her back as the creature roared, turning to attack her again.

But Mara was ready for it now. She matched the monster's cry with a roar of her own, the noise deafening around them as she raised the axe high and brought it down with a powerful swing. It slammed into the ground as the monster raised its taloned arm. There was a great rumbling and the earth around them began to shudder. Cracks of golden light erupted from the ground around the point of impact, snaking out from Mara's axe towards the creature as it destroyed the tunnel between them. The walls began to crack, reaching up into the stones overhead.

Mara leapt back as the rock came crashing down from above, creating an impenetrable barrier between her and the monster. She heard its muffled shriek as the earth drew still, heard it grow fainter and fainter as it left the caved-in tunnel. Mara was panting, wincing as her head throbbed. She could feel a bump raising on her skull from where the monster had slammed her into the wall, and the blood loss from her arm was making her sick to her stomach. She closed her eyes, forcing her mind away from the horror that was the desecrated Hopeful.

She ripped out the strip of cloth that held her hair out of her face, swearing angrily as she wrapped it around the gash. "Fuck, fuck, *fuck*." The magnetic pull inside of her had begun to thrum with renewed vigor, and Mara felt that she was getting close to whatever waited for her.

Her mind raced as she started back up the passageway, pointedly ignoring the blood and ooze from the Hopeful's

A PROPHECY OF UNDONE

body crusting on her leather. *How long till that thing finds me, now that it knows I'm here?* She had barely escaped, and cold sweat dripped from her brow at the thought of facing it again.

She had been walking for what felt like forever, unsure of how long she even had left, when the tunnel began to open ahead of her. Mara stepped cautiously into a cathedral sized room, gasping.

All around her, glittering with gold, gemstones, and foreign metals that Mara could not identify, were treasures beyond her wildest imagination. They were piled high, mountains of coins and diamonds; enchanted swords and chests bursting with riches. There was not a single bit of floor visible, and her heart skipped a beat as she realized there were tunnels leading away from the room all around the walls. The beast would surely emerge from one of them soon, ready to finish what it had started. And Mara wouldn't be able to cause a collapse in this room as she had done to the tunnel before.

She gulped, heart pounding as she stared hopelessly around at the infinite amounts of treasure. *How could I possibly hope to find one item in all of this?* As if in response to her panicked thoughts, she began to hear a low humming coming from somewhere deep in the room. She froze, listening.

The pull in her core hummed as well, vibrating with the same frequency as the one in the trove of treasure before her. She took a deep breath, closing her eyes and allowing her feet to follow the invisible string connected to her task. She stepped carefully through and around the piles of glistening gold, careful not to dislodge anything large for fear of attracting the beast sooner than was inevitable. The hum rocked through her, dimming every one of her senses to its sound. Suddenly, the string stopped

I.A. TAKERIAN

pulling her forward. The humming ceased. And Mara opened her eyes.

Poised atop a great mountain of golden coins, emitting an ominous energy that sent a cold shiver down Mara's spine, was a dark red throne. The velvet seat looked incredibly soft, inviting even, but Mara did not dare draw closer as her eyes took in every detail. Holding the chair together, framing its cushioned red material in ivory, was what Mara knew to be bone. Numerous human skulls sat like a menacing crown at the top of the winged back, and dark crystals filled with swirling black smoke accented the arms.

Mara glared at it, weary. *I don't understand. How am I supposed to retrieve a throne? Am I meant to carry it on my back?* She grimaced, spellbound as she moved up the golden mountain towards it. *Wavering here will do me no good. The monster could be here at any moment.* Hesitant, she reached her hand out slowly and placed it on the arm of the throne.

The world around her faded away instantly, and she was falling.

CHAPTER 10
CURSED CURIOSITY

Mara could still feel her feet planted firmly on the golden mountain through the darkness of whirring sensation. She realized with a sharp thrill of panic that she was being travelled through time, her consciousness rocketing backwards as her body remained in the treasure room. Vulnerable and undefended.

She slammed to a halt; hand still gripped with white knuckles on the throne. The room around her was well-lit, orb lights dancing about the high ceilings and casting glittering cascades of sparkles off the treasure below.

There were two women standing at the foot of the golden mountain, staring up at the throne with wide-eyed awe. They were beautiful, straight black hair laying sleek and long in curtains about their pretty faces. Mara could tell in an instant that they were sisters. Pointed ears stuck out from their heads, revealing that they were Odelian.

"Deliondra, please," the smaller one hissed. "You heard what father said. If we're caught down here again—"

I.A. TAKERIAN

"Father won't listen to reason, Tilly," her green-eyed sister replied. "If he won't let me in to the trials simply because I am a woman, I will have to prove my worth to him some other way." She stared through Mara at the throne. It was like she was hypnotized, pulled with the same irresistible intensity that had led Mara here.

"Being a Hopeful will not bring mother back!" Tilly squeaked in anguish. "Please! We must make haste! Something is very, very wrong here!"

But her sister was not listening. The woman started up the mountain, slipping a little on the golden coins beneath her feet as she went. She came to stand beside Mara, a child-like grin of excitement on her face. But instead of reaching forth with a hand as Mara had done, this woman stepped forward. Anticipation danced on her stunning face as she sat down on the throne.

Mara opened her mouth to warn her of the ominous feeling coming from the throne; the dark energy that almost visibly surrounded it. But she knew it would be no use. This was nothing more than a memory.

And a terrifying one at that.

The woman sat looking elated and at-peace, reveling in her moment of seeming triumph. Then, the smile began to slide from her face. A great gust of wind spun around the room, the orb lights winking out one by one as the girl upon the throne began to struggle. She pulled at her arms and legs, trying desperately to stand from her seat. But she was held steadfast by whatever darkness was infused into the throne.

She began to scream, thrashing violently like an animal caught in a trap. Tilly screamed in tandem, falling backwards in fright. Blood began to ooze from the woman's nose, her eyes, her ears. Mara heard a sickening crack as she fought to free herself, her forearm sticking out at an

A PROPHECY OF UNDONE

awkward angle. Her shriek of pain confirmed that her arm had broken in her struggle.

The shrieks echoed around and around, her eyes rolling into the back of her head as she frothed red at the mouth. The cracking noises went off like explosions, every limb in her body breaking by unseen force. Mara's eyes were wide as she watched the woman transform before her. It was a nightmare; one she was helplessly trapped within. The woman's skin began to crack, black slime rushing forth from the places they erupted. Her shuddering form writhed in her seat, her shrieks became more and more inhuman.

Cursed. This thing was cursed. By what, Mara didn't know, but she knew what was coming before the transformation was even complete.

The woman's fingers and toes had elongated into razor sharp talons, the whites of her eyes filling with the black ooze that fell from her cracking skin. Her mouth split across her cheeks, the flesh ripping like wet silk. Her teeth fell from the inside of the maw as sharp fangs forced them out from her gums. Great, long patches of hair fell from her head, the smell of burning flesh in the air. Mara saw tears fall from her blackened eyes before the last glimpse of humanity blinked out.

Two pin pricks of green appeared within the black voids, and she gave another mighty shriek as she shot up from the throne. The cursed woman threw herself down the mountain of gold, coins and treasure rushing to the ground in a great clatter. She charged with breakneck speed into her little sister, letting out a bloodcurdling scream.

Mara fell once more, her consciousness slamming back into her body and buckling her knees. She lurched away from the throne, eyes wide and panting as she slid down the golden mountain. The throne was pulsing with dark welcoming energy; begging her to sit as she drew further away, trembling. The woman's face was burned into her mind, screwed up in unimaginable pain as she fought to free herself. Her sister's look of terror and betrayal when her sister came in for the kill.

Mara had felt exactly as the woman had. The need to prove yourself worthy, by whatever means possible. To be seen, and respected. It had blinded her to the dangers of this place. Mara's heart ached for her, trapped, and forgotten below the temple for all time. Forced by cursed madness to feast on the flesh of those unlucky enough to be caught in her path. She had looked so triumphant in that moment on the throne. Filled with glowing pride and beaming possibility.

And it had been ripped from her in an instant by dark magick.

There was the sound of charging footfalls to her left, and Mara reached up to grab her axe. The monster crashed through a mountain of treasure in front of its tunnel, throwing its contents about with a deafening clatter. It shrieked as its eyes rested on her; the same sound Mara had heard in the memory. Her heart gave another pang of agony for the woman, eaten away by the beast. Her moment of hesitation was not missed by the monster. It shot forward through the golden hoard.

It moved too quickly, Mara barely having time to lift her axe before it was upon her. The taloned hand reached up, wrapping around the hilt in Mara's hands and yanking as hard as it could. It ripped the axe from her, throwing it aside as they crashed to the ground.

Mara cried out, pinned beneath it as the smell of rotting meat filled her nose. She gagged, struggling with all her might to escape. The creature shrieked, slashing at her

A PROPHECY OF UNDONE

torso. The leathers did almost nothing to stop the talons, and she felt them tear into her flesh. She screamed, her hand wrapping around the hilt of the dagger at her hip. She drew it upwards in a flash of golden light, ripping through the monster's face as it went.

The noise it made was ungodly, the hit catching it off guard for just enough time. Mara scrambled out from underneath it, launching to her feet as the creature stood to its full and considerable height. It towered over top of Mara, black ooze dripping from its massive jaws.

It lunged for her once more, Mara meeting its talons with a flash of black metal. But the monster did not flinch away from the strike. Still shrieking, it wrapped its long, patched-flesh fingers around the blade and squeezed. Mara saw black blood ooze from its fist as it gripped the sharp blade, pulling it from Mara's grasp with unnatural ease.

The violent shrieking at this distance was staggering her, blinding her with noise as the creature gripped the dagger between both hands. They bled freely, but it seemed wholly unphased. Dark clouds of ominous energy began to ooze from her palms, her eyes surging with glowing green light. And with a sickening *crack* that sounded like breaking bone, the dagger split clean in half.

She dropped the pieces to the golden ground, Mara's stomach an empty pit as she watched it fall. Its hand wrapped around Mara's throat before she could react. It squeezed her tight, lifting her off her feet and into the air as it roared. Mara sputtered, legs kicking as she flailed. Her vision blurred, tunneling on the glowing green dots of the creature's eyes. The pounding sound of her blood in her ears drowned out all noise as the world spun.

Mara felt a fire spark inside of her, stilling her body as it grew rapidly to a mighty blaze. She reached up, wrapping her fingers around the monster's wrist that held her

I.A. TAKERIAN

airborne. Her hands began to glow with bright golden light, nearly blinding in the darkness around them. There was a sizzling sound, the creature's shriek reaching new heights as the golden light began to stretch in lightning-like veins up her arm.

There was a mighty *bang*, and the monster was thrown backwards, dropping Mara into the pile of treasure below. She grabbed at her throat, coughing, and sputtering as the room came back into focus. Wincing from the pain, she moved towards the spot where the monster lay. It was writhing there, holding its arm, and screaming in agony. The bolts of magick through her patched flesh were still glowing bright. Mara approached it cautiously, torn as to what to do.

This creature was once an Odelian woman. She was trapped in this monster somewhere, her soul corrupted by the curse that had bound her. Mara had seen the light vanish from her eyes in the flashback, watched her body be torn apart and rebuilt into this abomination. It wasn't fair. She had been given no choice, bested by her own damned pride, as Mara had been so many times before.

As Mara stood, battered, and bloodied, the monster's shrieks faded into pitiful whimpers. It turned to stare at her, the pin pricked pupils of its eyes a little wider than they had been before. "*Please.*" The voice that came forth from its mouth was inhuman, but Mara could make out the ghost of a soft tone within it. Her eyes widened in shock as black tears began to fall down its face. "Please, you must. You must end this. The curse must be broken. The bond must be broken. *Please.*"

There was so much pain in her voice, and Mara felt a sob rip through her as she watched her writhe in agony. The pupils of her eyes were beginning to shrink, the

96

A PROPHECY OF UNDONE

shrieking starting up again as the monster seemed to fight with itself.

"*The bond must be broken.*" Mara's thoughts reeled as the words repeated in her head. *The bond. The curse. The curse must be broken.* Mara spun around as the monster began to struggle to its feet behind her. She bolted towards the mountain of treasure where the throne sat, snatching her axe from the ground as the monster roared and took chase.

She scrambled up the side, gold coin slipping beneath her feet and crying out in pain as her body objected. But she had no time to stop. The monster was at her heels, lunging up the golden slope towards her with breakneck speed. Mara swung her axe high, yelling as she brought it down upon the throne. It crashed through the velvet and bone, light erupting from the axe's head in tandem with her furious cry. Fire burst from the seat, a sound like children's screams ripping through the air. It cracked, splitting clean in two and sending the halves crashing to the gold below.

There was a scream, so loud that it forced Mara's hands over her ears and buckled her legs. She dropped to her knees, hunkering down against the energy exploding around her. The room grew pitch black, the air thick with the screams and the black magick the throne had been imbued with. It was crushing Mara from all sides, squeezing the air from her with its weight. It felt like every bone in her body was readying itself to shatter, her muscles tensed in anticipation.

Then, the darkness vanished. The screaming ceased, and the oppressive energy disappeared. Mara opened her eyes, pulling her hands from her ears slowly, and rising to her feet as she looked around.

The crumpled form of the monster lay feet from her, arm still extended to the spot where she stood. But there

I.A. TAKERIAN

were no longer talon tipped claws here. Only a human arm, covered in oozing black cracks and faintly glowing veins.

Mara fell to her knees, carefully pulling its head into her lap. She stared down at the beautiful woman from the memory, unaged from the centuries as a beast. Her breath came in shallow gasps, her chest rising and falling in great shuddering motions.

Her eyes fluttered open, back to their brilliant shade of green as she stared up at Mara. Tears welled in them, a faint smile on her face. "Thank you," she breathed.

"I've got you," Mara said, though her voice sounded choked. "You're going to be okay. I've got you."

The woman's smile broadened a little, a twinkle sparking momentarily in her gaze. Her eyes closed, her breathing slowing. There was a peaceful look on her broken face as her chest gave one final rattle, then ceased to move.

Mara held her scarred, frail form in her arms. Hot tears fell from her eyes and onto the woman's face, mingling with the blood and black ooze. She shook with sobs. Wind whipped around her, ruffling her curls gently.

"*Dawnbringer.*" The many voices she had heard on the breeze at the start of the catacombs circled her, caressing her cheek. Mara felt numb as she stared down into the woman's face, her tears drying as her blood went cold.

"This is the treasure I leave with," she said into the air, gripping the woman's body to her chest with dark eyes. "I will not leave without her."

The wind stilled, but Mara could still feel its weight around her. Without another sound, it whipped around them in a whirlwind, blocking Mara's vision as they spun. When it stopped and she could see once more, they had been transported back to the entrance to the catacombs.

A PROPHECY OF UNDONE

The dark archway hummed before them as she sat holding the woman to her.

Something clattered to the ground on the stone beside them. Her heart lurched as she saw the two halves of her mother's dagger appear on the slick rock. The wind blew down the passageway, taking its whispers with it. Mara unfolded the woman's body from her arms, using the sleeve of her leathers to wipe the blood from her mouth. She had been so small. It increased the agony spilling over in Mara. She swung her lifeless form across her shoulders, saddened by how light she was.

She reached out with tender hands and picked up the broken dagger, slipping the pieces into her hip pocket. Her legs shook violently as she stood, but she refused to falter as she stepped through the veil of magick towards the spiraling stairwell. The climb to the top was agony, but Mara gritted her teeth and forced her legs forward and up.

The smell of damp air faded, the faint sound of birds now drifting down to her. There was sunlight above, and Mara squinted against it after the hours spent in the dark. She emerged into the temple and could see the faces of the crowd waiting outside. Her companion's smiles fell from their faces as she approached, replaced with looks of worry and anger as they stared at her bloody wounds. Their eyes darted to the body on her shoulders, confused and curious. Whispers shot through the crowd.

Mara walked past them, face void of emotion as she came to stand before the wide eyed Caerani and Drake. She knelt to the ground and carefully slid the body from her back, laying it gently before them. She arranged the long black hair on her head, resting her petite hands on top of her stomach gently. Reaching slowly into her pocket, she removed the shards of dagger and lay them beside the body. The green gem had grown dark, no longer dancing

I.A. TAKERIAN

with its beautiful light. Mara felt the dark, numbness inside of her grow as she looked at it.

They all stared down at the woman's broken form, covered with blood and ooze and shattered beyond repair. Mara stood slowly, as if in a haze. "I bring the cursed protector of the catacombs as my treasure," she said, voice cold. "It was a woman trapped within the monster below. One of us. She is trapped no longer."

Her chin tilted up slightly as Drake and Caerani continued to stare with looks of shock and amazement. The entire crowd was deathly still with similar expressions on their faces. Mara turned on her heel, ignoring the silence of the crowd and the anxious faces of her companions as she began to march her way up the path towards the Grand Hall. She could hear the sets of four footfalls behind her as she walked, and she knew that Kain, El, Milios and Cyfrin followed.

She entered the house and turned down the hallway to her room without stopping. She walked in complete silence, almost trance-like, as she moved through the sunlit corridor. The sound of bird song and rustling leaves in the wind seemed distant as she entered her bedroom, not bothering to close the door. It didn't seem real, what happened in the catacombs, as well as her standing now in the crystal lined room. It was like she was still dreaming, watching it all from the outside.

Fully clothed in her armor, still covered in ooze and muck and blood, she lowered herself to the floor and laid down. She stared without really seeing up at her ceiling, ignoring her body's cries of pain against the hardwood.

There was a soft knock on her open door, and Cyfrin stepped silently into the room. His expression was solemn as he sat next to her on the floor. Mara's heart began to

A PROPHECY OF UNDONE

ache in his presence, her body trembling as every emotion she had been fighting to keep contained rose within her.

Cyfrin moved, and his arms were suddenly around her. He held her gently, pulling her to his chest. The tenderness in his touch tore away any hold Mara had. She took in a great, shuddering breath and began to sob.

The sound ripped from her, tearing through the room. The agony she felt for the woman in the catacombs, the absolute whirlwind of the last few months, the loss of her life in Delinval and of Adrian. The lies and deceit, the abuse of her youth, the intense expectations that lay on her shoulders and her fury at her inability to even control herself...it all cascaded around her at once as her walls crumbled.

Cyfrin pulled her into his lap, his arms wrapped tight around her as he rocked her gently. She buried her head in his chest, tears spilling from her as she cried. She gripped the front of his shirt like her life depended on it, and she felt his fingers press into her back. "I can't stand it," she sobbed. "It's all happened so fast and so violently, and I feel like I'm drowning. I can't stand it. I can't stand the thought of failing you all."

"I'm here." She felt his words more than heard them, so gentle was his tone. "I'm here for you, whatever you need. You're safe."

CHAPTER 11
FAITH IN THE STORM

Mara couldn't stop crying. It was like a great dam had burst, releasing a lifetime of grief. She had always thought her pain was well kept in a tightly sealed box within her. But with this final trigger, everything had been destroyed. She stood shivering in her bathroom, tears falling silently down her bloodstained cheeks. Cyfrin fiddled with the knobs to the massive bathtub, and steaming water began to cascade into it from the ceiling.

He turned to face her, reaching out slowly. "Mara, we need to get you cleaned off. El will have my hide if those get infected." His eyes lingered on her wounds, his expression angry. But his expression softened as he spoke next. "The water will help. It helps to wash it all away."

Mara took his hand through her haze, stepping towards him. He looked nervous, avoiding her eye. "Do you…may I help with your leathers?"

Mara blinked, looking down at herself. The leathers were so covered in blood and ooze, it was impossible to see where hers ended and the beasts began. Pieces of flesh

I.A. TAKERIAN

from the fallen Hopeful still clung to her. Her breath began to hurry again, her tears running faster.

Cyfrin put his hand under her chin, lifting her eyes to his. "We're going to get you cleaned off. You're safe, Mara."

Her hands were already fumbling with the closures of her leathers, shaking as her sobs mounted anew. Cyfrin's hands were over hers, moving them carefully down to her sides. Mara could see his head tilted back, staring respectfully up towards the domed ceiling as he undressed her. Mara helped as she could, ashamed of how helpless she was in this moment.

She stood naked now, Cyfrin holding her hand to steady her walk. He led her to the bathtub, helping her to ease into his depths while keeping his eyes ever-skyward. He knelt by the tub as Mara adjusted to the heat of the water. Cyfrin was right. It was already helping ease her out of her panic, the trembles melting into the warmth of the bath.

"If you'll turn your back to me and come to the edge here," he said in a low voice. "I can clean those wounds before we get you into bed."

Mara sank low into the water, starting to become aware of how very naked she was. And whose presence she was in. But she did as she was told, too exhausted to argue. The tears had finally begun to slow as she floated to Cyfrin's edge of the bath, placing her back against the smooth marble. She cleared her throat to alert him that she was in position.

She felt his hands sink into the water beside her, a soft rag brushing against her skin. He was being so gentle, it made new tears spring to Mara's eyes. She wasn't sure why. He took the soapy rag across her arms slowly, taking extra care as he came to her deep forearm gash. Mara

104

A PROPHECY OF UNDONE

could feel his breath behind her, sending a thrill down her spine.

His hand came to her cheek, wiping the fresh tears away with the rag. "Would talking about I help?"

Mara bit her lip. "I'm not sure. I've never tried."

Cyfrin was silent, patient as he poured water onto Mara's curls.

Mara closed her eyes as he worked suds into her hair. "It was like everything just crashed around me at once. I wouldn't even know where to start."

"Then start at the beginning," he replied, his tone serious. "Tell me everything."

"Everything?"

"Yes, Mara."

She shifted nervously in the water. She had never told anyone *everything* before. Not even Adrian. But perhaps that's exactly what she needed to move on. To part with the boiling anger and find who she was without it. And so, she started from the very beginning. From her childhood in the castle, to her days on the training fields. Her want to please her 'uncle', and the pain she felt thinking she was the reason for her mother's death. She told him of Lady Lenorei, and her horse, Balthazar, and her favorite barn cat, who she very much suspected was the father of most of the barn kittens. It was the first time she had truly spoken of Adrian. And though she missed him horribly, this seemed to loosen the grief.

She was laughing, trying not to pay much attention as Cyfrin's rag made its way to her cut belly. "So, Adrian becomes the newest Knight of Delinval, right? Oh, and he's the most pompous git about it too. Absolutely thriving off the attention from the swooning ladies of the court. He was impossible to deal with."

"Hmm, sounds like someone else I know," Cyfrin said,

I.A. TAKERIAN

and Mara could practically hear the smirk in his voice. But his hand trailed across her navel, and she was far too flushed to retort.

"When we get new Knights in Delinval, they're given their own set of armor to mark the occasion. It's got the crest of Delinval on it, and they're always as shiny as shiny could be." She gave a flourish with her hand. "It's like a bunch of birds. The more reflective the silver of ones armor, the more desirable one must be."

"And was Adrian's the shiniest of all?"

Mara gave a small smile, remembering. "No. No, Adrian hated the whole ceremony of it. Thought it got in the way of what being a knight is supposed to be about. 'It's the principle of the thing, Mara,' he said to me. I'll never forget him marching down to the blacksmith and demanding his darkest armor." Mara raised her hand, pointing towards the dark sky outside the window. "Dark as the night sky, he wanted. Never seen a piece like it in Delinval."

Cyfrin's hands had suddenly stopped moving. "Black armor? The crest of Delinval on his left pauldron?"

Mara froze, hearing the recognition in his voice. "Yes."

There was silence in response. It took everything in Mara not to spin around and expose herself to him.

"Why, Cyfrin?"

"I don't want to upset you."

Mara's lip trembled, fearing what was to come. "Too late."

Silence for a moment longer. "The Delinval forces have been gathering outside the Forgotten Wood for some time now. They're led by a man who is said to have fire for eyes. A man clad in black armor."

Mara's heart plummeted. "No," she whispered, feeling the tears welling again. "He can't be here. Not yet. I'm not ready." And it was true. She was haunted endlessly by the thought of what Adrian would do when he found out about Mara's secret. *But the pain he must be in,* she thought. *What would I do, if roles were reversed?*

She gulped. "I have to go to him. He probably thinks I'm dead, or...or *worse.*"

"I'd think death would be worst to him, from what you've told me," Cyfrin said, his voice low.

Mara shook her head. "The trials...I must finish the trials. I can't throw it all away when I'm this close to the end. And then..." Her voice trailed off. *And then what? I pop out of the woods, leader of the Odelians? "Oh, Adrian! Everything's been great since I've been gone, but Grathiel is built upon lies!"*

"And then you bring us to meet Adrian." Cyfrin's hand was against her cheek again, brushing his thumb across it slowly. "We'll walk you there together and help you to explain. I know he'll listen to you."

"And if he doesn't?" Mara whispered back.

"Well, then we cross that bridge when we get there." Cyfrin was holding a towel out behind her. "For now, you need rest. Let's get you dried off."

Mara got slowly out of the tub, Cyfrin standing with his back turned by the door. A silken nightgown had been set off to the side, and Mara slipped into it gratefully. Cyfrin helped her to the bed, moving the tomes and books onto the desk as she slid into the sheets.

He pointed down to the gashes across her arm. "El will be wanting to take a look at those in the morning. We've only cleaned them. They'll need to be sealed."

"Cyfrin," Mara said quickly, sensing him about to depart. "Please." She couldn't find the right words to say, or how to ask.

Cyfrin had frozen in place, watching her struggle. "Please, Mara?"

I.A. TAKERIAN

Mara dropped her eyes, face hot. She scooted over in the bed, placing her hand beside her on the empty spot. "Stay."

Cyfrin blinked. "Yes, ma'am." He moved forward without hesitation, slipping his boots off as he came to lay beside her on the bed. He was still, unmoving and straight as a board as he waited.

Mara moved closer to him, resting her head against his broad chest. She could hear his heart thundering beneath her, could swear it skipped a beat when she rest her hand against his stomach. He wrapped his arm around her carefully, pulling the blanket to her shoulder and taking a slow, deep breath.

The panic and anxiety were no match for the battle of emotion in Mara now. But nothing could compete with the feeling of overwhelming safety that had taken hold of her. And for the first time since she had been rescued for Delinval, Mara slept in dreamless slumber.

CHAPTER 12
SAVIOR OF THE DAMNED

The sunlight beat against Mara's eyelids, dragging her from her slumber. Her body throbbed, sore in places she had never imagined possible. She groaned and shifted her head away from the sun. The blanket beside her was covered in the smell of pine and honey, and Mara's eyes flew open. Cyfrin had gone, but the place he had slept was still warm.

The memories of the day before all came flooding back, and her face heated with embarrassment. *Sobbed. I absolutely dissolved a lifetime of trauma at Cyfrin's fucking feet.* She dragged her hands down her face at the thought. *And Adrian. Zenoths blood, poor Adrian. He fears the worst and here I am, being nursed to health by tall, dark, and irresistible.* She groaned even louder at this.

"Rough night then?"

El was leaned against the four poster, eyebrows raised as she stared down at her. Mara rolled over, letting out a heavy sigh and staring at the ceiling.

"I don't want to talk about it," she whimpered,

throwing her hands over her face. "I just want to shrivel up and die."

El laughed, sitting down beside her, and laying back to stare at the ceiling. "Surely it can't be worse than what you've just faced," she said.

"I've just spent a whole night crying into Cyfrin's arms. Like some poor, pathetic damsel." Mara groaned, wishing to disappear.

El's eyes flashed with merciless humor. "Oh my. I suppose you're right then. We'll just have to kill you."

Mara pinched her, both sitting up. "I don't want to talk about it!" Mara repeated, face very red.

El giggled. "You know, it's actually quite brave to cry and admit you need some help. Even if just for a moment. And especially with someone you have such loving feelings for."

"*I do not have feelings,*" Mara hissed but El ignored her, getting to her feet.

"You'll need to bathe before I can work on healing you. Looks like you only did a base job of it last night, and you need to be fully clean for this."

Though Mara had spent much of the night before in heart-wrenching sobs, she felt oddly good this morning. Not just good. *Great*. Her heart was clear of the emotions she had forced down, the high walls she had built now mostly vanished. Her mind focused with renewed intensity on the journey ahead.

It had been the first night void of nightmares as well, a fact she would be keeping to herself. Cyfrin appeared in

A PROPHECY OF UNDONE

her mind's eye, cocky and smiling wickedly at her. *"You slept soundly with me beside you?"* he would say, in his velvety soft purr. *"How utterly fascinating."*

She pulled her lace undershirt over her head, wincing with even the most subtle movements. El knocked on the bathroom door and opened it a crack. "I'm coming in!" she declared before pushing it wide. Her eyes narrowed as they looked at the many deep gashes covering Mara's body. She sighed, shaking her head. "It won't be pretty since they were made by a cursed beast. But I can close them all up; keep them from infection." El motioned for Mara to come stand before her.

She hovered her hands over the deep wound in Mara's forearm, her eyes beginning to glow. Mara felt intense warmth as her palms radiated with their green light, and she felt her skin begin to move slowly back together.

"You'll have to tell me sometime what exactly happened down there," El said in a soft voice, and Mara knew she was speaking about the catacombs. "Centuries. Centuries of warriors, including Alora, Caerani and Drake, and no one ever saw through the curse. Milios thinks she must have been one of the very first villagers."

El's hands moved to the inch long gashes covering her torso next. "You broke the trial. The last three Hopefuls passed automatically because there was no challenge left to complete. Caerani's not too pleased with it, but there isn't much difficulty in going down there now. You really know how to leave a mark."

Mara breathed a laugh. "I'm just happy to do something good for once. Something useful."

There was thoughtful silence, El's magick carefully healing the wounds on her chest and face. "The whole village has heard about it at this point. You know how quickly word travels here. They're calling you the Savior of

I.A. TAKERIAN

the Damned." El's voice was soft, watching Mara closely for her reaction.

She blinked, stunned. *Savior.* She had saved that woman from an eternity of nightmarish misery, released her soul finally to the Great Beyond. Mara's chest felt warm, filling with a sense of pride at the thought.

El had finished healing her wounds, stepping back to admire her work. There were thin white scars to mark the places each slash had been. But Mara didn't mind. They signified how far she had come; how hard she had fought to get here. Each scar told tale of her journey, and she would have it no other way.

She beamed up at El, who looked at her with an odd expression. She reached out and tucked Mara's curls behind an ear. "I was thinking…" El started hesitantly, eyes weary. "And I don't want you to be mad or strange when I say this but…I think I can heal your ears. Back to how they're meant to be."

Mara's mouth fell open slightly, reaching up to drag a finger across the scarred tip of her ear. El waved her hands hurriedly before her. "But only if you want me to!" she said quickly, mistaking Mara's expression for one of upset. "I had just been speaking to one of the healers about it whilst you were in the woods during your first trial. They taught me a spell that could work."

Tears were brimming in Mara's eyes, and she smiled up at El's worried face. "I would love that. Even just for you to try would mean everything to me," Mara breathed.

El returned her huge smile with a look of relief. "Yes! Please, it would be my *honor* to do this for you!" El proclaimed, clapping her hands excitedly.

She motioned for Mara to sit and El knelt before her, staring intently at her ears. "The healer I spoke to said it should be relatively straight forward. We're just growing

A PROPHECY OF UNDONE

back what's meant to be there already. Much easier than making something from nothing. Would you pull your hair back for me?" El rubbed her hands together as they began to glow deep emerald, green.

Mara pulled her hair back, holding it at the base of her neck with one hand. She was trembling slightly, in excitement and fear. Out of everything to happen thus far, this would be the most permanent. A definitive decision to accept her position here, as an Odelian. It would mean the end of hiding who she truly was.

El grabbed her free hand, squeezing it as the green glow heated through Mara's arms. Her eyes were sparking with a gentle determination. They nodded to one another, a silent confirmation of readiness.

El raised her hands to cover Mara's ears and began to chant in ancient tongues. Mara's ears were burning at the tips, the feeling very similar to being branded with a hot poker. She gritted her teeth, taking in sharp intakes of breath as El focused on her mumbled spell work.

Mara screwed her face up in concentration, squeezing her eyes shut and trying to focus on anything but the feeling. Her mind was dark and clouded, full of the pain now spreading from her ears into her skull. It stabbed at the base of her spine, sending her nerve endings into overdrive as she shuddered.

Then, through the fog of rising pain, she heard a wry laugh. Cyfrin's face floated out of the darkness, winking, and throwing a simpering smile to her. She was shocked by how detailed he was, wondering how she could possibly memorized him to this extent. She imagined him grabbing her roughly by the waist, pulling her close, whispering dark sweetness onto her lips as they met…

El had removed her hands from her ears, panting and sweaty but positively beaming at her. She grabbed the hand mirror from the table by the bath, giving it to Mara. With hands still trembling, she brought it up to stare at her reflection. Her eyes went wide.

Two perfectly tipped ears now sat on either side of her head, all prior scarring vanished. She released her hair, letting her curls fall and watching them settle around the soft points. And there it was. Her mother's face breaking into a smile, her father's eye winking beneath the dark curls. She squealed, El blinking in surprise.

Mara threw her arms around El's neck, squeezing her tight. "Thank you," she whispered tearfully against El's shoulder, feeling her redouble her squeeze. They held each other for a long moment, warm tears of happiness streaking down Mara's cheeks.

They released each other, both smiling so hard that Mara's wet face was starting to ache.

"We're due to leave on the Red Froth the day after tomorrow," El said as Mara pulled her bell-sleeved white top over her lace undershirt and leather pants. "We go with the Hopefuls nearly every year, just for the practice. Save for Milios, who wouldn't go out on the open water if their life depended on it, bless them. Keeps us all on our toes, going out there. Traditionally, we spend the day before we leave at the crystal falls, meditating." She smiled bashfully at Mara. "And by meditate, I mean we do a lot of drinking, a little dancing and some very intoxicated sparring. It's quite dangerous, actually...Want to join us?"

Mara did not even hesitate. She nodded, still smiling wide as she grabbed El by the hand and led the way out of the Grand Halls.

El had not been exaggerating when she said the whole village had heard of her trial in the catacombs. They had no sooner left the Grand Halls in the direction of the dirt path when a large group of people approached them. It

A PROPHECY OF UNDONE

looked as though they had been waiting on the bridge for Mara to emerge.

They were all cheering uproariously, some clapping her on the back while others outrightly hugged her. They congratulated her on her completion of the Trial and thanked her for ending it once and for all. Mara got the sense that many of these people had lost loved ones to this very trial, and the cursed monster in the deep. There were many tearfully exuberant eyes in the crowd around her as they cheered.

Someone had crowned her with a circlet of glowing flowers, and the barkeep of their favorite tavern had shoved an entire box of his house mead into El's arms with a heavy wink. Mara shook every hand, returned every hug. She felt a strange feeling inside of her, and with a bolt of pleasant surprise realized what it was.

Belonging.

It took them thirty whole minutes to finally pull away, off on the path through the woods to the crystal falls. The crowd waved after them as they departed, still beaming, and cheering one last time.

El was chuckling. "Don't let the others know you've just been given free mead," she said, shaking the box she carried so the glass bottles clinked against each other inside. "They'll never stop using you for free drinks if they find out."

They passed the temple, Mara keeping her eyes forward towards the edge of the falls as they did so. The feelings of peace and beautiful calm she had felt that day staring at the tapestries had died, replaced by only cold memory now. She doubted if she'd ever be able to look at it the same way again.

They reached the top of the stairwell that led down to the crystal lake below, the falls rumbling away beside them.

I.A. TAKERIAN

Mara could see Kain and Cyfrin at the bottom, swords already drawn as they danced back and forth by the lakeside.

Milios was seated on the water's edge, kicking their feet in the lake as they played a tune on the flute Mara could not hear over the roar of water. She could see bottles upon bottles of mead and wine sitting by the bottom of the rocky stairwell, waiting to be drunk. Boxes of pastries sat stacked high beside them.

Milios looked up as they reached the bottom, smiling widely at Mara. "You look radiant, Mara," they said, grey eyes flashing over her healed skin and lingering on the spot where her ears lay hidden beneath the curls. Kain and Cyfrin dropped their swords, approaching them breathlessly.

"Dawnbringer!" Kain called, arms held wide as he panted. "Breaker of the Trials! Savior of the Damned!"

"Today, we celebrate your hard-won victories!" Cyfrin added, sweat dripping from his beaming face.

Kain took the box of mead from El as Cyfrin came to stand toe-to-toe with Mara. She held her breath, flattening her expression as he studied her. His eyes flashed over the thin white scars tracing across her body. He lifted his hand, running his thumb across the one on her cheek as his gaze narrowed. Her heart hammered in her chest. He looked angry for a moment as he traced over the scarring, then he froze.

His eyes left her cheek, hand brushing across her skin as he drew her hair behind her ear. He stared at the pointed tips. His lips began to twist upward, breaking into the most painfully gorgeous smile Mara had ever seen. He cupped her face in his powerful hand, eyes smoldering as they bored into hers. Her breathing was shallow, face burning against his palm as he leaned closer to her.

A PROPHECY OF UNDONE

"You surprise me, darling," he murmured, heat pulsing in Mara's core at the gentle purr under his tone. "I didn't think you could be any more beautiful. And yet, here you are. Radiant and dazzling."

Mara stammered, her thoughts scrambling as his eyes glinted wickedly. He drew his hands from her cheek, glancing up at her crown of flowers with a chuckle. "Not only your ears restored, but a crown as well! Zenoths bless, you're on a roll today." He laughed and the sound filled Mara with a deep need.

It wasn't fair that he could make her feel this way, that he *knew* he made her feel this way. It brought him unending enjoyment to watch her squirm, and it drove her mad to know it. Her eyes narrowed as she stared up at his satisfied face. If he wanted to toy with her, she would no longer sit by without retaliation. *If it is a game he wants, it is a game he shall have.*

Mara softened her gaze, eyes hooded as she set a vicious smirk on her face. She closed the space between them, resting her hand on his chest and coming up on to her toes. She was inches from his lips, forcing herself to focus.

Cyfrin's breathing had stopped, his body rigged as he stared at her. His wide eyes darted from her lips back to her gaze with such speed that Mara nearly missed it.

Nearly.

She let out a breathy laugh, feeling his pulse quickening under her hand. "I do love surprising you, Lightcleaver," she murmured, her voice sultry in a way she did not think she was capable of.

She had never tried being seductive before, but from the way Cyfrin drew up to his full height, eyes flashing with something almost feral as he stared down into hers, she felt that she had been successful.

117

I.A. TAKERIAN

There was an excited "Ha ha!" proclaimed from some-where above them, tearing both of their eyes to the top of the falls.

Kain stood at the edge, shirtless and with both fists high.

"*I am the Slash Master!*" he cried into the air, cackling as he launched off the edge.

They all watched in amazement as she shot towards the water's deep surface, slamming through it with a great splash. The lake exploded from the place he hit, drenching them all in an instant.

The five of them roared with laughter as Kain's head popped up out of the lake, spouting a stream of water from his mouth like a fountain and glowing with child-like glee. For the first time in months, Mara felt completely and utterly at ease.

CHAPTER 13
BY CRYSTALS WATCHFUL REVERENCE

The autumn sun was setting over the falls, the multi-colored orb lights dancing happily around them. They had nearly demolished the entire stack of mead and wine over the course of the day, and they had all devolved into gleeful, giggling messes.

Kain and Cyfrin were both shirtless, as they so often liked to be. They wrestled in the light of the rising moon, growling at one another like wild animals. El was sighing happily, staring with wistful eyes and head-in-hands at Kain.

Milios played a spritely tune on their flute by the water's edge, and Mara sat with her feet in the dazzling clear waters beside them. Colorful specks of glowing light gathered around her skin under the surface, tickling her as they played. She turned with rosy cheeks to smile at Milios. "Is the flute the only instrument you play?" she asked, grinning as the twinkling notes flew about her.

Milios' eyes flashed playfully, removing the flute from their mouth and leaving the feral sounds of Kain and Cyfrin as the only noise echoing across the lake.

I.A. TAKERIAN

"You're quite good at it," Mara added, sighing. "I've not a lick of musical talent in my entire body."

Milios chuckled. "This? This is nothing," they replied. "I'll show you something *magickal*." Their eyes began to swirl with a stormy grey glow. The wind was starting to pick up around them, and Milios raised their hands.

It was something out of a beautiful dream. In time with Milios' careful strokes through the air, voices began to sing softly around her on the wind. She stood as they swirled about faster and faster, whipping her black curls high in the air as she laughed. The voices were like perfectly tuned bells; they reminded her of her favorite windchime from her room in Castle Delinval. The harmonies spun round about her, filling her with passionate glee. Mara spread her arms wide and began to dance.

The urge to move was irresistible. The singing winds were her partner, Milios their conductor. Her face ached from smiling, the laughter spilling forth from her mouth joining the music around her in a stunning sound. As she danced, she looked to Kain and Cyfrin fighting a few yards away. Through the whipping wind, petals joining the fray to spin around her, she could see Kain had toppled Cyfrin. He crouched above him, beaming with victory as he held him to the ground.

But Cyfrin was not looking at him. His full attention was centered on Mara, his eyes blazing with a hunger that made her heart leap. He began to struggle, thrashing beneath Kain as Mara closed her eyes and let the wind spin her. She twirled in place, the music growing louder now. It was ethereal, the notes sounding nothing short of pure happiness. She never wanted them to stop.

Then someone was grabbing her. A hand centered on her waist, pulling her close and sliding easily into the dance

120

A PROPHECY OF UNDONE

right along with her. She did not need to look to know who it was, but her eyes fluttered open. Cyfrin held her against him, his powerful grip hot on her skin. His free hand gripped hers firmly as they spun within the whipping winds. She stared up into his beautiful face.

His cheeks were flushed, eyes hooded and burning into her own as they moved. His jaw was clenched, the muscles taught. Her hand moved instinctively to his shoulder, sliding up to rest against the side of his neck. He raised his chin slightly to expose it further to her, staring down at Mara with animal-like intent. His hand slid from her waist to her lower back as they spun about, his fingers pressing into her skin and pushing her harder against him.

She felt the familiar heat rising within her, an aching need beginning to cry out in her core. But it was overshadowed by the joy, the happiness she felt in this moment. The wind blurred the crystal lake around them, the music drowning out any noise of the falls. And she began to laugh once more, a huge smile breaking across her face as she danced with Cyfrin. She threw her head back in carefree abandon.

He blinked down at her as if he had just been dazzled by bright light, his expression awestruck. Then, his eyes softened. The grip on her back and gentle firmness of his hand holding hers did not falter, but a brilliant smile was now shining across his perfect face. Through the blur of the singing winds as they spun faster, the world began to glow.

Every color imaginable pulsed to life around them, beaming brighter than the dawn. It illuminated them both in stunning splendor, and Mara became breathless as she beamed up at Cyfrin. The winds had begun to slow, the music becoming more and more distant as the spinning eased to a halt. Cyfrin released Mara almost instantly,

I.A. TAKERIAN

dragging his eyes away from hers and staring about them as the color raised higher in his face. Mara's eyes widened as she looked around.

Every crystal was lit from within with multi-colored facets. The ones sticking out from the walls of the canyon, the ones now glowing like starlight underneath the surface of the lake, the small pebble-like crystals all along the lake's shore. El, Kain and Milios were staring around in equal awe, the entire lake shining brightly enough to rival the sunniest of days.

"What's happening?" El breathed, spinning slowly in place with mouth wide as she took it all in.

Milios gave a broad smile to Mara and Cyfrin. "It seems the spirits of the lake quite enjoyed your performance," they said, and Mara blushed heavier, glancing at Cyfrin through her eyelashes.

He was already looking at her, eyes bright and burning.

"The magick is so heavy right now," Kain said, shuddering with a little smile. "It feels like it's pouring into me. Filling me."

"You're right," Cyfrin said, not breaking eye contact with Mara's bashful stare as he addressed Kain. "I've never felt more connected to Zenafrost. We should take advantage of the opportunity. We should invoke the Bond of the Brethren."

Kain's smiled widened. "I've been wanting you to take that bond with me for over two hundred years," he said, rubbing his hands together in excitement.

"It's not practiced in today's age," Milios said thoughtfully. "But long ago it was tradition. When warriors banded together in a War Party like ours—" They motioned around at the four of them. "When they banded together, they would partake in a sacred ritual that bound them for all eternity. The magick seals them in a bond that allows

A PROPHECY OF UNDONE

them to always feel one another, to find each other no matter where they were in the world. It helped to strengthen the party and make them an even more powerful force."

Their expression darkened slightly. "They stopped performing the ritual, stopped allowing the warriors to bind themselves to each other, because the pain of losing one of the bounded members was too great. And in times of war, death is commonplace. We lost many warriors to their own hands, the burden of the loss too much for them to bare."

The lake grew silent at Milios' words, as if in respect for the past lives lost.

"Yes, well done sharing all the *worst* parts of the bond, Milios," Kain scoffed, folding his arms across his chest. "Bonded war parties became coveted because of the power the bond invokes. When the Brethren were together in combat, the magicks would resonate with one another. It increases the power of each warrior's magick by a significant enough amount that the pain of potential loss was, for the most part, worth it."

"Until it wasn't anymore," El said softly, biting her lip.

Mara fidgeted uncomfortably. Her companions were hundreds of years old, already bonded together through battle and loss and love. And she was just the lost princess they had been tasked to rescue. She couldn't even control her magicks, let alone use them to assist her comrades.

"I am not worthy of such a bond." Mara's words hung in the air as they stood in silence. Cyfrin stepped forward instantly and took her hand.

His eyes were smoldering with blazing vindication, threatening to burn Mara with their intensity. But he squeezed her hand with a soft reassurance that made her stomach flutter. "Not worthy? You are the final piece we've

I.A. TAKERIAN

been waiting on," he said, and Mara's heart skipped several beats.

Kain came up behind Cyfrin, clapping a massive hand on his back as he beamed at them. "And what better time than right before another hair-raising, potentially deadly month of adventures!" He laughed.

El took Mara's other hand, smiling warmly at her. "Besides, I don't plan on myself or any of you dying. Ever," she said, eyes brimmed with tears.

Milios joined them as they formed a circle on the lakeside. They joined hands with one another, Mara still squeezing tightly to Cyfrin and El's grips. They all looked so beautiful, silhouetted by the crystal's glow and the stunning moonlight. The air around them had grown still, as if it could sense the powerful thing about to happen.

Milios met Mara's gaze with swirling grey eyes. "We stand before the purest magicks and spirits of old," they began, their voice echoing in the stillness. "We lay bare our hearts and souls to weigh and ask to be reborn within each other. We shed that which does not serve us, and welcome in the light of the new dawn. We invoke the Bond of Brethren."

A great ringing sounded in Mara's head. Cyfrin and El's hands were so hot clasped against hers, she felt they might catch fire. A dim glow started to pulse from each of their bodies, growing until they were all joined together by its radiance. Swirling lights of colorful magick whipped around them on the suddenly heavy wind, and Milios began to chant. It was a language Mara did not recognize, crisp and melodic. El, Kain and Cyfrin joined in, and Milios nodded to her in encouragement.

Though she knew not what she said, she mimicked their words into the air ripping around their circle. Their voices were becoming one and many all at once. The

124

A PROPHECY OF UNDONE

sound filled every inch of Mara's being, and she felt the very earth beneath their feet begin to tremble. This was ancient power, magick like she had never felt before.

Whispers filtered in through their chanting voices, unrecognizable voices intermingling with their sound. Goosebumps raised on her skin as a burning sensation began across the tops of the knuckles on her right hand. She looked down, continuing to chant as she stared at the place that was stinging like a fresh brand.

Shapes began to appear in her flesh, the sound of sizzling reaching Mara's ears as they raised. On the knuckle of her thumb sat three swirling lines, grey in color and looking like a depiction of the wind. Her pointer knuckle glowed with shocking shade of blue, a lightning bolt now etched into its surface. Her middle finger laid host to a brilliant, green orb; a tiny red sword appearing beside it on her ring finger. Last to appear as it seared into her skin was the marking on her pinky knuckle. The symbol of a glowing golden sun now sat upon it, appearing with a flourish as the sizzling ceased.

The ringing in her ears mixed with the clashing of their chanting voices was deafening. Mara looked around at her comrade's hands, seeing the same tattoos now glowing on their knuckles as well. The wind rushed suddenly upward, whisking the shining magick with it as it went. Mara's hair flew behind it, whipping her curls about in the pull. And then it was gone.

They stopped chanting, staring around at one another as the sound of the falls came back into focus. Smiles began to stretch across all five of their faces.

Kain began to laugh, dropping El and Milios' hands as he pulled his own to his face to examine. "That was *brilliant!*" he proclaimed jubilantly, rubbing the fresh tattoos with a finger.

I.A. TAKERIAN

"They don't typically take the form of specific symbols like this," Milios said with curiosity, poking the tattoos on their knuckles. "Most of the depictions I've seen have been bands of color, or dots like the ones beneath Cyfrin's eyes."

"Like I said," Kain called, grabbing El's hand from Mara's grasp to examine it. El blushed as he brought it close to his face, lips nearly grazing its surface. "Absolutely *brilliant!* This calls for celebration!" He hurried away to grab another bottle of wine from the dwindled stack by the stairs.

"As if we've been doing anything else today," El asked, raising an eyebrow as she followed Kain, her cheeks still flushed.

Kain popped the cork out of a fresh bottle, sending it flying across the lake with the force. And though neither acknowledged it, though their comrades now bonded by magick ignored it as well, Mara and Cyfrin's hands did not leave each other's for the rest of their jubilant, long night.

CHAPTER 14
THE BOND OF BRETHREN

The five of them stood in the morning light, groaning. The night before had been a complete blur after their binding. All of them woke up with the first flushes of sun to find they had fallen asleep on the water's edge. It had been with enormous effort that they dragged themselves up the stairs out of the lake's basin and to their bedrooms in the Grand Hall to ready themselves for the days' training.

Tomorrow, they would be departing aboard the Red Froth for an entire month at sea and on the island called Hope, and Caerani had declared their final day of training mandatory. Mara sat on the dirt in the training field, head in hands to block the sun. El was curled in a ball beside her while Kain, Cyfrin and Milios half-heartedly stretched.

"Whose idea was it to get completely wasted before the final trial, as a *tradition*?" Mara groaned, hissing the last word through her hands.

"Kain was the first to suggest it a hundred years ago. So, I blame him," Cyfrin mumbled, and Kain threw him an incredulous look.

I.A. TAKERIAN

"You were the one to bring the mead in the first place!" he shot back at Cyfrin's smug face. "I just wanted to meditate to focus our magicks before the journey! *I* am an innocent here."

"Oh, hardly," El replied, rolling on to her back with a grimace.

Milios chuckled. "Cheer up, all. We have new things to attempt today," they said, waving their newly tattooed hand before them all.

Mara sat upright, the throbbing in her head dimming slightly with the excitement. "Do you think the bond could help me with my magick problem?" she asked, getting to her feet with wobbly legs and helping El slowly to hers.

Milios smiled at her. "I think there's a decent chance it could," they replied, leading them all to the center of their training circle. "If anything can, it would be this." They motioned for Mara to stand in the middle, facing her body out towards the ocean. Milios gave her an apologetic look. "I'm not exactly sure what this sort of boost will do to your powers, so I want to make sure we do the least damage possible to the fields, should it go horribly awry."

Mara gulped. Her mind flashed with grim possibilities. Images of the fields on fire, the woods crumbling to ash, her friends smoldering on the ground all ran through her mind and she whimpered slightly.

Cyfrin, who had been carefully avoiding her eye all morning, was suddenly at her side. He slipped his hand into hers, holding it firmly. She looked up at his face, but he was staring out across the water pointedly, his jaw clenched. El took up her other hand, Kain and Milios coming to stand on either side of Cyfrin and her. Standing in a line, facing the crashing waves and bright sun on the horizon, Mara felt suddenly and completely at ease. She took a deep breath.

A PROPHECY OF UNDONE

"What do I do now?" she asked, feeling a wave of something powerful beginning to rise within her.

Cyfrin slid his hand from hers, bringing it to rest on her shoulder. El mirrored the motion.

"Try to focus your energy to your palms, as we usually do," Milios replied from the other side of Cyfrin.

She felt her heart rise to her throat, pausing as the usual anxiety that came with trying her magick sparked within her. Cyfrin squeezed her shoulder and leaned to her ear. His breath licked against the side of her neck, and she grew very still. "We'll support you, Dawnbringer. Don't overthink it."

His voice was soft, and it made Mara's stomach lurch with butterflies. She heard his breath catch for a moment, then he let out a soft laugh.

Kain cleared his throat. "Just a reminder, definitely not related to the situation at all," Kain began from beside El as she giggled. "The bond *does* allow us to feel each other's emotions when we're this close to one another. If anyone had forgotten."

Mara's face went hot, focusing down on her knuckles. Now that she was aware of it, Kain was right. The green orb representing El was pulsing with humor, Kain's sword mirroring the emotion. Milios' lines of wind seemed bemused as well, but Cyfrin's bolt was void of any feeling. Like a door was closed over that string in the bond.

It was strange, like having many different voices inside her heart instead of her head. Her cheeks were hot from embarrassment, sure from Cyfrin's look of smug pleasure that they had all felt her surge of emotion at his touch.

Kain cleared his throat once more. "We were focusing your energy to your palms, Mara," he said, and Mara got the feeling that he was attempting to change the subject on her behalf. "Close your eyes and recenter yourself."

I.A. TAKERIAN

She took a steadying breath once more, the bond growing silent within her. The glow of the sun shone through her closed lids, bathing her mind in golden light. She leaned into it, feeling the heat in her core start anew. But it was different than what she usually felt. Instead of the slow, steady uptake of rushing power she typically got when attempting to channel her magick, she was being filled from the ground up by an overpowering stream of heat. It surged through her, threatening to overtake her where she stood.

But just as she felt like she would be swallowed by its might, something gripped her tight and steadied her. It was like hands were grabbing on to her soul. Four sets of hands, raising her above the tidal wave of power to ride it instead of being consumed by it. The hands held her high, locking her in place atop the crest of the wave.

Mara could feel intense heat in her hands, and her eyes flew open with a gasp. She threw her arms out before her, aiming towards the horizon. Beams of golden white light shot from her palms, blending with the sun's rays as they rushed forth from her. The force nearly knocked her backwards off her feet, but Cyfrin and El had dug their heels into the dirt, gripping her shoulders and keeping her upright.

Beads of glittering sparks, like stars on a clear night, cascaded from the beams, chiming harmoniously as they fell to the waters below. Mara gritted her teeth, focusing all her might on maintaining the flow of magick that rocketed from her. But as the broad rays of gleaming sunlit power began to grow and strengthen, Mara's hands trembled violently. Her arms shook from the force, her nerves screaming under the pressure of it. With a gasp, the beam of light dimmed to nothing, and her arms dropped to her sides.

She was panting, knees buckling beneath her from the energy she had just output. Cyfrin's arms were around her in a flash, keeping her from collapsing to the ground. But Mara was beaming around at them all as she took great, deep breaths.

"Beyond's great mysteries, Mara, where have you been hiding all that?!" Kain exclaimed, rubbing his tattooed knuckles.

El was returning her smile with glowing intensity. Cyfrin steadied her, releasing her from his arms gently. Mara tried to ignore the way his touch made her feel, tried to keep it from spiraling out to the others through the fresh bond.

"That felt insane!" El said, as Milios examined Mara's hands for any sign of damage from the immense magick flow. "It was like I was atop a great mountain, sliding down to the bottom. Or maybe sliding up to the top. Either way, it was incredible."

"And you thought you couldn't produce your magicks," Cyfrin chuckled, and Mara bit down on her tongue to prevent the flutter in her stomach at his smirking face.

Kain patted on her back, giving her a wink. "Shall we give it another go then?" he asked, motioning out towards the ocean as Mara nodded with a look of fiery determination.

THEY HAD SPENT the entire day trying to get a proper control on Mara's powers. The celestial magicks passed from her mother was not something any of them had practice with, and its overwhelming strength, doubled by the

I.A. TAKERIAN

bond, was nearly too much for even the five of them to handle.

Though she had been able to produce beam after beam of golden rays when assisted by the other four, Mara was still completely unable to conjure any on her own. It enraged her to the point of tears at one point during the afternoon. She had wiped them away angrily, ignoring El's suggestion of taking a break. But her solo attempts had been to no avail.

She took the small victory of being able to use her magick with the assistance of the bond and felt content as they sat down for dinner that evening. The dining room of the Grand Hall was as it always was: Warm, welcoming, and filled with music from the village over the river. Caerani and Drake entered the room as they all took their seats, talking in animated voices about the day of training. Caerani held a long, black box in her hand and set it on the floor beside her chair.

Mara had not seen Caerani since the last Trial, and she looked exhausted. Mara knew she oversaw every bit of the Odelian's lives here, taking up Alora's mantle upon her passing and leading them. She had told Mara on numerous occasions that her heart lived for the clash of battle, not the steady necessity of being a ruler. But Mara could think of no one better to lead them than the powerful general who sat before her.

She gave a heavy sigh as she sunk into her chair, Drake filling her goblet to the brim with wine. Caerani cracked one eye, looking around at them all. Mara saw it flicker over the fresh, vibrant tattoos on their knuckles, and she sat bolt upright at attention.

"Where did you get those?" she asked, in a tone that suggested she already knew.

Cyfrin looked a little sheepish as he smiled at her. "We,

A PROPHECY OF UNDONE

uh…well, we're all about to be off for the month tomorrow and we thought it was best if were as powerfully prepared as possible."

Caerani's jaw dropped, but Drake laughed into his goblet. "Of course, you did," he chortled, smiling around at them all over the brim of his glass. "I'd expect nothing less from you five."

Caerani tsked but waved a hand before her. "I suppose boosting your abilities with everything to come, and learning to fight as one, isn't necessarily a bad idea." She swirled the wine in her goblet.

"And boy, did we get a boost!" Kain said, bouncing slightly in his chair as he burst forth with the information from the day. He told them about Mara's amplified celestial magick, how she had been able to maintain a steady stream of it for a solid minute by the time they finished their training today. Caerani raised her eyebrows to Mara, looking proud. Mara blushed, dropping her gaze to her plate, and smiling.

The tattoos on her hand were sending pulses of pride through her body from her companions as well. All except for Cyfrin, whose bond still seemed silent within her.

"I'm still not able to do it on my own though," Mara responded as Kain finished, and Caerani flashed a warm smile at her.

"That will come in time," she responded gently. "We're forcing hundreds of years of training down your throat in the course of just a few months. I never expected you to be using your magick in any form, let alone so soon. I'm glad you've got any, regardless of how it comes out. It will be paramount in your month on the island."

Mara had forgotten for a moment that the five of them would be leaving with Drake in the morning. Her first time ever on the ocean. She shifted uncomfortably. "Am I

I.A. TAKERIAN

allowed to ask what I should expect over this next month?" she asked. "I feel like the last few Hopefuls already know what's coming, and I know these four have faced it all already."

"Not I," Milios replied darkly, already looking nauseous. "But Caerani and I thought it wise I finally joined the lot. This will be my first time at sea, and on the island."

"And what fun we're going to have!" Kain said in an amused voice, and Milios glared at him.

Drake finished his goblet and refilled it with the last of the opened wine before addressing Mara. "The final challenge is designed to bring everything the Hopefuls have learned together in one harrowing month. Some pair up, some fly solo, others form groups like your own." He motioned around to them all, Mara listening intently. "We'll be on my ship, the Red Froth, for the better part of a week on our way there. Sometimes it's smooth sailing, other times we're fortunate enough to encounter sea monsters along the way."

Mara gulped at this. 'Fortunate' is not the word she would have used, but Drake continued, eyes full of wicked glee. "Once we dock on the island, you'll be transported inland by one of men. He'll drop you off at random, and you can decide whether to fight through the following few weeks on your own or set out to try and find your companions."

"Let's not forget the guardian, captain," Kain added, looking grim.

Drake's expression darkened. "Yes, well. The chances of meeting him are slim nowadays. Easier to track, he is."

"The guardian?" Mara asked, voice small.

"Aye," Drake replied, thumbing the hilt of his sword. "Old bastard keeps the entrances to the island. But there

A PROPHECY OF UNDONE

are too many for him to watch all at once. I've not had to deal with him in quite some time, the delusional fucker."

"He's not a big fan of our captain," Kain said, shaking his head. "Drake's the only one who's ever slipped past him undetected."

"Yes, and we'll keep slipping on past, so there's nothing to worry about on that front." Drake said in a biting tone that stopped Kain interjecting.

Drake took another drink of his wine, setting it down and looking at Mara thoughtfully. "The island is ever changing. When the Zenoths left these beautiful lands they created for us, they did so by magicking themselves to another realm entirely. The amount of power it took for them to do so left a tear in the very reality of our world, a slice through the fabric of space and time. Ever since then, all manners of beasties big, bad, and ugly have been appearing through it."

Mara felt a cold chill run down her back and Cyfrin's hand, already very close to where hers rested on the table, moved closer. His pinky rubbed gently against the side of her hand; his eyes still focused on Drake as he went on.

"Luckily, the Brisenbane has kept them all locked away on the island. And so, for thousands of years, the Odelian warriors have been braving the mighty ocean to prove their worth against the monsters' might. You never know what to expect when you're out there." He brought the goblet back to his lips, the rest of them mirroring the motion in the silence. Mara could see that El, Kain, and Cyfrin were lost in deep memory from their times on the island, Caerani smiling dreamily at Drake as they shared their own past moments silently between them.

Mara broke the silence. "Why is it you call the island Hope?" she asked, a question that had bothered her for weeks.

135

I.A. TAKERIAN

Drake smirked at her. "Because that is what you will need to survive it," he replied in good humor, though his red eyes flashed with steely seriousness. "Hope. Your mother thought it was a hilarious thing, naming it that."

"And on that note," Caerani began, reaching down to grab the box she had entered with from the floor. "I have a gift for you. We'll call it an early finishing present for completing the trials, which I have no doubts you'll do."

Mara blinked, surprised, as she slid the box across the table to her. Staring down at it, she had a sudden flashback to Grathiel presenting her with her mother's dagger as a birthday gift. Her stomach tightened uncomfortably. There was a pressure on her thigh, and she glanced down to see Cyfrin's hand on her leg. He was staring at her with the softest expression, and Mara had to remind herself that all four of them could now feel every intense emotion she had.

She gave him a small smile and opened the box. Mara gasped.

Laying within the box was a magnificent dagger. Its hilt was made of twisting, black metal; hints of gold swirling through it. The blade itself curved back and forth like a snake before ending in a menacingly sharp tip, the metal the same shade of black gold. Etched across its surface, stretching up the length of the blade, were finely swirling tendrils of vine and ivy. But it was not the daggers unique beauty that had left Mara breathless and staring in awe.

Encrusted in the hilt, glinting in the dancing flames from the fireplace beside her, were two dim gemstones. The first she recognized at once as the crystal she had retrieved in her second trial, though it was not glowing as it had that day. The second, seated right below it and just as dim as her own, was her mother's gemstone from her broken dagger.

A PROPHECY OF UNDONE

Mara's eyes fluttered up to meet Caerani's warm gaze, speechless.

"Cyfrin took the pieces of Alora's dagger and your crystal to Kain's parents' forge. Had them fashion you a new weapon." Caerani was smiling, nodding down at the box. "Drake and I couldn't determine exactly what magick your little rainbow gem holds, but the easiest way to find out is just by you using it eventually."

Mara's hands were trembling. Cyfrin squeezed her leg reassuringly as she reached down to grasp the hilt in her hands, raising it before her. Instantly, warmth shot from the hilt and through her body like an arrow. It flew through her, coming to settle somewhere in her heart as the crystals flickered to life and began to glow. Her gem was pulsing with its many colors, brighter than she had seen it that day in the lake as it gleamed in her hands. Her mother's crystal had also redoubled its glow, as if the joining of them together had created a force that surpassed time, reaching back to grip Alora's powers as well as Mara's.

She stared down at them, hands still trembling, and tears of overwhelming gratitude began to fall from her eyes. El took in a sharp intake of breath, tears falling down her face as well. Kain made a gentle noise of happiness.

Cyfrin rubbed his thumb across her thigh, and she beamed at them through her tears.

"Thank you. Thank you, all."

CHAPTER 15

THE RED FROTH

The morning was the coldest it had been since Mara had arrived in the village. Winter was coming quickly, and she shuddered at the thought of being out on the open water when the ice caps began to come down from the White North.

The five of them stood shivering in the training fields, dressed in warm cloaks and heavy boots with their sacks full of gear for the coming month. Milios was already tinted green from nerves and nausea, eyeing the thrashing waters with malcontent. The other three Hopefuls looking to complete their trials stood off to one side. They were throwing nervous looks at their group, speaking in hushed tones.

Cyfrin scowled at them, granting an inquisitive look from Mara. "They're some of Filigro's old lot," he replied, Kain and him both looking over at the three whispering with disdain. "They spent the better part of last night in the company of his brother and a pub's worth of mead. They're far from your biggest supporters." His eyes

139

I.A. TAKERIAN

narrowed as he called out loudly. *"And I know this because I can hear them."*

His voice was deep, almost growling as he spat the words at the trio. They all flinched back in unison, pulling the hoods of their cloaks over their heads, and backing away further. But Mara looked at Cyfrin with shock in her eyes.

"It's too early for this," El groaned, flashing a withering look at the three.

"Filigro had a brother?" Mara asked, a dull guilt twisting in her stomach. Filigro had left her no choice in the woods; it was kill or be killed. But the thought of his family, full of grief and never to see their loved one again, caused her great pain. Her heart ached for them. She watched the four of them wince, reminding her that the pain she felt was now reverberating through their bond in to each one of them.

Cyfrin leaned a little closer to her, the heat from his body warming the air around them. "Filigro chose his fate the moment he decided you were in his way," he said, his voice dark. "If it hadn't been you to end him, it would have eventually been me."

"Oh?" Mara said softly, forcing her face to look aloof even though her heart fluttered at his words. She tried to keep her emotions shrouded but could see at once that she was unsuccessful.

El, Kain, and Milios became very interested in the weapons rack a few yards away from them, loudly beginning to organize it. Cyfrin was smirking, glancing at her sideways as he stared out across the Brisenbane. "Oh aye, Mara. I will end anyone, or anything, that tries to stand against you." He had softened his tone, the sound coming out as the purr he took to rile her.

Mara straightened up, clenching her fists as her face

140

A PROPHECY OF UNDONE

went red. She gave him a nod of recognition, turning her eyes to the horizon beyond. He breathed a laugh. Out of the corner of her eye, she saw him flex his newly tattooed hand at his side. The veins became pronounced, the muscles roiling beneath the surface. It made the heat in Mara's core grow that much brighter. Voices reached them on the wind, and Mara forced herself to turn.

Drake and Caerani were striding towards them from out of the woods. Drake was nearly skipping as he hurried towards them, Caerani at his heels.

"What a beautiful morning, isn't it?" he cried, clapping his hands together as he smiled around at them all. "Perfect winds, steady waters… Wonderful."

Mara blinked at him. She didn't know what Drake was looking at, but it was clearly a different ocean than the one before them all. The waves crashed repeatedly into the rock face below them, the choppy waters in the horizon looking even less kind. She looked at him with dark eyes.

"Say goodbye to the comforts of home, all. Where we go, you'll find no peace," he said it with such pep, his eyes filled with wicked glee. He spun about and kissed Caerani's cheek. She flushed, pushing him away with narrow eyes as he laughed. He turned from her, setting out towards the stairs leading down to the dock with a wave over his shoulder.

Caerani gave Mara a crooked smile, squeezing her shoulder. "Don't let him, or any of these fools, torment you," she said with soft eyes. "You'll be done and back before you know it."

Mara smiled at her, but it didn't quite reach her eyes.

"Are you sure you can't join us, general?" Cyfrin asked her. "It would be an honor to watch you in combat again."

Caerani scowled. "You know bloody well I can't," she replied, and Mara could hear the regret in her voice at the

I.A. TAKERIAN

words. "I'll be here. Tending to run down buildings, and settling family disputes. And anyway, someone's got to stay behind to train the new round of Hopefuls. Since the four of you have decided to flit away to show off for your new friend." She kept her eyes steely as she stared at Cyfrin, who looked incredulous. But she turned to wink at Mara before giving one final wave and walking off towards her war tent at the edge of the field.

Mara had never been down to the ocean, and she marveled at how powerful it was as they stepped from the stairwell onto the dock. The waves had shaped massive craters into the cliffside leading up to the training fields, the sheer drop stretching for miles in both directions. She had seen Drake's ship from afar nearly every day for two months, but the distance had done it no justice. Now level with the water, she was awestruck at its magnificence.

The entirety of the Red Froth was made of dark red and black wood. It had been carved in such a way that it looked like scales etched into the sides. What Mara had originally thought was a wood carving lashed to the helm of the ship was much more impressive. Upon closer inspection, she concluded that this was actually the corpse of a dragon. Its eyes opened to reveal huge rubies in the sockets, and its wings were spread wide across the front. It was frozen with mouth wide, as if in attack.

She stared up, squinting against the sunlight towards the sails. The material from which they were crafted was like nothing Mara had ever seen, rippling like pieces of the darkest night sky on the sea breeze. A flag adorned with skull and crossbones waved high above them, and the waters beneath the ship were as still as always. Unnaturally so.

Mara's brow furrowed as they walked across the dock to the boarding ramp. "Is it magick that calms the waters

A PROPHECY OF UNDONE

around the dock?" she asked Drake, and she saw his eyes glint with mischief.

"Aye, but not like the magick you use here." He nodded towards the ocean with a loving gaze. "Dear Brisen and I came to an accord long ago, and she stills the waters below me to sail with moderate safety." He scratched his neck. "Though, it does very little when we're attacked by beasts from within its depths. Secretly, I think it's waiting for the day I'm thrown overboard."

Mara shivered at his words, following behind Drake as he led them up the ramp to board. She set her hand against the railing, the texture of the wood, strange and rough. She looked down. There were great gashes, made by some sort of massive blade, all along the rails of the ramp. Mara dragged her finger across a particularly deep one as they passed it.

Kain leaned forward, a boastful look about him. "I left those during my trials," He whispered to her, loudly enough for everyone to hear.

Cyfrin groaned. "Do you have to gloat *every* time we get on this damned thing?" he asked.

Drake threw a crippling look over his shoulder at Kain, eyes dark. Kain drew back a little. "Do not remind me, or I will lash you to the stern of my ship to watch our asses all the way to the island. Do you want that, Kain?"

Kain shook his head hurriedly, Mara opening her mouth to ask why he had carved such deep notches in Drake's ship. But she was silenced as she stepped onto the deck of the Red Froth, mouth agape.

The deck of the ship was expertly carved, veins of gold lacing through the wood below and around them. The sun reflected off bright gemstones molded into the carvings, accenting the designs. There were four levers in spots against the railing of the ship, and the masts were wrapped

I.A. TAKERIAN

in black metal chains that vibrated slightly. Mara could feel a great power emanating from the bowels of the ship and shivered in response.

There were dozens of crewmates scurrying about, and Mara saw races of all kinds. Odelians, Ylastrians, men that looked like they had been fused with beasts, and even a few forest dwellers hurried about, tending to riggings and checking all ties. Drake had his arms wide, beaming around at them all. "Welcome aboard!" he cried as a tall man with tusks jutting up from his bottom jaw approached him.

"Captain," he said, the voice guttural as he stood at attention before Drake. "We are ready to take our leave, sir."

Drake nodded at him, the man turning and disappearing into the crowd of the Red Froth's crew. "The best view for newcomers is on the back of the ship," he said, winking at Mara and pulling a large flask from the inside of his chest pocket. "Make sure you give the village a fond farewell. It may be the last time some of you ever see it." He laughed at this, taking a swig of his flask. He turned from their unamused faces, heading towards the large golden wheel at the helm.

The group of them, including Filigro's dejected looking friends, moved to the back of the ship, facing the cliff that led back to the woods. The ship creaked around them, giving a mighty lurch, and starting forward with a speed Mara did not expect. As they pulled away from the dock, the cliff growing further and further away from them, Mara felt her stomach clench with anxiety. Drake's words played again in her head as the cold ocean breeze whipped through her hair. *It may be the last time.*

Her palms were clammy. The village hidden in the woods was just starting to feel like home, the first place she

A PROPHECY OF UNDONE

had ever truly felt that way. And as it began to disappear into the fog hanging thick over the deeper waters, she couldn't help but feel a little panic. *What if this is where my luck runs out? What if I get lost once on the island? What if I get pulled into the rift and fall through nothingness for all eternity?*

Her thoughts were cut off as Cyfrin placed a hand on the middle of her back. It broke her from her spiral, focusing her attention solely to the place where it sat. The electric pulse was strangely warm, calming her despite her cold panic. She was dimly aware that the other three had drawn closer to her as well, sensing her distress down the bond. She turned her eyes from Cyfrin's stoic face to stare back out across the Brisenbane, back towards the home she now silently prayed she would soon return.

CHAPTER 16

TALES OF SWORD AND SEA

I f Mara had thought their rumbunctious behavior and late nights in the tavern back in the village were feisty, it was nothing compared to how they were all now acting at sea. She got the impression that Caerani was the only thing keeping the four of them, including Drake, contained in the village as they joined the crew on the deck that evening. There may as well have been hundreds of them aboard the Red Froth from the volume of their voices.

Someone played a fiddle, the hypnotic sound blocking out the sound of Milios retching over the side of the ship. Drake's men had brought barrels of mead to the deck an hour before, and they were already having to bring up more.

Mara stared up at the starry sky, enthralled. She had never seen so many stars, not even back in the village. But out here, there was only the moon, the cosmos, and the ocean to mirror them. In the darkness, it felt like they were flying. The fog of the day had dissipated, and though the waves crashed more violently than ever before, it gave no

147

I.A. TAKERIAN

sway to Drake's ship. Whatever deal Drake had reached with the Brisenbane, the magick kept the Red Froth protected from its chaos.

El and Mara were seated beside Drake on the steps that lead to the helm, drinking from their tankards as they watched the merry making. Cyfrin and Kain, markedly more inebriated than they were, stood crouched across from one another in the middle of the crowd. They were spinning around each other, growling through their smiles like wild animals. Much of the crew had gathered to watch them and cheer.

Mara could see Cyfrin's eyes glowing with vicious glee as Kain lunged for him with an exaggerated roar. He bowed beneath Kain, hiking his shoulder to connect with his chest as they collided. He rose quickly to his feet, flipping Kain to his back on the deck with a loud thud. The wind knocked from him, he remained on the floor as Cyfrin held his arms high in victory. The cheers grew in volume. Then Kain swept his leg out, knocking into Cyfrin and buckling him to the ground beside him as they all roared with laughter.

El was shaking her head. "You know, with every passing year I think they'll grow up a little. But honestly, I think they're devolving. More animals than men at this point," she said, finishing her tankard.

"Aye, but at least they're entertaining," Drake chortled. "Kain needs his ass kicked every now and again anyway."

El smirked at him. "Is this about the marks on the railing?" she asked, a playful glint in her eyes.

Drake grimaced over the edge of his glass. "It will always be about the railings," he growled. "And they weren't just *marks*, Eleanora. They are deep gashes in wood that was *incredibly* difficult to come by. The bumbling bastard."

A PROPHECY OF UNDONE

"If I recall, you were quite amused by him when it happened," El said, glancing at him sideways as they watched Kain toss Cyfrin high in the air.

"What exactly happened?" Mara asked, taking a sip of her drink, and looking at Drake.

El chuckled next to her. "Well, I've told you before that Kain's not a magick user," she began, motioning towards Kain being pinned down by Cyfrin as they laughed. "And non-users aren't really able to advance to warriors, because they're so easy to overpower. Drake's the only non-user I know to ever complete the trials all the way through."

Mara's mouth fell open. "You can't use magick?!" she asked, exasperated.

Drake winked at her, raising his glass. "Don't be so surprised, dear. I've had just as much training with a blade." He tapped the boarding sword at his hip.

El continued. "Kain barely finished his first three trials. He was heavily injured in the final challenge, trying to take a treasure from the catacombs, and literally crawled his way out before he lost consciousness. Even though he technically completed the trial, Caerani removed Kain from the group of remaining Hopefuls due to the extent of his injuries." El frowned. "He was near death when they pulled him out of the temple, and there was no way he was going to be well in time for the final trial."

Her eyes brightened, smirking in a dreamy way at Kain through the cheering crowd. "Cyfrin and I were here that morning, departing with Drake for our trials. There was this great commotion on the docks. Blades clashing and men being tossed into the ocean."

"That great, burly bastard had escaped the healer's cabin," Drake cut in, glaring at Kain. "Gotten himself all dressed up and was fighting *my* men to gain his way on to the ship. He took that great sword and swung it all about to

I.A. TAKERIAN

keep them back and caught my damn railing in the process."

El laughed. "He cleared a neat path, marched his way right up to Drake and demanded he be given the chance to complete his trials or die trying. Said it was the right and honorable thing to do."

Drake gave a half smile. "Not the brightest star in the sky, that one, but he's got balls. And heart. And really, what else could you need?" He finished his mead and shoved the empty tankard towards El. "Have the lads refill this, will you, darling?"

El took Mara's cup as well and pushed her way through the crowd towards the barrels. This was Mara's first time ever alone with Drake, who stared wistfully up at the moon. Her eyes flickered down to the box always at his hip, and she remembered her conversation with Caerani. Her rampant curiosity overtaking her, she cleared her throat.

"I don't think I've ever seen you without that thing," Mara said, trying to sound as casual as possible as she motioned to the black box.

Drake glanced down at it, an odd expression on his face. "Ah, well. That's because I never am without it." He gave a small smile, tapping the lid of the box a little aggressively. The golden chains gave a faint rattle.

"What do you keep in there?" she asked, not exactly sure she wanted the answer.

He cocked his head at her, fingers thrumming on the lid now. "It's my snuff box!" he said, giving her a wry wink.

She raised a disbelieving eyebrow, and he chuckled. He returned his gaze to the moon with a faraway look. "What do *you* suppose is in it?" he asked, and Mara shifted nervously.

She had heard many rumors from the other Hopefuls,

150

A PROPHECY OF UNDONE

as well as her companions, on what *they* thought was in the box. Fingers from men he'd killed, eyeballs he used in rituals to make him stronger in battle, strange plants he would smoke to commune with the ocean…she'd heard it all at this point.

"It…it isn't a heart, is it?" she asked, eyeballing the box as she voiced what Cyfrin's theory was.

Drake looked back at her, taken aback. He let out a huge laugh. "Perhaps it is! Or perhaps I just carry an empty box to make myself seem interesting." He smirked at her.

"Is it then? Empty, I mean?" she asked, brow furrowed.

His smile fell a little. "No. No it isn't." He looked down at the box, resting his hand against the lid. "Can you keep a secret, Mara?"

His voice had softened conspiratorially, and she nodded as she leaned towards him. He sighed. "This box was bound to me by a very old, very dear friend. Sealed away within its walls is a very powerful darkling. Old man said it would aid me on my journeys." He rapped his knuckles hard on to the lid, rolling his eyes. "So far, all he's given me is poor advice and bad attitude. He calls himself Tim, if you can believe it. Zenoths only know why. And Tim knows a great many things; Can sense a great many things. But he's not what you'd call a friend."

He grimaced, staring down at it. "The only reason he hasn't tried to kill me in earnest is because he's been bound to me. If I die, he'll be instantly destroyed. Keeps the great prat in line most days."

Mara was staring between Drake and the box, dumb-founded. "A darkling?!" she hissed. "Can he hurt us?"

Drake shook his head. "The magick that sealed him inside also prevents him from using any of his powers. Now he just spends the better part of my days and nights whispering naughty little things to me and prodding for a response."

"You mean...You mean you can hear him?"

"Aye," Drake replied, nodding solemnly. "It brings him endless delight at that."

Mara continued staring down at the box as El came elbowing back through the crowd with drinks full. Cyfrin and Kain had been joined in their rampant wrestling by several of Drake's crewmen, to the uproarious joy of the crowd around them. Mara pulled her eyes from the box holding the dark entity to stare at the group gleefully throwing each other across the deck.

Mara's eyes traced lazily across the runes covering Cyfrin's body, face hot from the drink and her staring. "Do those tattoos cover every inch of him?"

The words came forth from her mouth before she could stop them, and El snorted into her drink as she laughed. Mara felt the wave of embarrassment wash over her and saw her four companions react to it as it ricocheted down the bond. Milios' heaved with renewed vigor into the waters below. El threw an elbow into her ribcage, tossing her a playful look. Kain flailed and was knocked down by a charging Ylastrian man. Cyfrin, pinned beneath a growing pile of men, looked up at her with a flushed face and wild eyes.

She shot her stare to the sky instantly, trying to think of anything else but the way he had just looked at her.

"Yes. His father made sure of that." Drake's voice was dark, pulling Mara's attention back to him. His eyes were shadowed as he stared at Cyfrin over the rim of his tankard.

"Cyfrin told me it was necessary. To seal his powers," Mara said, surprised by the anger in Drake's voice.

He nodded slowly. "Aye, his father told us the same."

A PROPHECY OF UNDONE

His voice was grave, a heavy weight sitting in his words. "All Caerani and I heard was a father too weak to assist his son in learning control. He was the first and the quickest to assume the worst in Cyfrin. Got it in his head that his mother's blood, the blood of a forest dweller, had tainted his precious Lightcleaver bloodline. And that it was this that had Cyfrin losing control in such explosive outbursts."

There was a deadly look in his eyes as he took a steadying sip from his tankard. "Bullshit, if you ask me. That man abused Cyfrin from the moment he was born. His mother passed in childbirth. Their lot isn't supposed to bear children, you see. And it took her life, leaving Cyfrin with his terror of a father. Used to take his lightning whips and use them to train the poor boy."

"He'd lash him with them every time he failed to keep his magick perfectly clean and precise. Eleanora healed up his scarring on the outside, but the damage that sort of abuse does to your insides…it never really leaves you. Caerani, Alora, and I tried to stop him from sealing away his powers, begged him to let *us* help him. But he wouldn't listen."

Mara stared out at Cyfrin with cold sadness weighing in her heart. She tried desperately to rein in the pain she felt but saw El wince a little regardless as Drake continued.

"Then his old man led his war party into the Forests of Galion, looking for glory and riches. Aren't we all? But they happened upon a Reflector Beast. Poor saps never knew what hit them. Most of his party survived the attack, but Cyfrin's father tried to take the thing out single-handed. Whatever he saw drove him mad. Might have been better if he had just died, I reckon."

He paused, all three of them taking a drink as Mara shifted uncomfortably under the strain of controlling her emotions.

I.A. TAKERIAN

"He's *not* dead then?" she asked, and Drake shook his head.

"No, but he's as good as. The man doesn't know who he is, let alone who any of us are. Including Cyfrin. His mind was driven away by the beast's magick, and it will never return. Cyfrin pays one of the village healers to keep care of him. Which is more than I ever would have done in his shoes." He downed the rest of his drink and stood, smacking his lips. "Now, if you ladies will excuse me. It seems these boys need to be reminded who their captain is."

His red eyes flashed, dropping his long black jacket and weapons to the floor before letting out a mighty roar and charging forward towards the madness on deck. Mara was still staring at the place he had just been, her heart aching.

El nudged her arm gently. "Try not to look so grim." she said as Mara turned to look at her with misty eyes. "Milios practically raised Cyfrin. Then he got Kain and me, and now you. And we all know how much he likes *you*, oh dear Dawnbringer." She mimicked Cyfrin's soft purr as she said her name, smirking wide.

CHAPTER 17
LIGHTNING'S TONGUE AND WATERS BREAK

Three entire days had passed at sea before Milios could stomach an hour without hurling. Drake spent most of his time at the helm, twisting the ship's course through the fog that arrived with every morning. They had encountered nothing on their journey thus far, but with every passing day of calm Mara became more paranoid; more watchful.

It was eerie, watching the harsh waves rip around the ship but never feeling their push and pull. The waters surrounding them were a constant state of calm, and Mara wondered often why the ocean had gifted Drake with such a luxury. It was a topic he refused to give her answers on, which only furthered her hungry curiosity.

Being aboard the Red Froth did nothing to deter their training sessions, especially as it was practically the only thing they could do during the days.

Cyfrin and Kain had begun training her in close-combat techniques, mostly with her new dagger. It was strange to use, and it felt like it led Mara's arm. As if it was

I.A. TAKERIAN

controlling her. But it hit its target true and straight nearly every time, pulsing with a constant heat in her hands.

Drake had banned Mara from using her magick aboard after a near disaster the day before. Her beams of sunlit magick had rocketed forth from her during practice, wild and unmanageable as ever, and almost caught the entire mast on fire. One of the crew mates had whipped water high using magick, dousing the flames before it could take. Drake had scolded them all, lecturing them about "how fire and wood work together".

Their third night was going as it usually did: Loudly and full of heavy drink. The three other Hopefuls made it a point to avoid Mara and her companions, throwing her looks of disgust and disdain whenever Cyfrin was not near enough to see. It reminded her of the lords and ladies of the court in Delinval, their hatred nearly palpable in the air. And Mara did not blame them for it. In their shoes, regardless of the circumstance, she would never be able to forgive the killer of a friend. They had disappeared into the bowels of the ship as the sun set over the dark waters, and Mara knew they would not be seeing them till the morning.

Kain was standing by the railing, El sitting atop his shoulders to get a better look at the moonlight across the ocean. El's face was cherry red, a thrill shooting down the bond and burning Mara's hand with its intensity. Kain's tattoo pulsed with a deep satisfaction, and she smiled wistfully up at them.

Cyfrin's tattoo still felt oddly silent, like she was standing outside a heavily boarded door. Or an insurmountable wall. Mara couldn't help feeling it was on purpose.

Drake told animated stories to his crew at the stern, the orb lights dancing around him and casting long shadows

A PROPHECY OF UNDONE

across the deck. Mara finished her glass of wine and stood, head a little fuzzy from drink and the smoke from the many pipes on board. She wandered up the steps to the deck of the helm, empty and dark under the moon. Empty, save for the figure standing silhouetted at the very front of the ship.

Cyfrin stood facing out across the ocean, back to her and hands spread across the railing. Mara froze, heart skipping a beat. It had been days since they had been alone, and he looked so stunning standing there. Like a painting made of sun and moonlight. She could have stayed there for hours, just admiring his beauty. She took a deep breath, clenching her fists and walking forward toward the rail.

Cyfrin's body stiffened, shifting his gaze sideways to glance down at her.

"I thought you were down with the men listening to Drake's adventures," Mara said, maintaining a tone of cool detachment as she leaned against the rail.

Cyfrin breathed a laugh, the sound like warm honey through Mara's body. "I have heard every tale Drake has ten times over," he said, returning his gaze to the ocean. "I just wanted to get away from the crowd for a moment. Away from all the...bother."

Mara watched his eyes flick to her face again, his fingers thrumming against the wooden railing once. He had said 'bother' in such an oddly pointed way, and her eyes narrowed at him.

"The bother?" she asked, her stare flashing dangerously. "And what would the bother be, exactly, Lightcleaver?"

He gave a heavy sigh, tilting his head back as he turned to lean on the rail and stare at her. His cheeks were flushed from drink, and his eyes were coldly appraising. "You know damn well what the bother is, Mara."

157

I.A. TAKERIAN

His voice was low, threatening almost, and Mara's breath caught. She felt a thrill run through her, felt it pulse down the bond before she could stop it. Cyfrin smirked at her with the satisfied smugness that made her blood boil.

Fine. If he expected trouble, expected a *bother*, she would happily oblige him.

Mara dropped her chin, looking up at him through her long eyelashes as her gaze smoldered. His eyes widened as she leaned in closer. She could see the vein in his neck throbbing beneath his tattooed skin. The runes had begun to glow white. His jaw was clenched, one hand gripped so tightly on the railing that it turned his knuckles pale.

Mara laughed softly. "You're always poking fun at how affected I am by you. And yet here you stand, heart aflutter and face red as a rose." She took another step forward, closing the distance between them and reaching a hand up to rest on his chest. She could feel his heart slamming against her palm as she stared up into his dark face.

His blue eyes were flashing with a feral power that made Mara feel like mush underneath his gaze. He reached up and grabbed her hand firmly in his own, giving her a wicked smirk. "Are you trying to tempt me, Mara?" he growled softly. "Do you think that wise? This is a game you will lose."

"Oh?" she breathed, egged on by the speeding of his pulse and the way his eyes bored hungrily into her own. "So then, you don't mind my closeness?" She stood on tiptoes, both hands now on his chest as she hovered her lips inches from his own. Through her hooded eyes, she could see his stare beginning to glow dimly. Tiny bolts of lightning etched across his pupils.

His breath was coming in shallow bursts through his parted lips, and his face looked screwed up in deep concentration. Every rippling muscle in his body had grown very

158

A PROPHECY OF UNDONE

still, heat radiating into her palms from his chest. She could feel an electrical current starting to circulate through them both, pulling her magnetically closer to him. Her heart caught in her throat.

Perhaps this wasn't the best idea. Her brain was already starting to fog over, the way it nearly always did in his presence. A rumbling had started low within him, vibrating through Mara's hands with the unspoken promise of consuming her. She smirked, feeling her ego surge at his reaction.

"Are you bothered yet?" she breathed, tilting her head slightly to bring herself closer to his lips.

A noise came from him. A soft moan, and Mara felt she might go mad if she heard it again. "Damn you," he growled through his teeth. His hands were moving, leaving hers rested against his chest. One slid to the lowest part of her back, pressing her firmly against his warm body. The electrical static joining them ripped through Mara with renewed intensity. His other hand drifted upwards, twisting into the curls at the base of her neck and gripping her tight. Locking her in to his control. She gave a soft gasp, trembling. His lips brushed against hers, tingling as they made contact. Her breathing hitched and she felt his body tense at the reaction.

"Tell me to stop." His voice was impossibly soft as his words passed around her on the sea breeze. She could hear yearning there beneath the command, dark desire threatening to surface and destroy his control. "Tell me to release you and to never put your body against mine again."

Mara was breathless, the smell of him clouding every piece of rational thought in her mind. "I can't," she whispered against him. "Please. Please don't make me."

He let out a soft groan, as if it pained him to hear it.

I.A. TAKERIAN

But the grip on her back tightened, the fingers lacing deeper into her hair. And he pressed his lips firmly to hers.

Explosions of light went off behind her eyelids. She felt instantly charged, like she could take on any beast single-handedly. She was flying and falling, floating on air as her heart soared higher and higher on wings of lightning.

Cyfrin's first kiss was gentle, probing. His lips were so soft, in brazen contrast to the solid hardness of his body. But as he drew away and looked at Mara's face, hot and flustered in his hands, he lost all grip on his considerable control. His blue eyes flashed, his tattoos blazing like the sun.

Suddenly, Mara could feel everything through the tattoo that represented him on her finger. His need and desire, his protectiveness and animal-like emotions coursed through drawing a gasping moan from her lips pressed against his.

He spun her about, pinning her against the railing as he deepened his kisses. The world slipped away, narrowing only to the two of them as Mara felt her desire clash and double with his own. She was everything and nothing against him, happy to fall into the darkest void if it meant she could feel just this way.

His tongue flicked from his mouth, tracing her lips before entwining with hers. She was panting, her hands trying to grasp every bit of him as he pulled his lips from hers and trailed them gently across her jawline. He travelled down the curve of her neck, sucking softly along her collarbone as his hand moved down to cup her backside. There were deep, growling noises echoing from inside of him, sending Mara into deeper madness with every sound.

He brought his face back to hers, eyes burning as she melted in his hands. "Are you bothered, my darling Dawnbringer?" he asked, mimicking her question from earlier

A PROPHECY OF UNDONE

with a playful smirk before bringing his lips to hers once more with a wild hunger.

She clung to him, forgetting all together about the rest of the ship on the decks below. There was a great, rock-hard heat building between his legs; trapped against her body. She could feel it growing, pressed against her lower stomach as it throbbed. It rivaled the overwhelming, wet heat in her core. She wanted every inch of him bare and against her. *Needed* it.

Her hands fumbled with his shirt, and he chuckled breathlessly into her mouth as he moved to assist her. Then there came a sound like heavy thunder.

They both froze at the same time, Cyfrin's shirt halfway over his head and Mara's hands sliding against his hot skin underneath. The ocean behind them had begun to tremble, the deep rumble coming from somewhere beneath its surface. Cyfrin dropped his shirt back over his head, pulling Mara back from the rail and positioning her slightly behind him. The rest of the crew, Drake in the lead, had appeared next to them on the deck.

They all stared at the swirling whirlpool that stopped the Red Froth in its tracks. The rumbling noise grew louder, accompanied now by a great sucking sound. The whirlpool convulsed suddenly and sent a great pillar of water high into the sky. There was a roar from the water beneath the pillar, blood-curdling as it shook the timbers of the ship. The water fell with a crash back to the surface, revealing the beast that had drawn himself up before them.

It had to have been 300 feet tall, covered in deep black scales that blended with the night sky behind it. There was a many-barbed tail lashing through the water behind it, and a pair of mighty wings cascaded water to the ocean below. Its great red eyes were glaring down at them on the deck, a pair of spiraling horns stretching from its forehead

I.A. TAKERIAN

and into the sky. Mara had never seen anything like it and drew closer to Cyfrin by instinct. He reached back his hand, holding her against him.

The water beneath the beast seemed to flee at its presence, leaving a wide gap between the Red Froth and it. It glowered down at them before opening its fanged mouth wide and letting out a screaming roar that deafened them all.

Mara could see Drake laughing, hands over his ears. "Men! That head looks like the newest mount for my collection!" he cried, drawing his sword as his smile glinted wickedly under the moonlight. He took two steps back, and to Mara's great shock, ran forward to launch himself into the ocean's deathly grasp. Mara gasped as he shot down and out of sight.

The creature was raising one massive hand, a strange dark energy starting to swirl around it. The crewmen ran around, rotating the levers by the railing, and dropping the sails. Mara heard a loud creaking sound and glanced over the edge of the ship.

The levers had triggered slots to open in the sides of the Red Froth, and two huge blades jetted out on either side. Like great, metal wings waiting in the waters below. Mara turned her attention back to the beast, who looked ready to strike. But something rose to meet it.

Propelled upwards by a geyser of dark water, sword drawn and looking minuscule compared to the water monster, was Drake. The monster threw his hand forwards, aiming towards the ship. But Drake was too quick. The water flung him towards his outstretched arm, and before it could launch off its dark attack, his blade met flesh.

Mara wasn't sure how his sword, so small in comparison to the beastly arm, cut through so cleanly. But cut it did, driving undisrupted through the monster's wrist and

A PROPHECY OF UNDONE

cutting his hand clean from the body. The beast let out a high-pitched roar, the sound ripping through Mara as she threw her hands over her ears again. The hand dropped to the water, sizzling as it made contact and sinking slowly beneath the surface.

Black blood spattered through the air like heavy rainfall as it flung its stump skyward in pain. Drake was already readying to launch his next attack as the wound began to sizzle, smoke filling the air around it.

He turned back to look at the ship, eyes wild. "Well? Are you all just going to stand there or are we going to kill us a Water Fury?!"

CHAPTER 18
CAPTAIN OF SALT AND BLOOD

Mara's blood froze in her veins.

Water Fury. The words clung in the air as the beast shot a boulder of black magick towards Drake, missing by only inches. She had studied Furies in her history books in Delinval. They were gatherings of heavy, dark magick that corrupted the very elements around it with their polluting evil.

Fire Furies in the South, past the Forests of Galion, scorched the entire lower continent in their blind rage. Earth and Air Furies decimated the countryside from Delinval to the Forgotten Woods. Frost Furies to the North, created an unforgiving tundra of ice that none could pass. All they knew were death and destruction, the spawn of chaos and evil. They had all died out, killed by brave heroes and warriors of old.

Or so Mara had read.

Cyfrin was pulling her forward to the helm, grasping her hand firmly as he called out. "On me!"

Milios, Kain, and El appeared suddenly at their sides,

165

I.A. TAKERIAN

standing with looks of steel determination. Cyfrin pulled Mara beside him, releasing her hand. Drake was flying, the water below him reaching out to toss him high, again and again, as he attacked. The black blood flowing from the gashes Drake laid in the Fury's flesh hit the water with great smoke and burning sizzles. Milios' eyes narrowed, the wind whipping up around them.

"It's doing something to the water," they said, and all five of them stared down over the rail at the blackened surface.

Sure enough, the waters below began to boil violently, sloshing sizzling black liquid against the sides of the ship. Mara could see scorch marks on the places it touched, etching deep scars into the outside of the Red Froth. Something was moving just below the thrashing waves. She could see creatures rising from the darkness, eyes black voids as the water filled them. Controlled them. Possessed creatures of the deep come to fight at the Fury's call.

"Back!" Kain shouted, and they all leapt backwards with mere seconds to spare. Long tentacles with thorn-like pointed suckers slapped on to the rail where they had stood. The monsters from below began to climb them with unnatural quickness.

Sea creatures of terrifying size and stature started to haul themselves onto the deck, slipping in their own muck as they moved blindly towards their targets. Mercreatures, beings Mara had only ever seen in storybooks, with sharply filed teeth and grasping, webbed hands. Creatures with squids for faces, monsters with shark heads, beasts that looked like they had never once seen the light of day…They all moved forward as one, their eyes filled with the darkly swirling liquid that the Fury seemed to be using to control them.

"Enough of this!" Cyfrin called out, the railing before

A PROPHECY OF UNDONE

them completely blocked by the ascending creatures. He raised his hands, blue magick whipping around them as he aimed straight for the nearest monster. A bolt of lightning shot forth from him with a crackling bang, the residuals licking the surface of the deck and colliding directly into the beast's chest.

It staggered, seemingly untouched. Then there was another, louder, bang. White hot lightning shot from the creature's head, its arms, its feet. It ran into and through the two monsters on either side of it, not stopping till it had travelled through another pair on either side of them. All five creatures stunned to a halt, eyes rolling into the back of their heads as their sockets smoked. Then they all toppled in unison, clearly dead. Their bodies continued to smoke as the onslaught of creatures stepped on and over the corpses.

The clatter of shouts and metallic clanging resounded around them, clashing with the sound of the Water Fury's cries. Drake had mounted the beast's head and it flailed madly to get him off, throwing large blasts of magick into the air as it did. Drake looked to be having the time of his life, moving with the dexterity of a fox across the top of the Fury's head. His sword flashed like a falling star in the moonlight, slamming into the Fury's skull again and again. Mara could see what looked to be long swathes of water flying in tandem with the blade, elongating its blows to impossible heights.

The crew fought for their lives as monsters began climbing to the ship's deck from every side with gusto. The five that Cyfrin had destroyed were quickly replaced by five more, an entire second line of them already positioned to strike. Cyfrin swore loudly, the lightning stretching up his arms flashing dangerously in his eyes.

167

I.A. TAKERIAN

"Cyfrin, where do you want us?" El called out, blasting a ball of green magick through the creature closest to her.

Milios waved their hands, wind whipping forward and colliding with the monsters, tossing a handful back into the ocean below. Mara had momentarily forgotten that Cyfrin was the leader of their war party, but she saw no hint of the man she had just been nearly fused with as she looked up into his face.

His eyes were stone cold sober, deadlocked on the Water Fury, teeth grit and veins pulsing. She could feel all their heightened emotions down the bond. Including his. "Kain and Milios, with me," he commanded. "El and Mara, take care of this lot. Let Drake handle the Fury."

Kain, Milios, and Cyfrin broke off from them, flying down the steps to the larger battle below. Mara pulled her long, curving dagger from her hip, standing with knees bent as she had been taught to do. All their training for close combat over the last few days flashed through her mind, tunneling her attention to the monster closest to her. It was circling behind her position, emitting a low, wet growl as it slid across the deck. Trying to flank her.

It screeched, flashing finely pointed fangs lacing across four separate sets of gums as it lunged for her. Mara ducked low, swinging her leg out to stabilize herself as she slashed forward into the creature's torso. It gagged, halting as Mara's dagger sliced clean through its stomach. Fish-like entrails gushed forth from its insides to the ground as she leapt backwards, its cold dead form collapsing to the deck.

El threw orbs of green magick and exploding potion bottles at the creatures as Mara spun and danced through their backlines. She pretended to be sparring with Cyfrin, egged on by his taunting comments to be the best she could possibly be. To *win*.

She was slashing through throats, chests, limbs.

168

A PROPHECY OF UNDONE

Anything that found itself unlucky enough to be in her path was met with cold metal and swift death. And as she went, she felt a thrill begin to rise within her. The feeling was mirrored in the four tattoos on her hand, all five of them reveling in their power not only as individuals, but as one.

Pride swelled through her as she marveled at her own strength, at how far she had already come. From the scared princess, hissing and spitting like a trapped kitten, to the unstoppable mighty Odelian warrior that now rounded the deck. Strikes of lightning were resounding below, wind whipping around them all and sending Kain's mighty laughter echoing all about. The Water Fury let out a cry of renewed rage, drawing their eyes to the battle just beyond.

Drake had cut one of its massive eyes open, leaving it bulging and oozing in its skull. The Fury screamed, throwing its huge arms wide as darkness shot from it like an axe. The magick slammed into Drake, catapulting him through the air to crash with unnatural softness into the water below. Mara watched with wide eyes as he sank like a rock beneath the surface.

"*Mara!*" El yelled, and Mara spun to face her through the still-growing crowd of monsters on the deck. El roared, blasting green magick forth from her body and clearing a path to the place where Mara stood. She ran forward as the Water Fury yelled, throwing its head high and redirecting its assault to the ship.

"*On me!*" El cried behind her as she ran, reaching her hand towards Mara. "You have to kill it! We have to do it *now!*" Her hand collided with Mara's shoulder as she spun to face the creature, filled with dread. Black, swirling magick engulfed its arms, spilling forth from its roaring mouth.

A hand came to rest on her other shoulder, Kain

169

I.A. TAKERIAN

standing stoically at her side. Milios tossed another dozen monsters from the deck, joining Kain. Cyfrin was backing up the stairwell, sending bolts of blue magick into the crowds.

"*Mara, now!*" El screamed over the Fury's roaring and the sinister sound of its growing magick.

Mara swallowed hard, closing her eyes, and raising her hands high. The heat rose in her instantly, cascading through her arms and to her palms. She felt Kain and El's grips tighten on her shoulders as her eyes flew open. Golden, dawn-like light shot forth from her hands. Tiny stars flew from the beam and to the dark waters below, sounding like bells through the air. The places in the poisoned water that were touched by her light glowed bright, purifying on contact.

The beam slammed into the Fury, its roars morphing into blood-curdling shrieks as the waters trembled viciously below. The dark magick grew, engulfing its body as it thrashed against the brilliant magick. Mara's arms felt like glass breaking into a million pieces, begging her to drop them and her overpowering stem of light. She felt herself being forced backwards, her feet sliding on the slick wood as Kain and El struggled to hold her in place. It was too much. The might of the magick was going to destroy her, and possibly everyone on board.

Then a back pressed itself firmly against hers. Over the smell of fish, salt, and blood, she caught the notes of pine and honey. She could feel the force of his magick creating an electrical circuit through the two of them once more as he pushed against her, holding her up and protecting her back from the attacking monsters still coming for them.

The beam of sunlight seemed to double in size. The chiming became a deafening hum, filling Mara's heart with a strange peace and focusing all she was on the monster.

A PROPHECY OF UNDONE

She yelled through the pain in her arms, pushing everything she was into the attack. She could hear her friends yelling with her. Sparks of multi-colored lights shot from the beam, cracks of blinding white now etching across it. The Water Fury's screams overpowered theirs now, the black magick seeming to flicker around it. Mara's vision began to blur, the white gold magick starting to stutter as well.

Then the water erupted next to the beast. Like a bolt of darkness, Drake shot up into the Fury. His blade hit the edge of its thick neck, driving through its flesh like it was nothing. A jet of water slammed into Drake's feet, forcing him forward so fast that Mara could hardly believe he was slicing through that beast at all.

But as he splashed to a halt atop the jet on the other side, the Fury stopped screaming. Its eyes were wide and reflected the moon, hollow and unseeing. There was a great sizzling noise, smoke erupting forth from a clean slice through its neck. And its head slid sideways off its body and crashed into the waters below.

Mara's magick, dimming now, still poured forth from her and into the Fury's unbeating chest. The harmonious humming had reached a fever pitch, and the entire body began to crack with the same white light that lashed through her beam. The cracks grew, bathing them all in so much brightness that for a moment, it looked like midday.

There was a mighty *boom*, and the body exploded in dazzling, sparkling light. Golden ash hung in the air for a moment, still in the shape of the Fury's body. Then it caught on the sea breeze, drifting everything about them like glittering sunlight.

Mara's hands fell to her sides, staggering as her knees buckled. Cyfrin spun on the spot, arms around her. His hands were still covered in the ebbing blue magick, and

I.A. TAKERIAN

Mara expected to be shocked on contact. But the lightning laced across her skin like licks of warm wind, raising the hair on her arms and leaving tingling goosebumps where they touched.

The creatures, controlled by whatever corrupting properties the Water Fury possessed, had all fallen dead to the deck around them. There were piles of sea creatures lining the ship as Drake came level with them.

He stepped from the jet of flowing water and directly onto the rail, beaming around at them all. His red eyes flashed in the moonlight as another jet of water lifted the massive head of the Fury from its depths. They watched, wide eyed and mouths agape, as it carried the head to the side of the lower deck, dumping it with a crash on to the wooden planks. The crew were yelling, scraping bodies into the water, and rushing about to secure Drake's disturbing trophy.

"Ends be damned, Mara!" he was calling, stepping from the rail, and rushing towards them. "I've never seen anything like that before! Your mother was only able to shoot that sunbeam; I never saw her absolutely *destroy* something like that! I mean, you reduced it to *ashes*."

Mara was panting slightly, leaning in to Cyfrin's chest as he held her arms steady. "I've never done it to something like that before," she said breathlessly, feeling light-headed. "And I can't do any sort of magick, let alone like that, without these four with me."

They were all looking exhausted, eyes drooped and faces flushed. Mara got the impression that the same amount of power she had just expended came partially from them. It had left each of them drained. Cool sweat coated their skin, and Mara sent a wave of gratitude down the bond. It struck her in this moment how true those words were. How helpless she would be in a situa-

A PROPHECY OF UNDONE

tion like this without them. She felt a little ashamed at the thought.

Drake laughed jubilantly. "I had just been thinking about how dreadfully boring this trip was turning out to be. And now, I get to bring this beauty home to Caerani!" He looked down the steps to the head on the deck with pride. He puffed his chest out, watching them sealing it down with the black, vibrating chains from the mast. They gleamed, an ominous hum coming from them before they snapped tight around it like a lock.

He looked back at the five of them, practically slumped on the floor beside him. "Aye, it looks like it really took it out of you lot. Get some rest then. You never know when something worse could come along out here."

"Something *worse*?" Mara groaned softly, Drake's eyes flashing in delight as he descended the staircase.

El was reaching towards Mara, worry in her eyes. Cyfrin transferred her gently into her waiting arms, avoiding Mara's look as she turned to face him. She could sense the bond between the two of them had been closed off once more. Mara knew Cyfrin, knew he was full of regret for his lost control moments before the Fury appeared.

"*Tell me to stop.*"

His words haunted her as she stared at his back on the way to their bunks. Had he truly wanted her to? Perhaps his reaction had simply been due to the immense amount of drink, instead of any actual feeling. Maybe, to him, it really was just a game with her.

El squeezed her as the feelings rippled down the bond, and she saw Cyfrin square his shoulders. But she was too drained to give it any more thought. El eased her into the firm, scratchy bed below deck, her eyes closing as soon as she hit the pillow.

I.A. TAKERIAN

Her dreams were filled with deep waters, Mara swimming downwards as hard as she could while straining for a figure just out of reach. Lightning webbed through the darkness around her, as her name was whispered on the breath of a husky voice.

"Dawnbringer. Dawnbringer."

CHAPTER 19

THROUGH SHROUDED VEILS COLD EMBRACE

Much to Drake's obvious and outspoken dismay, the following three days went by without incident. The waters beneath the Red Froth were calm, in clashing contrast with the ripping tide beside them. The past two days, they were able to make out a massive, dark wall of stone through the mists that seemed to stretch the entirety of the ocean. Mara had been stunned by it.

"The island is surrounded on nearly every side by a great rock wall," Drake told her. "There are two passes on either side, just narrow enough for a ship to scrape through. One side is always open. The other one is always guarded by the being we spoke about. The Tide Master."

His voice was dark, distant. "An absolute relic left behind by the Zenoths. They tasked him with keeping the rift safe in case there should be any evil looking to manipulate it in the future. There were once two of them, he and his brother. Now only he remains. But he can only guard one side at a time, you see. And the side he stands watch

175

I.A. TAKERIAN

upon at any given time isn't *impenetrable*. Just *undesirable*." He grimaced.

Mara stared at him with mounting panic. "What in the End of All does that mean? How do we know which side is open?" Her voice was higher than usual with anxiety.

Drake gave her a wry smirk. "Ah, see, it'd spoil all the fun if we just *knew*." He thrummed his fingers across the box at his hip. "Tim's pretty good at sensing which side he's on if we're close enough. It's not fool proof, but it's the best we've got. And as I said: The Tide Master is not impossible to get past, on the off chance he's wrong."

Mara grimaced. "So, we're relying on your sealed darkling's word, and a prayer?" she asked, and Drake laughed.

"Aye, I suppose that's one way to look at it," he replied, his smile not quite reaching his eyes.

Mara had tried for days to get Cyfrin alone again, to no avail. He was pointedly making it impossible to do so, always attached to Kain's hip and careful to not catch Mara's eye. She felt nothing from the lightning bolt on her finger but cold darkness, having been blocked off from him yet again. But she could swear that she sometimes caught him looking away from her face in a great hurry when she'd turn.

The three other Hopefuls, who had remained below deck during the Fury's attack on the ship, had taken to whispering venomously as she passed; their eyes like daggers as they glared. Their words were never quite loud enough for her to hear, but the looks of disdain on their faces were telling enough.

Cyfrin and Kain were somehow always around her when the three were, even outside their consistent practices. Mara couldn't help but wonder if it was coincidence

A PROPHECY OF UNDONE

or intentional, to keep her from their possible confrontation.

She was lying in her bunk that night, wide awake and listening to Kain snore on the opposite end of the room. The cabin lay in darkness, the ship rocking softly back and forth on the gently rolling waves. Mara knew they were due to arrive at the rocky cliffs within the day, and her stomach twisted and turned over itself at the thought. She groaned, rolling over.

She hadn't stopped thinking of the Tide Master since Drake had mentioned him. He gave her very few details, beyond his powers being 'great and terrible'. The idea of some ancient beast once again blocking her path to completing the trials was sickening. Her nightmares were still haunted by every creature she had encountered on her journey here, and she wasn't in a hurry to add another to the collection. She closed her eyes, wondering if they would have to fight the Tide Master to pass.

Drake had said he wasn't an impossible obstacle, just an unpleasant one. She shivered, remembering his expression at the thought of it and imagining what could possibly make Drake so visibly shaken.

The door to their cabin suddenly burst open. All five of them shot from their beds in a flash, blinking in the orb light that flooded into the room. Drake entered in a cold sweat, swearing in words Mara recognized as Ylastrian as he pulled his long leather coat on. "Get up to the deck," he said, his tone hollow. "We're coming towards the pass." He turned and began to ascend the steps to the upper deck.

"Which pass are we taking?" El called after him.

"The wrong one," Drake said back, disappearing above them.

El whimpered, and Milios let out a heavy sigh. The

I.A. TAKERIAN

group surged forward as a unit, rushing up the steps in a single file line.

"What does that mean?!" Mara asked, heart pounding. "What's going to happen?" She could feel the resolve in each of her companions, feel the shadow of something dark and fearful within it. They emerged on to the deck and into the cool night air.

The moonlight shone brightly overhead. They were nearly upon the pass, the cliffside stretching high into the sky and blocking out the stars beyond it. Mara could see something strange, shimmering and opaquely swirling to cover the entirety of the pass. Like a great magickal veil.

Drake grabbed her as she stepped onto the deck, squeezing her shoulders, and staring with focused intensity into her eyes. "I need you to listen to me," he said, the crew running about and strapping themselves with ropes to the rails of the ship.

Mara watched them, saw their pale, placid faces. And her panic grew. Drake shook her slightly. "Mara, I need you to *listen*. The Tide Master uses very powerful spell work as his shield against intruders. It will create an illusion, unique to the individual. When you're within the spell, everything will seem very, very real. *Painfully* so." He glowered towards the pass, releasing her shoulders as they both turned to face it. "When we pass through the Tide Master's veil, it will weigh your soul. But not like how it happened in the crystal lake. There will be no fae spirit to guide you. The spell uses a hex; magick long dead to us. It will show you your darkest thoughts, the most desperate nightmares hidden within your heart. You must find the door to the illusion and escape. Or you'll be lost to us inside."

Mara's heart stopped, a cold thrill running down her

178

A PROPHECY OF UNDONE

spine. She had many nightmares, each more terrifying than the last. And she had repressed each one as they came, refusing to acknowledge their hold on her. She gulped, her legs beginning to shake.

"Mara!" It was Cyfrin who called out to her. Her four companions already had one hand tied to the railing each, Cyfrin reaching out to her with the other. There was a spot between him and Milios, the rope waiting for her.

Drake nudged her side, offering a gentle smile. "We tie ourselves down mostly as a precaution," he said, turning to walk towards the plank jutting from the side of the ship. "Try to remember it's only an illusion, Mara. No matter how convincing it may be."

They were almost to the pass, inching closer to the veil with every second. Mara rushed forward, kneeling between Cyfrin and Milios. She tied herself down beside them, facing Cyfrin but staring out towards the pass. Drake was stepping out onto the plank, dangling precariously over the water as they slowed towards the veil.

"What's he doing?!" Mara hissed, eyes wide.

Drake stared down at something by the entrance to the pass. Mara followed his gaze, falling upon a figure hovering inches above the water.

Drake hadn't been kidding when he had called the Tide Master a relic. His skin was tinted blue and cracked like the ancient vases that lined the temple back in the village. His eyes were a swirling milky white, his hair was a magnificent shade of dark blue. It cascaded down about his body, pulled into hundreds of intricate braids about his frail figure. He was dressed in billowing black robes, adorned with ancient symbols that looked like the ones on Cyfrin's body. He raised a hand as they approached, and the Red Froth suddenly stopped dead in its tracks.

I.A. TAKERIAN

Mara heard a hissing sound, and the Tide Master rose on a cloud of mist to hover before the plank. Drake folded his arms as he ascended towards him, a menacing grimace set on his ink-black skin. "Been awhile since I've seen you," Drake said, voice full of blank disdain.

The Tide Master looked at him with emotionless eyes. "You have been sneaking on to my island again, accursed one." His voice was a rumble like the waves around them, the ship swaying angrily against the sound.

Drake waved a hand, indifferent. "I never sneak, you rotted fish," he sneered. "I simply appear at the most opportune time for me."

But the Tide Master wasn't paying attention to his words. He sniffed at the air, nostrils flaring as he closed his eerily swirling eyes. Cyfrin shifted, angling himself slightly before Mara. His broad frame blocked her from view, but it was of little use.

The Tide Master's clouded eyes shot open, mouth breaking into a toothless grin at Drake. "You carry destiny aboard your vessel. I can taste them." His voice echoed around them, and Mara's breath caught in her throat. She shrunk towards Cyfrin's back, fear gripping her heart.

Drake kept his face cool and even. "If that destiny is me, kicking your ass...I can sense that its fulfillment is coming very, very soon."

His words sliced through the air, wiping the devious smile from the Tide Master's face. "It matters not whom you bring with you past my borders, Chaos Sealed." The rumble had deepened and increased in volume. It shook the cliffside, sending rocks crashing to the ocean around them and throwing waves threateningly against the sides of the Red Froth, drenching them all. "All must enter through the veil. All must pass or perish."

Mara shivered at his words, blood running cold in her

veins. "Through darkened night, and emptied light." The Tide Master said, his voice sounding like hundreds on the whipping wind. "Upon one's heart of cursed plight. Through shadows deep and whispers cold, through secrets wished once left untold—"

"Yes, yes, you decrepit bastard," Drake cut him off. "The veil will make us see terrible things and it's our job to get ourselves out. It's not complicated. We don't need you rhyming at us."

The Tide Master's white eyes darkened, reflecting the storm clouds that now rumbled threateningly above them. But Drake rolled his eyes at him, snapping his fingers impatiently. "Let's get on with it then," he said in a muted voice. "I've got a fiery woman waiting back in the village for me, and I'll not have you dragging this out."

The Tide Master let out a low growl, the sound followed by a growing hiss. The waves crashing before the Red Froth broke, and they were thrown haphazardly forward through the ice-cold veil.

"—AND ARE YOU *LISTENING*, MARA?!"

Mara's head shot up off her arms, eyes wild. She had fallen asleep on her desk again. The warm autumn sun cascading through the window caressed her face, and her black curls hung like a long curtain about her.

Dreaming. She had been having the most extraordinary dream. The more she focused on it, the cloudier it got. There had been magick, starlight, music... Heat and metal and lightning...

It was fading away, vanishing to whatever place dreams

I.A. TAKERIAN

went to when you woke. Lady Lenorei was shaking her head disapprovingly at Mara, tutting as she slammed her open history book closed on her desk. Mara winced at the sound.

"I-I'm sorry, Lady Len," she replied, groggy. She saw her tutor grimace at the name. "I was having the strangest dream—"

"Yes, Mara, that's the problem," Lady Lenorei cut her off, folding her arms across her chest. "You were *dreaming* instead of *listening*. What would your uncle say if he knew you were wasting away your time like this? You know what his wishes are."

Mara's brow furrowed. *My uncle.* There was an odd pang in her heart at the words. A scratch she couldn't itch, and she couldn't put her finger on exactly why. She nodded vaguely at Lady Lenorei as she lectured her, staring out the window. She could see the preparations for the Festival of End happening below them in the city, and her heart leapt suddenly.

She turned to Lady Lenorei's disapproving face with a wide smile. "Come on, Lady Len!" she crooned, pouting at her through wide eyes. "The festivities are taking place down there, and we're cooped up here discovering new meanings to the word boring!" She blinked, finishing the sentence slowly. Everything felt strangely familiar, as if it had happened once before.

Lady Lenorei was shaking her head. "In all my years, I have never met a more distracted lady—"

"Does that mean I can go?" She had cut Lady Len off, impatiently bouncing in her seat. Lady Lenorei gave a heavy sigh, rubbing the bridge of her nose. Mara shot from her seat, moving swiftly towards the door without waiting for an answer.

A PROPHECY OF UNDONE

"Be here bright and early tomorrow, Mara!" Lady Lenorei called after her. "An excess of drinking at tonight's ceremony will not excuse you."

Mara had said the words at the same time as Lady Len, chuckling at how incredibly predictable the exchange had been. She was back in her tower bedroom, the window thrown wide to let in the sound of swirling music and laughter from the excited city below. She stood in her padded leathers, staring at her reflection with a satisfied grin. She ran her hands down her body, reaching for the dagger at her thigh...

She froze, the smile slipping on her face. Why had she thought there was a dagger there? She never carried weapons in the castle, unless she was heading to practice with Adrian, and she didn't even own a dagger to begin with.

She shook off the odd feeling, squeezing her helmet on over her ponytail and heading off towards the courtyard. She walked in a fog to the fighter's tents standing at the entrance of the arena, desperately trying to pull herself from the drowsiness after her nap. It was jam packed with men of all kinds, raucous and loud as they waited for the tournament to begin. But she could see the handsome face of her friend, Adrian, at the very back.

She beamed, working her way through the crowd to stand beside him. He raised an eyebrow, staring down at her. Her heart leapt, as if she had not seen him for a very long time. But they had just been sparring the evening before.

"What's your problem?" he asked, voice rough. "Never seen a—"

Mara did not let him finish the sentence. Her body moved of its own accord, throwing her forward to hug

183

I.A. TAKERIAN

him. He staggered, stunned as a few of the men turned to stare with inquisitive looks.

"Don't let your ego get any bigger, Adrian," she giggled into his chest as his body grew very still. "You'll squash us all."

Adrian peeled her gently off him, face pale and eyes wild as he dragged her off to the side. He stared about them, paranoid. "Have you lost your entire bloody *mind*, Mara?!" he hissed at her, but she just continued to smile wistfully at him. His eyes fell on her face, and he blinked. "What's gotten into you?" he asked, his gaze tracing the entirety of her misty-eyed expression.

She giggled, Adrian raising an eyebrow at the sound. "I'm just really happy to see you is all," she replied, and she meant it. She didn't understand why, but her heart was doing backflips of excitement standing here before him, even more so than it did for the impending tournament.

He blinked at her again, a small smile breaking across his face as he flushed slightly. She dropped her eyes, avoiding the surge of hungry emotion in his.

"Don't think your soft words are going to make me go easy on you," he said in a husky voice. "If you're to compete, you'll do so with honor. I'd have it no other way."

She was standing before Adrian in the arena, a smirk on his face as he bowed low to her. Mara frowned slightly. Had she bested the other two men pitted against her already? Yes…Yes, she could remember her triumphs vaguely through her dream-like cloud. She returned Adrian's bow, raising her sword high before connecting with his.

They moved slowly about one another, blades meeting in a great clatter as they went. Mara felt strange, like she was floating through very hot water. The heat was filling her, a great humming beginning to resound in her ears as

184

A PROPHECY OF UNDONE

they went. She stumbled, distracted, and the sword tipped from her hands. She trembled, staring down at her palms as the crowd around her became hushed.

Something was growing inside of her, a fire in her blood as her entire being focused down to her palms. Adrian reached for her, a look of concern set deep in his face, and she raised a hand to step back. Golden-white light erupted forth from her outstretched hand, winging Adrian as they both cried out.

The crowd screamed, King Grathiel and his court leaping to their feet. She fell to her knees, staring at Adrian through panicked eyes. His arm was sizzling, bubbling, and burning like fat over fire. He turned to her with eyes black as night. They were filled with such hatred that Mara fell away from him, scrambling backwards through the dirt.

"*Dread.*" The word hissed from his mouth, echoed all around her by the crowd and court.

Mara trembled, shaking her head as tears sprung to her eyes. "No!" she stammered, an invisible weight preventing her from standing. She felt so incredibly small as they hissed around her, glowering. "No, I-I didn't mean to! Please!"

"*Martyr!*" King Grathiel shrieked in an animal-like voice, black smoke obscuring the bright sky and throwing them all into shadow. Mara closed her eyes, willing it to end. Praying it would stop.

She was kneeling now in the throne room. She stared down at her hands, joined by chains covered in darkly etched symbols. Rags hung from her body, barely covering her as she knelt on the cold marble floor. King Grathiel sat on the throne, a smug look on his face and eyes filled with black smoke. A voice rumbled from beside her.

"Bow before your king, wretch." It was Adrian, his words dripping in harsh disgust. He spit on her as she

I.A. TAKERIAN

looked up at him, slamming his foot into her back and forcing her face to the ground. He held her there, tears flowing from her eyes as the court laughed.

"You have been charged with the crime of dark magick, Dread," King Grathiel was saying over the jeers of the crowd. "And for this most heinous of crimes, your punishment shall be *beheading*."

A roar of approval from the onlookers as Mara sobbed. A hooded man was stepping forward, handing Adrian a massive axe as he removed his foot from her back.

She was nothing. She was less than nothing. She was unloved, and unlovable. She cried harder as he raised the axe high.

"*Dawnbringer!*" The voice came in like a soft whisper, floating almost soundlessly past her on the breeze. She froze, and the scene around her seemed to slow. There was a scent travelling about her on the gentle wind, something very familiar. Honey and pine.

The smell of home.

She brought herself upright, a strange pressure on her cheeks.

"Dawnbringer!" The voice was clear this time, deep and velvety as it echoed around her. Mara felt the heavy clouded weight trying to settle harder around her, making her eyes nearly impossible to keep open. "It's an illusion, Mara!" the voice called to her, growing fainter. "You must find the door! Find the door..." It vanished with the breeze, everything around her unfreezing at once.

Mara rolled forward, the axe swinging to the floor behind her with a deafening thud. The crowd gasped as she leapt to her feet, still bound. She spun around as Adrian lifted the axe again, advancing on her with murderous intent. Mara's eyes darted around her, fighting the crushing weight of darkness and deep hurt aching within her.

There was a small, inconspicuous door set in the wall to her left. It was glowing a very dim shade of blue, and she could hear the voice coming faintly from behind, repeating that same word. "Dawnbringer."

Adrian roared, taking a swing with his axe as he dove. She lurched forward, sprinting as hard as she could through the crowd of shocked courtiers and slamming her body into the door with all her might. It shuddered, giving way against the force of her collision. She flew forward through it, tumbling into a massive void beyond.

SHE SPUN DIZZYINGLY FAST, the sounds of the world around her rushing in all at once. The ocean waves against the steep cliffside, the many frantic voices of the crewmen, Drake barking orders. And then her name. She opened her eyes.

Cyfrin held her face cupped in his hands, his eyes panicked as he stared at her breathlessly. He let out a sigh of relief as her eyes met his, pushing his forehead against hers. Her skin tingled where he touched and she held still, savoring the warmth of his hands on her cheeks.

"That was terrible," she said hoarsely, and he pulled back to stare at her with a pained expression.

"I know," he replied in a low voice. "We could feel it. I could...We could feel you slipping into the darkness. I'm so sorry."

Her breath caught, tears threatening to spill forth. He was looking at her with such softness, such understanding.

I.A. TAKERIAN

She felt she would melt into a puddle where she sat. But she bit her tongue, nodding at him in acknowledgment. He rubbed his thumb across her cheek once, face unreadable, then stood and helped her to her feet.

Mostly everyone had emerged from the Tide Master's hex. The three other Hopefuls were looking at her with unfiltered disappointment, as if hoping she had remained trapped. El, Milios, and Kain looked deeply troubled, but otherwise unscathed. Cyfrin remained inches from her side, a fingertips length away, as they approached Drake.

He knelt next to a man who lay twitching on the deck. His eyes were filled with cloudy white mist, frothing at the mouth as he stared unseeingly up at the sky. Drake's face was dark, void of all emotion as he poured a potion down his throat.

The man shuddered, eyes closing as he fell completely still. Drake stood slowly, turning to face them. "Good to see you were able to pull yourself out," he said, and she flushed slightly.

She didn't know how to tell them all that it was Cyfrin who had led her from the clouded nightmare she was trapped in. Cyfrin who had kept her from being completely lost.

But Drake was staring over her shoulder now, towards the helm of the ship. The five of them turned as well, following his gaze. Through the lingering mists of the pass the ship was exiting, surrounded by crashing waves brought in on the heavy tides, was a large island.

It lay in the dark shadows cast by the rock wall locking it in, hundreds of yards away from its shore on all sides. It stretched far beyond what her eyes could see, but Mara got the strange feeling that there was much more here than her eyes could see. There was intense, heavy energy pulsing from the land, and Mara's skin crawled in response. Her

A PROPHECY OF UNDONE

nerve endings felt frayed as they approached, begging her to turn back. To retreat.

"Welcome to Hope," Drake said from beside her, stepping past them with humorless eyes to take up the wheel and steer them inland.

CHAPTER 20
SILENCE TO LEARN

Mara felt like she couldn't get a full breath of air, the things she had seen still resting on her heart. They stood beside Drake as he directed the Red Froth to port, all six of them lost in silent reverence.

Mara shivered, pulling her cloak tighter around herself. "What was the point of that?" she asked, voice still strained from the illusion. She did not feel she had been weighed at all, but instead tortured.

Drake grimaced, keeping his eyes forward. "When the Zenoths left Zenafrost through the portal they created here, they gave the Tide Master the task of protecting the island after they left. To keep the bad things in, and the greedy out." He scoffed. "Self-righteous bastard. His powers have been diminishing for centuries, and it only got worse once his brother passed on. Pretty piss poor excuse for a guard, if you ask me."

"That was his powers *diminished?*" Mara gulped, eyes wide.

Drake looked grim. "Aye. I haven't had to deal with

I.A. TAKERIAN

him in decades. As he said, I am very good at sneaking on to the island around his defenses."

Mara glanced back at the man once foaming on the deck, now being carried below by the crewmates. "What happens to those who become lost within the illusion?" she asked softly, trying to push the images of her kneeling in the throne room from her mind. It had been so real, so vivid. Exactly as Mara had imagined it if anyone had ever discovered who she really was. If she had ever even considered returning.

Seeing Adrian there had been bittersweet. She missed him so desperately, having spent nearly every moment of her life till now at his side. But she knew that to try and convince him of any of this would be an incredibly monumental task. Nearing on the impossible.

Emotion tore through her with no filter. Anger and sadness came together like a tidal wave, and she saw all four of her companion's flinch. Cyfrin, never having left her side, touched her arm gently. She took a deep breath, willing her anger to ebb.

Drake looked solemn. "If you're trapped inside the Tide Master's hex, then that's it. Your body lives on, but you're trapped in the darkness of your own mind." He glowered towards the island, angry energy rolling off him. "It may have been a worthy test once, long ago. But it's been twisted by time and his ageing mind."

They all fell silent, staring out at the shoreline and lost in deep thought. The closer they drew to the island, the more aware Mara became of the intensely heavy energy that was emanating from it. The air around it seemed to be waving slightly, blurring the details of the island as Mara frowned at it.

"It feels so...*powerful,*" Mara said, a thrill running through her as she stared out.

A PROPHECY OF UNDONE

Drake nodded in agreement. "The tear has created a strange environment on the island. It's constantly morphing the landscape, every second, and makes it absolutely impossible to map out. I've tried many times." He pointed towards the far shore, where a great, dark cloud swirled over the hills. "You can always see where the tear is, by that energy field there.

And I strongly suggest trying to avoid it as best as you can. Never know what it's going to spawn."

"I remember a few years back, it sprouted these great winged creatures that swept through and drank to blood of every living thing they encountered," El said, shivering at the thought.

Kain scoffed. "That was child's play compared to the year it turned every bit of sand on the island into lava. While we were standing on it."

Mara's stomach turned. "And we're just going to be thrown out into it? Without knowing what we're going to encounter?" The thought of appearing out of midair above a lava pit now hung in her mind.

Drake let out a wry laugh. "Tristan is an excellent Traveler," he said as the ship eased up to a small, makeshift dock. "He'll be the one teleporting you all out into the island, and to date he's yet to drop anyone into something immediately deadly. Though, I suppose there is a first for everything."

He let go of the wheel, the ship slowing instantly to a halt as he turned to face them all. Mara was still reeling, feeling ill-prepared to face the challenges ahead. *Perhaps that in itself is part of the challenge*, she thought to herself, sneering at her own dim attempt to feel better.

The three other Hopefuls had joined them at the helm, hoods drawn, and packs of supplies already strung to their backs. Drake's eyes were alight once more as he stared

I.A. TAKERIAN

around. "Right. Well, you all know by now how this goes. You'll be sent on to the island and expected to survive for the next two weeks, regardless of the conditions." His eyes flashed. "Be prepared for *any*thing. The rift isn't simply a tear in time and space. It's a connection to other dimenssions, other realms, and the things that exist therein."

He folded his arms behind his back, pacing across the deck as he continued. "You'll be travelled individually. It will be up to you whether you continue your journey alone or attempt to group up for your survival. Both options have pros and cons. I suggest you weigh them accordingly." He stopped, looking at each of them in turn. "This is your final test. Your last stop on the way to being deemed a warrior of the Odelian people. Our highest honor. In two weeks' time, your body will be travelled back aboard my deck, dead or alive, and we will return to the village to honor our survivors and bury those of you who do not make it."

The silence following this was heavy, Mara's heart thundered in her chest. El threw her an encouraging smile, trying to ease the panic echoing down through their bond.

Drake nodded to them. "Gather your supplies, your packs, your cloaks. Tristan will be sending you each out shortly. Do not leave anything behind; I will throw it overboard."

They returned to the upper decks a few minutes later, packs full on their backs and weapons strapped across their bodies. Mara was cold, her brain feeling very distant from her. Adrian's face still swam in her mind, encompassing all her thoughts.

"You're going to do great," El was saying to her as they waited by the railing.

The three other Hopefuls glared at them from across the deck. Kain slapped her on the back, knocking her

194

A PROPHECY OF UNDONE

forward slightly. "Just remember to hunt us down as quickly as you can," he said, eyes glinting with excitement. "I don't give a damn what Drake says. That island's a beast not meant to be travelled alone."

Mara gulped, and she felt a squeeze on her shoulder and her opposite hand at the same time.

Milios stood at her shoulder, gazing at her calmly. "Just focus on the bond," they said, waving their tattooed hand. "You'll be able to feel when we're close. It will guide you to us."

It was Cyfrin grasping her hand firmly, eyes burning into hers with an intensity she hadn't seen in days. "You are mighty, Mara," he said in a low voice, while the other three looked away. "Even if you were to take the island on your own for the entire two weeks, I have no doubt that you would conquer it with ease." He smirked down at her blushing cheeks.

"Then why does it feel like I'm walking to my own grave?" she asked, her throat tight.

His gaze softened, like fresh snowfall coming down around her. "Mmm. If only you could see yourself the way I see you, my Dawnbringer." His words sent electricity through her body, erasing everything from the world but the two of them. She blinked up at him, face getting hotter under the steadiness of his stare.

She remembered back to the first time she had seen him in her room at Castle Delinval. How she had been just as struck then by his beauty as she was now. She bit her lip, pulling her eyes away from him as he released her hand.

El took his place at her side, lacing her arm through hers. "I agree with Cyf," she said, hugging her. "You doubt yourself too much, Mara. We watched you blast your way through an entire Fury earlier, and here you are worried."

"I wouldn't have taken out the Fury without the four of

I.A. TAKERIAN

you," Mara replied. "I'm practically magick-less without you all." She bowed her head in embarrassment, El gripping her arm tighter as her three companions pulled instinctively closer to her.

Drake was approaching the three Hopefuls across the deck from them, a tall lanky man dressed in a brown leather duster following behind. His long green hair had been pulled into a braid down his back, shining as the first rays of morning edged above the cliffs. Mara recognized him as a forest dweller.

Drake spoke swiftly to the three, bowing low as they each returned the gesture. The forest dweller stepped forward; eyes glowing pure white as he waved his hands smoothly before the first Hopeful. There was a loud *pop*, and the first Hopeful vanished in the blink of an eye.

Mara could feel cold sweat on her back as he moved forward to the next one, repeating the motions till all three Hopefuls were gone.

Smiling wickedly, an ornate flask in hand, Drake made his way over to the five of them. He beamed, reveling in the anxiety on Mara's face. He waved back at the forest dweller standing behind him, staring at them all with a small smile. "Mara, I believe you're the only one that's not met my resident traveler," Drake said as the man gave a little wave at her. "This is Tristan. He will be placing you each on the island, as you just saw. But first!" He brandished the flask and they all groaned.

"I am not drinking deep wine before we start this," Cyfrin said, eyeing the flask with wearily.

El and Kain nodded in agreement, Milios matching his look of hesitation. Drake looked shocked, eyes narrowing. "It's not deep wine," he began, pulling the lid off and sniffing it. "It's mead, thank you very much. And even if it

A PROPHECY OF UNDONE

was deep wine, who wouldn't want to start their trial with an extra pep in their step?!"

They exchanged dark looks and Drake scowled at them. "I wanted to toast you all, seeing as it's our Mara's first time on the island," he continued, and Mara froze.

"*Our* Mara," he had said. She had never been anyone's anything, really. Never belonged to something bigger than herself. Not like this. A smile broke across her nervous expression, one that Drake returned enthusiastically. He raised the flask at her, passing it to Kain beside him who took a swig and passed it on.

"To Mara!" Drake said as they each took a drink. It tasted oddly bitter as it slid down Mara's throat, leaving the familiar burn of the mead from the taverns in the village. "May your time on Hope be vivid, full of growth, and void of life-threatening injury!"

The flask got back around to him, and he lidded it, eyes flashing with an odd look. Kain opened his mouth to add something to the toast but sputtered. His eyes went wide, hands flying to his mouth as he stared around frantically. Puzzled, Mara opened her mouth to ask what was wrong.

But no noise came out.

She tried again and again to speak, mouthing the words soundlessly as she stared around at her companions making similar motions. Cyfrin turned on Drake, eyes wild and fists engulfing in furious blue lightning.

Drake raised his eyebrow at him, chuckling. "Put those away, boy, before you get hurt." His voice was humorous but threatening. Cyfrin hesitated, magick still surrounding his hands as he glowered at Drake. He shook the now empty flask, winking at them. "The four of you have travelled this island many, many times before," he said as Kain looked close

197

I.A. TAKERIAN

to tears, poking his own tongue. "The three other Hopefuls have never been here, the same as Mara. I know the five of you will be joining together out there, and it would be wildly unfair to those three to not give you *some* form of handicap."

He shook his head, eyes still alight. He looked like he was thrilled at this final twist he had given to them. "So, I had the healer in the village whip up a Potion of Undying Silence for me before we left. I have the antidote aboard as well, and I will give you each a dose when you return. In two weeks."

Cyfrin looked murderous, Kain still poking into his mouth sadly. El made a helpless face of desperation.

"Look on the bright side," Drake was saying. "This will teach you all how to communicate without words! Which is an invaluable skill on and off the battlefield. It will bring you closer as a unit. That's what you all want, isn't it? To be the best?" His eyes gleamed, all five of them nodding begrudgingly at him.

It's not as if we have much of a choice, Mara thought disdainfully, grimacing at Drake's smile. Tristan had stepped forward, coming to stand before Mara. He gave her a soft smile as panic flashed through her eyes. She wasn't ready. She didn't have the time she needed to process any of what had just happened, let alone the silence had been forced upon her.

"Do not be afraid," Tristan said, and Mara felt an unnatural calm wash over her at his voice. She wondered vaguely if it was some sort of magick that silenced the anxiety within her as she stared at him. "Look around you to your comrades. They have all passed this trial once before, and then a hundred times again."

Mara looked around at them all. The harsh stares towards Drake were gone, all of them looking to her with encouragement. Kain, El, and Milios flashed brilliant

198

A PROPHECY OF UNDONE

smiles at her, Drake giving her an excited wave from behind Tristan.

Cyfrin had a strange look on his face as he stared at her, a cross between steel acceptance and worry. But he too gave her a smile as Tristan's eyes began to glow. His hands were moving, a hum starting to emit from them. "You should close your eyes," he said, a strange pull beginning to tug at Mara from all sides.

She squeezed her eyes shut, clenching her hands in to fists at her sides as she felt her feet ripped from the dock. The wind whipped around her, swirling faster and faster, and she was shot forward through the ocean air.

CHAPTER 21
ALONE AND WITHOUT

Mara had the feeling of being pushed through an impossibly tight tunnel, at least two times too small for her body. She couldn't breathe as it shot her through the air, her eyes still squeezed closed as her stomach threatened to empty its contents. Right as she started to feel like she may pass out, the world stopped moving.

She had slammed to a halt on solid ground, her senses overwhelmed by the landscape. Cold air nipped at her exposed face, whispering through reeds as it flew past her. Mara opened her eyes slowly, taking in her surroundings with wide-eyed wonderment.

She stood in the middle of a stretch of wetlands. Her feet had come to rest on a small patch of spongy grass, surrounded by oddly purple waters. The reeds swaying all around her were topped in light blue fuzz, soft seeds expelling into the air with each large gust of wind. The air was filled with strange glass balls, floating lazily through the weeping willows dispersed through the waters. They floated like the orb lights back in the village, and Mara

I.A. TAKERIAN

could hear a soft twinkling sound emitting from them as they passed.

Everything was tinted slightly pink, and the waters seemed to be heavily perfumed with something sweet. It made Mara's head spin. There was noise coming from the waters to her left, and she knelt low to make herself small. The reeds hid her cloaked figure as she stared out towards the source of the sound.

Walking through the waters a few yards away, pushing through the low hanging leaves of the willows, were four creatures. They were covered in strangely iridescent fur, long ears sticking out from the sides of their heads and small ivory horns jutting up from either side of their skulls. They had nubby tails, fat webbed feet that ended in razor-sharp talons, and hands that looked like softly padded paws. Paws that were tipped in blade-like nails.

Their beady black eyes shined out from the mass of fur on their faces, large dog-like noses wiggling as they chittered to one another. Mara could see whiskers waving on their cheeks, sticking out from their ears, and their words sounded like bird song as they passed her. The waters beneath them seemed to part as they walked, closing behind them as they lifted their feet to step. Mara ducked further down as she watched them embarked deeper into the wetlands. She had never seen creatures like these, and she knew they would be far from the only ones she would encounter on her journey.

At least these ones weren't inherently scary, she thought, standing slowly from her spot hidden amongst the reeds. *Could have been big, shadow-like and teleporting around. Those just looked like walking teddy bears.* She sighed, looking around her at the waters with weary eyes.

Its shade of purple, coupled with the unnatural smoothness with which it moved, made her hesitant to step

A PROPHECY OF UNDONE

in. Puffs of pink fog emitted from the surface, sending the sweetly dizzying perfume into the air. She bit her lip, looking back at the spot the bear-creatures had been. The waters had parted for them. Perhaps they would do the same for her.

She took a steadying breath, listening to the soft twinkling of the orb lights and sounds of cricketing bugs all around her. There was a throb in her hand, brief and fleeting, and she looked down at the tattoos across her knuckles. It was gone now, but she could have sworn she had felt something like a yell ripple down the bond from Cyfrin. Like a scream on the wind, almost indiscernible by the time it reached your ears.

Indeed, the more she focused on the tattoos, the more she could feel them pulsing softly with their shared energy. She closed her eyes, willing them to guide her forward. There was a slight tug on her chest, pulling her irresistibly northwards. *Right,* she thought, resolved and clenching her hands into fists. *Better get a move on then.* Cautiously, ready to yank her foot away at the smallest sign of trouble, she took one step into the mystical waters.

Just as they had done for the fuzzy creatures before, they parted to reveal white sand below their surface. Mara stepped forward quickly, watching as it created a small path for her through it before closing behind each footstep. She began to march, letting the bond between the five of them pull her unthinkingly onward.

Mara walked for hours, feet growing sore as she hurried through the wetlands. She ducked behind trees and in large patches of reeds whenever another fuzzy beast would pass, careful not to make a sound as they spoke to one another in their trilling voices. The sun, tinted in the strange pink of the air around her, was low in the sky when she finally stopped for a break.

203

I.A. TAKERIAN

She plopped down on a large rock embedded into the earth, pulling her water pouch and rations from her pack. Her feet throbbed angrily in her boots. The warnings about the island from Drake, Caerani, and her comrades seemed disproportionate as she sat underneath the willows, listening to the soft sounds of the environment around her.

But the fact that this place had been so calm and almost beautiful up to this point was far from making Mara feel better.

She had learned from experience within the Forgotten Woods that peaceful, beautiful things were often the deadliest. They led you into a false sense of security, creating the illusion that you were safe before taking advantage of your relaxed state. She refused to let it get to her. Refused to become prey for some horror waiting to strike.

"You are mighty." Cyfrin's words played in her head again as she ate, staring wistfully out through the trees.

If those four warriors, trained and battle-hardened over hundreds of years, thought that she was powerful... Then why could she not see herself as such? Her anxious heart betrayed her, wondering if they were all just saying such things to make her feel better before her trial. There was noise beside her, pulling her from her musings to stare at the moving patch of reeds feet away.

She set her bread down, reaching slowly for her dagger, eyes narrowing. The reeds parted, and something bounced out. Mara startled, blade already in her hand as she stared.

It looked like a baby of the fuzzy creatures she saw walking around constantly. Its completely black eyes were huge compared to its tiny head, looking like an oversized cotton ball as it stared at her curiously. It tilted its head, chittering softly as it sniffed the air.

The grip on her dagger loosened. Mara smiled softly at it, eyes passing over its talon-less feet and softly padded

204

A PROPHECY OF UNDONE

paws. It hopped closer to her, its nub of a tail wiggling excitedly. It was inches from her leg, wagging its butt and looking up at her with the sweetest of expressions in its large eyes. If Mara could have crooned at it, she would have.

It rested its paw against the broad side of her blade, making an inquisitive squeak. She smiled, waving it a little in the air so that the glowing gems sparkled on its face. It reached out, as if asking to hold it. Mara raised an eyebrow, amused, shaking her head gently as if telling a small child 'no'.

She knew in an instant that it had been a mistake to let this tiny thing so close to her.

As she shook her head, it rose up on to its back legs. It tilted its head back, opening its tiny mouth wide as it stared at the sky. A sound like a siren erupted forth from it, sending birds shooting into the clouds from the willow trees. Mara leapt to her feet at once, sensing movement all around her as the siren sound was returned by much bigger creatures in the distance.

She swore inside her head, hesitating for only a moment as she stared down at the small creature now alerting the wetlands around her. She threw her foot forward, kicking it hard and sending it flying into the trees. It continued to scream as it flew, and Mara began to run.

She could hear large beasts crashing through the trees behind her as she went, the howl that the baby was making now mirrored in their cries. She smacked one of the glass balls floating in the air out of her way as she bolted, and it exploded on impact. It looked like snow as it fell about her, a soft sigh filling the air as it popped. Several of the glass balls around it popped like a tidal wave, the sound of sighs clashing with the screams of the beasts behind her. She crashed through the reeds and

205

I.A. TAKERIAN

trees, throwing caution to the wind as she struggled to get away.

Something large slammed into her, sending her flying sideways to land with a hard thud against a particularly large willows trunk. Mara groaned as the creature roared before her. It was a fully grown bear-beast, beady eyes wild as it slammed its fists against its mighty chest. The roar ceased, the beast dropping to all fours and barreling forward towards her. Mara leapt to her feet, her axe in her hands in an instant.

She swung it high as it lunged for her, bringing it down to collide directly with its skull as it slammed into her again. She smashed back against the tree as the creature crumpled to the ground, dark blue blood gushing forth from its skull. She stepped around it, the sound of more creatures growing closer as she stared, panting. *If I can get them to attack me one at a time like this,* she thought as she began to back away from the bleeding beast. *Then I can fight my way out.*

But something was happening as she stared at the creature. Hundreds of the tiny glass balls were cascading down upon the place where it laid, covering its body entirely. They began to shatter one by one, bursting into its furry body. The white snow-like powder enshrouded it.

Mara eyes grew wide as the beast got to its feet slowly, turning to face her. Its wound had been completely healed, its eyes now glowing a pearly shade of white as blue smoke billowed forth from its ears and nose. It roared again, the cry sounding oddly metallic.

Mara swore to herself once more, throwing the axe back into its sling as she turned from the beast. She began to sprint, as fast as her feet would carry, back through the trees. She could feel the steady, dim pulse of their bond still

206

A PROPHECY OF UNDONE

pulling her as she ran, the sound of many creatures crashing through the wetlands hot on her tail.

Her chest felt like it was tearing open, the air growing thin as more bubbles of glass popped around her. She wondered if they had anything to do with the sudden dizzying in her head, but only for an instant as she moved. She could feel how close they were to catching her, hear the low pants of their hungry breathes in between their shrieks of fury. She could see light up ahead, maybe a clearing in which she could gain a little more distance on them.

She cursed herself, enraged that her magick would not even come to her aid in a time like this. She tried focusing her energy down to her palms as she sprinted through the reeds but was met only with clammy silence. The light grew closer, the wetlands opening ahead of her.

She gasped as she came barreling through the tree line, trying to slow herself down. But it was too late, her momentum too great. She shot out of the wetlands and ran herself straight off the cliff before her.

There was a moment where she floated in the air, suspended high above the shimmering clear waters below her. She heard the beasts chasing her grind to a halt as they appeared from the trees, roaring in unison as she began to plummet.

Mara opened her mouth in a soundless scream. She wondered if her companions could feel her down the bond as she dropped, resolved to what was surely her death waiting in the water below. She slammed through its surface, sinking quickly as her body ached. Her back felt like someone had dropped a boulder on it, the backs of her arms and legs stinging in the crystal-clear waters around her. A bubble of air escaped her; the wind knocked from her chest with the force of the collision.

207

I.A. TAKERIAN

Her head throbbed as she righted herself, forcing her legs to kick painstakingly upwards. There were tiny, gem-like fish swimming away from her, the waters where she fell still full of the bubbles from her impact. She burst through the surface, gasping as she flailed to stay afloat.

The water dragged her quickly backwards, towards what sounded unmistakably like a waterfall. There was dense forest surrounding the river taking her onward, and she swam furiously towards the shore. The struggle was painful, draining her to the point of exhaustion as the current pulled hard at her arms and legs. She grabbed on to the roots sticking out of the shoreline, hauling herself up to solid ground.

She crawled her body through the dirt, across the rocks and vines covering the earth, till she was fully away from the ripping waters behind her. She slumped against a tree shooting seventy feet into the sky above, panting heavily. There was a stitch in her side that shot sharp pain through her, and she grabbed at it, wincing. She looked up to the cliffside high above where she had just fallen, squinting to try and see any figures. But it was impossible through the fog clinging to the air.

This landscape was different than the one she had just come from, darker and less whimsical as howls and strange, throaty calls echoed from the depths of the dense trees. She remembered Drake's words of caution, about how the island was ever changing and evolving. Mara closed her eyes, leaning her head against the tree as she tried to catch her breath.

It had been less than a day so far, and she was already almost killed by things that had looked like overgrown children's toys. She grimaced, thinking of how she would never tell her companions of this. Of how she let her guard down because that thing had been small and cute.

208

A PROPHECY OF UNDONE

There was a deep howl uncomfortably close to her position, and Mara stood with wobbly legs. The sun started to drop below the trees, threatening the night that was to come. Her eyes were heavy from exhaustion, staring ahead into the dark forest with trepidation.

It wouldn't be wise, setting up camp for the night in a place she knew nothing of, full of creatures that would surely love to take her for their dinner. Nor could she stomach the thought of trekking forth through the dark night into the same dangerous landscape. She grimaced, staring up at the massive, knobby tree she had just collapsed against. At least from higher off the ground, she'd be able to see if something was coming for her. Have a better chance at mounting an attack before it could.

She gave a mighty sigh, rubbing dirt into her hands to make them less damp. She grabbed on to a large knot in the tree, hoisting herself up and beginning to climb. Ignoring the cries of outrage from her battered body, she continued upwards until she was high above the ground. The bark of the tree was black, its leaves a strange shade of matte purple as they waved in the cold breeze. Mara shivered into her damp cloak, climbing out onto the branch a short way and sitting down. She leaned her back to the tree behind her, letting one leg drop off the side of the limb as she fought to stop her hands from trembling. Sleep wouldn't be easy, but it seemed inevitable at this point.

The underbrush beneath her shuddered, the sound of heavy pawprints resounding around her suddenly as she glanced down. Three creatures stepped out from the dark forest, crouched on all fours as they moved almost silently forward towards the shoreline. Their fur was impossibly green and looked like moss from where she sat high above them. Their beastly talons left deep gauges in the ground

209

I.A. TAKERIAN

where they walked, and Mara could hear low snorting noises coming from them.

They had no eyes, but their snouts ended in wide noses that took in every scent as they went. They had cat-like tails, swaying softly from side to side, and Mara could see long fangs jutting from their mouths as they began to lap from the ripping river.

Mara froze in place, barely breathing as she watched them.

The two smaller beasts drank, while the biggest began to sniff at the base of her tree. She watched it track her scent from the edge of the river and back to the trunk, extending its neck high as it followed her path upwards. Cold sweat covered the back of her neck as she stared down at it, clawing the base of her tree and leaving deep gashes in the bark. She prayed to the Zenoths that whatever this thing was, it could not climb.

After a few minutes of this, it seemed to grow bored, returning to the river to drink with its companions. Mara's heart thundered in her chest, watching them carefully until they disappeared out of view further up the riverbank.

High atop her branch, as safe as she could have been in that moment, exhaustion tore through her. It forced her eyes to droop, the feeling impossible to fight. She slipped slowly but irresistibly into a restless sleep, the sounds of howling, growling creatures still drifting softly through the woods around her as she dozed.

CHAPTER 22
THE SPRITE'S SONG

Mara awoke the following morning as the sun appeared over the cliffside. The air was unnaturally warm, drying her damp leathers as she sat on her branch. She stared wearily at the forest floor beneath her. The howls of the night before had gone, replaced by loud bird song in the treetops all around. She tapped the dagger at her hip, focusing hard on the bond. It pulsed a tiny bit harder than the day before. She sat upright, excited.

If she could find even *one* of them, she knew they would be unstoppable. Capable of whatever challenges the island had planned for them. The thought was enough to drive the aches of her body from her mind. She pulled the dagger from her thigh, gripping the blade between her teeth as she descended. She dropped softly to the vine covered ground, crouching on impact, and scanning her surroundings.

There was no movement, save for the softly flowing leaves on trees and hanging ivy before her. It looked markedly more inviting than it had the day before, almost

I.A. TAKERIAN

as if it were a new forest entirely. She took a steadying breath, rising slowly and starting forward through the wood.

The further she walked, the more mesmerizing the forest became. She lost sense of time, the sun like swashes of honey through the leaves. The dark trees sparkled with gold in the daytime, glittering dust cascading about her from the whispering leaves. The birds darting about were all different colors, their songs making strange harmonies as they flitted this way and that. She kept seeing rainbows, reflecting off small puddles through the trees and shining dimly across her skin.

Her head felt light, like the way Cyfrin's smoldering gaze made her feel. Breathless, happily drifting. She was dimly aware that she had fallen on a path, glowing stones leading her through the wood in a softly twisting trail. Music drifted towards her, the hypnotic notes swirling about through the gentle breeze. She closed her eyes, the smell of wildflowers clouding her senses.

The air was warmer here. A strange heat rose in her core like softly burning flame. Mara opened her eyes, face flushed. She had stepped into a beautiful glen, the sunlight above pooling on the stunningly green grass.

This is what she imagined the Beyonds to look like. She stood before a great lake sparkling like rays of starlight as a waterfall cascaded into it from a small cliffside. Its rounded rock face cut through the trees and out of sight. There were thousands of glittering orb lights, pulsing with every color as they swirled through the air around her.

There were people dancing on the grass by the lakeside, across the flower filled green field. No, not just dancing. *Flying.*

She watched in awe as the stunning figures flew about one another, each with a pair of dazzling wings flittering

212

A PROPHECY OF UNDONE

behind them. The music was so loud here that Mara felt her heartbeat fall into rhythm with it. One of the figures, spinning along through the open air, turned to face her.

He was perfect in every way, down to the very last detail. His skin was dark, golden brown, glistening in the glowing lights about him. His silver hair fell softly across his broad shoulders, his long arms covered in thick bands of muscle. His eyes were void of the whites, glowing with a dark pink pulse. He wore very little clothing, just two very long strips of fabric covering the front and back of his manhood. He smiled wide, descending from his place in the air to stand before her.

Mara stared up at him, eyelids drooping as he reached out his arms to her. She felt herself pulled forward, stumbling irresistibly into his grasp as he grinned. He gripped her waist, pulling her close and taking her by the hand. Her other hand floated up to his shoulder of its own accord, resting on it softly as he stared down at her with hungry intent.

She couldn't escape. She wasn't sure she wanted to. He began to swirl her around in a rapid dance, eyes a blur of color in her dream-like state. She was only vaguely aware of her feet leaving the ground, his wings humming as he pulled them into the air.

They were surrounded by perfect, dancing couples. They smiled and laughed as they passed, Mara limp in the man's arms as he spun her. The world whizzed around them, the music filling her to the brim as it kicked up faster, faster. She was being passed off to someone else, their body pressing hard against hers as she fell into their arms. Her eyes travelled slowly to his face.

Cyfrin's face.

His hand slid to her lower back, fingers pressing into her skin. His other hand moved to her face, caressing her

I.A. TAKERIAN

cheek as he pulled her in close. His hot breath drifted across her. "*Mara*," he purred in his husky voice, eyelids hooded as his gaze darted to her lips.

He was dizzyingly close, Mara's breath came in shallow pants as his mouth paused an inch from hers. "*Kiss me, Mara*," he breathed.

But she didn't move.

Something was crying out from within her; screaming to be heard. She pulled back slightly, frowning. *Something's wrong*, she thought distantly, feeling his body grow still against hers. The usual woodsy sweet smell that always saturated his skin was nowhere to be found. And it was something she had always been able to pick up on from a mile off. And he could speak. *How can he speak, when Drake gave us that damned potion?*

It felt like a thick cloud was dissipating from Mara's mind. She blinked hard, realizing she was several feet in the air. She tried to pull away, trapped in the man's uncompromising grasp.

"What's the matter?" he asked, but Cyfrin's voice was echoey and warped. The body pressed against hers shifted, leaning out before her very eyes. "Is this better, Mar?"

She drew her gaze from his body to his face, horror-struck. She was now pressed against Adrian, his voice low and sweet. He ran this thumb across her bottom lip, smirking. "Would you kiss me now?" he breathed, leaning back into her.

But Mara was lucid, fully aware of whatever strange magicks were at work. She felt rage boil over inside her, reaching down to grab the dagger off her hip. His eyes were closed, the mask of Adrian's face inches from her own and closing in. She brought the dagger swiftly upward, slashing through his cheek.

The illusion ended at once.

A PROPHECY OF UNDONE

The man's skin turned grey, his eyes now completely black. His features were elongated, his chin as pointed as his sharp cheekbones. His silver hair whipped around him in an angry fury as he cried out, green blood spilling from the cut on his face.

He released Mara, and she dropped the several feet to the grass below. The sky above was dark now, filled with threatening clouds as thunder rolled past. The man above her hissed, a sound echoed by the many still-spinning beings around him. He brought his hand high, the air around it twisting and writhing. Mara could sense the immense power radiating from it as he threw the ball of energy at her.

She had barely any time to move, raising her arms defensively before her. The dagger still clutched in her hand shook violently, heating up in her grasp. The rainbow gemstone glowed like a beacon, shining directly at the harsh energy that rocketed towards her. The magick collided with the blade, shoving Mara backwards several feet.

But she felt no damage to her body. Instead, the dagger shuddered in her hand before erupting in a solid beam of golden light. It shot directly at the man still airborne above, knocking into his chest and sending him tumbling through the air.

He let out a shriek of pain, the dancers whipping up into a frenzy of screams as they slammed to a halt. The man lunged at her from above. He grabbed her arms, twisting them roughly as he attempted to grab the dagger. His fingers grazed the metal, sizzling and burning as they made contact. He cried out, eyes furious. The people above began chanting, conjuring magick like the ball from earlier.

Mara moved instinctively, grabbing the grey creature

I.A. TAKERIAN

around the neck with her arm and brandishing the knife to his throat. He immediately tried to tear himself away, but she pressed the blade hard into his flesh. Blood beaded beneath it, smoke hissing from the wound. The creatures above them froze, their magick wavering. The rainbow gem pulsed threateningly, and the man in her arms fell still.

"Bornbane," it hissed through gritted fangs. "Dawnbringer. Destiny's End. Fate's Blade." He sniffed the air loudly. "You smell of mortal men and fright, spawn of Yvanar."

Mara pushed the blade more firmly against his throat, silencing him. *Let me out of here,* she thought as loudly as she could, glowering at the many winged creatures ready to strike. *Let me out of these woods, or I will tear your throat out where you stand.*

He hissed louder, confirming her suspicion that he could hear her mind. She pressed harder into his neck, feeling warmth as more blood poured across the blade and down the hilt. It sizzled like meat over flame as it touched the metal. *I will not ask a second time.*

The man in her arms said something in a language Mara was unfamiliar with. He raised an arm and snapped his fingers. Mara was yanked backwards, too hard to resist. An invisible hand grasped at her collar, pulling her back through the woods with tremendous speed as the creatures flew to the ground to surround the man she had held captive. The clearing vanished from view in an instant.

The forest was no longer mesmerizing or beautiful, replaced instead by darkly twisting vines and blackened bark trees. All the glittering, golden dust had disappeared, along with the sweet smell of flowers. She was tossed unceremoniously through the tree line, landing hard on her ass. She winced, making a rude gesture towards the forest as she slowly got to her feet.

She was standing at the base of a hilly landscape, feet from the dark wood. She could see the mouths of caves scattered about the rolling countryside as she looked around. It stretched, treeless and open, for as far as her eyes could see. A welcome change from the dark shadows of the last two days.

She threw a final, haunted look behind her at the forest. The sound of music had started up again, faint and ghostly as it whispered through the thicket. Mara shivered, setting out into the hills as she tried not to think of the things the man had pulled from her mind to use against her.

NIGHT WAS BEGINNING to fall on the island. The rolling hills, though void of the threatening mystery of trees, were twice as tiring to walk through. Uneven rock, tightly winding grassy paths through sheltered hills, slants, and slopes...all made it nearly exhausting to continue. The bond on her hand pulsed steadily still, though Mara couldn't tell if she had drawn any closer to her companions. The thrum was constant, and she had lost track of any changes in its pull.

Every cave she passed looked to be already inhabited by some form of beast, thunder rolling in from overhead as she searched for a safe place to make camp. The moon had already risen over the hilltops when she heard movement coming from the darkness ahead.

She froze, pressing herself into the hillside to try and hide in its shadow. The movement had ceased as well. Whatever it was seemed to copy her actions. She stood

I.A. TAKERIAN

frozen against the grassy hill for an immeasurable amount of time. The longer she stood, the more convinced she became that she had imagined it entirely. The silence pressed in on her, eyes straining ahead to catch any motion. When none came, she stepped forward cautiously into the moonlight.

White hot energy shot into her chest, rippling through her body, and freezing her where she stood. Her eyes went wide. Three figures emerged from the darkness beyond, grinning maliciously at her.

The three other Hopefuls.

They laughed at her, the tall blonde man's eyes glowing white. "Aw, just like a deer in a trap," he sneered over their vicious laughter.

Mara tried to move, but only her fingers twitched as she watched them approach. One of the other men, a red head with freckles covering every inch of his skin, placed a finger against her arm. Instantly, smoke began to billow from the spot. Mara screamed inside her head as pain ripped through her. Pure fire seemed to radiate from the spot he touched, lacing under her skin, and setting her heart ablaze. It was torture. He removed his finger, a perfect circle brand left where it had been. Burned tendrils stretched from the mark, like angry purple veins. The red head looked gleeful as he admired it.

The third man, a tall ranger with a black ponytail resting on the bow across his back, smirked at her. But she could see discomfort flicker across his face as he stared at the burn.

The blonde man's eyes flashed, glowing brightly as he brought his hands before Mara. She could feel cold energy flowing from them. "I've been trying for weeks now to figure out how you did it," he snarled at her, dragging his ice-cold fingers across her cheek. "How did you, weak,

A PROPHECY OF UNDONE

pathetic, practically mortal *you*, defeat Filigro. And then it dawned on me."

He leaned in close to her ear, sending a shiver down her spine as she fought desperately against whatever magick held her. "You must have known he was planning to usurp you," he whispered to her. "Must have brought something powerful with you into the woods. Gotten your bastard friends to help. You must have *cheated*."

He drew back, slashing through the air before her. She winced, tears of pain beading in her eyes as his magick drove into her flesh. She could feel three distinct, deep scratches across her chest, ice cold from his power. The blood that rushed to spill froze instantly, creating sharp shards of icicles in her flesh. He smirked. "We were so hoping to find you out here, you know," he continued, circling around her while his friends cackled. "I think it's time we return the favor, for what you did to Fil."

Mara watched his eyes flash, sending a thrill of panic through her as he raised his hand high once more. She thrashed desperately against the magick binding her as his hand dropped down, aiming for her throat.

The spell broke as his magick whipped towards her. Mara threw herself to her knees, the attack flying over her head as she grabbed for her dagger. The three of them yelled as she shot upwards, blade held before her. She slashed at the blonde man as he jerked back, catching him across the middle of the face. He cried out, hand flying to the cut as it split open and bled. His friends had stopped laughing; looking to him for direction.

He roared, grabbing the sword from his back as his eyes flared white. Thick ice cracked up the blade, covering and elongating it into a sharp point. The ranger raised his hands, backing away slowly. "I thought we were just going to beat her up and take her gear," he said, slight panic in

I.A. TAKERIAN

his voice. "Do you know what Caerani, and Drake would do to us if they found out we tried to actually kill her? What *Cyfrin* would do to us?!"

"You're pathetic!" The blonde yelled at him, the ranger flinching back. "She's no better than the Delinvalians. She was *raised* by them. She could be a spy! She *killed our friend*."

And at this, he dove for her. She had no time to grab her axe, forced to meet his sword with her dagger as she stepped back. They clanged against each other, but she was much too close. She saw his eyes flash, a shard of ice shooting from his blade and into her shoulder. It drove through her flesh like butter, and she fell back, feeling the blood beginning to run from the wound.

She cursed to herself. The two men with him had drawn back against the hillside, watching with shadowed eyes as they fought. Mara looked desperately around for an escape. No axe, no magick, none of her companions. She was dead in the water, surrounded by sloping hills and moonlight.

His sword came flying for her again, Mara dove out of the way this time to avoid it. *Come on,* she thought angrily, leaping backwards from another deadly strike. *We need our magick! Come on, dammit!*

But no heat came to her palms, no power rose in her core. She spun about, meeting his sword with her dagger as he slashed at her back. Shards of ice flew from the blade, embedding themselves in her body as she launched backwards away from him. They drove deep into her body, freezing her blood where they met.

She couldn't keep this up long. Blood flowed heavier from the wounds through her armor as the ice shards melted, revealing deep gashes in her flesh. The blonde man's eyes glinted wickedly as he admired his work, like he knew her time was running out.

A PROPHECY OF UNDONE

Her arms were like lead, bleeding freely as she screwed up her face in concentration; willing the magick to flow forth. She was pinned with her back against one of the steep hills, staring over the blonde's shoulder at his two friends watching them.

He was closing the distance slowly, savoring this moment. She gripped the dagger in her hand tighter, panting as she stared him down. He flashed a manic smile, raising his sword high above his head. Mara held his gaze unfaltering, ready to meet his blow with her dagger regardless of the consequences.

There was a great *crack*.

The man's eyes grew wide, the sword dropping from his hands to the ground. Blue lightning shot from his fingertips, his eyes rolling back into his skull as he convulsed on the spot. The magick crackled through him before his body gave a final shudder and crashed to the dirt. Behind him, eyes flashing with electric blue power and face contorted into a mask of terrifying anger, was Cyfrin.

He was covered in mud, leaves and a great deal of blood. She couldn't tell if it was his or someone else's. He didn't even look at the man now laying at their feet, his eyes burning into Mara's bleeding face. Darkness clouded his expression as he dropped his eyes downward.

Mara saw Kain behind him, his great sword out as he held the other two men in place. They looked petrified. Cyfrin stooped low, lifting the blonde man into the air as he groaned, stirring. He shook him hard, forcing the man to wake up as he held him off the ground.

He woke up slowly, eyes clouded. But as soon as he looked down into Cyfrin's murderous face, as soon as he realized the situation he had put himself in, he began to thrash.

Cyfrin pulled his gaze slowly from the blonde's face,

221

I.A. TAKERIAN

looking at Mara. His eyes were completely taken over by the blue lightning, flashing like a storm on the sea. Mara was reminded of a creature looking to its master, waiting for the command to strike.

To kill.

CHAPTER 23
VENGEANCE/MERCY

Cyfrin's gaze was unfaltering, his body barely moving as the blonde man thrashed desperately against his grip. His eyes were almost inhuman in their wrathful focus, waiting for her command.

Mara stared at the blonde man, his eyes wild with fear and panic. He had tried to kill her. Probably would have succeeded, had Cyfrin not found her when he did. But she kept hearing his words in her head.

"She killed our friend."

And he wasn't wrong. Regardless of Filigro's actions, she had dissolved his body to ash in an instant. There was nothing left to bring home, no scrap of him remaining for his family to mourn. He had a *family*. People who loved him. She thought of what she might do if someone killed one of her loved ones, how mad with pain she would go. Her eyes filled with sadness as she returned to Cyfrin's cold fury.

She shook her head once at him, denying him the kill he so obviously wanted. His eyes flashed, gripping the blonde man tighter for a moment. Then he spun on the

I.A. TAKERIAN

spot, launching him through the air at break-neck speed to collide hard with his friends.

His body slammed into theirs with a crack, knocking all three of them winded to the ground. Mara didn't even offer them a second glance. She leapt forward, momentarily forgetting the bleeding cuts all over her body. As Cyfrin turned back to face her, she launched. Her arms wrapped tightly around him, burying her face against his dirty leather armor. He froze as she took a deep breath.

The smell of dirt and dried blood drifted through her, but it was mostly overshadowed by the overwhelming smell of pine and honey. A smell she hadn't realized she missed so desperately. She pressed herself harder against him. His body relaxed slightly.

She felt his hands grasp her shoulders gently, pushing her away far enough to examine her. His angry, electrically pulsating eyes had dimmed to a faint glow, and Mara could read worry and panic underneath the growing fury. His gaze swept over the cuts across her face, the ice chunks in her arms still embedded as they slowly melted. He gripped the arm that held the finger shaped burn mark, pulling it up to the level of his eyes to more closely examine it. His eyes traced the vein-like burns lacing out from it.

There was dark, ominous power emanating from Cyfrin. She could feel electricity licking the air around her. Thin bolts of lightning cracked from his arms, breaking into the earth below them and leaving small burns in the grass. He pulled his thumb slowly across the bottom of a cut on her cheek, wiping away the trail of blood oozing towards her lips.

He moved from Mara in the blink of an eye, leaving only the electricity still surrounding her to caress her aching skin. He appeared beside the three now cowering before Kain's mighty frame. They all three screamed in

A PROPHECY OF UNDONE

fright, Cyfrin reaching down to where they sat huddled together and yanking the red head straight into the air by his collar. He choked, gagging, and flailing as Cyfrin marched him with wild eyes to the place where Mara stood.

He smashed his feet to the ground, keeping a grip on his collar as he whimpered, wide eyes staring panicked at her. Cyfrin waved his hand. A vine came rushing up the redhead's body from the ground, twisting like a snake around his arm and forcing his index finger into a pointing position.

Mara rarely saw Cyfrin use his earth magicks, thinking back to their first encounter when he had bound her with vines like this. He grabbed Mara's arm tenderly in his free hand, his grip on the man's collar still firm. Cyfrin pulled her towards the redhead, towards his outstretched finger. He matched the purple burn on her arm up perfectly with his fingertip.

The air around them crackled with lightning, the bolts dancing with tingling energy as they bounced off Mara's skin. But the redhead was screaming as they touched him, shaking as if electrocuted. Cyfrin raised him high, brandishing him pointedly at Kain. Kain's eyes flashed wickedly, and he swung his sword high. There was a glint of dark metal, blurring through the air as it slashed downwards. It sliced with a wet crack through the redheads still-outstretched finger.

He shrieked, blood gushing forth from the wound. Cyfrin hovered his hand above it, eyes glowing bright. White hot lightning shot from his palms, like a storm cloud born in his hand. The bolts combined into one as they pulsed in to the newly made nub on the redhead's finger. There was a sizzling like cooking meat, smoke billowing up from the wound. When the lightning stopped and Cyfrin

225

I.A. TAKERIAN

threw him to the ground, Mara could see that the wound had been cooked closed. He scrambled backwards, face gauntly pale as he huddled against his friends. Cyfrin returned to the place where they cowered, Kain stooping with gleeful eyes to retrieve the severed finger. Mara watched him drop it into his pouch, winking at her.

Cyfrin grabbed the blonde man again, pushing him roughly against the hillside to his back. Vines appeared from the grassy wall behind him, twisting around his arms and legs and pinning him down.

He trembled, sweat dripping down his horror-filled face. "P-Please," he begged as Cyfrin cocked his head, a mindless beast ready to strike. "Please, don't kill me! Please!"

Cyfrin raised both his hands, blue magick surrounding them both as the blonde cried out, struggling to break free of the vines. He hovered his crackling hands over his, pulled open by the vines that bound him. Lightning shot from Cyfrin's palms, travelling into the blonde's hands as he shrieked. His two friends shook with fear, looking away as he writhed. Cyfrin's magick ceased after several long moments, the vines releasing the man as he slumped to the ground. Mara could see his hands smoking as he brought them trembling to his face.

"What...What have you done to me?!" he sputtered, staring down at them with more frantic panic than Mara had seen this entire time. "Why can't I use my magick?! *What have you done?!*"

Tears fell from his eyes and onto his smoking hands. His friends rushed forward, grabbing him under the arms and hoisting him to his feet. He shook from head to toe, throwing a look of murderous, vengeful fury at Cyfrin and Mara as the three of them ran as one into the darkness beyond.

226

A PROPHECY OF UNDONE

Kain clapped, his eyes alight. He too was covered in all manners of muck and blood, as he beamed at Mara. There were newly stripped pieces of strange furs attached to his belt, the pouch he had thrown the finger into full to bursting.

Cyfrin turned and walked to her, stopping when they were toe-to-toe. His eyes were no longer balls of lightning, glowing gently as he stared down at her with pride. His face softened into a look of relief, and he pulled her swiftly against his chest.

He hugged her tightly, a deep breath easing from him as he buried his face in her curls. She wrapped her arms around him once more, closing her eyes and reveling in the happiness and calm now vibrating down the bond to her from both of them.

He pulled away, eyes darting over her face once more. She saw the white-hot rage threatening to surface again, threatening to carry him back to hunt the three Hopefuls to their deaths. His eyes flashed blue, waving a hand over the particularly deep cuts in her armor.

Lightning drifted with unnatural slowness into the gashes. It licked carefully at the skin around the wounds, numbing them with soft electrical pulses before zapping into the flesh. She flinched as cold, fire-like burning happened in each one for a second, before vanishing entirely. She looked down; every wound now closed with odd zig-zagging scars. Like lightning bolts.

Her eyes flew to his, beaming. He returned her smile with equal intensity, and she felt her heart skip to an irregular beat at its splendor.

Kain's arms were suddenly around them both, squeezing them together as he hugged them tightly. Mara sputtered as Kain shook with silent laughter. He released them, miming to where the three had sat cowering before

I.A. TAKERIAN

shadow boxing the air. He motioned to her dagger, then gave Mara two thumbs up, as if indicating she had done a good job for the situation. She blushed, shaking her head, and pointing between the two of them to show that they had saved her. She looked at Cyfrin, pointing to the blood on his armor, and then to his face.

"Is this yours?" she said through her expression, raising an eyebrow.

He smiled wryly at her, shaking his head slowly. He opened a pouch at his hip, pulling something from its depths and handing it to Mara.

It was a thick, barbed fang, longer than her hand. She could still see bits of dried flesh from where it had been forcibly removed from a mouth, and the ivory bone was covered in twisting cracks. Cracks like lightning.

She looked up at him, eyes wide. He and Kain were beaming jubilantly at her. Kain was pointing enthusiastically at the tally marks along his great sword. There was a new one at the end of Cyfrin's score. Kain clapped him on the back, looking proud. Mara gave the fang back to Cyfrin, who returned it to his pouch.

She couldn't wait for them to return to Drake's ship. To hear their stories, and to tell them her own. Possibly edited to remove the small fuzz creature that had almost gotten her killed, or the beings that had morphed to Cyfrin and Adrian's faces.

It was strange, not being able to speak to them. She missed their banter, missed the husky purr of Cyfrin's snide comments. The way he would say her name. *"My darling Dawnbringer."* His voice whispered through her mind like a distant memory as they settled in to camp for the night. They had found a small cave, dry and abandoned by whatever had left all the bones strewn across the rock floor. Kain had made a small fire, and the three of

A PROPHECY OF UNDONE

them ate as they listened to the sounds of the night outside.

Mara was once again exhausted, missing her bed in the Grand Halls desperately as she eyeballed the hard ground. Kain flopped back on to it unceremoniously after food, waving a hand idly at them before drifting off almost immediately. His snores echoed around the cave in minutes, eliminating the noises outside. She frowned at him, wishing she could drift off as easily. There was movement against the cave wall across from her.

Cyfrin sat up against the rock, legs in front of him and cloak wadded up like a make-shift pillow atop them. His eyes glinted in the dying flames from their pit, patting his lap as he smirked.

Mara's mind flashed back to falling asleep on him after the third task. Her face went hot, the feeling shooting down the bond. She saw his smile widen, his head tilting at her as hunger flashed through his eyes. She shook her head hurriedly, trying to ignore the butterflies flitting across her stomach.

He frowned, leaning himself back to nearly lay on the stone floor. He brought the cloak up about himself like a blanket, his eyes holding hers as he extended an arm out to his side. He motioned at her; face set in a mask of smoldering command as he pointed from her to the spot on the ground beside him.

She bit her lip. The fire was nearly extinguished, and the dark cold of the night was settling around them. She would be freezing till morning if she didn't share his warmth.

Or at least this is what she told herself to further deny the excited fluttering of her heart.

She crawled forward to him, laying down slowly at his side. His body emitted a great deal of heat, trapped under-

229

I.A. TAKERIAN

neath his cloak as he lifted it for her to curl underneath. She pressed into his side, laying her head in the crook of his arm and his chest. She could hear his heart slamming quickly against his ribcage, feeling the irregular pattern of his breath as she settled in. It would have driven her wild, had she not been so unbearably tired.

He brought his arm down and around her, pulling her closer to his body as it wrapped around her shoulder. His thumb rubbed against the exposed skin at her bicep in gentle, smooth strokes. His breathing evened out, setting the pace for Mara's own as they held one another.

Her hand drifted up to rest against his chest, and he grabbed it, holding it to him with a firm security that made Mara's exhaustion double. Her leg hiked up, coming to rest on top of him. She felt his body grow very still at this.

Her eyes closed, the burning heat in her core at his touch dimming into gently smoldering embers within her. She could feel his breath against her face, his thumb continuing to stroke her arm slowly as she fell into a deep, dreamless slumber.

CHAPTER 24
KING OF THE FAIRIES

The morning sun leaked in through the mouth of the cave, stirring Mara from her slumber. She frowned, stretching from under Cyfrin's warm cloak and feeling the cool air lick across her flesh. Her eyes opened slowly, squinting against the light. She could see Cyfrin sitting up next to her, his body still as the stone around them. He was staring with a mixture of fury and panic at the wall across from them, eyes glinting with blue bolts.

She sat upright, pivoting to face whatever held his attention. Kain was sitting on her other side, his stare full of the same dark fury as Cyfrin's. Across from the three of them was a tall man, sitting cross-legged on the ground. He had to have been an Odelian, his face was so flawlessly handsome. Two long, swooping ears came out of his thick purple braids; many sparkling charms hanging from his hair. His features were all gently slanting, with eyes the shade of Brisenbane's depths. He wore a shining silver shirt, the sleeves billowing out around his long arms. It was

231

I.A. TAKERIAN

opened down to his stomach, revealing perfectly carved muscles beneath.

Many golden chains, all with various pendants, dripped from his neck. One hung much lower than the rest, dropping down to his mid torso and ending in a strangely swirling crystal. He had several dazzling rings on each finger, each more ornate than the next. But it was none of these things that struck Mara breathless.

He was exuding an incredible amount of raw magick, like the kind that rolled off The One Who Sees. It filled the entire cave, nearly suffocating Mara under the feeling.

He was tilting his head at her, smirking. "Ah, excellent!" he said in a voice that seemed to come directly from Mara's head. "We've been waiting for you to wake. You're well rested now, I trust?"

Mara glanced between Cyfrin and Kain. Neither of them had moved an inch since she had awoken, sitting with unnatural stillness as they glared at the man. Mara got the distinct impression that they had been enchanted to stop them moving.

The man laughed lightly. "I'm so sorry, how foolish of me! I had already gleaned from your friends here that you've fallen mute." He looked at Cyfrin, eyes narrowing. "I will release you from your binds, but I do suggest you keep a level head while I say my piece."

Cyfrin glowered at him, but his eyes flickered to Mara, and he nodded curtly.

The man smiled, snapping his fingers. Both of their bodies relaxed, tensing back to strike in an instant. Mara glared at the man, eyes cold.

He smirked. "I've been watching you all for several days," he said, brushing dirt from his black boots. "All of you. I saw the one who dances on wind floating over treetops. The girl with acid breath out in the blighted

232

A PROPHECY OF UNDONE

swamps." He pointed towards Kain. "I saw you kill an entire swarm of vampyres with absolutely no magick. Very impressive."

His eyes flicked to Cyfrin, snarling at him like a caged beast. "I watched *you* drive your entire body through a basilisk, like lightning through a storm cloud. I even heard the air crack around you like thunder, you were going so fast." He laughed at the look on Cyfrin's face, the thought that someone was watching him without his knowledge nearly driving him into a rage. His eyes came to rest finally on Mara, flashing with curiosity.

"And you," he said, head tilting once more as his eyes burned into hers. "You managed to escape the sprites in that damned illusionary forest they've got over there. No easy feat. Especially when they wanted your soul so very badly." He took a deep breath, Mara grimacing as she felt strange magick twist around her, probing. "I can see why," he breathed, his eyes alight.

Mara felt Cyfrin tense suddenly beside her, deathly energy pouring from him as he glowered. But the man held Mara's angry stare, eyes bright with delight.

"You smell like the *divine,*" he said, twirling the long crystal necklace absently as he stared with wide eyes. "Like you've been touched by the heavens themselves. Or whatever it is that's your equivalent in this cursed place." He pointed at Cyfrin, eyes narrowed. "*You* have a strange tinge to you as well, boy. But I imagine that's just the incredibly potent magick you seem to possess. What do they call you three?"

They continued to glare with increasing fury at him, all too cautious to attack when such intense power pulsated about. He blinked, then burst out with laughter. "Ah! That's right! Blasted, it's so easily dumped from my mind!"

He rubbed his hands together, bright sparks cascading

I.A. TAKERIAN

out from them. Cyfrin drew slightly in front of Mara, Kain's hand twitching towards his great sword.

"I can't do anything about that potion that's blocking your speech. It is *very* beautifully crafted; I should love to meet the master who brewed it." His hands were sparking like tiny fireworks, zapping the air around them as his energy began to grow. "But I do know a nifty little enchantment that we might use to better communicate. It's a party trick, really, but efficient for a time." His eyes flashed, reflecting the bursts of energy as they erupted throughout the cave. Sparks flew into Mara's skin, the same happening to Cyfrin and Kain beside her. She winced as she felt the white hot magick rush through her. The man beamed at them, arms wide.

"That should do it!" he said happily. "Now tell me. What are your names?"

"Rip your throat out. Throw it in the stew pot for tonight's dinner."

Mara gasped, a familiar voice echoing in her head suddenly. Her eyes flew to Kain's face, still glaring at the man before him.

"Set you ablaze. Watch the pieces burn. Bury them so you can never come back."

A thrill ran down her spine as the growling, raspy voice of Cyfrin filled her mind, whipping about to stare at him.

The man tsked disapprovingly. "Now, really," he said, offended. "Such senseless violence."

"Beyonds bless me, his voice. We're about to be burned or eaten or Zenoths knows what, and all I can think of is how much I miss his voice." The thought resounded in Mara as she stared at Cyfrin, barely hearing the man's words.

Cyfrin's concentration shattered, his eyes shooting to hers with a strange expression. His face flushed slightly, the corner of his mouth twitching as if to smile. She saw the

234

A PROPHECY OF UNDONE

smoldering fire that filled her with such desperate yearning begin to glow behind his eyes.

The man laughed as Mara began to piece their situation together. "That's more like it!" he said excitedly, clapping his hands and sitting up straighter. "I like you. Not afraid to really *feel* things. Not blinded by stupid, arrogant anger." His eyes flashed to Cyfrin, but he kept his unfaltering stare on Mara.

"Her voice. Music. Like beautiful music, gracing my ears. Blessing me beyond what I deserve." His eyes widened, dropping them from Mara's face as his voice sounded in her head. There was a buzzing sound now, and Mara heard Kain's laughter in her head.

"Tension," the man said in a sing-song voice, winking at Cyfrin. "I am, once again, very impressed by you. Not many are able to control my spell work, especially this enchantment. And yet, here you are! Causing interference so the rest of us can't hear your fleeting, fascinating little thoughts." He frowned at him, looking disappointed.

"Is that what's happening?" Mara thought. *"We're reading each other's minds?"*

She felt panic rise in her throat. There were many, many things that passed through her head when Cyfrin was present that she would be mortified for him to hear.

"More or less," the man said. "Really, it broadcasts your most immediate thoughts in a textile that is understandable to every and all. Regardless of language or species barriers." His eyes become misty, a faraway look in them. "I can't tell you the number of times this spell has helped me to, erm...*further* relations in my favor." He dropped his gaze back to Mara. "Please. I'll have your names."

"You'll have my sword at your throat," Kain's voice growled through her.

235

I.A. TAKERIAN

The man's eyes flashed to Kain's face, his smile not faltering. "There's another spell I know," he said, his voice dripping with cruel intent. "One where I forcibly invade each of your minds and draw the names from your writhing bodies. Very painful and, in my opinion, rather drastic. Wouldn't you say?"

The growling continued from both Kain and Cyfrin, but Mara's brow furrowed.

"*Mara,*" she thought, Cyfrin and Kain both staring at her incredulously.

The man perked up, getting to his feet. The boys on either side of Mara did the same, at practically the same time, and Mara stood with them.

The man bowed low to her, grinning. "Mara. What an absolutely strange name," he said, winking at her as she sneered.

"*Cyfrin.*" The growling beside her dimmed as his name floated through her. She closed her eyes, repeating it back a hundred times as it echoed through her head.

Cyfrin glanced at her, flushing, and she could tell they had all heard it. She felt heat rise high in her cheeks as the man bowed with less bravado to Cyfrin.

"*And I am the man who shall kill you, bejeweled fool. My name is Kain. Remember it.*" Kain's voice was intermingled with his growling, but the man bowed to him slightly regardless.

"Brave warriors!" he proclaimed, smiling at them all. "My name is Dewin. I am King of the Fairies, and I beseech you to aid me!"

There was silence, the buzzing from Cyfrin's mind the only sound around them. "*There hasn't been a fae in Zenafrost for centuries,*" Cyfrin thought, frowning at Dewin. "*They all fled through the tear in reality after the Zenoths left us.*"

The man grinned at him, looking pleased. "Excellent! Then you know the first half of my story," he said happily.

236

A PROPHECY OF UNDONE

"We *did* flee Zenafrost all those years ago, crossing the portal to the land we now call home."

"*Oh good. I was so hoping to be pulled into a fucking fairy history lesson this morning,*" Kain thought angrily, granting him a glare from Dewin.

"My great-great-grandfather was the ruler of all the fae that had come with us, the crown passing down from one descendant to the next," he continued, ignoring the growling resounding once more from both Kain and Cyfrin. "My father, Gods rest his soul, passed on from ripe old age. Which passed the crown on to me." He gave a hearty sigh, looking dejected as he went on. "But sadly, the way I ruled didn't sit well with some of my court. I'll admit, there was a lot of drinking. Quite a few parties that ended in several deaths. The brief orgy, or ten, in the throne room."

He shrugged, eyes sad. "I see now that I wasn't entirely focused on the things that were my responsibility. Not exactly the best trait for the man who would be king. My cousin, Balinfort, was second in line to the crown behind me. And possibly the most outspoken about how terrible a king I was. As I said, he wasn't entirely wrong. But he never once tried to guide me, tried to actually speak with me about it. So, one night he and his damned sorcerer cult came for me in my chambers."

He scoffed, offended at the thought. "I mean, I was drunk. Drugged. Exhausted from the day. And they took advantage of that. Hog tied me, hexed me, dragged me out to the rip on our side of reality and tossed me on in." His smile fell from his face, pulling the long crystal necklace up before him. "But that wasn't enough for them. It wasn't enough to usurp my throne, abandon me in this...*hellscape.* They had to make sure I couldn't come

237

I.A. TAKERIAN

back to reclaim my title as king. So, they whipped up this lovely thing."

He shook the crystal necklace before him, swirling the smoke within it like iridescent liquid. "I know I could figure out a way home through that portal, but this necklace has been cursed. Bound to me with blood magick that I cannot break. I cannot remove it myself, and the enchantment placed upon it is infuriatingly clever."

He drew his eyes to Mara, hanging from every word. "Should someone attempt to remove the necklace from my body and rid me of its curse, the spell work forces me to stop them. As if my life depended on it. It's caused a disturbing number of deaths over the years. All consensual, I assure you!" he added as lightning sparked around Cyfrin's hands. "I've encountered many Hopeful warriors like you over the years. Each more determined than the last to earn glory through combat. To find and defeat the biggest challenge they could. That's why you're all here isn't it? To grow beyond your best?"

He pointed towards Mara, holding Cyfrin's glowing stare. "In all my years trapped upon this island, I have never *once* felt something as powerful as her. You feel it as well; I know you do."

Mara felt a chill run over her body as the growl redoubled in Cyfrin. Kain shifted nervously on her other side. *"Destiny,"* his voice whispered through her head as he struggled to hold it in. *"Prophecy. Dawnbringer."*

Dewin's eyes lit up, smiling broadly at Mara while Cyfrin turned his angry stare on Kain. *"Destiny,"* Dewin repeated. "Yes. Yes, that's what it feels like. You *have* been touched by the divines. How wonderful."

He knelt before her, taking her hand in his and bowing his head. A snarl ripped through Mara, reverberating from Cyfrin. He looked murderous as Dewin held her hand.

A PROPHECY OF UNDONE

"Mara. I beg you. Will you aid me in removing my burden?" His voice was soft, but firm; filled with an intense yearning. Yearning to be free. Mara recognized the sound, having heard it from herself for twenty years without knowing what it meant. "If you succeed, I will, in turn, reward you with a favor. Anything you ask of me, just once. Whatever you could ever need, within my ability to give it. It is yours."

Mara heard Kain scoff, watching his eyes roll as he folded his arms. Cyfrin looked even more deadly at his words, the same look as he had when he nearly killed the blonde hopeful. Mara stared down at Dewin, eyes wide.

His magick was obviously stronger than nearly anything she had encountered in Zenafrost, let alone the three of them standing around him. And if the prophecy was true, if they would soon be at war with Mezilmoth and his dark forces...

"*Fine,*" Mara thought, the growling from Cyfrin ceasing instantly as he blinked at her.

Dewin's eyes flew to her face, gleeful. "You'll do it?!"

Mara yanked her hand from his, frowning. "*You'll hold true to your word?*" Mara thought, raising an eyebrow. "*Any one favor I ask of you, regardless of what it may be?*"

"*Mara...*" Cyfrin's voice purred in her mind, a soft warning in his tone.

But Mara ignored him as Dewin got to his feet, smiling. "Yes! Yes, of course! If you can free me, destined one, I will owe you my life." His eyes flashed. "And my life means all to me."

Mara continued to stare at him, hesitant. But she let out a sigh. "*You have a deal, Dewin,*" she thought, feeling a rush of energy flood through Cyfrin's tattoo, scalding her.

Dewin stepped back, clapping excitedly. "Well then! No better time like the present!" He motioned towards the

239

I.A. TAKERIAN

mouth of the cave, out at the sunny hilled valley beyond. "Shall we?" He set off outside at a bouncing pace, leaving the three to stand in discomfort.

"Making deals with fairies is never wise," Kain thought, shaking his head. *"Nor is inserting ourselves into their troubles. They are powerful, unpredictable beings."*

"He is a man trapped by people who could have simply taught him self-control," she thought heatedly back, reminded irresistibly of Cyfrin's father binding his powers in lieu of teaching him. *"And do you feel his magick? Imagine that owing us a favor in the war to come."*

"There's nothing for it now," Cyfrin added, looking grim. *"Our Dawnbringer has made a deal, and it must be honored. Come."*

The three of them trudged together out of the cave into the grassy field and glowing sunlight, Dewin waiting for them with a wide smile.

CHAPTER 25

GARNERING FAVORS

O ut in the valley, Mara got a full sense of just how powerful Dewin was. It was like he had it dampened in the cave, massive wings of energy furled in to keep from suffocating them. But here, in the broadness of the hilly landscape, he gave off a staggering amount of magick. The sun cascaded down upon them all, bathing them in golden light, and there was an aura of shimmering energy that surrounded Dewin's entire body. She eyed the crystal at his throat. The ominous power that oozed out of it made her skin crawl. She wondered if all curses felt this way: Unclean and strangling.

Dewin beamed at them, raising his hands. "Whenever you're ready," he said, as if this was just a typical sparring session.

Cyfrin whipped around to Kain, eyes wide as he barked an order. "*Wait,*" he yelled down their connections, but too late.

Kain had not even hesitated, charging at Dewin with his full force. He moved with startling speed as he rocketed forward, eyes flashes of fury and victory as he threw his

241

I.A. TAKERIAN

sword high. Mara moved to join him, but Cyfrin grabbed her arm. She turned to face him, incredulous, but he stared with a grim expression at Dewin. Mara followed his gaze to watch as Kain drew level with him.

Dewin's face was bright with humor, unmoving as Kain charged forward. The great sword glinted furiously in the morning sun before colliding hard with Dewin's shoulder. Mara winced automatically with the force of the impact. Kain stood for a moment, suspended with eyes full of prideful glory as his sword drifted through Dewin's body.

But something was wrong. The sword moved *too* swiftly, as if cutting through a cloud. Mara saw Kain's smile falter, and Dewin's body erupted suddenly into a thousand purple butterflies. They flew around Kain, spinning into the air as Mara watched in awe. There was a trill of laughter behind them, and they spun about.

Dewin leaned against the steep base of a hill a few yards back, arms folded in relaxation as he watched them. "It will take much more than brute strength to best me," he said in a sing-song voice. "Though, I quite enjoyed you charging for me with no care. It was rather attractive…like a bear in heat."

Kain's voice roared through Mara's head, his face contorted in rage as he shot past Cyfrin towards the spot where Dewin stood. His great sword collided with the grassy hill, Dewin vanishing once more.

"*Stop, you mad bastard!*" Cyfrin barked through their heads, and Kain whipped around to face him with furious eyes. "*We need to advance together, or he'll just keep running us around!*"

"Ah! Tall, dark, and wildly attractive here is right!" Dewin was behind them again, back atop the hillside he and Kain had stood upon a moment before. He grinned flirtatiously down at Cyfrin. "I wasn't kidding when I said

A PROPHECY OF UNDONE

the curse forces me to try and stop you. Regardless of my best efforts to not. Speaking of, I wouldn't stop to have a chat if I were you. Once the crystal is threatened, it will not stop till you are all dead."

He said it so calmly, so casually, but his hands waved about him in a graceful ark. The air around him rippled, and he threw his arms forward. The ground beneath him cracked, sending deep scars through the earth in every direction. The air, shining like the iridescent bubbles Mara had seen in the wetlands, shot out before him like massive whips. There was a *crack*, and Cyfrin was throwing Mara aside.

He raised his forearm to his face, his voice crying out in her head as the lash of magick connected with flesh. Mara saw blood splatter the ground from the gash it tore effortlessly in his armor. She turned to glare with furious eyes at Dewin.

He shrugged, looking apologetic. His moment of brief distraction as he looked at Mara granted Cyfrin an opening. He shot up the hill like the wind, faster than Mara's eye was able to catch. He flew forward into Dewin, whose eyes widened with mild surprise. Bright blue lighting cracked through Cyfrin's arms as he sent bolts straight into Dewin's chest. Mara saw him freeze, saw his body convulse slightly. His eyes rolled back and Cyfrin made to grab for the necklace.

Dewin's hand shot up, grabbing Cyfrin's wrist. Furious lighting lashed at his grip as Cyfrin struggled to get away. But it was as if Dewin was made of pure stone, the hold on his arm unwavering. He brought his eyes back to stare at Cyfrin, smiling wide. "Now, *that* is the kind of power you'll need to win this!" he said excitedly.

There was an odd energy in the air, emanating from Dewin as he held Cyfrin in place. Lightning, the same

243

I.A. TAKERIAN

lightning that filled Cyfrin, began to spark in Dewin's eyes. Mara gaped as it laced down his arms, blasting in to Cyfrin with twice the power he had used to throw it. He flew backwards through the air, colliding hard with the hillside opposite as Kain and Mara rushed to his aid. He stood slowly from the ground, wincing as they approached. A trickle of blood oozed down his face, but none of the fury had left his eyes.

Dewin whipped his arms about once more. Cyfrin grabbed Mara's wrist. *"We need your magick,"* he thought, glowering at Dewin. Panic flashed through his eyes for the first time as he said it, his gaze darting to Mara's face. *"I don't want to put you in danger. But you're stronger than we are, we all know it. It's our only option."*

Dewin threw his hands onto the ground, still looking apologetic. The earth beneath them began to ebb and flow, as if made of water. They struggled to maintain their balance, Mara nearly toppling backwards as Dewin began to march smoothly down the hill at them. Cyfrin grabbed her arm, steadying her and offering a nod of stern determination. Kain raised his great sword towards the beaming Dewin, his other hand wrapping around Mara's opposite arm as he readied himself to attack.

Mara took a steadying breath, closing her eyes and allowing herself to ride the ground beneath her as if it *was* water. The heat in her core ignited instantly, rushing through her body in great swathes of furious power. It beat at the sides of her soul, roaring to be released. She frowned, grimacing as she focused her full might on channeling the magick into her arms. She shook as the heat flowed down into her hands, burning in her grip. Her eyes flew open, falling on Dewin who stood frozen a few feet away. His head was tilted, looking at her with fascination as she threw her hands forward.

244

A PROPHECY OF UNDONE

Beams of sunlight shot from her palms, ricocheting a harmonious humming all about them through the valley. It blasted into Dewin's chest, hitting the crystal directly. His arms flew wide, a cry of pain reaching them through the blinding power. She felt her body tremble with energy, squinting through the growing pain in her extremities.

Her arms fell to her sides, the rays of bright white magick extinguishing in an instant. The ground had fallen still, patches of grass laying uprooted all around them. Dewin stood where he had a moment before, head dropped and purple braids curtaining his face. A thin stream of smoke was billowing out from his back. They stood frozen, waiting.

Bang.

Mara cried out as iridescent power exploded from Dewin's body. She felt an ice-cold slash slap her hard across the face, snapping her to the side. The three of them flew backwards, slamming into the hillsides surrounding the valley. Mara's head slammed back into the solid earth, popping stars across her vision. There was a mighty ringing in her ears, and she could feel something wet and hot dripping from her face.

A hand cupped her chin, pulling her face upwards with a soft touch as the world spun. Her eyes came into focus, settling on Cyfrin crouched above her. He was staring with hot rage at a bleeding gash in her face, lightning cracking in his eyes. The two of them were surrounded in a blue dome of protective magick, and Mara could vaguely make out Kain and Dewin in combat behind them.

"*Stay.*" His voice was murderous as it breathed the command through her mind.

He was gone in a flash. Mara heard the familiar *crack* of his magick as he left her side, surging towards Dewin as she watched through the shielded dome. Mara blinked

245

I.A. TAKERIAN

slowly at them, trying to focus her dizzying vision and dim the ring in her ears.

Diminished flashes of light shot around the battling men, sending bolts of white and blue magick high as they went. Mara forced herself to her feet, pushing her way through Cyfrin's shield and charging forward to the place where they fought.

Kain and Cyfrin moved in perfect tandem, slashing at every opening Dewin gave as he zapped around them. Kain's sword seemed to make no contact with flesh, even with his masterful precision. But Mara could see tiny glowing cuts of blue light in the spots Cyfrin's blade drove through again and again. He was no longer using his magick, baring his teeth and releasing a torrent of blows from his dual swords instead.

Dewin's face was set in a mask of deep concentration, all apologetic humor gone. Cyfrin and Kain were obviously giving him the challenge he had so craved. Mara entered the fray beside Cyfrin, slicing at Dewin's back. The gems in her dagger glowed bright as it hit the iridescent aura surrounding him, and she watched with surprise as it sank partially through the shield.

Dewin lashed forward with an axe-like blow of his magick, colliding with Kain and Cyfrin and sending them crashing to the ground below. Mara spun to the front of him before he could recoup his attack, raising the dagger high and setting it hard through the aura above his face. It pushed through the magick surrounding him, the tip glancing off his cheek before being forced away by the regenerating shield.

Blood beaded out from a slice in his skin. Mara saw the crystal swinging at his chest swirl with menacing dark energy, like the corrupted waters of the ocean below them the night of the Fury's attack. Dewin's eyes widened as

A PROPHECY OF UNDONE

the world slowed. His arm shot out towards her with break-neck speed, latching on to her forearm. Another apologetic look flashed across his face as he tightened his grip.

There was a crackle of electricity as the remaining magick he absorbed from Cyfrin shot through his hand and into her. She cried out through the psychic connection. Cyfrin's lightning had touched her before, lacing up and down her skin and leaving teasingly heated licks of goose-bumps across her. But never like this.

She realized in this moment that Cyfrin must have been controlling the power that grazed her skin whenever she was close to it. Because this unfiltered magick of his was blood-boiling, tear-jerking pain. She watched tree-like roots of stained magick crack under the skin in her arm, setting her teeth on edge as she tried to pull away.

Wham. A blur of black and blue fury shot past Mara, rocketing into Dewin and ramming him away from her. It was only by the icy glow of his eyes as he whizzed past that Mara knew it was Cyfrin. She fell backwards, tumbling down the hill as her arm throbbed.

By the time she landed on the ground, Kain had joined Cyfrin atop the hillside. There were storm clouds gathering overhead, the lightning surrounding Cyfrin's body lashing about wildly. Uncontrolled. He and Kain launched at Dewin as he flew back towards them over the hillside. All three were yelling, moving headlong at each other with impossible speed. The earth shook beneath her as they met his magick with cold metal.

Black smoke burst forth from the crystal on his neck, surrounding them suddenly in an impenetrable dome of screaming darkness. She saw Cyfrin sucked into the earth, still shooting blue lightning from his body as he thrashed. Kain was slammed back into the rocks, straining every

I.A. TAKERIAN

muscle in his body against the force of the power pinning him.

Dewin was looking sad, both arms extended out towards her companions to keep them grounded. "It's a real pity," he said, and it sounded like he meant it. "I was so hoping the three of you would be the ones to do it. And I truly do *hate* having to kill your lot. You're always so noble and full of passionate mission."

He sighed, resigned as he squeezed Cyfrin and Kain tighter with his strange magick. Dewin closed his eyes, and the ominous dark energy began to gather around him, readying for the killing blow. But Mara had a sudden idea, a fleeting thought that whispered through her mind as she leapt to her feet and began sprinting up the hill towards them.

The black liquid-like smoke that filled Dewin's crystal looked just like the corrupted waters from the Brisenbane. The memory flashed through her head, starlight cascading down to the ocean in streams of purifying light. She didn't know if it would work, wasn't even sure she could do it on her own. But her companions were slowly having the life squeezed from them before her eyes, and she had to act.

She focused her intent, screwing up her face in concentration as she arrived at the outside of the black, smokey magick field. Her eyes shot to Cyfrin, gasping for air as the earth squeezed him tight. Kain, red in the face as he pulled helplessly against the magick holding him down.

Mara raised both hands before her, pushing desperately against the force field around the three of them. It felt like solid rock as she leaned into it, willing her magick to come forth. And for a moment, despite her most desperate efforts, she thought she would fail. But then, like the dim flickering of a fire starting in a hearth, she felt it.

She grasped firmly to the heat in her core, twisting her

A PROPHECY OF UNDONE

fingers about the feeling and forcing it up, up, up. It swelled from a flicker into a full-blown blaze, shooting through her arms as she pushed hard against the barrier. She could feel the earth beneath her feet begin to tremble, her heart thundering against her chest as she pushed. Her hands were pulsing with blinding golden light, cracking in longs veins against the bubble. Then, like the popping of a seal, she crashed through the darkness to the other side.

She closed her eyes as she dove blindly towards Dewin's body, reaching her golden glowing hands towards his chest. Mara felt magick surge around her as she snatched at the necklace, falling to the ground as the earth waved furiously beneath her. There was a mighty *boom*, and Mara dropped several feet into the hillside from her crouched position on her knees. She hugged her hands in towards her chest, ducking her head over top of them as the world shook. A massive wave of magick blasted through them all, winding Mara as it flew by.

There was silence, sudden and deafening, after the chaos moments before. She lifted her head slowly, peaking out through her eyelids. She knelt in a huge crater, blasted out in a perfect circle around her. Tiny pieces of dirt and debris still fell from the sky as she looked around.

Cyfrin and Kain had been released from their magick tethers, the two of them staring at her in awe. Dewin was between them, eyes wide in shock. She pulled her hands from her chest, cracking open her tight grip as they all looked down. Sitting in her palm, a huge crack shattered through its now-opaque surface, was the crystal necklace.

She was suddenly in the air. Dewin squeezed her against him, spinning her round as he lifted her high. He was laughing in great, bellowing " Haha" s, Mara growing dizzy as the world spun past.

Another pair of arms were around her then, unfurling

249

I.A. TAKERIAN

her from Dewin's grasp with deliberate firmness. Cyfrin held her against him for a moment, glaring daggers at Dewin as he skipped over to Kain. He was still laughing as he planted a kiss against his cheek. Kain pushed away, looking enraged.

"*Back, you rat!*" his voice growled through Mara's head over Dewin's boisterous excitement. "*You just tried to kill us!*"

"Yes, and you're still *alive!*" Dewin cheered, leaping into the air to hover feet above them. "And I am *free*. Finally free! Isn't it absolutely wonderful?!"

He landed before Mara, taking her hand in his and bowing so low that his nose nearly brushed the tips of his boots. He kissed the back of her hand softly, his eyes burning into hers as he grinned up at her. "I knew it would be you," he said, pulling up to his full height and taking both of her hands in his own. "It had to be. No darkness could ever hope to stand against something as blindingly bright as you."

He beamed at her. "Daughter of Prophecy!" he declared. "You have done me a great service. Released me from centuries of this torment. A favor I'm not sure I can ever fully repay with the same gratitude I feel now. But I will do my utmost to try." He slid a ring from his finger, one made of white silver and twisting ornately up towards his knuckle. He placed it on Mara's pointer, and she felt the cool metal tighten as it molded by magick to her finger. She could see tiny, dazzling gems all along its spiraling surface, sparkling in the sun overhead.

"I owe you a debt. One that must match the life you have freed me to live." He squeezed her hands, eyes bright. "Whenever you are in great need, Mara, rub this ring and call out my name. I will come to your aid, one favor, whatever it may be."

He kissed her hand once more and Mara felt Cyfrin

A PROPHECY OF UNDONE

growl beside her as he took a step forward. *"We have completed your task, fae-born,"* he thought, the voice thick with venom. *"Now remove your enchantment from us and be gone."*

"Yes, ends be damned, how much longer do I have to keep myself focused away from——" Mara cut her stream of thought short, heat rising instantly in her face. She glanced at Cyfrin, who gave no reaction other than to flex both his hands at his side.

Dewin looked amused as he faced him. "Ah, yes. That spell will last for a few hours yet before it fades off." He smirked at the look of disdain Cyfrin shot him. "But worry not! It seems you quite enjoy my little charm anyway. Appreciate it while it lasts."

Dewin winked at him as Cyfrin snarled. He turned his eyes skyward, staring over Mara and Cyfrin's shoulders off into the far distance. "Yes, I really should be off," he said, his voice thoughtful. "That portal will be an offensively difficult puzzle to crack."

He dropped his eyes to Mara, bowing low once more. "I bid you adieu, my saviors! Till next we meet again, and may it be much merrier." And with a wink and a flourish of his delicate hands, he was gone.

They stood in silence for a moment, the buzzing from Cyfrin loud in her head. Mara brushed the caked mud from her leathers awkwardly, trying to focus her attention on how filthy she was instead of the intrusive thoughts begging to betray her.

"We should find a water source," Cyfrin thought in response to her intense focus. *"Mara's right. We're all disgusting at this point."*

Kain raised his eyebrows, smirking. *"A hundred years we've been coming out here."* He thought, the humor in his voice clear. *"Never once have I seen you take more than a splash bath during our stay."*

I.A. TAKERIAN

Cyfrin shot him a venomous look before starting out through the valley. *"There was a small lake in the woods Kain and I came out of,"* he thought through the constant buzz. *"I could feel El and Milios out in that direction as well. Might as well kill two birds with one stone."*

"You can't make me bathe, you bastard," Kain thought as they followed him. *"I like a little grit on my skin. Helps me stay camouflaged."*

CHAPTER 26
YOU AND I

It was an exhausting, painstaking task trying to keep her thoughts hidden. Cyfrin's buzzing wall of sound had remained constant throughout their hours of walking, never once faltering except to speak when he intended. Kain had been regaling Mara with their encounters thus far, in vivid detail. How he had not just killed, but dismembered all thirty vampyres he had found himself up against. How he had stumbled upon Cyfrin, elbows deep in the basilisk he slayed. Cyfrin looked smug at this, flashing a smirk back towards them.

Mara had told him about her experience in the woods before she was attacked by the three Hopefuls, and Kain was staring at her in awe. *"Sprites are absolute bastards,"* he thought, shivering. *"They deal in soul magick. Wicked stuff, very old. Taking mortals and immortals alike as their slaves for all eternity."* He paused, eyes glinting with mischief as he looked at Mara. *"I also know for a fact that they like to use illusion magick. Lure in their prey with enchanted flower powder before morphing themselves to look like their deepest desires."*

He thumbed a knife on his belt, his eyes narrowing

253

I.A. TAKERIAN

sideways at Mara. "*They need their captives to seal the magick with a kiss, see. It's how they bind your soul to them. And they can't take it themselves. No, you must give it willingly for the magick to work. So, tell us, Mara...Who did they make you see?*"

Mara shot him a fiery look, knowing full well he knew the answer from the smirk on his face. She fought with all her might against the images flashing through her mind, against the name trying to escape her. But it was no use, already exhausted from the effort of keeping her mind silent for hours.

"*Cyfrin.*"

It circled around her head like a whisper on the wind, repeated over and over again. Kain looked away, a smug smile on his face. Mara pinched herself, drawing her attention to the sharp pain. She watched Cyfrin's shoulders square ahead of her.

"*We're here.*" It was the first she had heard him in hours, sending a thrill down her spine. Mara could hear running water, see it glistening through the thick trees ahead.

Kain gave her a sly wink, stretching his arms dramatically overhead. "*I'll be damned if I wash off my well-earned grime. If you two will excuse me, I think I'll just take a walk till this fae fuckery wears off.*" He waved a hand behind him and hurried away into the forest.

Mara felt her heart rise in her chest, gulping as panic set in. She turned slowly to face Cyfrin. He was staring at her with an eyebrow raised.

"*You can wash off first,*" he thought, his voice low and gentle over the buzzing. "*I'll sit with my back to you. No need to look so flustered.*" He smirked at her, pulling his eyes away from her red cheeks and leaning against a tree beside the lake.

Mara gulped again, cursing the butterflies flitting frantically around her stomach. She moved to walk past him,

A PROPHECY OF UNDONE

pine and honey drifting around her on the soft breeze. She grimaced, willing her thoughts to be still.

He reached out as she moved, grabbing her arms lightly to stop her walking any further. Mara's eyes widened as he leaned forward, stare set on her cut cheek. He ran a thumb gently across the slash. Mara felt the familiar, tingling numbness of his magick, his hot lightning closing her skin like cooked meat. He released her as soon as it was fully shut, breaking eye contact and waving his hand behind him. *"Make sure you wash the area around all of your wounds, regardless of it its closed or not."*

The lake was smaller than the crystal falls back in the Forgotten Wood, but not by much. The water was a deep shade of blue, nearly violet. The surface moved in strange, twisting patterns. It was mesmerizing, but unnatural. The entire lake was surrounded by dense trees, tiny white balls of light flickering on and off across its surface. Mara threw an anxious glance at Cyfrin, his back to her against the tree.

Taking a steadying breath, she began to undress. She peeled the grime covered leathers off, piling them neatly on the ground by the water's edge. The air nipped against her bare skin, sending shivers down her spine with its touch. She eased into the water, pleasantly surprised by how warm it was. Her muscles sighed in relief against the floating weightlessness. Mara closed her eyes, dipping her head back into the water and laying on its surface. Her black curls fanned out around here, and the forest sounds were dampened by the water in her ears.

She might have been able to ignore Cyfrin's electrical energy mere yards away, were it not for his buzzing. It had grown in volume, distracting Mara from her momentary peace. She frowned. *"Do you have to keep doing that?"*

"Doing what?" His voice replied through the noise.

255

I.A. TAKERIAN

Mara could practically see his expression of mock-innocence in her mind's eye. "*The buzzing, Cyfrin.*"

There was a brief pause, then the buzzing began to die off slowly. "*I cannot control my thoughts.*" His tone sounded strained.

"*Well, neither can I,*" she shot at him, irritated. How many times just in the last hour had she thought tender things about him? How much had he already heard? "*At least this makes it fair.*"

There was nothing but the sound of harmonious bird song in the trees for several long moments. Then whispers began to drift softly through Mara's head. They were almost inaudible at first, forcing her to screw up her face in concentration as she floated.

"*—a glance. Just a glance.*" Cyfrin's voice breathed. A deep growl resounded immediately after, scolding. "*Control yourself, you bastard. You're better than this. You have better control than this. But, oh what bliss just a glance of her would be.*"

Mara floated upright in the water, staring at the place where Cyfrin stood with his back to her. She could see his hands folded behind his back as he leaned back into the tree, his eyes skyward.

Mara bit her lip, feeling the fluttering heat within her grow. This was something out of her dreams, something she would have never dared wish for. She released her grip on her wildly spinning thoughts, just enough to let a few set forth. "*The way his arms felt wrapped around me last night. The scent of his skin. The way my name sounds on his lips. The way his lips moved against mine. I could go mad just thinking about it—*" She cut herself short, heated and flushed.

She saw Cyfrin freeze, the movement from his breathing stilling. "*You're a cruel woman, Dawnbringer,*" he thought. "*Control yourself.*"

But Mara couldn't tell if he was talking to her, or to

256

A PROPHECY OF UNDONE

himself. Whispers were still whirling forth from him, dancing around Mara's head in dizzying circles. *"Her skin. Like fresh flowers and sunlight. The smell of her...I want to touch every* **inch** *of her. I want to kiss and claim every piece as my own. All my own. I would kill for her. I'd kill any man who tries to touch her."* His thoughts were growing in volume, wild and unfiltered.

Mara was so hot, she felt she might burst. Her nipples perked up as the wind slid across her exposed body.

"I want to bury myself in her. Lose myself inside of her. Push deeper till there's no separation between our souls. I want to know her by the slightest touch, so that even if I am laid blind, I will still **know** *her. I would bring her to the edge of oblivion again and again and again, till she's screaming my name, clawing at me, begging for me-NO. Damnit, no. I'm sorry. Ignore me, please. Please. Ends be, if I could just hear her ask me please-"* The thought disappeared beneath an angry snarl.

Mara's eyes were wide as they stared at the clear, blue sky. If her heart hammered any faster, it would be in danger of exploding from her chest. The heat was threatening to overtake her, a dull throb mounting between her legs.

"And what would you do, Cyfrin? If I asked you nicely. If I said please. If I begged."

She felt the tattoo on her hand burn, saw his head twitch as if to turn in her direction. His fists clenched at his sides, sparking with tendrils of lightning. *"Don't."* His thought came through like a rumble of thunder.

"Come in here and make me." Mara couldn't imagine how red her face was by now.

Cyfrin's head turned, his eyes stopping just shy of looking at her. *"Mara, this is your last warning."*

Mara giggled, feeling him startle at the sound through their bond. *"Can't do much to stop me from way out there though,*

I.A. TAKERIAN

can you, Lightcleaver?" She felt a disproportionate amount of power in not having to actually speak these thoughts. She wasn't sure her mouth would ever allow her to form the words.

There was movement from the shoreline, and he was on Mara before she could even turn around. Cyfrin had ripped his shirt from his body, kicking his boots off and only bothering to untie his leather pants halfway before he had dove in. His arms wrapped around her torso, his hot skin pressing against her bare flesh and sending a shock-wave of electricity through her body.

Mara gasped, feeling his chest and stomach press against her bare back. He splayed his fingers across her stomach, grabbing her throat with a gentle grip in his other hand. She felt the fire roaring within her, crashing about as it yearned for release.

Cyfrin's lips grazed against her neck, travelling upwards as his thoughts pounded in her skull. *"Take her. Take her here and now."* Mara lost focus of the world, dissolving into the places he kissed. *"Claim her as your own. Entwine her body with yours. Feel every bit of her. Fill her to the brim from now until forever and destroy anyone that even dares look her way."*

Mara moaned, feeling his body grow still behind her.

"That sound. I'll have a thousand more just like it from you," he thought, the hand pressed against her stomach drifting upwards. He cupped one of her breasts, flicking his thumb across her nipple as he bit gently at the base of her throat. She shuddered, dropping her head back to rest against his shoulder.

"Please," she thought, breathless. *"I'll beg you. I **am** begging you, Cyfrin. Please."*

He spun her to face him, holding her slightly away from his body. His eyes were burning in a feral way, the runes on his skin nearly blindingly white. She could practically feel the spots where his eyes passed over, and that was every exposed inch of her sticking out of the water. They took her in with a hunger that made her womanhood throb, overheating under his gaze. She blushed, bashfully bringing her arms about herself to cover some of her bareness.

But Cyfrin grabbed her wrists gently, pulling them away from her body as he continued to stare. His eyes returned to hers after what felt like forever, pouring into them. *"You are breathtaking,"* his voice breathed, reaching for her. His hand slid to her lower back, fingers pressing into her skin. His other hand came to rest on her cheek, pulling her lips to his.

Mara had thought of his kiss a million times since their first, but none served it justice.

His lips moved expertly against hers, parting them with a gentle sigh as he slid his tongue inside. Mara's wet hands twisted up into his disheveled white hair, moaning into his mouth. She felt a rumble deep in his chest.

His hand shot from her face to her waist, lifting her out of the water in one fluid movement to straddle him. His hands cupped underneath her, his hungry kisses leaving her breathless. She could feel the thick, hard length of him poised beneath her, the fabric of his pants the only thing separating it from entering her.

She swirled her hips on instinct, grinding against him. She felt him twitch, throbbing from the motion as he let out a throaty moan against her mouth. Mara was ablaze with the feeling of electrified fire. Cyfrin's emotions slammed against her own down the bond, like the Brisenbane against the cliffs of the Forgotten Wood. But beneath this terrifying passion, something was beginning to rise. It started like an itch she wasn't sure how to scratch. Like

I.A. TAKERIAN

something trying to escape. And the more fevered their moment was becoming, the more torturous it started to feel.

But Mara couldn't bring herself to care. She felt wild, her entire being boiling down to the heat, the noises he made and his body against hers. One of his hands slid up to the back of her neck, tangling it in her curls and gripping tight. He pulled her head back, exposing her breasts to him. He kissed down her throat, across her chest, pausing just before her nipples, peaked from his touch.

"*Say it again for me. Say my name.*" The command rippled through her, reducing her to a trembling puddle in his hands.

"*Cyfrin.*" She was struggling to catch her breath. It was overwhelming how he made her feel, like the world started and ended only with him.

He breathed a laugh, flicking his tongue across her breast. Mara trembled, unable to contain herself. She'd touched herself before, exploring with curious touch. But she'd never felt anything like *this*. Cyfrin's hand sank more firmly against her backside, locking her in place. His teeth grazed her sensitive flesh, sucking her into his mouth and pulling a gasp from Mara. The length of him throbbed more powerfully underneath her.

He pulled back from her breasts, releasing the back of her hair so he could stare into her eyes. His were glowing white-blue, mirroring the intense light from his tattoos. He searched her face, hungry. "*Why do you make me feel this way?*" His voice sounded breathless, deep, and panting as his fingers traced the inside of her thigh.

"*What way?*" Mara thought, but it sounded so distant. Her focus had become lost on his fingers, trailing up ever further.

"*Like my heart is not my own.*" He held her eyes, sliding his

260

A PROPHECY OF UNDONE

hand between her legs to where her entrance sat pressed against him. His finger brushed gently against her, finding the weakest spot in one try. Mara's head fell back, her eyes rolling slightly. Cyfrin's face was so focused. He watched her every move, studying the complete control he had over her. Learning what made her body react the most. Two of his fingers slid slowly inside. He pressed them upwards into her walls, drawing them slowly down against her wet warmth. Mara writhed, from both the feeling, and the way Cyfrin was looking at her.

"*I need you,*" she thought, the words echoing around a hundred times. The feeling of something scratching down the bond was becoming almost unbearable.

He froze, sliding his hand out from between her legs. Mara could feel him pulsing angrily against her once more. He let out a gentle moan that made Mara feel like she could die happily right there. His lips pressed into hers, sunbursts exploding behind her eyes. He tasted like honey, his tongue twisting and sliding with hers in a sort of dance. It was a much more deeply passionate kiss than he had offered her before. Something beyond lust, or hunger.

The scratching was in her very soul now, reaching, digging. It was driving her crazy. Mara felt Cyfrin tense against her, and he was suddenly pulling her legs gently from around his waist. His lips never left hers as he lowered her carefully back into the water, hands at her waist. He pulled his face slowly away from her, looking pained.

Her eyes searched his strange expression. "*Do you not need me?*" she thought in a very small voice.

His eyes flew to her face, shocked. He breathed a laugh, incredulous. "*Mara, I have feelings for you that I cannot even begin to express or understand. Things I have never once felt; Not in all my years in this life.*"

He brushed his hand against her cheek, eyes staring

261

I.A. TAKERIAN

determinedly into her own as he tried to keep from looking down the length of her. From losing control again. *"But that doesn't matter. Nothing matters but you. What's best for you and your happiness. I am but a broken man. The pieces of my blackened heart laid rest their hollow dreams long ago. And you, my beautiful Dawnbringer. Light, and stars. Being from the Beyonds themselves. You deserve nothing but wholeness in the love given to you. Fierce passion and fiery grip. I have only lust and need and feral hunger."*

His voice sounded faraway, muffled. Mara realized the spell craft from the Fae was beginning to wane.

"To keep you in my shadow, to act on these things…It would be selfish of me. Beyond selfish." He released her, taking a step back as she stared at him, dumbfounded. *"I will not taint you with my misery. I will not diminish your light."*

His voice was nearly impossible to hear now. Mara stood in shock, waist deep in the water. He closed his eyes, turning away from her with what looked like monumental effort. He trudged from the lake, disappearing beyond the tree line, and leaving Mara alone behind him.

She stared, gaping, at the spot he had just been. Her skin still felt alight with electricity, the heat in her core burning bright. The scratching had vanished, and it was like a great weight had been lifted from Mara. Cyfrin's string of the bond had gone silent once more.

This was it. The reason for his hesitance, his briefly stolen glances and looks of sad longing. He thought himself unworthy of her love. Of her everything. Mara scoffed. *He thinks himself too broken for* **me**. *The lost princess. The nameless one of prophecy.*

She had been struck by his beauty from moment one, the second she saw him in her tower bedroom at castle Delinval. And slowly through the course of her journey, through their snide comments and rough edges, she had

A PROPHECY OF UNDONE

slipped. Without her knowledge, she had fallen hopelessly lost in feeling for him.

Hopelessly lost in love.

"Nothing matters but you, and your happiness," he had said, and she scoffed once more at the thought. There was not a single thing in her life, ever, that brought her the sort of happiness his smile did. The kind of joy his laugh gave her, or the thrill of hearing his voice for the first time on any given day. Not to mention the way his briefest touch made her feel. She sunk into the water to her lips, blowing angry bubbles as she let out a frustrated sigh.

She wasn't letting him get away that easily. If this was truly his reason, then she would show him how worthy he was. Whether it be by talking it out, or by her throwing herself completely naked at him, she did not care. It had been Cyfrin, after all, to tell her there was no use in wallowing. Cyfrin, to pull her from her darkest hours when she first arrived. His wounds, his scars, his healing…She wanted to stand beside every part of his journey. To help him grow past the darkness that still weighed so heavy upon him. She would break through that wall of his and tell him the truth: That she was in love with him, body and soul. The dark bits, and the light.

The heat dimmed in her core, simmering to a low thrum of anger at being left alone with her thoughts. Her fingers traced across her skin, memorizing the spots where his hands had travelled. She wondered if the strange scratching was something to do with the Bond of the Brethren, and made a mental note to ask Milios about it when they returned to the Red Froth.

Mara closed her eyes, sinking back into the water and letting it float her feelings away for the moment. Her thoughts settled on the repeated image of Cyfrin, tattoos aglow and panting as he threatened to devour all she was.

263

CHAPTER 27
WAR PARTY

Mara trailed at a distance behind Kain and Cyfrin, walking through the forest the next day. The silence after the hours of hearing one another the day before was infuriating, but Mara couldn't help being slightly relieved. It was doing no one any good, hearing their most unfiltered, sudden thoughts. And she couldn't begin to imagine the things she'd be thinking after yesterday's encounter.

Kain knew something was amiss, throwing weary glances between Cyfrin and Mara as they walked through the trees. They had encountered nothing but small woodland creatures thus far, hopping across their path with no care to them or their size. The bond pulled them forward, leading them towards where they knew El and Milios must be.

Mara was ready to be off this Zenoths forsaken island, ready to be aboard the Red Froth and able to properly confront Cyfrin. *What does he expect me to do? Pretend the sun does not rise and fall with him? Act as if the mere mention of his*

I.A. TAKERIAN

name does not throw me into madness? She scoffed at the ludi-
crous impossibility of it.

They travelled in strained silence, all pantomimed
stories and spelled-out hand motions from the day prior
gone. Mara was reminded irresistibly of her first few weeks
with them on their mission back from Delinval. Angry
silence, stolen glances, furious stares whenever Cyfrin did
manage to catch her eye. Suddenly, a noise pulled Mara
from her musings. The three of them stopped in their
tracks, listening.

There was a great booming sound in the distance, the
ground trembling underfoot. They drew their weapons,
hunching with caution as they inched forward. The
crashing sounds were growing louder with every step
northward, sending shockwaves through the earth and
shaking the mighty trees free of their leaves. The forest was
opening ahead, the sunlight glinting at them through the
underbrush. The sounds were deafening now, accompanied by strange cracking and whizzing noises as they drew
closer.

Cutting through the terrain was a deep canyon, the
cliffside the three stood upon serving as the highest point.
Standing before them, towering two-hundred feet high and
nearly as wide, was a massive rock monster. He was made
up of huge boulders, connected with what Mara could
only assume was very ancient, very powerful magicks. He
had no discernable eyes, but the large boulder serving as
his head did have a crack across its middle acting as a
mouth. It was presently grabbing at the cliffside beside it,
ripping huge pieces of earth from its walls and throwing
them to the ground below.

On the valley floor, dancing and dodging around the
mounds of earth cascading down upon them, were too
familiar figures. Milios was flying, whipping chunks of rock

A PROPHECY OF UNDONE

and hard earth back at the rock golem with harrowing speeds. Mara could just make out El by the golem's feet, clouds of green and purple smoke pluming up from her position. There were deep craters in the golem's legs from where she had tossed her many acid attacks.

Cyfrin put his fingers in his mouth, breathing out a shrill whistle that pulled even the rock golem's attention. El leapt into the air in celebration, Milios beaming up towards them. The golem seemed bored by their exchange, ignoring the three on the cliffside as it continued tossing boulders at El and Milios.

Kain and Cyfrin exchanged a look, a twisting smile breaking out nearly identically on their faces. Mara had no time to decipher the nod they gave. Each of them grabbed one of her hands. They gripped her tightly, breaking out into a run as they shot towards the cliff side. Mara had no choice but to keep pace with them, eyes wide as they flew off the ground towards the golem.

The three of them landed unceremoniously atop its head, causing it to pause mid throw. Kain ran forwards, sliding down the length of the rock golem's face as he drove his blade through the solid rock. The golem dropped the rock it carried, swatting at Kain like he was an annoying insect buzzing about. He was seemingly unphased by his attack.

His hand collided with Kain's sliding body, sending him flying backwards. Milios waved their hands, slowing his body slowed to a stop before it landed softly on the ground below. Cyfrin gave Mara a wink, raising his blades high and driving them through the top of the golem's head. His eyes glowed blue, lightning shooting from his hands and down the swords into the rock below.

The golem shuddered to a halt, freezing for a moment. Then it opened it's great, stony mouth and roared.

I.A. TAKERIAN

Mara fell to her knees with the force of the sound, Cyfrin grabbing her hand to keep her stationary as he gripped to one of his swords in the golem's head. It began flailing, slamming its feet into the ground as it reached frantically for Cyfrin and Mara. It was akin to being atop a wild horse, untamed and enraged. But Cyfrin's grip on her hand was strong, holding her in place as the golem shook. He pulled her towards him, placing her hand onto his second sword. She held on to the hilt as they were flung about, looking to him for a plan.

His eyes flashed, grabbing her free hand in his. Mara felt his lightning shoot down his blade, moving through her arm. She flinched, waiting for the pain she had felt from Dewin's attack yesterday. But none came.

Heat ignited within her. There was harmonious humming resounding around them, like a million tiny bells on the wind, all perfectly tuned with one another. Cyfrin's lightning was morphing, resembling frost blue constellations as they mixed with Mara's sunbeam. The golem shrieked, flinging itself about as their magick coursed through it.

The rock beneath their feet began to crack, beams of light spilling forth into the fissures. Cyfrin pulled Mara away from the blades. He gave her a wicked smile, pulling her along behind him as he launched off the top of the golem. They plummeted several feet together, hands still clasped, before the wind whipped up underneath them.

Mara felt their decent slow, drifting with feather-like weight to the earth. Cyfrin released her hand as they touched down, turning to face the golem. Its shrieking had been cut short; its body nearly invisible through the blinding white lights pouring forth from what was now hundreds of cracks. There was a loud *bang* that shook some rocks loose from the surrounding cliffs. Then the golem

268

A PROPHECY OF UNDONE

exploded into a torrential downpour of golden dust. It shimmered in the sunlight, drifting all about them on the wind as it carried the ash up and away.

Someone slammed into Mara, pulling her in to a tight hug and rubbing their cheek against hers. Mara beamed, squeezing El back as she nuzzled against her face. Another set of arms wrapped around her from the other side, Milios holding her gently. A third and fourth set of arms joined the fray, Mara smooshed in the middle as the five of them hugged. Kain lifted the tangle of them into the air with his embrace, the breath squeezed from Mara before he released them back to the earth.

El smiled dazzlingly at Mara, eyes scanning her face. Her grin faltered as they passed over the many haphazardly closed cuts given to her by the blonde hopeful. Her jaw dropped as she leveled on to the sealed gash in her cheek.

Kain stepped forward, brushing El's brown hair aside and staring at her neck. His face was more serious than Mara had ever seen it, anger flickering to life beneath his steady gaze. There were three, deep claw marks in El's skin at her throat, still red and angry even after being sealed by her magick. Kain drew his finger across her collarbone, glowering down at her injury with fire in his eyes.

El blushed, pushing his hand aside gently and smiling at him. Milios was staring at Cyfrin with a raised eyebrow, eyes flickering back and forth from him to Mara and back again. Milios always gave her the feeling that they knew much more than they let on. Mara suspected it had to do with their whispering winds, and the things it saw and told Milios in secret.

El grabbed Mara's hand, tugging her gently in the direction of the mouth of the valley. It seemed to dip into another canyon, the ground disappearing out of view a few

269

I.A. TAKERIAN

feet after the exit. She pulled her, nearly skipping, all the way to the edge. Mara's eyes went wide.

They were standing looking down at an oasis. There were hundreds of different species of vines, trees, flowers, all growing straight out of the green canyon walls below. They trailed off into the mists that blocked their view a few hundred feet down. A massive waterfall was cascading over the edge across from them, throwing dazzling rainbows off its surface and into the air. It disappeared past the cloud cover beneath as well.

El had a cat-like grin on her pretty face, turning to Mara with her back to the canyon. She waved at her, then leapt suddenly backwards off the edge. Mara gasped, rushing forward to try and grab her. El was shooting down-ward, rocketing towards the wall of fog as Mara watched in horror. But instead of whizzing through it to whatever lay beyond, she collided with the top of it. She sank into the cloud slightly before it bounced her off, throwing her back up the entire length she had fallen. She hovered in the air before Mara for a moment, giving her a wink before shooting back towards the bottom.

If Mara could have laughed, she would have. Without a second thought, she launched out into the open air. She saw Cyfrin's eyes fill with panic as she shot towards the cloud cover. The air become warmer the closer she drew to the fog, and she found it to be soft and spongey on impact. She sank into it a little way before being ricocheted high into the air beside El.

As they flew up, Cyfrin and Kain plummeted down past them. They were tangled up with one another, tumbling in a spinning ball as if Kain had tackled Cyfrin off the cliffside. Both of their eyes looked alight with laughter, Milios hovering above them all looking delighted.

They bounced up and down on the cloud's surface for

far longer than they probably should have. There was something so pure about this moment, free of the weight of the world. Mara closed her eyes, imagining herself flying as she raised and dropped through the open air. There was a burst of beautiful smell around her, like a million wildflowers in bloom. She opened her eyes, bouncing high.

Flower petals had appeared all around her, rising and falling as she did as if magnetized to her. They were all bright, fantastic colors, swirling magickly through the air. A few swept through her hair, getting lost in her curls. Cyfrin whizzed past her, waving his hands towards the petals as he flashed a wry smile. The petals burst into bloom all around, morphing into full flowers before disappearing with tiny *pops* of color.

When they were finished leaping and tumbling about, Milios hovered them each safely across to the other edge of the canyon. It stood in stark contrast to the whimsical greenery behind them.

The landscape here was dark, the ground like black cooled molten beneath their feet. Smoke curled softly from the earth, twisting through the air like tendrils stretching towards the sky. There was a deep rumbling far in the distance, shaking the earth underfoot. The energy of the group shifted instantly, all carefree abandon vanished..

Mara could just make out the silhouette of mountains beyond through the thick air, her eyes stinging against the smoke. Cyfrin stepped forward, positioning himself at the front of the group with a solemn look on his face. They took up their places behind him, following his path in a single-file line across the harsh terrain.

Through the swirling smog, Mara could hear inhuman noises circling around them. Growling, snarling, snapping sounds, echoing off the rock below and warping the noise.

I.A. TAKERIAN

It gave the illusion that they were coming from everywhere, all at once. Mara was reminded of their trek through the swamps on the outskirts of Ylastra, glad to have a weapon with her as they moved.

They walked in careful formation for an indeterminate amount of time, throwing weary glances about themselves as they went. They were nearly upon the mountain range, the moon hanging in the sky, when an ominous noise came from behind. They spun around in unison, Kain at the rear raising his great sword. The smoke was so thick, it served as a wall to obscure their vision. El raised a hand, shooting green orb lights onto the path behind them and illuminating the surrounding area in their eerie glow.

Through the smoke, Mara could see many figures moving about. Circling them. The orb lights threw them into sharp relief, revealing a small army descending almost soundlessly from the sky to the blackened ground below. Mara's eyes fell upon the man standing at the front, clearly leading this force. He threw a dark smile at her, and Mara felt her stomach plummet. She recognized the grey, sharp face, taking in the bandage wrapped tightly around his throat.

These were the sprites from the woods.

CHAPTER 28

A FORCE TO BE RECKONED WITH

Chaos erupted. The sprites began to shriek, launching forward as the five of them reacted in unison. Kain met the first wave of them with a great, arcing slash of his sword. He flew forwards into the fray, dodging as bolts of magick whizzed past him.

Milios grabbed El's hand, launching her into the air and using their magick to hover her above the forces. She released a torrent of acid bursts upon them, their screams mixing with the sizzling of their flesh as she flew. A bolt of magick shot through the air, hitting her in the gut and sending her tumbling through their backlines. Milios rocketed in after her, sending sprites flying as they passed.

Cyfrin's hands burst with crackling lightning, winging several sprites with his bolts as they went for him. Mara dodged as a powerful ball of magick flew past her. The sprite who she had held hostage stepped into her path. He cracked his neck to the side, looking from Cyfrin to her with an evil smile. Mara blinked, and it was suddenly Cyfrin's face staring back at her. She felt her heart sputter,

273

I.A. TAKERIAN

eyes widening. The sprite, enchanted to look like her companion again, dove for her with a roar.

His hands glowed blue, the same blue as Cyfrin's magick. Mara stumbled backwards, raising her dagger to meet his fists. The blue energy shot down the blade, past the gemstones pulsing violently in the hilt and into her shielding arms. It felt like fire as it filled her to the shoulders, forcing her back as it burned her skin. She looked down, shocked. Her arms had gone completely blue. She tried to raise them to defend herself once more. But they remained hanging at her sides.

Her eyes shot to the sprite's face, still morphed to look like Cyfrin's. He shook his head, pointing towards her limp arms. "No more of that for you, *Bornbane*." He raised his hands, blue energy surrounding them once more as he fired off at her.

Her feet left the ground, her body lifted into the air and spun out of the way.

Cyfrin placed her on the earth yards away, his arms both covered in green blood. His eyes flashed over her face before he disappeared, surging forward to the bandaged sprite. Mara saw him pause for a moment, studying his face mirrored upon the enemy. Then Cyfrin's hands flashed, hitting the sprite like a hammer across the jaw. He tumbled backwards over a sprite's corpse.

Mara was fighting against whatever enchantment the sprite had used. But it seemed to be no use. Her arms continued to swing, long and limp, through the air beside her.

Kain was crashing through the crowd of sprites, his great sword cutting clean through them as he went. Milios had tossed El high once more, her acid magick raining death down upon the massive crowd still gathering through the smog. Tornadoes of vicious wind lashed out through

A PROPHECY OF UNDONE

the forces, tossing screaming bodies skyward before sending them crashing to the unforgiving earth.

Cyfrin was backing away from the bandaged sprite, eyes wide. Mara looked to the shapeshifting enemy, but he was no longer wearing Cyfrin's handsome face. She felt a thrill run through her.

Cyfrin was stepping slowly back from *her*.

The sprite was identical to her in every way, down to the uneven cut of her black curls bouncing with unnatural slowness around her green eyes. "*Kiss me,*" it crooned in a warped voice, stuck somewhere between Cyfrin's tone and her own. "*Won't you kiss me, my Lightcleaver?*" The sprite lunged for him, golden magick cascading into Cyfrin's torso as he tried to leap away. He collapsed to the ground in an instant, eyes rolling as he lay motionless.

Mara felt cold panic, ignoring the battle and her helplessness as she ran to his side. She fell to her knees, pivoting her body between the sprite and his unconscious form like a human shield. His skin was glowing slightly, swirls of golden magick just visible beneath the surface. He wasn't moving, and she could see no breath rise and fall in his chest.

There was an irresistible tug from behind her, pulling her roughly into the air. She fought against it as she raised above Cyfrin, the air around her thinning. She felt her head spin as she stared wildly down at his body.

The sprite leader stood on the ground behind her, cackling as it raised her into the air. Mara was trapped in some sort of invisible bubble, limiting her oxygen supply, and preventing her escape. She saw Kain step onto the back of a bleeding sprite, face set in stone as he launched through the air towards her. Her captor waved a hand lazily towards him, iridescent magick stopping him dead. His body was thrown backwards a hundred feet.

275

I.A. TAKERIAN

El was surrounded by sprites, exploding in clouds of acid as they tried to trap her. Milios shot from their position towards Mara. Wind whipped out from their outstretched hands like a blade, cracking through her magick prison. Mara began to tumble towards the ground now 20 feet below her, as another bolt of invisible magick hit Milios square in the face. They startled, freezing in the air before being slammed into the ground with enough force to shatter the earth around them.

The magick prison circled Mara again, inches before she collided with the ground next to Cyfrin's unmoving body. She screamed as loudly as she could through the bond, staring wide eyed down at him as she was shot back into the air. He began to stir, Mara watching as she flew up twenty, thirty, fourty feet. His eyes opened slowly, blinking as he looked up at her.

He was on in his feet in an instant, diving for the sprite who held her aloft. Cyfrin collided with a barrier of shimmering magick that surrounded him, and the sprite laughed even louder. He still wore Mara's face, but it looked distorted now. Twisted into a corrupted version of what she could be. Cyfrin launched backwards, looking skyward as she flew higher and higher. She had to strain her eyes to see what was happening below.

Cyfrin lunged for the sprite again, blue lightning whipping out of him with deadly intent. But the barrier surrounding the sprite seemed unbreakable. It threw Cyfrin through the air, the Sprite taking the chance to flee into the air. It came level with Mara in seconds, morphing back into a corrupted form of Cyfrin as it smiled at her through pointed teeth.

They were beginning to move back through the air, towards the area they had just come from. Back towards the illusionary forest.

A PROPHECY OF UNDONE

Mara could see Kain, El and Milios overwhelmed in the army of sprites, throwing anxious and panicked looks upwards at her through the fray. But Cyfrin had stood from the ground slowly, and Mara watched as he drew a knife from his belt.

He wrapped his hand around the blade, blue lightning enshrouding it. Sparks of red cascaded from the silver, the blade growing white-hot under his powers. He was staring up at her, face far too distant to make out. He drew the blade across his arm, from bicep to wrist. Mara felt sharp pain rocket through their bond.

Instantly, the air around them all became electrified.

The sky went black. Thunder rumbled from the many threatening clouds. The hair on Mara's arms stood on end, a cold chill running down the back of her neck. Great, impending warning filled her body, urging her to escape. There was a deafening, cracking *boom* and a pillar of lightning shot through the sprite leader beside her.

His screams ripped through the air, mixing with the sounds of flailing, sizzling flesh. The pillar vanished, lightning still cracking through the clouds towards the ground. The sprite's entire body was charred and smoking. His eyes were bubbling in their sockets, tongue lolled out from his bloody, frothing mouth. He hung suspended for another moment. Then his body dropped, disappearing through the clouds as it raced towards the ground. Mara felt the bubble of magick around her burst, and she too began to plummet.

She broke through the thundering cloud cover, cold wind cutting at her face. Deadly blue pillars of lightning were slamming into the battlefield, burning the sprites alive and making deep craters in the earth where they hit. Some sprites were attempting to flee as their comrades fell in droves.

I.A. TAKERIAN

El, Kain and Milios were huddled together, protected by a vortex of wind that whipped around them from Milios' outstretched hands. Milios threw a hand towards her position as she fell. A pillar of lightning grazed her arm, burning her as Milios' wind caught her mid-fall. She sped forward through the air, dodging past the massive strikes of electrical magick. She landed inside the wind vortex, squeezed against her friends as they watched.

There were at least eighty charred corpses of sprites scattered all around them in the madness. The pillars of blue lightning were growing more intense, smashing through the earth with furious strikes. Milios' arms shook with the struggle to maintain their shield.

Yards away, head thrown back in a silent scream, was Cyfrin. His entire body was covered in lightning, his eyes glowing white. His hair whipped around him as rocks rose from the ground to hover about his outstretched arms. The earth below his feet was cracking as it gave way partially. Mara could just make out the strip of flesh on his arm that he had taken the burning blade to. The skin had been melted away, removing a large chunk of the rune tattoos that kept his magick in check.

He tore away some of his protection, she thought with dawning understanding. *He ripped off part of his barrier to save me.* She realized by her hands now covering her mouth that the blue magick binding her arms had vanished, gone with the spirt leader's demise. Her mind zeroed in on Cyfrin's tattoo on her hand.

It was in *agony*, her hand trembling under the pain. Kain, El and Milios were staring at Cyfrin too, terror in their eyes. And she knew what she must do.

Pushing hard against the vortex of wind keeping them safe, Mara shot out the other side and dropped to a knee on the ground beside a pile of burnt corpses. El and Kain

A PROPHECY OF UNDONE

both reached for her at the same time, panic on their faces, but Mara was already on her feet. She ran through the lightning crashing, diving out of the way as a few narrowly missed her. She was feet away from Cyfrin, the earth beneath him breaking off in huge pieces and rising to hover about him.

His face was void of emotion, mouth wide in his noiseless scream and eyes wide beams of white light. Mara squinted, gritting her teeth against the power bursting forth from him. She raised her hand to block her face from the debris in the air. It threatened to destroy her by the sheer magnitude of it. Lightning covered every inch of his skin, crackling in grave warning as she stepped forward.

She shouldered through the rubble flying around him, wincing as burning bolts of lightning hit her. His arms were held out from his sides, his entire body shaking from the overwhelming power. She reached out her hand to grab him. Lightning shot through her as soon as their bodies connected. It felt like her blood was boiling underneath her skin as she gripped him, squeezing her eyes shut. The magick ripped through her, threatening to tear her apart from the inside out. But she did not falter.

She leaned forward, forcing her way through the aura of deadly power surrounding him. Her hand released his as she threw herself against his body, wrapping her arms around his waist.

It was pain like she had never felt before. It etched through her, zapping at her soul, and carving through her entire being. She could feel the lightning, an unforgiving current of mighty power, cascading through her. Just like the fire she felt in her own abilities. And something suddenly clicked into place.

She willed her mind, crying out as wave after wave of pain took her, to be silent. Her body grew still against his

I.A. TAKERIAN

as she took a shaky, deep breath. She focused on his lightning within her, feeling its screaming fury as it tried to escape through any part of her it could. She reached out to it in her mind, feeling it lash angrily against her as she did so. She clenched her jaw.

"Be still," her voice whispered from deep within her, reaching out mentally towards the overpowering waves of magick. *"Be still and come to me."*

The magick seemed to stop. Like it was taken aback by her. She imagined herself atop the crested waves of its cold madness, hushing its roaring. She felt the magick shudder, unsure, as she caressed it. Then, it began to flow.

It felt like a great circuit, connecting her to Cyfrin as the lightning spun through them both. She felt his arms drop to his sides, felt him take in a great shuddering breath. The lightning was calming, and Mara swore she could hear a kind of purring in her head as it began to dim. She felt its fury smolder underneath her focus, the lightning now licking long stretches of warmth across her skin. It felt like it was petting her, apologizing for any pain it had caused.

The debris around them crashed to the ground, the slam of the lightning into the earth ceasing entirely. The booms of impact still echoed around them as the magick circuit stopped spinning and the power retreated into Cyfrin.

Mara was suddenly more exhausted than she had ever been in her life. Cyfrin swayed against her as both their knees buckled at the same time. The world tipped sideways, her head spinning. She felt him topple to the ground beside her as she collapsed, and she was thrown into the darkness of unconsciousness.

CHAPTER 29
REFLECTIONS IN FEAR

"*Mara.*"

Mara turned to Adrian, blinking in the dazzling sunshine. His eyes danced with laughter. He splashed water on her face. They were by the river in Delinval, and the summer heat had them both in loose cotton clothing. This…This was her sixteenth birthday.

She remembered it so clearly. Two of Lord Xertas' daughters had pelted her with dirty wash water as she passed below their window. Their laughter, hag-like and shrill, rang in Mara's ears. She could feel the sting of tears still in her eyes.

Adrian smirked at her, jumping into the river fully clothed.

"Adrian!" Mara called, her crying now mixed with laughter. "What are you doing?!"

"Joining you in your immense wetness, your highness," he called back, giving a dramatic bow in the river. He beamed at her, shaking water from his brown mane. His

281

I.A. TAKERIAN

eyes flashed, sinking to his neck in the water. "Will you be joining me then, princess?"

Mara shook her head, smirking at him. "I think I've had quite enough wetness for the day, thank you," she replied, raising an eyebrow.

But Adrian shot towards her from the water with a mock roar. Mara squealed, both laughing as he dragged her down into the river's current. The water was colder than she remembered it being, and the flow seemed to pick up around her.

She stopped laughing, her smile faltering. "What is this?" She turned to face Adrian, struggling against the relentless tide. But he was nowhere to be seen.

The sunshine had gone from the sky, replaced by dull, gray darkness. The water was at her throat as it rose rapidly. She cried out, but too late. Something below her wrapped its way around her ankle, giving a mighty tug and forcing her under. She couldn't breathe.

The cold water felt oddly airy, like falling through freshly fallen snow. Everything was darkness; empty, deafening darkness. She was being pulled further and further down, not even bothering to struggle against it.

"*Mara.*"

Her eyes flew upwards, staring at the black void beyond. She had heard him. Not the low, soft drawl of Adrian. No, this voice was much more animal than man.

"*Mara!*"

She could see blue light now, pulsing dimly above her in the distance. She reached out with both hands, stretching her fingertips towards the glow.

"***Mara!***"

The voice was so clear, it felt as if it came from within her. The darkness shattered, bathing her in warm, frosty light as the pulling ceased. She felt electricity slam through

282

A PROPHECY OF UNDONE

her, and she gasped, shooting upright as her eyes flew open.

She had been dreaming. Lost somewhere deep in her subconscious. She blinked hurriedly, staring around. She was sitting on the hard ground, a cloak tucked underneath where her head had been. Rain was pelting down from above. Her companions sat around her, faces pale and drawn.

Cyfrin sat beside her, holding her hand loosely in his. He looked grief-stricken as he stared at her. Mara gripped his hand, yanking his arm towards her and pulling him closer. She pointed down to the strip of raw flesh he had burnt away with his knife. It looked like El had already begun mending it, fresh pink skin covering its surface.

He pulled his hand gently from hers, and Mara became very aware of their companions studying them. It had felt like powerful, raw magick, whatever happened out there. Soul joining and universe unravelling. Milios was staring at Mara with an annoyingly knowing look, like they had already figured out exactly what it was that occurred.

They were seated at the base of a great mountain range. It was taller than the Krakenbär Mountains, stretching up and through the gray clouds pouring above them. There were no foreseeable passes, and Mara felt a twinge of relief. She had never really gotten over the suffocating feeling of Bardro's Gash. Sometimes, she still had nightmares of being stuck in there with the Necromancer. The thought of climbing across the mountains was less than pleasant, but far better than the alternative in her mind.

Cyfrin was standing from the ground, staring at a trail beaten through the underbrush of the mountain. Milios looked wearily at the darkening sky, raising an eyebrow at him.

Cyfrin snarled, waving behind him as if to say, "We can't stay here".

Milios look skeptical still, but gave a curt nod regardless before starting forward after him. Begrudgingly, painfully, they began to march their way upwards into the forested mountain.

MARA STILL FELT STRANGELY TINGLY as she walked, the aftereffects of the lightning still clinging to her insides. She glanced at Cyfrin, tall and resolute as he led them. He had only burnt away a small portion of his tattoos, barely anything compared to the coverage on the rest of his body. And yet he had lost complete control over his magick, the power overtaking him the instant it was given the opportunity.

Mara had often wondered if magick had its own emotions, thinking on how she had felt Cyfrin's power bow to her. If he was trapping it in there, perhaps his loss of control was simply a magickal temper tantrum. Not unlike the ones she herself used to have so often, locked away in her tower in Delinval. She was so lost in this train of thought that she barely heard it as a scream ripped the air.

They all slammed to a halt, pulling their weapons as they positioned themselves for an attack. The sound had come from somewhere far off in the trees, drifting through the shadows like rumbling thunder. There was silence for a long moment, everyone straining their ears to listen.

A second scream, this one more pronounced. It was blood-curdling, chilling Mara to the core before it was abruptly cut off. She could see Cyfrin scowling, eyes

A PROPHECY OF UNDONE

narrow as he stared through the wooded landscape. He began inching forward, swords at the ready in his hands as he led them in the direction of the sound.

Whoever it was had obviously been in great pain, perhaps fallen prey to any of the numerous monsters inhabiting the island. They moved nearly noiselessly through the trees, Mara's breathing shallow as she crouched behind Cyfrin. A great, ominous energy had begun to slither about them in the underbrush, pulsing with dark magick as they drew closer to the source of the sound.

She could see the trees thinning out ahead, opening to a small clearing just beyond. Milios brushed suddenly past Mara, gripping Cyfrin's shoulder and forcing him to halt. They weren't looking at him, instead staring ahead with placid calm.

Cyfrin searched their face, crouching lower. There were bushes surrounding the entirety of the clearing, and the group moved behind their shadows, peaking out through the leaves. They were met with a horrifying scene.

Mara was glad she couldn't make noise, sure that she would have at least whimpered at what lay before her. The clearing was bathed in cloudy moonlight, casting long shadows across the flowing grass. There were two men cowering on their knees in the center, and Mara recognized them as the two Hopefuls that attacked her. Laying on the grass at their knees, crumpled and twisted into odd shapes, was a headless body. Blood still sputtered from the gaping neck, splattering up from the ground and onto the black-haired Hopeful's armor.

Looming above them, waving like the shadows in the grass all around, was a beast Mara knew well from her nightmares. It had no face, an endless abyss under its thick hood. Black, smoke-like limbs were shooting from random

I.A. TAKERIAN

places on its body, retracting before appearing suddenly elsewhere. Its shimmering, waving aura sent thrills of terror through Mara, and she felt the feeling reflected through their tattooed bonds.

This was a Reflector Beast.

Held aloft in one of its long, crooked hands, was the head of the body between him and the men. Its face was contorted into a look of wild fear, eyes rolling back in his head. The bottom part of his jaw had been ripped off, leaving a bleeding open space where his mouth had once been. This was the blonde Hopeful who had been intent on killing her.

The Reflector Beast tossed the head to the side, the five of them watching as it whizzed past through the trees. The beast was grabbing the black-haired Hopeful off the ground by his hair, his feet flailing in the struggle. He was letting out panicked cries, his eyes looking like they were about to pop from his skull. There was a noise coming from the beast, like a hundred screams through thick liquid. It drew goose-bumps across her skin as it leaned towards the Hopeful.

"Dawnbringer."

Mara froze as she heard her name echo around the clearing, the beast speaking in many different voices at once. She felt Cyfrin grow still beside her, his eyes narrowing.

"I know you have been with her, foul flesh," the beast wheezed, black smokey tendrils reaching forth to wrap around the Hopeful's neck. *"I can smell her aura on you. You reek of her. All of you **reek** of her."*

Cyfrin's eyes flew to Milios, who nodded. Mara felt the wind shift around her, pushing backwards through the trees. Carrying her scent away from the Reflector Beast. Her pulse was flying, cold sweat on her neck. It had come

A PROPHECY OF UNDONE

all the way to the island to find *her*. To hunt her down like an animal, no doubt to be brought before Mezilmoth for slaughter.

Cyfrin drew closer to her, keeping his dark eyes fixed on the clearing as the Hopeful began to speak.

"P-please!" he stammered, tears falling from his face as he sobbed. "Please, we were only with her for moments! I swear! We were there to scare her and things got out of hand and-"

"***Silence,***" the Reflector Beast's voice roared all around. "*Your tongue trills lies, and I shall rend it from your hide!*" The black void beneath its hood began to swirl, the Hopeful's eyes going wide and glassy as he stared at it. Then he began to scream.

Mara threw her hands over her ears, mouth moving in a silent yelp. It was the same spine-chilling sound that had drawn them here in the first place. The sound that the blond Hopeful beheaded on the ground no doubt had made before his death.

The Hopeful thrashed against the beast's twisting grip, and blood began to trickle from his nose and ears. Mara watched in horror. These three had attacked her, would have killed her if Cyfrin hadn't shown up when he did. But the one now shrieking as he fought for his life had been disquieted by the idea. Had even attempted, however meekly, to stop his comrades. And even with their hatred of her, even though she was sure they would not be the first to stand opposed to who she was, she could not help the feeling now rising within her.

These were her people, the title of Queen her birthright. Despite the circumstances surrounding the first twenty years of her life, the entirety of the Odelian race was hers to guide and protect. *How am I to lead them, if I*

I.A. TAKERIAN

cannot even protect them? And in this moment, Mara felt the overwhelming power of her responsibility.

She moved as if in a daze. She was on her feet before anyone could stop her, charging forward through the bushes and launching towards the beast with her dagger outstretched. It turned its faceless void on her as soon as she emerged, following her as she slashed upwards through the arm holding the Hopeful.

It vanished like a puff of smoke, the black-haired man dropping to the ground as he gasped for air. Mara heard the four shoot out after her, Cyfrin diving for her with hands covered in lightning. Kain swung his sword in tandem with Milios whipping magick, El tossing a purple potion bottle towards the beast's face.

Darkness erupted around them. It knocked the breath from Mara, dropping her to a knee as it lashed out across the clearing. Cyfrin collided hard with it like a wall, rocketing backwards through the tree line. Kain, Milios and El were tossed with equal intensity, all flung away from the center point. Mara was surrounded by a dome of impenetrable black magick. It was just her and the Reflector Beast now.

A patch of undarkened land surrounded just the two of them, the thick darkness around them swirling. Mara remembered their near encounter with the Reflector Beast in the Forest of the Fallen. Her companions had warned her to never look at its face, lest you be trapped in their magick. But it was too late for that. Her eyes had already fallen with wide panic on the black, swirling void. She froze in place; sure she wouldn't be able to move even if she tried.

The beast had begun vibrating very fast, a near blur of black smoke and flailing limbs as it stood above her. She blinked as it stopped, mouth agape. It was like staring

A PROPHECY OF UNDONE

through a mirror. A perfect replica of herself had appeared before her, her skin oddly shadowed as if she stood in a dark room. But her face was *too* perfect as it smiled back at her.

Her curls were no longer tangled haphazardly about her, falling instead in beautifully glistening ringlets about her shoulders. Her eyes, slanting delicately upwards, were shining with dark delight, long eyelashes batting down against her arching high cheekbones. Her body, usually full and muscled, was slimmed out. Leaned and long underneath tight-fitting armor. She smiled at Mara; the look twisted as a deep male voice echoed forth from her mouth.

"You've caused me quite a lot of trouble in finding you, Dawnbringer."

CHAPTER 30
DARK IMAGE

Mara took a step back, stunned. The deep voice laughed, the sound echoing all around her in a full octave of pitches before falling deathly silent. It shook itself off, dusting her shoulder and cracking her neck at Mara.

"I have seen a million deep, dark fears over my many centuries," it spoke as it began to circle her, studying her. "Fear of the darkness, fear of death, fear of heights of drowning or burning alive...But I think you are the first I have seen who is truly afraid of *themselves.*" The word whispered around Mara as she pivoted to keep the beast in her vision.

"The lost princess. Scared and alone her entire life. And now she finds her destiny is far too big to carry; finds herself too scared to use her powers. And yet afraid that she won't be able to in a time of dire need." It glanced over its shoulder, towards the flashes of blue magick slamming dimly into the darkness yards away from them. "You fear you'll either hurt them or let them all die. You fear that they'll *leave.*"

I.A. TAKERIAN

There was such gleeful venom in their words, green eyes glowing with an eerie tinge. Mara shied away instinctively. A smiling was growing on its face, stretching far past where it should. "You fear that they'll discover how pathetically *weak* you are. How truly incapable and *insignificant*. Then once they see your true self, they will abandon you, and you shall be left with *nothing*."

Cruel laughter filled the air as her heart sank. The beast wasn't wrong. She *did* fear herself; feared her weakness and what it might mean for her companions. They had already risked so much for her, and Cyfrin…Mara looked over the beast's shoulder to where the lighting cracked against the side of the dome. Cyfrin would gladly throw his life down for her. And this scared her perhaps most of all. The willingness they all had to stand beside her, to guide and shield her.

The fear gripped with unnatural strength to her heart, the Reflector Beast's dark magick increasing the feeling tenfold. She gasped, feeling breathless. Her pulse hammered away in her ears.

"I searched high and wide for you, pet," the deep voice rumbled, the beastly Mara looking bored. "I had hoped to catch you before you entered the mountains. But your friends are much more clever than I gave them credit for."

Mara's blood ran cold. This beast *was* the one they had seen that day in the forest months ago. He had confirmed her worst fears, been there not by accident, but in search of her. "*My master*", it had said. The beast was speaking of Mezilmoth. And if he wanted Mara, then he must already know about her quest to seal the Dark Gate once and for all.

The beat took a step toward her. Mara raised her dagger, and the beast's smile widened. "We could make you happy, you know. We could give you everything you've

A PROPHECY OF UNDONE

ever wanted. I can see it all, your entire future laid before me in vivid splendor. ***Let me show you***." It waved its hands, and the darkness swirled about them at dizzying speeds. The world slammed to a halt and Mara blinked against the sudden, bright sunlight.

She was in the throne room of Castle Delinval, the stained-glass windows throwing dazzling colors all about her. She was seated on Grathiel's grand, wingback throne, facing out towards a crowd of bowing Delinvalians. She turned to see Adrian seated at her side.

He was slightly older, his features chiseled out and the finest robes adorning his body. A golden crown glinted on his head, and he was beaming at her. He grabbed her hand, and she gasped. It felt so real, the rough callouses on his palm pressing into her skin as he squeezed her.

"You are so beautiful, Mara," he said in a soft voice, his eyes shining. "I can want for nothing when you are seated by my side."

She stared at him; eyes wide as she opened her mouth. But no sound escaped her, unable to pull herself from her seat as he caressed her cheek. The great double doors to the throne room burst open, a stoic crowd of knights bustling in. They came to stand before her and Adrian, seated above them all.

In the center, held at sword point on all sides and bound by black metal cuffs, were her four companions. They were all bloodied, bruised and half conscious. One of the knights held El from her hair, another's sword pushing into Cyfrin's flesh and drawing blood.

"*No!*" she thought, eyes wild as she fought to move. "*No, please! Don't do this!*"

But she was standing now, pulled forward like a puppet on strings and unable to break the grip. There was suddenly something heavy in her hands. She looked

I.A. TAKERIAN

down to see King Grathiel's great sword glinting in her grasp, sharp enough to cut the wings from a fly. She was drawn to El, whimpering on her knees against the marble floor.

The sword raised in Mara's hands as she fought furiously against it, screaming in her head. Her arms drew downwards, the blade slicing clean through El's neck. Her head fell to the ground, rolling across the marble and dousing everything in blood.

The crowd cheered, Adrian's voice loudest of all. Kain stared furiously at her, betrayed. She raised the sword a second time, slashing through Kain's neck with ease as his head fell to the floor with wet thud.

"*It's not real!*" she thought against the frantic fearful panic forcing her heart into fits. "*It's an illusion! It's not real!*" She stared down at Milios, stormy eyes sad as they met hers.

"Please, Mara," they breathed as she raised the sword again. "Please, you don't have to do this. You can fight this. Please-" She cut their pleading short, sending their head crashing to the ground in one fell sweep.

Mara was shaking, tears cascading down her face as she stood finally above Cyfrin. He gazed up at her from his knees with a calm acceptance in his eyes. He offered her a small smile as the sword swung high.

"I love you, my Dawnbringer," he breathed as the sword slammed through his neck.

His eyes rolled, blood flying across Mara's face from his open neck. She felt like she was dying. Her breath was coming in shaky gasps, her entire body nearly convulsing as something hot mixed with her tears rolling down her cheeks. She looked down, watching blood fall to the ground below her from her face. The sword vanished from her hands in a plume of smoke.

294

A PROPHECY OF UNDONE

There was laughter all around, Adrian on his feet clapping as the Delinvalians cheered.

Mara's legs buckled, falling to her knees as the tears continued to rain. It was hopeless. All was lost without them. She had worked so hard to grow strong, to defeat the enemy that was to come. And she had been the villain the entire time. The monster they sought so desperately to destroy.

The world began to spin, her heartbeat high in her throat.

There was a great crackling sound, followed by a resounding *boom*. The earth around Mara shook and cracked, a flash of blue light slamming into the ground before her. Wind whipped around her in an instant, pulling her up and out of the way. The Reflector Beast shrieked. Cyfrin stood from the crater he had created in the ground, his eyes flashing with lightning as he faced Mara. The dome of darkness wavered, then vanished in a cloud of thick smoke.

Cyfrin's electric eyes zipped across her body, settling on the look of panic still strewn across her sweating face. He stepped to the side as a ball of black magic shot by him, the Reflector Beast's roars echoing around the forest. It had shifted back to its original, vibrating black form, the void under its hood swirling violently. Mara kept her eyes from it, scared to be sucked back into the all-too-real illusion she had just been trapped within.

Kain charged forward, swinging at the beast with a flurry of great slashes. The sword connected, drifting through the monster as if it was made only of shadow. The beast moved in eerie, unnatural dashes, whipping behind Kain, and sending him flying across the clearing. Milios conjured a tornado of lashing wind, El tossing a glistening pink potion into its depths.

I.A. TAKERIAN

The air instantly began to flash with a violently pink glow, thundering towards the beast and whipping it high. Cyfrin raised a hand towards the sky where the Reflector Beast hung suspended, shrieking in fury. A pillar of white-hot lightning shot from the clouds above, ramming through the beast with a flash of unbridled power.

The beast vanished in a cloud of black smoke, reappearing out of nothingness before Cyfrin. An arm shot out from the beast's chest, grabbing Cyfrin by the throat and raising him into the air. Cyfrin sent lighting down the arm, the sky above them rumbling with deadly warning. Mara could feel his control on his power wavering down the bond, could feel his grip on his conscious state of being slowly ebbing.

The beast was cackling madly as the lighting was met with nothing but smoke, the dark tendril around Cyfrin's neck growing thicker as he sputtered.

Kain and El flew towards the beast from opposite sides, sword and acid-laced hands held high. There was a sickening *crack* as a wall of darkness shot from the beast's body, slamming in to Kain and El and dropping them stunned to the ground where they stood.

Milios dove at them from above, wind slashing wildly about them as they flew. The beast raised a hand at the last moment, slashing through Milios' magick and into their arm. Blood spattered across the earth as they flew backwards into a thick tree. Strikes of lightning were beginning to crash to the ground around them, cracking and frying the earth where they hit.

Mara looked to Kain and El, still held fast by dark magick yards away. To Milios, who looked dazed as they tried to pull themselves from the cracked tree trunk. The two Hopefuls cowered in a huddle together, staring with wide eyes at Mara as the lightning crashed closer to them.

296

A PROPHECY OF UNDONE

The crackling magick erupting from Cyfrin was doing nothing to the beast, slipping with a great sizzling din through its smokey body as it squeezed the last breaths from him. Mara's dagger was suddenly in her hand, face resolute as she charged forward. Heat sputtered to life in her core, roaring in her ears with furious intent. It felt white-hot, laced with the same panic she had felt during her first trial with Elise. When their lives had been at stake.

Golden light surrounded her hands as the Beasts arm extended to stop her, the strikes of lightning growing thicker and more powerful as Cyfrin struggled. There was a bright flash, blinding as it threw the clearing into golden relief.

The black magick that erupted from the beast glanced off Mara as if she was surrounded by a brilliant shield. It dropped Cyfrin as she closed the remaining distance, all three of its limbs reaching out to fire at her. She stabbed at the beast's chest, twisting the dagger as she felt it drive through true flesh.

Black smoke exploded from the beast, slamming into Mara with so much force that it felt like her ribs cracked. She shot back through the air, landing hard on the ground yards away. The beast had thrown everyone away from it, smoke whipping in a frenzy about its body as it screamed to the Beyonds.

Through the thick cover of darkness, Mara could just make out what looked like a hole in its chest, black sludge oozing from it. The fluid hit the grass, sizzling, and disintegrating it on impact. The beast launched into the air, shooting past the treetops in seconds. The cloud of smoke that enshrouded him vanished beyond the grey cover above them, the noise of its screaming still echoing through the wood.

Cyfrin was at her side, his expression dark. He helped

I.A. TAKERIAN

her sit up, the world still spinning around her from the impact. There was a deep purple bruise in the shape of the beasts twisted hand circling Cyfrin's throat, blood dripping from his head and a deep cut beneath his eye. He grabbed her face in his hands, staring intently.

She understood his voiceless command from the look he gave her: Don't ever do that again.

She nodded, her cheeks tingling beneath his hands as their companions joined them. Milios' arm was bleeding freely, El trying to hurriedly mend it with her already-strained healing magicks. Kain was covered in deep gashes, blood spattering across the armor on his chest. They all looked solemn, eyeing the sky nervously for the beast to re-appear.

The Hopefuls were standing a few feet away from them, still holding one another as they shook. Cyfrin helped Mara to her shaky feet, taking her dagger gingerly from her hand to examine the black blood that still dripped down the blade. She offered a small smile to the petrified Hopefuls, neither of whom returned it.

"You saved me," The black-haired Hopeful said so softly that Mara barely caught it. "You...why?"

She shrugged, still not fully sure herself. She motioned to the two of them, to herself, then to her four companions glowering at them. "*We're all in this together,*" she thought, hoping they understood her point.

The black-haired Hopeful's eyes widened, his bottom lip quivering. He gulped, turning to his red-headed friend. "I can't do this, Basil," he whispered. "It's not right. None of this is right."

"Be silent, Henry," Basil hissed at him, looking fearfully between Kain and Cyfrin. "You'll see us both killed!"

"I would've been killed already, if it wasn't for her!" Henry cried back, tearing himself from Basil's grip and

A PROPHECY OF UNDONE

rushing forward to Mara. Cyfrin moved to intercept him, his expression deadly. But Mara held out a hand, stopping him.

All four of them continued to glare as Henry flew past them, coming to kneel before Mara. He was trembling, tears falling from his face to the grass below. "Your highness, I beg your forgiveness," He began, bowing his forehead to the ground at her feet. "But I must speak. I should've spoken sooner but I...We were made aware of a plot most heinous against you and the people of the Hidden Village."

"Silence, you *fool!*" Basil shrieked, stepping forward. But he was stopped short, looking petrified once more as Kain placed the tip of his great sword to his chest.

Mara stared down at Henry, a cold sweat breaking out across her neck. He looked up at her slowly, his eyes brimming with tears and his face screwed up in pain. "When your highness defeated Filigro during the first trial, it caused great outcry amongst those who would wish to see you gone." His voice strangled around his cries. "None more distraught than Filigro's eldest brother, Aro. He... The pain of his loss tormented him, driving him to *madness*, my lady. He..He...Oh." His voice trailed off as a sob shook him. Cyfrin kicked his leg hard, glowering as he pulled a yelp from Henry's lips.

Henry steadied himself as best he could, returning his eyes to Mara's. "The night before we left aboard the Red Froth, we met Aro at the Darkmoor tavern. I knew he wasn't doing well. His own mother had come to us asking to check on him. To try and pull him from his misery. But Aro is beyond grief. Beyond *reason*. He...He made us swear not to tell anyone." He stared helplessly at her. "But you aren't at all what I expected you to be."

His voice had dropped to a whisper, the little remaining

299

I.A. TAKERIAN

color in his face vanishing. "You are kind, and caring, and strong…You saved me. Saved my life." He gulped. "There is a great army that has amassed outside the borders of the Forgotten Woods, covering the Deep Walk with their dark forces. Grathiel's army knows that you are here, but they cannot get inside to retrieve you. None can, without being invited in by those of us who call it home. And so…So Aro plans on meeting with the dark knight that leads their forces."

His eyes closed, fresh tears falling. "He told us he was going to lead them into the woods. That he was going to use their invasion to turn the tide of the people in the village, to show how unworthy and ill-suited you are. And finally take the throne in Filigro's name."

Movement erupted all around her. Milios raised their arms into the air, lips moving, and eyes closed as wind whipped up and out of sight past the trees. Kain lunged forward, punching Basil square in the face. His head snapped back, collapsing unconscious to the ground. Cyfrin's eyes sparked to life, his hands waving before him. Vines twisted around Basil and Henry, binding them together as Henry continued to sob.

"I'm so sorry!" he cried, panic-stricken. "I never wanted to hurt anyone!"

There was strange pulling sensation starting at Mara's back. She felt it grip to her insides, forcing her backwards into what felt like a very small tube. The air left her as she was squeezed with great force and speed from all sides. She recognized the feeling at once. She was being travelled somewhere.

The ground steadied beneath her feet, rocking slightly, and she heard the great clatter of the ocean rush around her. She opened her eyes, her companions appearing on the deck beside her and the two bound Hopefuls.

300

A PROPHECY OF UNDONE

They were all standing aboard the Red Froth, swaying gently in the waves of the island's dock. Drake stood before them; his dark face distorted with rage like Mara had never seen it.

"If this is a joke," he growled. "Then I will make a new coat from the strips of skin I flay from your bodies."

CHAPTER 31
UPON OCEAN'S MIGHTY STEAD

Drake continued to glower at them each in turn, taking in their gaunt looks and pulling a flask from the inside of his cloak. He tossed it at Kain, standing closest to him. "Drink. Now," he commanded, motioning for Kain to pass it down as he took a swig.

It passed to Milios, to El, then to Mara who took a drink and grimaced. It tasted like grass and dirt, grit clinging to her teeth as it oozed slowly down her throat. Cyfrin finished off the flask, handing it back to the furious Drake.

"Speak," he barked.

Mara opened her mouth, surprising herself as a small noise escaped. All five of them began to talk at once, the loud voices clashing with another as Drake cringed. He raised a hand angrily, grinding his teeth. He pointed to Cyfrin.

"*You* speak," he clarified as the rest of them fell mute.

"It's Filigro's brother," Cyfrin said hurriedly. "He's planning on going to the Deep Walk. To let in Grathiel's

303

I.A. TAKERIAN

forces and lead the dark knight's legion. He intends to burn down the village before he sees it in Mara's hands."

Drake's face went emotionless, somehow more terrifying than the look of fury a moment before. "How do you know this?" Mara could have sworn she saw dim purple light flash within his red eyes.

Cyfrin kicked Basil, who was tied against Henry at his feet. He yelped and Drake was on them in an instant.

He crouched an inch away from Basil's face, nowhere for him to escape. "Then it is *your* flesh that will make my new cloak," he growled, Basil whimpering softly under the heat of his stare. Drake stood, walking to the edge of the ship as he waved his hand behind him.

The crew began running around, closing latches, and hoisting the sails. Four of them ran forward, grabbing the vine-tied Hopefuls from the ground. Mara watched as they dragged them to the base of the mast, binding them against it with the black, vibrating chains wrapped around the wood. Drake leaned over the rail, teetering dangerously close to falling. He seemed to be speaking to the ocean.

Mara felt like she was dreaming, still trapped within the beast's illusion. She pinched herself hard to prove she wasn't, wincing against the pain. The ship lurched beneath them, ripping away from the dock, and rocketing forward. The wind whipped against her face as they flew, her feet held to the deck by what she could only assume was magick.

Drake returned to them, face set in stone. "Send a message to Caerani," he said in a low voice to Milios. "Warn her. Tell her we are coming."

Milios nodded before closing their eyes and murmuring to thin air.

Drake turned to face the direction they were headed.

A PROPHECY OF UNDONE

"The Brisenbane is going to get us there as quickly as she can. Pray that we arrive before they do."

"They're coming for me," Mara said, and they all turned to look at her. "That's all they want. Me."

"Aye, and they'll not have you," Cyfrin growled.

Drake nodded grimly. "There's nothing to fear. We outpower them, even if they outman us." But Mara could hear the hesitation in his voice, like he didn't fully believe his own words. "Who is the dark knight that leads them?"

Mara's companions froze. She felt sick to her stomach. She wasn't ready to face the very-1real possibility that Adrian was at the forefront of this charge. "He's my friend. He was my *only* friend." Her throat closed around the word, tears stinging her eyes.

Drake gave one final, solemn nod. "At this pace, we'll be at the cliffs within a few hours. If Aro's already entered the woods, we'll mount our defenses and re-enforce the wards at the village edge."

"And if they have already invaded?" Milios voiced the question they were all thinking.

Drake's brow furrowed. "Then we shall launch from this ship and rain fiery death upon them all," he replied darkly, gazing out towards the horizon as they sped along. "Zenoths help them if they reach the village first. They'll find no mercy from our general."

Mara watched a shiver run through her comrades at the thought of Caerani, enraged and shielding the Hidden Village. A dragon protecting her brood.

It was a terrifying thought.

Drake turned his eyes back to Mara, frowning. His knuckles wrapped along the lid of Tim's box. "You are not incorrect, you know," he said, raising an eyebrow. "They *are* coming for you."

Mara felt pain rip through her once more. The thought

of the entire beautiful haven she now called home burning to the ground with all her people inside…It was too much. She dropped her eyes to the ground, flinching.

"And you can choose to stay on this ship, safe and well-kept till we extinguish the threat," Drake went on. Mara glanced up to see the ghost of a smile tugging at his lips. "Or, you can take up arms with us, as you've been trained to. And you can show those pompous bastards exactly who you are. Show them the light they tried your whole life to extinguish."

Mara blinked up at him. She thought back across all those days training with Adrian, her only escape in her misplaced existence. She saw his face smiling at her, and she felt her heart throb with another wave of misery. This would not be like their sparring sessions. It wasn't practice they would be engaged in this time, and she felt a flash of panic at the thought of having to use magick against him.

No. I would never resort to that. He would never make me. He will listen to me. He **has** *to.* If she could make him see how wrong they were about everything, then perhaps he would fight beside her in the coming war.

Perhaps then, he would stay.

THE TRIP back to the cliffside was rough. Though magick held them firmly to the boards of the deck, the wind still lashed hard against their faces, stripping them raw and trying to force them backwards. Milios attempted to ease the flow of air, but it was of little help.

The sun was rising over the water's edge, casting a dim glow through the storm clouds above. Mara would have

A PROPHECY OF UNDONE

been exhausted from their encounters and lack of sleep, but the panic and anxious anticipation of what was to come kept her wide awake.

No one spoke, but the five of them stood nearly shoulder to shoulder the entire journey. The thought of confrontation with Cyfrin had completely left her head, replaced entirely by the dim roar of overwhelming emotion racing through her. These were people she knew, people she had grown up with. And they, like herself, had been lied to about nearly everything. Tucked away behind their marble walls, in their white city.

It made Mara sick.

Drake suddenly leaned against the rail, squinting into the distance. His eyes widen. "Zenoths golden fucking blood."

Through the foggy morning air, shadowed by the dense cloud cover, Mara could just barely make out the silhouette of the great cliffs protecting the village from the waters reach. Immense gatherings of smoke were erupting into the sky from the top, joining with the stormy clouds and creating a swirling area of darkness above the village. As they stared, a swirling inferno of fire exploded into the air from the training fields. An echoing **boom** raised the hairs on Mara's skin.

"Ready yourselves!" Drake yelled to the crew, marching away from the rail where they stood. He began barking orders as they raced towards the dock, the crew flying about them through their yelling.

El turned to face Mara, looking disquieted. "Mara…" she began, wringing her hands together and biting her lip. "I know what Drake said. And I know you want to help, but…"

"But you should stay here in the captain's cabin," Kain finished the sentence for her, looking more serious than

307

I.A. TAKERIAN

Mara had ever seen him. "If they're able to take you and can manage to get you out of the woods...I'm not sure if we'll be able to get you back. Not without heavy casualty."

Mara stared between the two of them, incredulous. "I am the reason the village *burns!*" she cried out, louder than she had intended. El flinched and Kain grimaced against her anger. "Grathiel's forces, Mezilmoth's beasts, Adrian... they come for *me* alone. They were only able to enter because of the pain I caused Filigro's family, and there's no denying that," she finished sharply, as El looked like she might interrupt. "I will not sit cowering in a hiding place while my people *die* in my stead. We fight as one, or we fall as one."

A hush fell through her as Cyfrin's hand grasped her shoulder. "You will not die here today, Dawnbringer," he said, the gentle tone to his voice silencing the anxiety within her for a moment. "I would be honored to fight beside you. I will protect you with every piece of me."

They were pulling up against the dock, Drake returning to their side. He had pulled both swords from his person, gripping them tightly as he stared up at the cliffside. The five of them unsheathed their weapons alongside him.

"Milios," Drake said quietly, his tone deathly calm. "Get us up there."

Milios nodded once, waving their hands in great arks about them. The wind whipped into a frenzy, creating a gust beneath each of their feet that began to rocket them upwards. Mara's hands were clammy, gripping her dagger. The smoke stung her eyes and throat as they shot towards the cliffside. The six of them landed on solid ground, taking in the scene before them.

The training field was on fire. The war tents surrounding the outside were smoldering on the scorched

A PROPHECY OF UNDONE

earth, the ground completely black and crystallized in places. The woods had great patches of flame scattered throughout, the smoke nearly impossible to see through past a few yards. Screams echoed in the distance. There was another earth-shattering **boom** and flames cascaded out from a spot by the war tents.

There were at least two hundred Delinvalian soldiers gathered here, Mara only recognizing them from the emblems etched in their armor. Everything else about them was inhuman, dark, and twisted as corruption changed the very core of who they were. They fought with swords and bursts of dark magick, falling like ash to the ground as the pillar of swirling fire lashed out at a few closest to it. The blazing vortex died off, revealing the slender woman at its center.

Caerani was dressed in full war-gear, the red metal covering her entire body flashing venomously in the blaze around the fields. She had a massive lance-like sword in one hand, fire etching across the black blade as it poured from her palms. Her other hand was outstretched, shooting balls of flame at the encroaching crowd. She roared as a blast of fire blasted forth from her palm, dropping an entire row of corrupted soldiers in a line before her. Dark magick shot towards her from several places, colliding with her armor and nearly buckling her as she was forced to take several steps back.

Ominous energy ripped around Mara, reaching out from beside her. She spun around, backing in to Cyfrin. Drake was surrounded in a black aura. It was stretching his features, distorting him in odd ways as his blades became nothing but thick black smoke. His eyes were glowing purple, raw magick slashing at the air around him as he shot forward with impossible speed.

He rammed through the gathering crowd of soldiers,

I.A. TAKERIAN

sending ten flying with one slash of his swords. Their bodies tore apart in midair, barely leaving time for them to scream. Drake was beside Caerani, her fiery sword reducing the three nearest them to ash. Mara stared in disbelief at the magick tearing from Drake.

It was growing, the darkness reaching up around him and creating a horned silhouette shadowing his body. She remembered back to their conversation on the ship, when he had told her he couldn't use magick. But, no...no, it had been *her* to suggest he couldn't. And he had neither confirmed nor denied it in his answer.

Milios shot into the air, darting towards the forest, and attempting to extinguish the uncontrollable blaze tearing through the trees. Mara could hear screaming and explosions from the village beyond. A group of eighty dark soldiers had noticed them, racing across the fields with warped roars as they raised their weapons high.

Mara dipped her chin, allowing the angry heat in her core to burst forth. The golden light surrounded her hands faster than it ever had before, engulfing her blade. Cyfrin lunged forwards into the crowd. Kain let out a great battle cry, joining Cyfrin as his crackling lightning ripped through the crowd.

El gave Mara one final look of resignation before they too shot forward into the fray of light and dark magicks.

310

CHAPTER 32
ABLAZE

The enemy forces seemed endless. Mara couldn't figure out how they were growing so rapidly in numbers, each fallen body replaced by three, four, five more. Her gold-lit dagger flashed as she drove deep into their backlines. She recognized the armor on some of the corrupted soldiers, many of them having grown up with her within the walls of the castle. But none of their faces were their own, horribly stretched and contorted; the chaos inside of them mutating rapidly.

Her dagger sunk through body after body, a blur as she weaved and dodged. Through the crowd around her there were bright flashes of blue lightning, twisting their way from one target to the next. It dropped charred, foaming corpses in its wake, leaving long streaks of warm tingling down her body whenever they glanced off her. She could hear the sizzling of flesh as El threw acid rain down upon them, Mara sunk too low in the rear of their forces to be hit by the poison. Kain was somewhere in the middle of the ever-growing crowd, tossing bodies with his great sword and roaring over their shrieks.

I.A. TAKERIAN

Dark magick whizzed past her from all sides, stinging as it grazed her body. She could see thin burns sprouting up all over her flesh, every place the dark bolts touched her. She shot out of the crowd, close to the path that led to the village. The ground shook as she whirled around to stare into the enemies gathered in the fields.

Though a great majority of them wore the glinting metal armor of Delinvalian knights, a growing portion of them were not any form of man at all. Scattered throughout the thrashing mass of soldiers, screeching as they flailed bolts of darkness out of their bodies, were darklings. Huge, lurking creatures, blended in with the smokey energy of the corrupted knights.

Kain and Cyfrin noticed at the same time. Kain leapt backwards out of the crowd; Cyfrin shot a flurry of white lightning from his body. He backed away towards Kain, whose body angled slightly before El as the enemies closed in. The darkling's magick was much more potent than that of the corrupted knights. They had all witnessed firsthand what even a glancing blow from the darkness could do to a person. Her companions backed up towards the cliffside, weapons and magick raised towards the encroaching forces. Mara made to run forward to them.

There was a mighty *boom*, the earth beneath the corrupted forces splitting with the force. It shook them to a halt, a great shadow stretching ominously across the fields. Mara saw long horns curving above the growing darkness, a low growl rumbling through their feet. Her eyes flew to the base of the shadow, to the figure flying towards the crowd with blades outstretched.

Drake was surrounded in a pitch-black aura, his features indiscernible beyond the flashing purple lights she knew were his eyes. She saw the ocean over the cliffside roar, a massive wave rushing forth in time with Drake. He

A PROPHECY OF UNDONE

shot through the crowd, the shadow rising. The air went cold with the energy and there was another mighty *boom*.

The ground below Mara cracked, her feet almost giving way with the motion. Droves of the corrupted creatures exploded, throwing fluids and parts everywhere as they burst. They fell in a huge half circle, arcing out from Drake who stood motionless amid the crowd. There was a deafening ***fwoom*** as fire shot skyward out of Caerani again, blazing some of the still-growing crowd into ash around her.

Drake's shadow tendrils were thrashing wildly, like a kraken trapped inland. It lashed out at everything near it. The corrupted knights and darklings, Kain, Cyfrin and El at the cliffside, and Mara by the forest's edge. It had no prejudice as it sliced and burned through everything it could, the low rumbling still trembling from the ground below it.

Mara cried out, leaping back as one tendril shot at her, slapping her across the arms as she raised them in defense. Her bracer tore like wet cotton, the leather thudding to the ground as they completely fell away. She could feel warmth running down her forearms as she leapt back from the shadows, knowing it was blood. She bared her teeth against the pain, watching her three comrades dive away from the lashing darkness. She glanced down at the gashes running the full length of both her arms. They were incredibly deep for how light the initial blow had felt, and her eyes widened a little in shock.

Drake crouched, the horned shadow concentrating in around him for a moment before he launched back into the air. He landed in the space of a heartbeat beside Caerani, like a zombie guard as he mindlessly lashed at the creatures surrounding her.

Mara rushed forward through the opening Drake had

313

I.A. TAKERIAN

created in the crowd. Cyfrin reached out and pulled her forward as the gap surged shut with the new wave of men. He spun her behind his body, locking her between the cliffside and him as his hand flashed. He sent a wave of lightning rocketing into the crowd, its bolts cascading through the bodies as it ripped them apart from the inside. Mara put her hand against the small of Cyfrin's back, his gaze flicking over his shoulder at her.

She bent under his outstretched arms, aiming her palm towards the creatures nearest to them. The heat in her core burned with power, crashing against her insides harder than it ever had before. She felt super charged, the hair on the back of her neck standing on end as the magick burst from her palm.

A beam of golden light shot towards the dark forces, but it was different than its usual form. Instead of tiny stars cascading off the beam, there were small pops of glittering explosions erupting from it. The sparks flew into the crowd, burning through flesh as they went. The beam burst six men into golden ash, sparkling dimly as it flew into the smoke surrounding them.

Every time they took out one man, it was as if ten more took his place. There was barely any space between them and the dark things, their feet inching dangerously close to the cliffside as they fought like caged animals. Mara could faintly see Caerani through the army, no longer engulfed in her tornado of fire.

She had driven her great sword through the earth before her, gripping the hilt with both hands as Drake's chaos form kept the forces back from her. Mara realized that the ornately twisting helmet Caerani wore, covering her entire face in golden red metal, ended in two horns atop her crown. They were nearly identical to the ominous shadow aura that currently consumed Drake.

314

A PROPHECY OF UNDONE

The earth beneath them began to tremble, shaking the cliffside and sending loose rocks crashing to the violent waves below. Caerani was ablaze with a strange, dark purple fire. It whipped viciously skyward, a roar ripping through the air as she drew her sword from the earth. She held it high above her head, screaming as thunder rolled in the sky. There was a crashing **boom**, and fire exploded from her.

It burst in a great circle, covering the entire field in an instant as it burned. Cyfrin drew Mara further back behind himself as it rushed for them, El crying out. But the flames curved around them in a great ark as they torched the throngs of darklings and soldiers.

Their screams mixed with the black smoke, horrifying in its energy as the ground continued to quake. The fire did not stop till the entirety of the crowd had been reduced to ash, piles of it now whipping up in the winds. Caerani stumbled, leaning on her sword as she nearly toppled.

The shadows around Drake writhed. He gave a howling cry that sounded metallic, distorted. He shot into the blazing forest, the horned shadow disappearing with him as he went.

They met Caerani halfway across the blackened field. The fire had burnt deep cracks of shimmering dark purple in the ground, the piles of ash still swirling through the air.

"What happened to Drake?" Mara asked, staring at the blaze in the smoldering trees where he had crashed through.

Caerani removed her helmet, shaking her long white braid loose. Her face was smeared with black soot and flecks of blood. "That is a very long, very sad story that we have no time for right now. Drake's body lays host to a tremendous amount of chaos magick. A curse, trapping the shadows inside of him."

315

I.A. TAKERIAN

She said it so matter of fact. Like she was discussing the weather, or the state of the grounds. "He's able to keep the beast it manifests inside of him at bay, for the most part. It's gotten much easier for him with age, time, training. He's worked his ass off for the better part of six centuries, trying to get it completely under control. It becomes harder for him when we...while, when *I* am in danger."

"He'll be wandering the woods for the next week to shed that shell off him," Kain said, shaking his head in disapproval.

Cyfrin punched his shoulder hard, glaring. "You knew?! You knew he was a chaos beast?!"

Kain raised his hands defensively. "He threatened me with *horrible* things if I ever told! He only told *me* because of how well I hold my own using no magick at all. I told him how much I idolized him for fighting with no magick abilities, and he told me of his plight. And it wasn't my place to tell!"

"He didn't look human," Mara murmured, and Caerani's eyes flashed.

"He's not entirely," she said, her voice cold. "That shadow being takes control of him, makes him lose focus on everything but the need to kill. Or, in my case, protect. At all costs."

Her final words were weighted, sitting heavy about them. Mara could still see Drake's blackened, ominous form in her mind, his face a void with glowing eyes. He had been so mindless in his attacks, narrowed down, as Caerani said, to just the need to kill. And the need to protect her. There were noises coming from the forest path behind them, drawing their attention from where Drake had gone to the mouth of the trail.

A crowd of screaming, terrified villagers burst forth

316

A PROPHECY OF UNDONE

into the blackened fields. They were all covered in varying degrees of soot and ash, some clearly wounded as they began running towards them. Many of them were reduced to sobs. Behind them were a few of the older warriors and failed Hopefuls from this year's Trials. They were blasting magick through the tree line as they dove backwards into the field. Mara saw Elise among them, eyes wild and face bloodied as she whipped magick bolts loose.

The crowd of villagers gathered behind the five of them, cowering and crying as a nightmarish creature crashed out of the woods off the path.

It looked like three corrupted knights, fused together into a mesh of pulsing flesh and metal. Magick blasted forth from an arm that jutted straight out of its stomach, flying towards the warriors fighting to keep them back. It collied with one of the failed Hopefuls as they all doze out of the way, stopping him midair. His skin turned black, his eyes swelling and looking near to bursting in his skull. He gave a great shudder, then collapsed dead to the ground.

Caerani and Kain roared in unison, following at Cyfrin's heals as he shot instantly towards the monster. El positioned herself between the crowd of villagers and the battle, hands glowing green. Mara took a step forward, ready to dive into combat. But someone grabbed her arm, stopping her.

She turned to face one of the villagers, who she recognized vaguely from one of their many nights drinking and dancing in the village. His eyes were watering, shaking from head to toe as he stared at her with a strange look.

"I have to," he whispered around a shuddering sob, gripping tighter to her. "He told me that if I did it, he would spare my family. Spare *us*. You must understand that. You must. I'm so sorry."

Mara felt a chill run down her spine. The man was

317

I.A. TAKERIAN

reaching for something, and every nerve in her body sounded off at once. She made to tug out of his grip, El lunging forward as she cried out. But the man had flung a small vial of dark red liquid at Mara's feet. It shattered, releasing red smoke into the air around her.

She heard a crack behind her, heard Cyfrin screaming her name. But the world gave a shuddering lurch, throwing her off her feet as she flew through the air. She knew this feeling well now.

Whatever had been in that potion bottle was travelling her. She was being whisked off the battlefield and away, into the dark unknown as the magick threw her uncontrollably forward.

CHAPTER 33
LIGHT AND DAWN

Mara's knees collided with ashen ground, her head throbbing. The world slowed to a halt around her. The smoke was thicker here, the screams sounding desperately close as they ripped through the dense black air. She couldn't tell where she was through the glowing blaze of fiery smog, barely able to make out her hand inches from her face. She stumbled blindly forward, cupping her arm around her mouth to muffle the poisonous intake.

Mara could see sunlight ahead, the wind pushing towards her and clearing the air slightly as she hurried towards it. She emerged into semi-clearness, whirling around to get a full view of the damage beyond.

The village was completely engulfed in smoke and flames. Dark figures were rushing forth from the forest on all sides, and she could see flashes of magick lighting up the suffocating air all through the streets. She turned back to face the forests edge, watching darklings clawing their way through the underbrush as they ran alongside the stragglers of Grathiel's forces. Her eyes moved across the

319

I.A. TAKERIAN

tree line, scanning to get a count on how many there were rushing in. It was a truly staggering amount.

Her stare stopped atop the hillside ahead. Her eyes went wide, a cry ripping unstoppably from her chest. There he was, silhouetted by the sunlight and smoke of battle as he glared out towards the village. He looked like a conquering king, menacing and powerful.

"Adrian!" Mara cried.

He stopped dead. His handsome features were gaunt and drawn, as if he hadn't slept in weeks. But his eyes were filled with nothing but pulsating hatred, his armor drenched in Odelian blood. It dripped from his sword in long, thick streams and Mara felt a sob tear from her. He looked nothing like the boy she had seen mere months ago. Her last image of his face, smirking at her as he bade her goodnight, flashed before her eyes. She had watched his back as he walked away from her down the hall, tilting his head for her to catch his smirk.

There was not even a hint of that man here.

He was looking at her as if he didn't believe she was real. He lowered his sword, blinking furiously as the black smoke surrounding it dissipated. He took several steps down the hill towards her. The sounds of battle, of the screams and blasting of magick, ebbed away suddenly. There was a loud ringing in her ears, threatening. Warning her as Adrian approached.

"Mara..?" His voice was hoarse and distant. As if it had not been used in weeks. Mara felt tears brimming in her eyes as he reached for her. His hand grazed her arm and he pulled it back as if shocked. "I...we thought...are you hurt?" His eyes darted wildly across the white scars along her face, the blood leaking from cuts all over her.

She shook her head, grasping his free hand in hers. Tears flowed freely down her cheeks. "Adrian, please," she

A PROPHECY OF UNDONE

pleaded. The screams and cries of the Odelian filled the space between them. "These people are not our enemies! Please you must *listen* to me, Adrian!"

She grabbed his face between her hands. His expression looked suddenly relaxed and even a little calm as she held him. She was struggling to find the right words to say. "We've been lied to, my dear friend. Please, you must call off the forces and listen to me!" She breathed the words; her voice strangled against her tears.

It all tumbled forth from her. Mara had spent so many nights now thinking of what she might say to him if she had the chance. How she could break all of this to him, in a way where he might understand. Here, in the heat of battle and bloodshed, was hardly what she had imagined. He had to listen, though. She needed to make him listen.

But something had shifted in his eyes while she explained. His face became twisted with a mixture of anger and disgust. It reminded Mara of his expression in the Tide Master's illusion and she shrank away slightly.

"Your uncle was right." His voice sounded wrong. Like it was echoing from inside her head. "They've enchanted you. Ensnared you. ***Bewitched you***."

Mara made to draw away, the dark smoke beginning to encompass him once more. But Adrian had grabbed her wrist, the skin his long fingers wrapped around burning like a brand. She cried out as it sent a shock of pain through her.

The smoke seemed to drown out the noise around them, leaving her with only the vibrant ringing even as the Delinvalian soldiers raged past. Adrian began pulling her towards the forest's edge, away from the battle. Kain's words from aboard the Red Froth echoed in her head. "*If they can get you into the woods, I'm not sure how we'll save you.*"

Mara struggled and pulled and yelled, but it was no

I.A. TAKERIAN

use. He held her with some sort of dark magick, her flesh sizzling against his palm as he dragged her to the trees. There was a roaring behind them, and a bolt of white-hot magic shot past Mara's right ear. It hit Adrian square between the shoulder blades. He faltered, and Mara was able to twist her wrist out of his grip. She stumbled backwards and slammed into something hard. The smell of pine and honey surrounded her and Cyfrin had her by the shoulders, spinning her around. His eyes were still glowing as they raced across her face, down her body. The runes on his skin started beaming bright white. He grabbed her arm and his stare fell on the spot Adrian had gripped so tightly.

There was a searing red burn wrapping around her wrist, in the exact shape of Adrian's hand.

The air around them grew cold. Cyfrin's expression became that of deathly calm. "Listen to me." His voice rocked through her. "I know you want to fight. And you can, you've proven that, but right now I need you to *run*. Find Caerani, El, Kain. They'll protect you."

Mara's eyes grew wide. She could see Adrian turning slowly to face them over his shoulder. "I...I can't," she breathed, her eyes transfixed on the face of her best friend, so unrecognizable with the darkness now surrounding him. He looked hollow.

"You can, and you will," Cyfrin said, shaking her gently. His eyes were sadly knowing. Like he understood exactly how much it pained her to see what Adrian had become. "If you're taken, if they're able to bring you back to that place...everything we've done, all of this will have been for nothing. You're the last hope for us all, Mara."

A dark tendril shot from Adrian like an arrow. Cyfrin's eyes flashed, and he threw out his hand, his blue magick blasting forth to intercept it. They crashed together and sent dark blue sparks high into the air.

A PROPHECY OF UNDONE

"Go!" Cyfrin yelled, positioning himself between Adrian and her.

It was an order, not a request. The image of his back to her, standing as her sole guardian against the darkness, was seared into her brain. He had stood just this way so many times before, without a second thought. Mara turned on her heel and began to run.

"You will give her to me!" The voice that came from Adrian was not his own. It was the stuff of nightmares, dripping with cruel intent and malic. Mara felt magick collide with magick behind her again. *"She is mine!"*

"She is no one's but her own," Cyfrin boomed back. "I will not let her be taken again."

Another *crack*. Mara felt the hairs on the back of her neck stand on edge with the energy radiating around them. She ran as fast as she could, choking on her tears as she looked at the once beautiful village.

Everything was burning. The smoke was so dense, she could only make out shapes through it as magick threw flashes of light. Her pulse was like a war drum in her ears, drowning out the screams that cut the air. Cyfrin's words still rang in her head.

"I will not let her be taken again." Cyfrin and the Odelian people had risked everything to find her; to rescue her from the prison King Grathiel had created. Kain, Milios and El's faces swam through her mind, laughing as they had that night around the lake. Dancing and drinking, reveling in the moonlight and Milios' music. Her family-

Mara stopped dead in her tracks.

My family.

Her feet were turning her back, back towards Adrian and Cyfrin.

They came to save me against all odds.

I.A. TAKERIAN

She was running as quickly as she could, blindly slipping through blood and ash.

I tried to escape at every turn. Wanted nothing more than to hurt them. To kill them.

The screams and sounds were growing more and more quiet. Mara tried not to focus on who may be walking out victorious from the raging battle.

And still they took me in. Treated me as if I was I had been with them my whole life. Gifted me with the truth, no matter how difficult.

She skidded to a halt as she came to the clearing at the forest's edge. Oppressive, overpowering darkness stood in a massive dome around the spot Adrian and Cyfrin had been. It trapped all sound and light within its grasp and sent a shiver of warning down Mara's spine. Her feet willed her to turn back, to flee from its might. But Mara was resolute. She grit her teeth and ran forward.

This is what evil felt like.

It made her skin crawl and body ache. She moved blindly through it, wincing as the very air seemed to cut at her. She squinted against it, eyes burning. The muted, stifled atmosphere was dense in her ears, increasing the powerful ringing tenfold. But she could hear something in the distance. Muffled, mighty roars were coming from ahead, and she swore she could see dim flashes of bright blue light cracking through the thick fog. Mara barreled towards it and stepped out suddenly into a pocket of light and sound.

A bubble surrounded Adrian and Cyfrin, the darkness trying desperately to push in. Cyfrin was hunched, his armor torn completely away in places to reveal raw flesh underneath. Blood was streaming steadily down his face, but his stare was steel. Mara looked at Adrian and let out a sob.

His skin was cracked, a thick black slime oozing out of

324

A PROPHECY OF UNDONE

the wounds. His eyes had changed to slits, black as a void, and magick so ominous rolled off him that it made Mara's knees buckle.

Cyfrin turned as she cried out, his mouth agape. And Adrian seized the opportunity as his attention turned from the fight. A shard of darkness slammed into Cyfrin's chest, knocking him to his knees. Mara saw the darkness gathering in a massive spike before Adrian. Cyfrin bared his teeth like a beast with his back to the wall. He raised his hands in defense, even as the glow of his eyes faltered. And Mara knew then that he wouldn't survive the next hit.

Her legs moved before her thoughts caught up. She ran for Cyfrin, her hand outstretched in desperation. The spike shot to kill and Mara threw her arms around his neck, shielding his body with her own.

Time seemed to stop. The air around them became still and Mara felt that even her blood ceased flowing. Cyfrin's scent surrounded her as she buried her face against his neck. There was something building in her chest. It felt like a million dazzling explosions. Like a torrent of flame and lightning setting off in the depths of her soul. This was elation like she had never known, her heart trying to fly out of her chest in its exuberance.

If this was death, she would enter it gladly. She heard Cyfrin's breath catch, the familiar electrical circuit whizzing to life connecting them. Then a force shot through her, and she gasped. Golden white, blinding light erupted from Cyfrin's outstretched hands. It cast what looked like tiny, sparking blue constellations from its beam as it blasted towards Adrian. The softly popping stars hung in the air all around them, looking like the night sky framed against the darkness.

The ground where its sparks touched sprung forth with life, patches of grass and wildflowers popping up all around them through the ash and blood. Lightning shot through the darkness from above, crashing into the earth in a concentrated pattern around Adrian. It obliterated the black spear of darkness and threw them all backwards with a mighty **boom**.

Cyfrin wrapped his arms tightly around Mara as they slammed into the ground, softening her impact. The darkness around them sputtered like a flickering flame. Mara's head spun and she felt her eyelids grow impossibly heavy. Cyfrin unfolded her carefully from his body, kneeling beside her and staring like he had seen a ghost. There was a scream across the clearing from them, and they looked in unison.

Adrian was crouching on the ground, his hands covering his face, black ooze pouring from between his fingers. Mara's vision blurred and the image swam in front of her. She fought the crushing darkness of exhaustion, trying to stay conscious. Cyfrin stood slowly, his body blocking her once more. Adrian screamed again, and the sound was inhumane.

Rage was filling Mara's head, but it was odd; distant and disconnected from the exhaustion now taking her over. She watched as golden white light engulfed Cyfrin's hands, as he broke into a run towards Adrian. The ground underneath his feet cracked as he lunged for him.

Then the world went black.

CHAPTER 34
REBIRTH OF A HEART

CYFRIN

There were noises coming from the forest path behind them, drawing their attention from where Drake had vanished,. to the mouth of the trail. A crowd of screaming, terrified villagers burst forth into the blackened fields. They were all covered in varying degrees of soot and ash, running towards them as a few sobbed. Hot on their tails were a few of the older warriors and failed Hopefuls from this year's trials. They were blasting magick through the tree line, driving backwards into thyfrine field.

Cyfrin swore loudly as a corrupted beast crashed off the path behind them. His eyes flew over its body, fused together in horrible ways by magick. The Delinvalian emblems on their armor were still blaringly clear. Cyfrin flinched at the sight of them, glancing at Mara for her reaction. She was staring at the beast with a look of abject terror and pain.

The villagers hurried behind them, cowering and

I.A. TAKERIAN

crying over the sounds ripping forth from the beast. There was a great wave of energy that washed over Cyfrin, pulling his gaze back to the monster. A ball of dark magick shot forth from its core, rocketing towards the warriors standing to fight. Nearly all of them dove and dodged out of its path, but Cyfrin saw it hurtling towards the slowest of them.

He knew it would collide with him before they could stop it, knew what that level of dark magick would do to his body. He was rushing towards the monster before the warrior even hit the ground. Cyfrin heard Kain and Caerani roar in unison behind him. He sent cracks of angry lightning into the beast. It shrieked. Cyfrin ducked as it flailed wildly towards him.

Kain swung low as he came upon the creature, his sword driving partially through its stomach. It screamed like a stuck pig, black sludge oozing forth from the wound and burning the ashen ground. The hairs on the back of Cyfrin's neck stood on end as there was another powerful wave of magick. He leapt backwards just in time for a burning wall of fire to rocket past him. The monster stumbled backwards, skin crackling under Caerani's power as it let loose another bolt of dark magick. Cyfrin turned, ready to reach out to Mara for her assistance.

But she was nowhere to be seen.

Cyfrin's heart stopped, staring around wildly for her. His eyes fell on the crowd of villagers still cowering in the middle of the field. El was shielding a few of the women sobbing in a huddle on the burned ground. The beast erupted in a wave of dark magick and the three of them were once again forced to leap out of its path. Cyfrin's eyes narrowed, straining towards where Mara stood yards away. He could just make out that one of the villagers had her by the wrist, his face pained.

A PROPHECY OF UNDONE

Something was desperately wrong. As if in slow motion, the villager raised something above his head, slamming it to the ground between Mara and himself. El was running towards her, Mara fighting to pull away. A cloud of dark red smoke plumed around her.

Cyfrin's blood ran cold, panic gripping his pounding heart. He leapt to his feet. **Crack.** Lightning surged beneath him, shooting him forward with arms outstretched. "***Mara!***" he yelled, mere feet from her now.

He watched her head turn to look at him, his fingertips brushing her arm. But he stumbled forward through thin air. Mara was gone, vanished into nothingness by whatever magick still clung to the spot. Her scent, the softness of rosemary and honeysuckle that always signaled her presence to Cyfrin, had disappeared in a flash. It left no trace.

El gasped in horror. Cyfrin looked up at the man now trembling and pale before him. The cold panic in his heart was replaced by white-hot fury and murderous rage. He grabbed the villager by his tunic, raising him straight into the air. He did not fight, hanging limp in Cyfrin's grip as small bolts of lightning lashed from him. They burned thin marks across the villager's body where they touched, and he whimpered softly.

Cyfrin shook him as the other villagers backed away. "*Where. Is. She,*" he demanded, putting emphasis on each word. The power inside of him was roaring, racing from end of him to the other as it scraped just below the surface of his skin. It begged to be released, begged for the blood of the man before him. Cried for the head of whoever had taken its Dawnbringer, *his* Dawnbringer. But Cyfrin forced it back, tiny bolts still crackling off him uncontrollably as he glowered at the man.

The villager shook his head slowly, still crying as he dangled in the air. "I was watering the herb gardens by the

I.A. TAKERIAN

forest when they came," he gasped around Cyfrin's unrelenting grip. "They brought me before a man with black armor and...and *terrible* powers. He turned my friend to rubble right where he stood. Like he was made of soft stone." He was shaking with sobs. "He told me that all of this would stop, that we could all be saved, if...if we just gave him what he came for."

He had breathed the last bit of the sentence, so quietly that Cyfrin nearly missed it through the sounds of the battle behind them. His eyes flashed, a bolt flying from his hands irresistibly and shocking the man. His body convulsed slightly in the air, his eyes starting to roll. Cyfrin bit down hard on his tongue, the pain forcing his control back into focus. The lightning receded slightly, the man groaning.

"Where did the potion send her?" Cyfrin said through gritted teeth, his head throbbing as he fought not only with his power but also his panic. He could feel fear and confusion ripping through the tattooed bond on his hand, resonating from the small sun at his pinky. Wherever she was, Mara was in trouble. The feeling gripped at his heart, throwing pain across his chest. His magick scratched tortuously beneath his skin, raking against the wards.

The man looked dazed, his head rolling on his neck. "Took her...to him," he mumbled, his eyes rolling as he fainted.

Cyfrin dropped him unceremoniously, his body thudding to the ground. He began to run. El was left beside the villagers, her eyes wide with the panic Cyfrin felt coursing through him. He flew past Caerani and Kain, both still attacking the corrupted creature with the warriors.

The burning woods whizzed by as he ran down the path to the village, ignoring the sharp pain in his lungs from the heavy smoke. Mara and him had spoken at great

A PROPHECY OF UNDONE

length about Adrian. Her only friend. Her confidant. Her eyes lit up with such a strange combination of joy and pain when she spoke of him. It nearly broke his heart each time.

Adrian had been the only one to treat Mara with a shred of human decency during her life in Delinval, let alone kindness. Her sword skills had been taught, in large part, by him. She had expressed her concerns about what he, specifically, might think of her being the very thing they were taught to fear. To hate. The thought of her being forced to confront him alone, while his mind was sick with the corruption, was making Cyfrin nauseated.

Mara's tattoo shot a bolt of agony up his arm, and he cursed loudly. He felt power wash through him, calmer than the lightning still threatening to rip him apart. His palms angled towards the ground, a wave of energy rushing out of them and into the earth. The ground beneath him trembled, pieces of rock springing up underneath each footfall and tossing him forward with great force.

He was moving faster than he ever had before through the cobblestone streets of the Hidden Village. Buildings all around him were ablaze, places he had known his whole life now piles of rubble amongst the ash. The air was so thick with smoke that even with his excellent vision, it was impossible to see through. Screams lashed the air around him, his hair standing on end as flashes of magick erupted through the smog.

Cyfrin couldn't tell who was winning, the cries of his people mixing with that of the beasts in the crackling air. But his mind was barely focused on that as he was pulled forward towards where he knew Mara must be. Faintly through the smell of burning wood and dense smoke, he could make out the scent of rosemary and honeysuckle. A shiver of fear and panic rushed up his arm from the bond.

I.A. TAKERIAN

There was light breaking through the smoke ahead of him, towards the border of the Forgotten Woods. He shot past the last of the smoldering buildings, bursting through the smoke and into semi-fresh air. He whipped around, searching desperately through the crowd of darklings. Two of them spotted him, shrieking as they dove. His eyes fell on a place towards the tree-line yards away from him.

Mara was thrashing hard, a man pulling her towards the woods. A man in all black armor, glinting dully in the firelight behind them. Heavy corruption oozed from him, so much so that Cyfrin's body begged him to pull away.

Pure, unfiltered fury ran through Cyfrin as he watched Mara fight to break free of his unrelenting grasp. He felt his control slip on his magick as the two darklings lunged for him. Lightning surrounded his hands, shooting into the earth below. He sliced through the air at the creatures. They let out gurgled cries as his hands cleaved through them, feeling the wet tear of their flesh as they burst. He used the force of the magick to throw him forwards up the hill, towards where Adrian dragged Mara. He heard her cry out, and the magick within him raised its deadly maws in response.

Cyfrin roared, electricity tearing through his arms. It shot from his extended hand, the bolt bright white. It whizzed past Mara's ear, almost too close for comfort. It collided dead-on with Adrian's back. He stumbled forward, catching himself before he hit the ground. Mara toppled backwards, slamming in to Cyfrin's chest as he grabbed for her. The crackling magick within him smoldered slightly, bowing in her presence as it always did.

He felt relief wash over him, everything else falling away. He spun her around. Her perfect face was ashen, spattered in blood from battle and pale with shock. Her eyes were wild, darting over his shoulder to the place

A PROPHECY OF UNDONE

Adrian was composing himself. Cyfrin couldn't see any new wounds on her face, but his eyes trailed down to her arm hung limply at her side. He grabbed it gingerly. Wrapped around the entirety of her wrist, an angry shade of purple against her freckled skin, was a burned handprint.

Wrath flooded Cyfrin as he examined it. The man behind him had not only hurt his Dawnbringer. He had *marked* her. Laid a permanent brand against her pure, soft body. Cyfrin was nearly blind with the red-hot rage crashing in his chest, swallowing hard as the beast in his core threatened to break free.

"Listen to me," he said in a low voice, fighting to keep his tone calm. Mara stared up at him with wide eyes. "I know you want to fight. And you can, you've more than proven that, but right now I need you to *run*. Find Caerani, El, Kain. They'll protect you."

Nothing mattered more in the world to him than keeping her safe. The village could burn, he could be ripped apart by the darkness gaining in power behind them, he could fall to the corruption cascading forth from the woods. As long as they got her away and kept her protected, he would take it all. As it should have always been.

Mara's eyes swam with tears, staring at Adrian over his shoulder. "I...I can't."

Cyfrin's heart cried at the agony in her voice. He knew this pain well. The pain of watching someone you love be torn from you by forces out of your control. Forces of *darkness*. It was an impossible feeling.

"You can, and you will." He shook her gently. She looked back up at him, her gorgeous green eyes overflowing with shimmering tears. They left long streaks of cleaned skin through the grime on her cheeks. "If you're

333

I.A. TAKERIAN

taken, if they're able to bring you back to that place… everything we've done, all of this will have been for nothing. You're the last hope for us all, Mara."

Cyfrin felt the great bubble of dark energy growing behind him burst, rushing for them. He threw his hand back, firing off a bolt of blue lightning. It slammed against Adrian's dark magick, exploding in a shower of sparks and shadow in midair. He spun about, positioning Mara behind him as lightning surrounded his hands.

"*Go!*" he ordered, facing the twisted knight. He felt her turn and begin to sprint back towards the burning fields. *Zenoths hear me,* he thought. *Protect her. Please, please protect her.*

Adrian had clearly been a handsome man. He was nearly as tall as Cyfrin, though much leaner than his broadly muscled body. But the corruption was tearing across his face, contorting his features as the magick changed him from the inside. The ornate longsword in his hands was wrapped entirely in dark magick. Cyfrin's skin crawled in his presence. Adrian raised his hand high, pointing it towards Cyfrin. The intense wave of magick washed through the air again.

"*You will give her to me!*" His voice was strange and rasping. Dark magick rocketed from Adrian's outstretched hand.

Cyfrin fired off another bolt of crackling lighting. Their magick collided in the air, sending more sparks of darkness to the grass below.

"*She is mine!*" The rasps were coming through in many different tones, high and low.

The furious beast howling to be released raised up at his words. Cyfrin loosened his grip further. The blue lighting around his hands turned almost white, cracking the earth below him.

A PROPHECY OF UNDONE

"She is no one's but her own," Cyfrin boomed back. "I will not let her be taken again."

He had failed her once, twenty-one years ago when he was the last line of her defense. *I will lay down my life before I allow that to happen again.*

Adrian roared and another spear of dark magick shot from him. There was a *bang* and Cyfrin's angry bolts of lightning wrapped themselves around the shadows before it was even halfway to him. The combined energy vibrated in midair before exploding with enough force to blow a small crater in the ground below it.

The clouds above gave a threatening rumble. Cyfrin's entire body covered with electricity, the sky swirling above him. Adrian raised his sword high in the air. There was a ripple of terrifying power, then the shadows around his blade flew into the clouds.

It was like a tornado of screaming shadows. They expanded as they rose, covering them in a dome of impenetrable darkness. Cyfrin swore loudly, blasting magick from himself. The white lightning flung from his body, lashing and slicing at the encroaching darkness. The shadows spun like a crackling whirlwind in a great circle around the two men, creating a bubble of earth untouched by the dome of swirling darkness.

Power was surrounding Adrian's sword, building. He began to walk towards Cyfrin. "*You took her from me,*" he rasped, his darkly swirling pupils filled with blind rage. "*You stole her from her room in the night like a **coward**.*" He dashed forward suddenly, closing the distance between he and Cyfrin in one bound.

Cyfrin leapt back, tossing lighting forth from his hands. Shadows whipped off Adrian's sword. They grazed Cyfrin's hands as he flew backwards, searing the flesh

I.A. TAKERIAN

where it touched. He cursed, glowering at Adrian who was readying another attack.

"I saved her from the corruption that now eats you!" Cyfrin growled through his teeth. "She was imprisoned there by the man you call King!"

Adrian screamed in response, a mighty blast of dark magick ripping from him in a great fan. It slammed into Cyfrin's torso. Pain shot down every one of his nerve endings. His heart sputtered, his feet stumbling backwards. He fired off another burst of angry white lightning at Adrian.

"*Liar!*" Adrian screamed. "*You came exactly when you knew there would be little resistance. Bested the weakest of our soldiers, mere palace guards. You took Mara, and I didn't even stand a chance of protecting her.* **You took my Mara.**"

Another spear of dark magick loosed from Adrian's hands. Cyfrin leapt aside, clutching his chest. His heart was throbbing after the last attack, like there were a hundred daggers stabbing it again and again and again. But he had frozen at Adrian's words, momentarily distracted. He stared at Adrian's face, so twisted by corruption, but he could see true and real pain behind his darkly slitted eyes.

Mara spoke of Adrian as if he was her brother; the family she always wanted and never had. But it was clear to Cyfrin in this moment that Adrian's feelings for her were much deeper. Much more. He recognized that blind fury, that need to protect. To protect *her*. In Adrian's shoes, his love being stolen from him by those he knew only as his enemies...what *wouldn't* he have done to save her?

And Cyfrin felt a deep sadness for Adrian, even as he readied another attack. He dove out of the way of the next bolt of magick, backing away from Adrian as far as he could. And as he began circling closer, Cyfrin felt

336

A PROPHECY OF UNDONE

compelled to try to save him. To give Mara's dearest companion one last chance.

"Adrian," he began, surprised when Adrian faltered in his approach, his eyes widening. Cyfrin forced his lightning to retreat, raising his hands in surrender. "Please. For Mara's sake, please listen to me."

Adrian had frozen in place, the dark magick wavering slightly.

"There was no other way than to take Mara from the castle in Delinval," he began, unsure of how much time he had. "The history you've been taught is a lie. Your king began the Great War, stole our princess from us at the end of it all. He brought her to the castle and raised her under his wing, for reasons that are entirely his own."

He paused, searching Adrian's face for any sign of humanity. He could have sworn he saw a flicker of recognition pass through his eyes, and his heart skipped a beat. Perhaps he *could* fight off the corruption working to consume within him.

"For twenty years, we thought her dead," Cyfrin continued. "And when we found out otherwise, there were very few options as to how to proceed. But she was a prisoner under Grathiel's thumb, and she needed to be rescued."

The arm holding Adrian's sword twitched, and Cyfrin's body tensed.

"*You're lying,*" he rasped, but he did not move.

Cyfrin shook his head. "You know I'm not," he replied softly. "I know you can feel the magick coming off her, Adrian. Just as I know it is love that has driven you so blindly to this madness. Please, let us show you. Let us *help* you." He extended a welcoming hand.

Adrian shifted his head, glancing over Cyfrin's shoulder through the dome of darkness to where Mara had disap-

I.A. TAKERIAN

peared. There was a long moment in which they both stood motionless. Then, the ominous evil magick began to roll in droves off Adrian's body, even heavier than before.

"*Then you have corrupted her,*" he growled, and Cyfrin couldn't help but sneer at the irony of his poisoned lips speaking the words. "*I will rend the sickness from her body. I will burn away your hold on her, flay every piece you have touched from her figure, and she will be pure once more.*"

Bolts of dark magick shot from every inch of Adrian's body, leaving no place to escape within the torrent of shadows. Cyfrin stood defenseless against the attack, not even his lightning now growing forth from him quick enough to stop it. He felt multiple bolts connect with his body, buckling his knees. His head filled with sharp pain. The world around him spun, and he felt blood trickling from his head and nose. He grit his teeth, forcing himself to stand. His flesh was raw and bloodied across every inch the dark magick had touched.

Cyfrin felt cold calm rush over him as he accepted the inevitable. *What a beautiful way to meet the Beyonds, in the place of the one I love.* The largest gathering of darkness he had felt yet was building between Adrian's hands, and he knew he wouldn't survive this last attack. He tried to force his magick to surround him, but the lightning seemed to have been momentarily bound by the dark magick of last attack. He closed his eyes, taking a deep breath and imaging Mara's face once last time. There was a small sob a few feet away from Cyfrin, and his eyes flew open. He turned in horror.

Mara had flown through the darkness, small cuts covering her body. He felt icy fear rise in his throat, his heart stopping. *No. No, you damned fool. Why didn't you run?!*

A shard of the darkness surrounding Adrian fired off at Cyfrin, knocking him to his knees as he continued to stare

A PROPHECY OF UNDONE

at Mara. His ears were ringing with pain, but he ignored it. He could not die now. Not with Mara here to witness. Not with Mara here to be taken when he feel. He focused every bit of himself onto his magick.

He felt it flicker, the electricity starting to flow through him as Adrian readied his final attack. He wouldn't be able to conjure up enough power to save him, but he could at least deal enough damage to Adrian to grant Mara her final escape. He bared his teeth against the feeling rocketing down the bond from Mara. The darkness fired off towards him. He raised his hands in defense.

To his immense horror, Mara flung herself at him. She slammed into the side of his body, wrapping her arms around his neck and clutching to him. Protecting him. She buried her wet face into the nape of his neck, his breath catching. A sudden warmth exploded inside of him.

The world slowed. Everything seemed to stop as many things happened all at once.

The feeling of dim electricity in his core shifted, erupting suddenly into a blaze to rival the burning forest. The beastly magick in his core purred against the bright flames within him, weaving itself into the energy. There was a powerful tug on his soul, like a thick tether entangling him tighter to Mara hanging from his neck. He felt mad, like he could burst out laughing right here and now. His vision filled with light. His heart was dancing, his body feeling like it was floating through air.

The electrified fire was running up his body, through his arms. He felt crackling magick connect him to Mara like a great circuit, and power erupted from his palms. A beam of golden-white light exploded from him, identical to Mara's magick. What looked like constellations of sparking light cascaded from the beam, dazzling him as they fell to the ground. The places they touched burst forth with life,

339

I.A. TAKERIAN

covering the earth beneath the beam in bright green grass and patches of glowing wildflowers.

The air smelled strangely sweet and electric, every hair on his body standing on end. There was a great rumble from overhead, and stellar pillars of blue lighting cracked through the ceiling of the shadow dome. They shot into the ground around Adrian, splitting the earth beneath him as they went. There was an odd feeling in Cyfrin's heart, like it suddenly had two distinct beats.

The beam of golden magick slammed into Adrian's sword, and there was deafening *bang*. The force blasted all three of them backwards in a shockwave. Cyfrin wrapped himself around Mara to protect her. His back slammed into the ground a few yards away, sliding through the dirt. The darkness around them cracked like glass.

Cyfrin unfolded Mara from his body, staring down at her with wide-eyed disbelief. That was the most powerful magick he had ever felt, leaving him breathless and with an intense tingling sensation all over. It was like he had been super charged, increasing his powers to God-like potential. But the strange scratching at his insides that he always felt around Mara had increased tenfold. A scream came from across the clearing and they both turned to face it.

Adrian was crouched on the ground, hands covering his face. Black ooze poured out between his fingers. Cyfrin felt a huge rush of pain and sadness mix with his fury, but it was disconnected; strained.

Adrian stared at them through his fingers, his eyes mere slits of swirling darkness. Cyfrin knew he would take another shot as soon as he regained composure. *He could have killed Mara with the last one. He **would** have killed her.* Cyfrin stood slowly from the ground, putting himself between Mara and Adrian. Golden bolts of lightning

340

sprang forth from his hands, filling him with that feeling of caressing flame.

He charged forward, the ground cracking underfoot. He felt the sadness inside of him cut off suddenly, the tether tied around his very being shuddering. He slammed into Adrian, who was covered in black blood and cracked flesh. The sun-infused lightning sliced through his dark armor, spinning him backwards as Cyfrin tore through the metal with ease. Cyfrin raised up for a second attack. The dark shadows surrounding Adrian sputtered, his body falling suddenly still. He looked up at Cyfrin, who froze with hands ready to strike.

Two very human, golden-brown eyes stared at him through the cracked and twisted face of Adrian. Tears sprang to them, and he reached out towards Cyfrin, not in attack. But in surrender.

"Do it," he wheezed, his voice sounding incredibly strained. His entire body was shaking, the tears mixing with the thick black blood dripping from his face. "I cannot hold on any longer. I cannot fight it. Please. Please, while she's not awake to see. You have to do it." His eyes flickered to Mara, who lay unconscious behind them. The darkness was beginning to swirl underneath their surface, and he turned to face Cyfrin one last time.

Adrian had given every piece of himself, body and soul, to come and rescue Mara. He had thought her to be in great danger, maybe even dead. And the furious fear of this thought had driven him to pure madness in his quest to save her.

And Cyfrin's eyes welled with tears. He nodded, kneeling to the ground beside Adrian. He took his blooded, morphed hand, the electricity snaking into his skin. Golden threads of light laced through his veins, overtaking the darkness. "There is no greater honor than laying down your life to protect those you love," he said in a low voice. "You are truly as legendary a warrior as Mara told us."

Adrian shuddered, the golden lightning reaching his heart. His eyes flew open, and shadows burst out of him. They escaped from his mouth like bile, soaking into the ground and vanishing. The darkness left his eyes, his skin still cracked. The black blood gushing from him turned red. His hands were ice in Cyfrin's grip.

He was taking shallow, shuddering breaths. His eyes fluttered to Cyfrin's face, squeezing his hand in a vice-like grip. His brow furrowed in concentration. Blood leaked from his open mouth. "Keep...our princess...safe..." he gurgled, the color draining from his face as he struggled to speak.

Cyfrin nodded, his tears falling onto Adrian's face. "With all I am. Forever."

Adrian gave another rattling breath, his eyes turning to stare at the smokey sky above. Cyfrin could hear a noise coming from him, like a strained humming. A song he couldn't quite catch the melody of. His grip on Cyfrin's hand went suddenly slack. The humming ceased.

And Adrian was gone.

Cyfrin cried, continuing to hold his hand gingerly. He stared down at Adrian's destroyed face, a man who had given everything he was, doing what he thought was right. Cyfrin took a gentle hand and closed Adrian's empty eyes, resting his sword on his chest. The fallen white knight. Mara's family. And he had been forced to end his life all too soon.

Thunder rumbled overhead, lighting cracking across the sky, and great drops of water began to rain down on the smoldering village beyond.

CHAPTER 35
A WARRIOR'S END

MARA

There was a loud humming in Mara's head. She could see a dim green glow through her eyelids. She cracked them open slowly, wincing. Her chest throbbed. She was home, back in the Grand Halls and bathed in the multi-colored orb lights. El was seated beside her on the large four poster, hands hovering across Mara's body and face gray. Caerani stood at the foot of the bed with Milios, both frowning. They spoke to one another in hushed tones. A soft breeze floated in through the open balcony, brushing against Mara's cheek and bringing the heavy smell of smoke with it.

She sat bolt upright, gasping. The chain of events that led her here came crashing down. El reached out to her with calming eyes, but Mara was already on her feet. "Where is Adrian?" she demanded, her heart shuddering at the look on her face.

She knew the answer by the dimming of her eyes but refused to believe it.

I.A. TAKERIAN

Mara lunged forward like a wild animal, gripping the front of Caerani's blouse. Caerani looked down at her with wide eyes. "*Where is Adrian?!*" Mara repeated, much louder this time.

Caerani looked pained, grabbing her gently around the wrists as she shook her head slowly.

A noise ripped from Mara, a mix of a sob and a strangled scream. Her legs wobbled as tears clouded her vision, and Caerani pulled her tightly to her chest. Mara shook with her cries against the embrace.

This was what dying felt like. Her heart was breaking into a million tiny pieces, scattering across the hardwood floor with her tears. She would die here in Caerani's arms, for there was surely no way she'd survive the shattering pain tearing through her. She heard El let out a sob behind her, and Milios flinched as they looked away.

"He was brave, your friend," Caerani murmured into Mara's curls, rubbing her back gently. "From what I was told, he fought the corruption valiantly. He stood against the darkness and met a warrior's end."

"No..." Mara wept. "No, no, no...*please* no..." She couldn't breathe. Couldn't think. She had hoped, selfishly, that Adrian would hear her. That he would abandon Grathiel and Delinval and all he ever knew to stand beside her in the battle to come. They would have trained in the fields from dusk till dawn. He would have loved sparring with Kain and Cyfrin, maybe even found an Odelian woman to place his romantic feelings with. *My fault. It's my fault he's dead. If it wasn't me, he never would have come here. If it wasn't me, he never would have fallen...*

It was strange. Even as her thoughts ran wild, she was settling into the odd feeling of disconnection she had become so accustomed to. It was the same feeling she had upon arriving to the Hidden Village and discovering the

A PROPHECY OF UNDONE

truth. But she clung desperately to the agony as her brain tried to shut down. This agony is where Adrian now lived, and she would be damned before she gave herself the kindness of disassociating from that.

"The site around his final stand…" El said in a strangled voice beside her. "It's a miracle Cyfrin and you even survived."

Mara remembered the battle so clearly, it could have been happening at that very moment. The brilliant flashes of blinding gold, sun and stars shooting from Cyfrin's outstretched hand. "Something happened while Cyfrin and I were trapped in Ad-" Her throat closed around his name, unable to finish it. "When we were trapped in the darkness. It looked like my powers came from *Cyfrin*. My sunbeams shot from his hands when I touched him."

Caerani frowned. "Yes, the entire village saw it," she replied, folding her arms across her chest. "It looked like the Beyonds were opening wide, shooting straight towards you three. With the high energy of the moment, and that blood bond on your hands, it's entirely possible that you two resonated with one another. It's not unheard of in situations like that, magick mixing."

"It was very strange," Milios added, studying Mara with their stormy eyes. "I've not seen anything like it, in all my years."

But Mara was suddenly standing very straight, forcing her tears away with the back of her hand. "The village. Our people, are they alive? How many fell in the battle?"

The energy in the room shifted, the air growing cold. It was eerily still, now that she was focusing on it. There was no music coming from the village beyond the balcony. Only heavy, hard silence.

"We will rebuild," Caerani said, voice dark.

"Surprisingly few lost their lives," Milios offered softly,

I.A. TAKERIAN

seeing Mara's face contort in pain. "The warriors were able to evacuate a good portion of them. I was able to control the blaze and eventually stop it entirely. The woods are quite ashen, as is the village. Many of the oldest buildings fell to nothing."

Milios looked around them, smiling sadly. "The flames never crossed the river," they continued. "It kept the temple safe, the falls, and the Grand Hall. We'll house anyone who needs it here, feed and clothe anyone we can. And Caerani is right: We will start to rebuild."

Mara gulped, swallowing the renewed round of sobs that threatened to take her. Her anguish and desperation at the loss of her friend would have to wait. Now was the time for action. Now, more than ever, the Odelian's needed a leader. She stood a little taller. "And what of the corrupted ones? The knights and their darklings?"

"Most escaped," Caerani said, thumbing the hilt of her dagger. "That light show you and Cyfrin set off really put the fear of the Beyonds in them. Ran like cowards into the woods."

"They'll find the forest to be most unforgiving," Milios added.

"Small blessings, I suppose," Caerani growled. She raised an eyebrow at Mara, looking hesitant. "We did, however, manage to apprehend one of the knights during their escape. El was able to slow the corruption from the dark magick, just long enough for us to, erm...*question* him."

Mara's heart hammered in her chest. "Take me to him."

Caerani eyed her wearily. "I'm not sure that's wise-" she began, but Mara cut her off.

"These are *my* people too, Caerani," she breathed,

A PROPHECY OF UNDONE

feeling strained. "If we are gathering information that may be useful to us, then I wish to be present for it."

Caerani studied her face for a moment longer before giving a small smile. "As you wish," she said, bowing her head slightly and moving to leave the room.

Mara took a step forward to follow, but El grabbed her arm gently. Mara froze, feeling her thumb trace the wound on her arm. The handprint Adrian had burned into her skin.

"I can heal this for you," El said in a muted tone. "It would only take a moment."

Mara jerked away. "**No**," she said, much harsher than she had intended.

El stiffened, taken aback.

Mara softened her tone before she spoke again, eyes apologetic. "Please, no."

Silence followed her words. Tears brimmed in El's eyes and she gave a curt nod.

Caerani led them through the doorway and out into the silent hall. They turned and began walking towards the end of the house Mara never went to, having no reason to do so. She knew Kain's room was back here, and Cyfrin's. Her stomach fluttered at the thought of his name, her mind repeating it over and over again in a siren-like symphony. Mara could smell overwhelming honey and pine coming from behind one of the doorways they passed.

They were approaching a door at the end of the long hallway, its black wood standing in stark contrast to the dark red walls around it. Mara saw runes, like the ones at the entrance to the catacombs, etched all around the threshold. Immense power pulsated from the door itself, sending a shiver down Mara's spine. Caerani waved her hand as they approached, her eyes flashing orange red. She whispered in a language Mara did not understand. The

347

I.A. TAKERIAN

door gave a soft shudder, and Caerani stepped right through the wood as if it was made of smoke. Milios followed behind her, Mara, and El taking up the rear.

They had entered a dark passageway, its narrow corridor lit on all sides by simple candlesticks instead of orb lights. They descended what felt like an ever-spiraling staircase, the air musty and thin as they walked lower and lower. They emerged suddenly into a massive chasm, its ceiling too far above them to see in the darkness. Caerani led them out onto a small stone path that stretched across the chasm. Mara could see it led to a single black door beyond. They stepped forward with cautious steps on the narrow walkway. Mara's eyes darted about as they walked, taking in her surroundings.

All along the high stone walls, built directly into the rock face, were heavy barred off cells. They had no doors, no discernible way to reach them. But Mara could feel strange, dark energy emanating from the shadows of some. She felt like they were being watched from all sides, shuddering as they continued forward.

"What is this place?" Mara asked in a quiet voice to no one in particular.

It was Caerani who answered. "We are in the Underbelly of the Grand Halls," she said over her shoulder to Mara. "Your great grandfather built down into the earth below his home after the Shadow Wars, to hold dangerous creatures or enemies to the crown. The whole place is warded out the ass, but we've not had the pleasure of using it for many years now." Her voice dripped with cruel satisfaction.

They approached the door at the end of the path. Caerani waved her hand once more, and the four of them stepped through the vanishing doorway.

They had walked into a bloody scene. Noise lashed at

A PROPHECY OF UNDONE

Mara as soon as she entered the room. Screams, growls, snarls, snaps. They all crashed through the air. It made her ears ring. The room was covered across every inch in faintly glowing runes that pulsed every few seconds. The high ceiling disappeared into the darkness beyond.

A blonde-haired man sat in a chair in the very center of the circular chamber. Mara recognized him as the son of Grathiel's most loyal friend. Desmond was shrieking and spitting, thrashing like a beast against the black chains that held him to the seat. His mouth foamed with dark grey liquid, eyes blood shot and rolling. Every muscle on his body was strained against his binds.

Kain stood to one side of him, a flail with many razor-tipped tails in one hand. Cyfrin stood to the other, his hands crackling with electricity. Both of their faces were dark and menacing, the glowing of Cyfrin's eyes looking more deadly than Mara had ever seen it. They did not look up as they entered, continuing to glower at the struggling Desmond between them.

"Mara requested to be present for this," Caerani said simply, her voice echoing back to them many times.

"*Deceiver!*" Desmond spoke in a voice that was more monster than man. It gurgled forth from him as he snapped his teeth towards Caerani. "*Putrid, foul, fallen ones. Tucked away, all nice and safe, in your little homes.*" He threw his head back and cackled; deranged. "*We burned your beds and defiled your lands, as you have burned and defiled ours! Rotten! Vile! Murderers!*"

He snapped at the air, a trickle of blood leaking from his nose. His eyes flashed, darting to the place where Mara stood watching. He froze, his panting breath ceasing. His eyes narrowed on her. "*Betrayer.*"

The word rocked through Mara. He shrieked, becoming markedly more violent. He spit in her direction.

349

I.A. TAKERIAN

The ground his saliva touched sizzled in response. "*You have created unholy union with the Dreads! You walk among them, you fight beside them, you have abandoned your people. Your soul will burn for eternity for your transgressions!*"

Cyfrin shot a bolt into his chest, Kain flexing his hand on his flail. Desmond screeched, the sounds mingling with his laughter. Cyfrin's magick cracked madly, untamed, at the ground beneath Desmond's feet. A beast begging to be freed against the enemy.

But instead of shying away from the evil thing in the chair, Mara took a step forward. She stood a few feet away from Desmond, who was trying unsuccessfully to bite at his wrist cuffs. Mara watched him with cold eyes.

"You will tell us what happened, from the time your forces left Delinval until now." She spoke in a calm, even tone, ignoring the raging fire within her. It was the voice Lady Lenorei had taught her to speak in when addressing royalty or the court. Cold, assessing. "How did you and your men become corrupted?"

Desmond spit at her feet, shrieking in pain and laughter as she leapt back from its acidic touch. "*You stink of death,*" he hissed, venom dripping from his words, mouth twisting up into an evil grin. "*Death and pain and flame and ash. You are the reason we come, conniving whore. You are the reason your friends burned-*"

Crack. Cyfrin grabbed Desmond's face in one hand, squeezing his cheeks hard as lighting lashed into his flesh. "I advise you to think very carefully about your next words to my Queen," he growled, Desmond convulsing slightly as the energy shot into him. "Lest you wish your sharp tongue to be boiled inside your foul mouth."

Mara raised her hand to Cyfrin, her cool eyes not leaving Desmond's face. Cyfrin bowed his head instantly,

A PROPHECY OF UNDONE

releasing Desmond and stepping back to pace beside the chair.

"I will not ask you a third time, Desmond," she said in her emotionless tone, tilting her chin to stare down her nose at the knight. Even as a man, he had been distinctly unpleasant. He had cornered Mara at many of Grathiel's parties, drunk and pushy; pawing at her. The corruption merely amplified that which was already inside of him. "Tell me how you came to be this way."

The command echoed around the room, Desmond continuing to thrash against his binds. He hissed menacingly as Kain cracked the flail in warning beside him. *"The King wished you brought back, no matter the method or cost,"* he rasped, glaring between Kain and Cyfrin. *"Adrian, poor, sweet, sad, Adrian...He never did recover from your kidnapping."*

He grinned viciously at the look of pain that flashed in her eyes. *"Your forever protector. Adrian would do anything to retrieve you. His precious, his only, his Mara. So, it was he who bore the honor of taking the darkness first. The King gifted us each with magick and shadow, to make us perfect in his vision. And sweet Adrian led us here. Here to you, sitting like chickens in their fox-stalked pens."* He shrieked again, the sound becoming more inhuman as his face began to contort.

"What do you mean he gifted you each magick?" Mara demanded, disgusted. Black ooze began to drip from Desmond's panting mouth.

"It's as it was in the Great War," Caerani answered Mara over the echoing din of Desmond's monstrous sounds. "Grathiel has struck a deal with Mezilmoth. It is the only way he could have obtained such terrible powers." She stared darkly at Desmond, grimacing. "This is what happens when magick is forced into a body that is not meant to hold it. Especially something as soul-altering as dark magick."

I.A. TAKERIAN

Desmond let out another cackling shriek. "*We will not stop till your body lay at the All-King's feet, oh blasphemer. Oh betrayer. Oh **monster**!*"

Cyfrin's fist collided with the side of his face with such force, that his neck snapped to the side. Desmond made a sickening gasping sound, eyes popping with terror as he convulsed on his seat. There was a faint glowing underneath his cheeks and Mara knew that Cyfrin was holding true to his promise to burn out his tongue.

Dark energy tore from Desmond. A hand was on her shoulder, turning her back towards the door. It was El, leading her gently through the threshold and back into the chasm beyond. "You don't want to watch this next part," she said quietly to Mara, the screaming cut short instantly as the door became solid once more.

They all stood in the silence on the narrow walkway, Mara's pulse pounding loudly in her ears. Grathiel had known Adrian's feelings for her. He had known he would do practically anything he could to save her. How easy it must have been for Grathiel to convince him to do this, to turn to darkness to somehow "rescue her". He had used Adrian, her best friend, against her. Her one weakness he had at his disposal. Mara's fists clenched painfully tight at her sides, her companion's eyes widening as golden light throbbed around them. Hot rage filled her entire being, driving her towards the absolute need for justice.

Justice. Not only for her dear friend, but for all the lies and lives lost in Grathiel's blind madness.

She faced Caerani, hands still aglow with sunlit energy. "I wish to address the people," she said. "All of them. As soon as I can. Is that possible?"

Caerani looked slightly taken aback but bowed her head in response. "Of course," she replied, inclining her

352

A PROPHECY OF UNDONE

head to Mara. "I shall have everyone in the Crystal Falls basin by noon tomorrow, if that is what you wish."

Mara nodded fervently, focusing her magick back inside her body. Grathiel had made perhaps his biggest mistake yet when manipulating Adrian, using his good heart and pure intensions to his advantage. And the price of his death was one she would gladly carve from Grathiel's flesh. In fact, she looked forward to it.

CHAPTER 36
GOODNIGHT

Mara was frozen, stood at the edge of the path that led to the training fields. They'd been left scorched and desolate, huge craters taken from the ground in places. The sun was setting over the Brisenbane, smoke still hanging in the air far above the crashing waves. It was the first time she couldn't hear noise coming from the Red Froth. The deck lay in darkness, the ship unmoving in the port. Her destination lay on the furthest edge of the cliffs, but her feet refused to move.

She was swaying slightly on the spot, unsure if she was going to faint or be violently ill. She had asked Caerani to have him brought here. To have him lay facing the ocean and the cosmos beyond. He deserved to be put to rest properly. He deserved a knight's grave-

She gasped as pain ripped through her anew. Tears cascaded down her cheeks, hot and unstoppable. Mara clutched at her heart, and a sob tore from her. It felt like she was moving through a dream. A terrible, cruel dream. There were hands on her arms suddenly, steadying her

I.A. TAKERIAN

from behind. She didn't need to turn to know it was Cyfrin.

"How can I help you?" he asked. The softness in his voice made her tears fall even harder.

"I don't know," she whispered, unable to pull her eyes from Adrian's distant form. "I feel like I can't breathe." Her head was spinning, the world tunneling down to just his body on the cliffside.

Cyfrin came to stand beside her, taking her hand gently in his own. "It's getting late. Let's get Adrian settled into his new home, okay?"

Mara's heart stuttered. She looked up at him, stunned by Adrian's name.

Cyfrin looked exhausted, closing wounds patterned across his body and face. But he gave her a small smile, squeezing her hand and beginning to lead her forward. They walked in silence towards the cliffside where Adrian lay. His body had been covered by a large tapestry, hiding him from sight. They stopped just beside him, Mara shaking hard with her sobs. Her knees buckled, and Cyfrin lowered her carefully to the ground.

The sun was low in the sky, practically flush with the Brisenbane. Constellations were winking to life above them, heralding the coming moon. Mara reached out to touch Adrian's form, but stopped short, dropping her hand to the grass beside him.

She stared up at the stars, the tears racing past her ears and dampening her curls. "He would have loved it here," she breathed. "We don't get clear skies like these in Delinval. He used to stare at the old tomes for *hours*, memorizing the placements of the stars. He'd point up at the darkness and tell me where they were all meant to be. Promised we'd see them one day-" She couldn't continue.

"I can think of no better place for him to rest then,"

356

A PROPHECY OF UNDONE

Cyfrin said, and there was a great shifting of the earth beside Mara. He waved his hands, and the ground hollowed out a large, deep hole. Just big enough for Adrian.

Not yet, Mara thought, gasping for air. The pain was making it impossible to bottom out her breath. *Not yet. Please, you can't go yet. I need you.*

She drew her hand towards the bit of tapestry covering his face, making to draw it down. To look at him one last time. But Cyfrin's hand was holding hers again, knelt beside her and preventing her moving any further. His face swam in her teary vision.

He gave a very slow shake of his head, looking pained. "No, Mara. He didn't want you to see him this way."

She yanked her hand away from him, her strangled cries echoing out across the Brisenbane. "That isn't fair!"

"You're right," he replied softly. "It isn't fair that your last image of Adrian was marred by this corruption. So, let's think back to the time you saw him before that. The last night you saw him in Delinval."

Mara blinked, remembering it as clearly as if it had happened. Adrian, first upset and then amused, fighting with her at the tournaments. He was disapproving, but proud-none-the-less. At the banquet that night, he had not worn his family's colors, as was traditional for the knights. No, he had worn Mara's chosen colors of silver and green. The way he had smiled at her before trailing off down the hallway that night outside her bedroom. The way he'd ruffled her curls in his calloused hand. She could still hear his voice in her head. "*Happy End Day, Mara. Things will look brighter in the morning.*"

She curled her knees into her chest, wrapping her arms around them. She didn't know if she'd ever stop crying.

I.A. TAKERIAN

How am I supposed to go on without you, Adrian? What am I supposed to do?

Arms wrapped around her shoulders, but it was not Cyfrin this time. El buried her face against Mara's back, and Mara could feel tears soaking through her shirt. Kain was at her side, placing a reassuring hand on top of Mara's head. Milios was knelt down beside Cyfrin, staring down at Adrian's body.

"He was my only friend. My whole life," Mara managed to choke out to them. "And I am the reason he is dead. It's my fault."

Cyfrin shook his head once more. "Adrian chose to give his life, to keep you safe. Do not disrespect that by blaming yourself. He came here out of love. And it is with love that he left this world."

"Aye, and a warrior's departure is never a demise," Kain went on, his usually booming voice very low. "They live on in every moment we choose to fight. In every chance we get to protect the ones we love."

"The Beyonds are a beautiful place," El murmured into Mara's back. "He is surrounded with love and light. And hope."

Milios reached out and took the hand Mara still held clutched to her chest. They rubbed it gently, offering her a warm smile. "Why don't you tell us about him, Mara?"

Mara's lip gave a violent quiver. Milios was waving their free hand, ushering the wind to gather beneath Adrian's body. It floated him off the ground, moving him slowly and carefully towards his final resting place.

"Adrian was kind," she began, her voice cracking. "He gave me hope everyday that tomorrow would be better. And it always was, with him there. He showed me how to use a blade, trained with me when no one else would, stood by me when everyone mocked my trying. And when I

A PROPHECY OF UNDONE

started being able to keep up with him, he didn't get odd about it. He wasn't jealous or envious or heady. He was... he was..."

"Proud," Cyfrin picked up as she trailed off.

"Yes. Yes, I think he was. I *hope* he was." His body was being lowered into the ground, easing towards the soft earth at the bottom. "I loved him. I loved him so much. Maybe not in the same way that he loved me, but mine was just as fierce. He would have loved this place. Loved all of you and what we are fighting for."

Adrian had reached the very bottom, and Mara stood to keep his body in sight. Her friends followed suit, coming to stand around the grave beside her. The moon was rising over the water now, and the waves seemed to have grown oddly calm. The dirt was beginning to cascade like dark snow on Adrian's form, covering him. And Mara had a sudden vivid memory of her best friend's face, beaming at her.

"Ah, won't you sing it for me one last time, Mar?" he had asked her, referencing a silly little tune Mara could never seem to get out of her head. She had sung it to him again and again, growing tired and annoyed after hours of the repeated request.

Here, above Adrian's resting place, she began to hum it again. She swayed slightly on the spot, ignoring her ever-flowing tears that spattered the fresh earth above him. El knelt down and placed a large crystal from the falls at the head of the grave. Cyfrin waved his hand, and glowing wildflowers sprung to life all about them. Intricate, scrolling ivy made its way around the grave, marking it. Kain stepped forward last, unsheathing something from his hip as he went. It was Adrian's sword, cleaned and dispelled of all corruption.

He offered it to Mara, bowing his head. "It is tradition

I.A. TAKERIAN

that a warrior be laid to rest with his weapon. My parents made sure to fix his up, good as new."

Mara took it gently from his hands. She had held it so many times before, it felt like greeting an old friend. She remembered its weight, the perfect balance, the way the blade reflected the light. She kissed the hilt and placed the tip into the dirt before the crystal marker. It drove with ease into the ground, standing stoic in the glow of the moon.

Mara knelt into the wildflowers, watching them lean towards her slightly. Clouds were rolling in overhead, rumbling with distant thunder. Soft drops of rain spattered the ground. She placed her forehead against the broadside of the blade, closing her eyes and taking a deep breath. She couldn't bring herself to say goodbye. It was too final. Too eternal. And so, with one last great sob, Mara whispered, "Goodnight, Adrian."

CHAPTER 37
BECOMING WHO YOU ARE

Mara sat in her room the following morning, staring at nothing. Her mind reeled, but she found herself wholly incapable of latching on to a single thought. She had awoken in her bed, with the balcony doors wide as they always were. But there was none of the familiar sounds of early activity from the village below. Mara had yet to peak out at it, afraid of what she would be met with. The smell of smoke and burning wood still clung in the air, agitating her throat.

There had been many villagers in and out of the Grand Halls all morning, whatever magick that ran the kitchens whipping out meal after meal till everyone had their fill. They had been given clothing, blankets, pillows, rooms…anything they needed in the aftermath of yesterday's nightmare.

Here heart ached with grief, and anxiety over the coming gathering she had called. Mara felt in the deepest recesses of her being that she needed to stand tall, and finally address the matters at hand. The occupants of the Hidden Village were her people, her responsibility. She

361

I.A. TAKERIAN

hadn't grown up with them, was still working to learn and understand everything she could about their ways and histories. But the Dawnbringer legacy had led the Odelians for centuries, and she wasn't about to let that stop with her.

Filigro's face swam across her mind, her body shivering in response to his cold grin. His plot to take the crown had been supported by others. How many, she did not know. But even *one* Odelian being that vehemently against her on the throne was one too many.

She would have a lot of work ahead of her, proving to them that she could, and would, be a great Queen. Maybe not as great as her mother before her, but she would work herself to the bone to be damned close. Her eyes flitted to the portrait of her mother and father, smiling at her from the opposite wall.

They had given their lives for the Odelians. Her mother had rested not only their fate, but the fate of the entirety of Zenafrost, on the hope that Mara would be the hero of prophecy. Though they were gone, she wanted nothing more than to make them, *all* of them, proud.

There was a soft knock at the door, and Caerani stepped in. She was in an outfit very similar to Mara's, black leather pants and a billowing shirt tucked into them. She had soot on her face, indicating that she'd already been helping in the village that morning.

Mara scooted to the side of the bed. Caerani came to sit beside her. Her pale green eyes gazed at her parent's portrait. A small smile broke on her face. "What you don't see in that picture," she said with a faraway look. "Is that your father kept grabbing Alora's ass, and she pinched him so hard on the back of the arm that he cried a little." She laughed. It was a sound Mara had never heard from her before. Joyous and unbridled. Mara couldn't help returning

362

A PROPHECY OF UNDONE

her smile, watching Caerani lost in the memory of her best friend.

"She really did hate those portraits," she continued, her smile growing sad. "We were prepping to go aboard the Red Froth for a month when your grandfather made her sit for that one. Oh, she was so impatient about it too. Kept telling the artist that he could just work from memory, and that she'd give him *any* sum of gold if he'd let her and Yvonar go."

"What was she like?" Mara asked, studying the smile of her mother. Caerani was right, her face *did* look vaguely agitated. Looking more closely at Yvonar's face, his eyes had been captured with tiny glints of mischief in them.

Caerani turned to look at her, appraising. "She was a lot like you, actually. Brave, determined, brings out the best in others. She never wanted help with anything, never wanted for much at all, outside of love. And she had a fire blazing in her that rivaled even mine. She was the only one I ever knew who could withstand my tantrums in my much younger years. The only one who wanted to be my friend."

Mara's heart swelled at the comparison, blushing. "She sounds wonderful," Mara replied in a gentle tone. "I hope to do them proud. To do you *all* proud."

Caerani rubbed a hand over her back, giving her an encouraging smile. "I know she would be beyond proud of you. Both of them. And Mara, you have done nothing but grow and thrive since arriving here. We ripped the rug out from under your entire existence, tossed the weight of the world on your head, then asked you to fight beside us against people you've known your whole life. You could have drowned beneath it. But you've taken it all in stride."

Her gaze drifted out over the balcony, towards the village. "You are a warrior, and the blood of the Dawn-

I.A. TAKERIAN

bringer's beats within your heart. Your rule shall be one of peace and prosperity. I can feel it in my bones."

Mara nodded, but her palms were still slick with nervousness. She shook her head clear of the doubtful thoughts, changing the subject with the next question weighing heavy on her heart. "Has Drake returned yet?"

Caerani grew tense, her jaw setting in place. "No, he has not," she replied, heaving a sigh. "Drake was born in Ylastra to a very powerful bloodline, much like yourself. But they took him, and his incredibly volatile chaos magick, and made him into a weapon. He was only a child when he fought in his first war centuries ago."

Her eyes were cloudy, her expression dark as she went on. "Your grandfather, your mother and I travelled as part of a royal convoy to Ylastra when we were still quite young. It was a training mission, as well as an act to keep relations with our neighboring kingdoms. Your grandfather was called Lionas the Giving, so beautiful was his rule. He was known for helping those who were in need. And when we found Drake, he was in great need."

She stood from the bed to walk to the balcony doors, leaning against the frame and gazing out with arms folded. "Our first night there, Drake begged King Lionas to leave the Underkingdom. He warned us that his mad king, Normigone, wanted our heads. Not that we were much surprised by that. But Lionas spoke to Drake like he knew him. Like he could see the goodness in his heart. Ends be, all of us could. He was like a light in their abyss, down there. And when we made our escape from Ylastra, we stole Drake away with us."

She trailed off for a moment, looking thoughtful. "You should've seen their faces when they knew they'd lost, the arrogant bastards. Your mother stood toe-to-toe with the

364

A PROPHECY OF UNDONE

dark king and didn't even bat an eye." She laughed aloud at the memory.

"Is that why Ylastra is at such odds with us?" Mara asked her, cutting her laughter short.

"That, among some other disputes over these many centuries. And there was a time when your War Party destroyed a large portion of their more religious buildings in a drunken tirade. Though, in their defense, Normigone had insulted their Queen. Your mother. And they took none too kindly to that." She wiped a tear of laughter from her eyes. "When we got back here all those centuries ago with Drake, he asked King Lionas to perform a very ancient binding spell. To seal the weight of his powers away within him."

"Like Cyfrin," Mara said quietly and Caerani nodded, looking grim.

"Exactly the same spell, as a matter of fact. Lionas sealed away Drake's untamable chaos beast as best as he could, and Drake quickly became one of us. But that sort of magick is temperamental. None of us knew it at the time but locking away that much power came with a price. Over the years of being imprisoned, the magick within him began to change. It started to take form, become harder to control."

"Is that what that horned shadow was?" Mara asked, the hairs on the back of her neck standing on end.

Caerani gave her a half smile. "Yes. It's harder for him to control when he's under emotional turmoil." Mara remembered the look on Drake's face when he had seen Caerani being attacked; surrounded by the enemy.

"It's one of the biggest reasons he so vehemently fought against Cyfrin's father when he wanted to seal his magicks away," Caerani continued. "He knew what horrible things could happen to a person, when they tried to force their magick away instead of learning to harness it."

"He'll return soon though, won't he?" Mara asked, the vision of Drake surrounded by that lashing shadow-beast haunting her.

Caerani nodded reassuringly. "Usually takes him about a week to shake it off when he gets like this." Her eyes were sad. She gave a mighty sigh, the ghost of a smile on her lips. "The villagers have almost finished gathering at the falls. Are you ready?"

Mara wasn't, but the longer she waited the more anxious she became. She nodded slowly, getting to her feet, and trying to ignore how quickly her heart flew in her chest.

MARA HAD ONLY EVER HAD to speak publicly once before, and it had not gone well. Grathiel had made her prepare a speech for his birthday toast, had written exactly what she was supposed to say down on a piece of paper. But it had been stolen from her pocket by one of the teenaged lords, laughing and mocking as he ran off through the castle with it.

She had tried to make up a toast on the spot but ended up sweating and stuttering before the entirety of the court. Grathiel had made light of it, laughing mockingly at her as the rest of the dining hall had joined in. She still had nightmares about it and standing now at the base of the Crystal Falls, she felt like she was twelve years old and trembling again.

The villagers had all arrived in the basin, their voices

A PROPHECY OF UNDONE

creating a loud buzz across the lake side. Mara leaned against the stairwell in the rockface, arms folded, and brow furrowed as she ran through what needed to be said in her head.

Caerani was standing beside her, talking to Kain about the recovery efforts happening in the village. El listened from her other side, looking weary. The two of them were both covered in ash and soot, having spent the entirety of their mornings helping the villagers. Cyfrin and Milios were nowhere to be seen, but Mara had no time to focus on that.

She hadn't realized how little words she knew. Big, lavish words that made for strong speeches. The kind that King's gave before battle. She thought she was well-read, well-learned. But standing here waiting to address all these people...words utterly escaped her.

Mara's heart slammed somewhere high in her throat, her breath speeding up. Panic sent a cold wave through her. Kain and El drew closer to her instinctively, not breaking stride in their conversation as the bond called out to them on her behalf.

Mara's ears were overwhelmed with the sound of the crowd and the waterfall. She was becoming overstimulated, her entire being focusing down to the cascade of ever-increasing noise. There was movement above her and she glanced back at the stairwell.

Cyfrin and Milios were descending from above. They both looked exhausted, equally as dirty as Kain and El. Cyfrin's black, flowing shirt was rolled up to the elbows, his chest exposed to reveal lightning shaped burns against his tan flesh. She glanced away quickly as his gaze travelled to hers.

"Sorry for the hold up." Cyfrin said as they reached the

I.A. TAKERIAN

bottom of the steps. "Milios and I had last minute business to attend to."

Caerani nodded, stepping around Kain and smiling at Mara. "They're ready for you."

Mara's body stiffened, her eyes going wide as she turned to stare at the crowd. The buzzing chatter had reached a fever-pitch, their many bodies shuffling about anxiously. Mara took a deep breath, starting towards a small rock platform that had been wrought in the ground before them.

The crowd grew silent at her approach approached, turning as one to face her. Mara's face burned under their stares, her hands trembling. She stood in the center of the platform, nearly gasping for breath now. She felt woozy. They stared at her expectantly, all of them disheveled and dirty from the past 24 hours.

Mara opened her mouth to speak, but only a small squeak came out. She snapped her mouth closed, cursing herself. The anxiety was throwing her system into a full-on panic, her stomach lurching under the many expectant eyes as words failed her. There was movement from either side of her and she glanced around.

Caerani stood to her left, arms behind her back and standing tall as she stared out across the crowd. Standing beside one another behind her were Kain, El and Milios, all with steely gazes. Cyfrin was standing by her right side, turning to meet her wide eyes. She saw something flash beneath the ice blue surface, felt a strange warmth in her core that soothed the pounding of her heart.

Cyfrin grinned at her, turning to look into the crowd as Mara took another steadying breath. Standing here, looking around at the faces of her people, she was reminded instantly of the memory she had been shown of her mother. Alora had stood in this very spot, flanked in

368

A PROPHECY OF UNDONE

the same way by Caerani and her friends as she addressed the Odelians. And suddenly, Mara felt courage.

"I know we are all frightened," she began, stepping forward slightly on the platform. "And we have every right to be. We were invaded, our village raised to the ground, our beautiful forest set ablaze." She paced from one end of the platform to the other as she spoke.

"We lost people. *Great* people, whose lives were cut short by darkness and madness and corruption. I know we've all barely just met. I know that I have brought these things upon us, and I know that many of you feel hesitation because I was raised by our enemy."

She stopped in the middle of the platform, face set in stone. "Hear me now, and know I speak only truth. My eyes have been shed of the lies that shrouded them. I was taken by Grathiel's dark forces, and I am still learning all there is to know about our people. But I can swear to you on my life that I will give my *all* to protect the Hidden Village and your families, as my parents did before me. We will rebuild our home, and I will work tirelessly to earn your trust and bring the joy back to your hearts."

"Our land is sick. Corrupted by the darkness that leaks from the Dark Gate. We are *all* in danger, every life in Zenafrost. Grathiel's forces showed us just how powerful that darkness is. And I will stop at nothing to close the Gate and save us for good. I have spent twenty-one years in the shadows, believing the lies that were told to me about our people. Please. Allow me the chance to atone."

Mara dropped to her knee, bowing her head low to the crowd. "I vow this to you. Not just as your Queen, but as the daughter of Alora Dawnbringer. As an Odelian, and a child of Zenafrost. I will save us."

There was silence, even the waterfall behind them seeming to grow oddly still. After a long moment, Mara

I.A. TAKERIAN

glanced up through her curtain of black curls. The entire crowd was on their knees, every one of them bowing low to her. She got to her feet slowly, eyes widening as she took them in. Her friends had dropped to their knees around her as well, leaving Mara alone gazing out at her people.

"We vow to stand beside you till the end," Cyfrin spoke from the ground, drawing Mara's attention to the top of his disheveled white hair. "We will aid you in ending this darkness and saving our world. Always."

Mara felt tearful as they all stood, the crowd's eyes glittering like the crystals around them in the afternoon sun.

"*Long live the Dawnbringer!*" Caerani called, raising her fist high into the air.

"*Long live the Dawnbringer!*" the crowd echoed back, cheering, and whooping roars of approval.

Mara beamed at them all. Her heart felt like it was growing to three times its size. This is what home felt like. *This* is what family was. She would give everything to protect it. *No harm will ever come to my lands again.*

CHAPTER 38
A QUEST BEGUN

Mara was back in her room, the sun beginning to set over the edge of her balcony. The orb lights had come back, fluttering around above her and casting dancing, colored streams off the hanging crystals. Mara had stood in the basin of the falls for nearly four hours after her speech, shaking hands and taking notes on who needed help with what. Many had lost their homes, and Mara invited each of them who had to stay in the Grand Halls with her.

She spoke with each grieving family, mourning with them for the losses throughout their beautiful village. She held them as they cried, listened as they screamed. She sat through each burial, sending prayers to the Zenoths and speaking on behalf of those who could not.

El had practically dragged her up the steps of the falls as the sun lowered over the cliffside. She had brought her back to the Grand Halls, acting skittish and barely speaking. When Mara had pressed her about this, she had told her only that they would be dining all together that evening and she needed to clean up.

371

Mara had changed into a loose hanging, dark green lace dress, the light fabric drifting about her body on the breeze. Her curls were clean for the first time in weeks, ringleted and bouncing across her face. Her finger traced absent-mindedly across Adrian's burned handprint, lost in thought. There was a single sharp knock at the door, and El skipped into the room.

She was wearing a tight-fitted, pale orange satin dress. It shined in the sunset, hanging down across the wooden floor in a trail behind her. Her jaw dropped as she looked at Mara.

"You look fantastic," she exclaimed, circling around Mara. "I haven't seen you this clean in months!"

"Hard to keep clean and fight for your life at the same time, oddly enough," Mara said, sticking her tongue out at El.

"Is that so?" she asked sarcastically, looping her arm through Mara's as they stepped into the hall. "You see, I can't relate to that at all. I simply move so fast; I never get dirty!"

"Oh really?" Mara sneered, pinching El's arm. "You've never once been oozed on in battle?"

"Nope! Not even one tiny speck of blood."

"Oh, to be as powerful as you, Eleanora," Mara jeered and they both laughed on their approach to the dining hall.

El pulled them to a stop, putting her back to the door as she faced Mara. Her eyes glinted mischievously, and Mara raised an eyebrow.

"Why are you looking at me like that?" she asked, hesitant.

El smirked. "I just wanted you to know that all of this was Cyfrin's idea," she said with a relish, flipping her short brown hair out of her eyes. "Thought you'd get a real kick

A PROPHECY OF UNDONE

out of that." She turned and pushed the doors wide before Mara could question her.

She gasped. The dining hall had been decorated with hundreds of vines, thick with ivy and white glowing lilies. They hung down about the orb lights, casting soft glowing shadows across the room. The fire was warming the room, a huge feast laid out on the round table.

Her friends were all here. Kain, dressed in beautifully crafted brown leather armor. Milios in flowing robes, the same color as the ivy around them. Caerani, in her black leather pants and a long-sleeved, red corset.

And Cyfrin. *Zenoths be, Cyfrin.* He wore beautiful black leather armor, thinner than his usual set and ornately decorated with scrolling vines. He looked like a portrait, painted painstakingly by the hand of an artist in love. They beamed at her as she entered.

"What...What is this?" Mara asked, breathless and gaping around at it all. There was a sudden sound drifting up across the patio and into the open hall. Mara's breath caught in her throat.

Gentle notes of music, growing louder and more boisterous by the minute, floated past her on the evening air. She could see orb lights gathering across the river, hear the clinking of glass and growing laughter. The villagers were celebrating in the streets, gathering despite the circumstances. Mara felt the familiar sting of tears in her eyes.

Cyfrin bowed his head low, kissing the top of her hand and sending a shockwave of electrical pull through her body. A weight she hadn't known was there lifted suddenly from her chest, allowing her to take a full breath. He glanced up at her through his white bangs, his blue eyes smoldering with a strange look.

"Breathtaking," he said softly, standing up straight and

I.A. TAKERIAN

still grasping her hand. "I'm afraid I have no words magnificent enough for you."

He was pulling her forwards to the fireplace, to where the four of her friends stood smiling. Caerani was holding her great sword aloft. She bowed her head slightly to Mara as she came to stand before her.

"Mara Dawnbringer," she began, but Mara raised her hand to silence her. They all looked surprised, eyes widening.

But Mara raised her chin; Resolute. "That name no longer serves me," she said into the dancing music around them. "Please. Call me by my true name."

Caerani's gaze softened, bowing her head once more to her. "Yvaine Dawnbringer," she started again, holding her arms wide. "You have stood against every Trial, stared down every foe, bested every enemy and then some. You have proved yourself worthy and beyond of serving the Odelian people and protecting that which we hold dear. Kneel."

She motioned to the heath by the crackling fire, and Yvaine took a knee beside it. Caerani raised her sword, tapping each of Yvaine's shoulders. "I bestow upon you our greatest honor. The honor of fighting for what is true and just, the chance to defend the light with all you are. Yvaine Dawnbringer. Savior of the Damned. Daughter of Prophecy. Bringer of the Light. Rise."

Her friends erupted in applause and cheers as she got to her feet, beaming with tears in her eyes.

"Yvaine!" Kain said thoughtfully, rubbing his chin. "EEE-vain….hmm. It'll take some getting used to. Are you sure there's not something else you'd rather be called?"

El threw her elbow into his ribs, glaring. "Your opinion on names is unwanted, *Slash Master*," she sneered at him. Kain looked incredulous as they all burst with laughter.

A PROPHECY OF UNDONE

"Ah, there is one more thing before we sit to eat," Cyfrin said, nodding to Milios as their laughter at Kain died down.

Milios smiled, waving their hands above them. Descending from the ceiling, held aloft by a long tendril of ivy, was a magnificent wreath of flowers. Yvaine hardly recognized some of the brightly glowing petals wrapped throughout it. It dropped down into Cyfrin's hands, the rest of them taking a few steps back as he stood before her.

His eyes were alight, staring wistfully as they took in the entirety of her confused expression. He knelt before her again, head bowed and crown held above him.

Yvaine blinked, stunned. Cyfrin had been the one to take her from the castle, despite her best efforts to prevent it. It had been Cyfrin who protected her at every turn, from the moment she was brought into this world. Always ready to lay his life down to save her, whatever the cost. This warrior. This powerful, beautiful, unstoppable man.

She dropped to her knees in front of him. Cyfrin met her eye with a look of shock. Yvaine flashed a broad smile, feeling a thrill as his face flushed. "You saved me," she breathed. "It is *I* who should bow to *you*."

Cyfrin blinked at her, an odd expression on his face. This close to him, she could feel the electrical circuit rushing through them. Connecting them to each other. Her heart felt ready to burst. Cyfrin's face softened, and he flashed the most dazzling smile Yvaine had ever seen. She could have wept from his radiance. It was something she would never tire of seeing, something she would do anything to see every moment of every day forever.

He raised the wreath, setting it atop her head. Her skin tingled where his hands brushed against. "Your mother's crown was taken during the war," he said, his husky voice making Yvaine's pulse quicken. "So, Milios and I made you a placeholder. Just for the time being, until we can get you a new one made. I hope it's acceptable. Your highness."

He said the last part with such snide humor that Yvaine couldn't help throwing him a wicked grin in response.

"You know, I take it back," she said as they stood. "You *should* bow to me. But only you, Cyfrin."

He let out a heady laugh, echoed by their friends. They all seated themselves at the table. He pushed her chair in behind her, leaning in towards her ear so that only she could hear him say the next words. "You had me on my knees long before you accepted your crown, Dawnbringer."

Yvaine felt like she had been shocked, sitting up straighter in response. Heat throbbed in her core, her cheeks turning red as Cyfrin took his seat beside her.

El filled her goblet with eyebrows raised, giggling softly from her other side.

THE CONVERSATION at dinner centered around one thing: What was the next step?

Grathiel would feel the fury of Yvaine's power, would bow before her and the memory of Adrian. He would pay for what he did to her. What he did to her best friend, and all the people of Zenafrost. But their efforts were better spent focusing on the Dark Gate first, a fact that Mara accepted begrudgingly.

"I've been giving a lot of thought to that," Caerani said, folding her arms neatly in front of her. "I'm going to share something with you lot that I've never shared with anyone before. It's time."

A PROPHECY OF UNDONE

They all stopped moving, staring at her with silent expectation.

"The night before your mother surrendered, she called me to her tent," Caerani began, staring at Yvaine with cloudy eyes. "She knew that her surrender spelled her death, knew that it would barely be enough to grant us time to escape. She entrusted me with you, asked us to bring you back here to the Hidden Village. But what no one else knew is that Alora had a plan. A fail safe, of sorts. She knew of a ritual, one that came from the Zenoths themselves. Legend had it that Zenafrost could absorb magicks from the Zenoths, and from the Fae. It could store it somewhere deep, deep into her depths." The room was deathly quiet, even the music from the village ceasing for a moment in between songs. "Alora planned to give up her powers, to pray to the Zenoths and beg them to keep her magick safe until you were grown. Until you could take it as her own."

Her face was dark, lost in the memory of that last night with her best friend. "I told her it was insane, that the Zenoths had abandoned this place long ago. I begged her to reconsider, that maybe her magick could save *her*. But she refused. It was impossible to talk her out of things once she was set on it. She needed a second for the ritual, someone of blood or as good as. And it was her final request. How could I refuse her?" She paused, her words catching in her throat.

"We sat in that tent and prayed and prayed. We went on for hours like that, when there was this…this feeling. Like a thousand wings beating against your body, and a million whistles in your head. The tent grew bright as the sun, then it stopped. All of it. When the light vanished, so did Alora's powers."

They all stared at Caerani, aghast, as she took a long drink of her wine.

"So...where did they go?" Yvaine asked, on the very edge of her seat.

Caerani shook her head. "I'm not sure. I've searched for it for nearly twenty years, scouring the entire continent. I've yet to find even a hint of where it could be." She leaned forward, gazing at Yvaine over the tips of her fingers. "But if we could find it, if it is waiting somewhere out there...I think it could give you the power you need to shut the Dark Gate for good."

Yvaine felt a thrill run through her. This was it. The answer to her fear of not being strong enough for the journey ahead. She slapped her hand on the tabletop, eyes burning. "We'll help you find it then."

Her companions nodded approvingly. She had a direction once more, a quest to guide her forward towards her destiny.

Caerani swirled her glass, eyes glinting. "I'll be going to the woods tomorrow," she said over the rim of her cup. "To find Drake...and the One Who Sees."

"Why in the great End below would you ever want to do that?" Kain asked, flabbergasted.

Caerani smirked. "Well, Kain. As her name suggests, she does 'see all'. She may have the answer we're looking for."

"But at what price?" Milios asked, raising an eyebrow.

"Better you than me, I suppose," Kain scoffed, granting him a warning look from Caerani as she drank deeply of her cup.

A PROPHECY OF UNDONE

Yvaine stood on the patio after dinner, looking out towards the village across the river. She could see some of the ruined buildings at the water's edge, the blackened streets still dusted in ash and soot. The music had reached a fever pitch, the shadows of dancing villagers stretching towards the bridge. The smell of smoke had faded, replaced by the sea breeze and pines swaying around the Grand Halls. She was leaning over the railing, eyes skyward towards the twinkling stars.

Cyfrin stepped out of the dining room behind her, full of the sound of boisterous drunken voices from her friends. She felt him before she saw him, his woodsy scent flying about her.

He stood beside her at the railing, following her gaze upwards. The tugging circuit of magnetic electricity between them whizzed to life, and Yvaine gasped softly against it.

"You're glowing," he said, his eyes dropping to stare at the side of her face.

"So are you," she replied, motioning towards his pulsing white tattoos.

Cyfrin chuckled. "I don't think I've ever seen you look so alive."

Yvaine flushed, returning his smoldering stare. His eyes darted to her lips for a split second, and she felt hot fluttering in her stomach. "It seems wrong," she said in a quite voice.

"What does?" he asked, confused.

"You're right. I *feel* more alive than I ever have in my entire life. How terrible is that when there is so much death around us?"

Cyfrin gave her a knowing look. "I think that the closer we are to death, the more we appreciate the things that

I.A. TAKERIAN

make us love living." His voice was rough, low, and hypnotic to Yvaine's ears.

She smiled at him, and his eyes darted to her lips once more. "This place is my home," She looked out at the village again with love in her eyes. "I've never felt right, no matter where I was or what I did. But being here with you all...being here with *you*..." She glanced up at him through her lashes. "I'm so happy. And I feel so guilty for that, given everything that's happened. But I really am. I finally feel like I belong."

He breathed a laugh. Yvaine had to fight the urge to reach out and press the sound against her lips. "We're an awfully ragtag bunch for a Queen," he chuckled. "But I suppose you're not a normal Queen, are you?"

He brushed a hand across her cheek, sending electricity through her skin. She shuddered slightly against the warm caress, eyelids drooping. He looked almost lost staring down at her, his eyes searching hers with a strange expression on his face. "My beautiful Dawnbringer. You'll be the ruin of me, you know."

Her lips parted slightly, and hunger flashed through his eyes. He leaned closer, every piece of Yvaine crying out to be kissed by him. There was commotion behind them as Milios, Kain and El stumbled out onto the patio. Cyfrin's hand dropped from her face, and Yvaine frowned slightly.

But instead of pulling away completely, he slid his hand down to grasp hers, placing them both atop the railing as their drunken friends slammed into them. Kain was hiccupping, mocking Milios as they spoke in heated words about the difference between a longsword and great sword. El was giggling, wrapping her arms around Yvaine's neck, and draping partially from her. Yvaine laughed, wrapping an arm around her waist to steady her.

"Still want to belong to this?" Cyfrin asked as Kain

380

A PROPHECY OF UNDONE

licked the side of his cheek. Cyfrin grimaced, smacking him across the face. Kain simply boomed with laughter, slapping him back.

"There's not a place in the world I'd rather be," Yvaine laughed, watching Milios disentangle Kain from Cyfrin.

"It'll be nothing but doom and gloom from here on out," Kain pouted, slouching to the ground with his back against the railing.

"But at least it'll be an adventure," Yvaine said, letting the weight of the world drop away for a moment.

It was just the five of them, together against the evil ahead. And even against the forces of darkness gathering their corruption at the Dark Gate, even as Grathiel plotted in his white castle in Delinval, Yvaine liked their odds.

Fin

Join our intrepid band of heroes in the third book of the series,
Bornbane: The Tower of Wrought Time

BONUS CHAPTER

ADRIAN

A thousand times I had thought of her face since last I saw it. I thought I had memorized each detail down to the individual freckles on her cheeks. But not even the most vivid of memories could have done her justice. I had been living in darkness, *agonizing* darkness since she had been stolen from me. And here she was, a beautiful beacon amidst the battle. She was like the sun, bright and glowing. Like a dream.

"Mara?" I couldn't remember the last time I spoke. It hurt to say the words. My throat stung with the effort, but I didn't care. She was here. She was *alive*. "I...we thought... are you hurt?" There were cuts all over her perfect face. She was spattered in blood. My eyes rushed across her, looking for signs of it being her own.

Mara was crying. How was it possible for someone to look so beautiful and so anguished all at once? "Adrian, please," she pleaded. Her voice was like home. "These

BONUS CHAPTER

people are not our enemies! Please you must *listen* to me, Adrian!"

Her hands were suddenly on my face, and the world melted away. She was so warm. Like a nice hearth after a day of combat training. I wanted to grab her, hold her, kiss her. I *needed* her to survive. I had only just realized how gray the world had been without her. But now, everything was filled with cosmic life. Zenoths bless, she was radiant. She was talking hurriedly, but I could barely hear her words. Mara. My Mara, I have found you at last. I have come to save you, and...and....

And I was catching some of her words now. She wasn't commending me on saving her. No. No, she was begging me to *stay*. She was pleading with me to call off the attack and spare the Dreads the fate they so deserved. The fate they should have been wrought twenty years ago. I studied her harder, looking for signs of an enchantment or curse. But instead, my eyes fell upon her ears. Two perfectly pointed ears, jutting from the sides of her head like a fucking Dread monster.

I wanted nothing more than to chop them from her body like the mutations they were. "Your uncle was right." I will burn this entire forest to the ground for what they've done. I will kill every last one of them. None will be spared. "They've enchanted you. Ensnared you. **Bewitched you**." I didn't think it was possible to hate this much. To despise something so deeply that it could infect even my love for Mara.

I had to get her out of here. Had to return her to Delinval. They'd be able to make her normal, ears and sanity and all. I could feel her trying to pull away from me, the enchantment on her clearly too deep to fight. I redoubled my grip. Not even magick would be enough to steal Mara from me this time. I had found her. I had saved her. I

BONUS CHAPTER

heard a noise like a bear behind me, and something hit me in the back. It knocked the wind out of me, sending a ringing through my ears and dislodging the grip on my Mara.

And there he was. The beast who had haunted my every waking moment for months. His smirk, taunting me as he launched out the window of Mara's bedroom…It had served as my catalyst when all hope seemed lost. The thought of slicing his head clean from his body was enough to drive me through even the worst of times. He was holding Mara. *Touching* her skin as if it was *his*. Death would be too easy for him. I'd keep him in the smallest cage in Delinval's dungeon, and each day carve a little piece of flesh from the bone to feed to Mara. She'd eat it gladly, once her enchantment had worn off. Once he no longer had hold of her.

I could feel my new-found magick inside of me, welling in my chest and begging to be set free. It felt so good to release it. Almost orgasmic. I aimed true at the Dread, and a black spear flew towards him. He didn't even have the honor to turn and face me. A bolt of lighting shot from his backwards extended hand, knocking into my magick and creating an explosion.

"*Go!*" the man yelled at Mara, finally turning. I couldn't wait to rip that skin off his face, to hear him scream for a mercy that I would never grant. Mara obeyed like the perfect pawn, fleeing into the smoke behind him. No matter. I'd punish him for starting this horror to begin with. Then I'd burn down the whole damn world if I had to, leaving her no where left to hide when this was all over.

I concentrated my magick into my chest again. "You will give her to me! She is *mine!*" Our magick collided in the air. How dare he stand there like some sort of protector. Like *he* was shielding Mara from *me*. How dare he lay

BONUS CHAPTER

his filthy hands on her? She was unsullied before him. She was *pure* and *dazzling*. The King promised her to me, and though I know my Mara and know she will protest at first...She will come around to it in the end. We were meant to be. I had always known it. Always.

"She is no one's but her own," the man growled. "I will not let her be taken again."

Taken? **Taken?!** I threw yet another blind attack of magick at him. He had no idea the heartache of having her missing. He had no idea what I had done, who I had *killed* on my way here to her. My pain was all-mighty, but it was *nothing* compared to what I would bring upon him and his fellow monsters.

He was covered in lighting, and the clouds above us had whipped up into a storm. This Dread's magick must control the weather. So I will cut off all access he has to the skies. I was still working out how to use this borrowed magick of mine. Sometimes, I felt like the rider on the back of a horse with the power of a thousand. It led me, dragged me to what I needed to do. I asked it to block the Beyonds from the Dread. And my prayers were answered.

My magick swirled around us, creating a dome of darkness that blocked all light. I raised my sword, concentrating my magick onto the blade. "You took her from me," I said. But my voice sounded odd. "You stole her from her room in the night like a *coward*." I launched at him, begging my blade for his blood.

Even in this moment, I had to admit: The Dread was a formidable opponent. He leapt out of the way of my attack with near ease, glaring at me as he came to a halt a few yards away. No wonder Mara hadn't been able to overcome them. If he was any indication of what the rest of them were like, this might actually be a worthy challenge. And what a great story it would be to tell back in Delinval

BONUS CHAPTER

years from now. They'd tell tale of the mighty Adrian, legend and savior of the crown.

"I saved her from the corruption that now eats you!" The Dread growled through his teeth at me. "She was imprisoned there by the man you call *King*!"

I'd cut out his tongue for that one. My magick slammed into him, knocking him backwards as I advanced. "Liar! You came exactly when you knew there would be little resistance. Bested the weakest of our soldiers, mere palace guards. You took Mara, and I didn't even stand a chance of protecting her. **You took my Mara.**" *My* Mara. My princess, my little warrior, my future wife and Queen. He had stolen her from me. He had tried to rip away our future right before it began.

Another attack made connection with his chest, forcing him back further. But he was looking at me in the strangest way. Not in anger, or with the smirk he had thrown my way that night in Delinval. No, this was…This was *pity*. Sad, understanding, pity. It made me want to be sick. Stop looking at me like that. *Why are you looking at me like that?!*

"Adrian." This stopped me cold. He knew my name. Mara told him my name. Or, more likely, they tortured it out of her upon arrival. But he was pulling back his lighting, disengaging from me with hands held up in submission. How strange.

"Please. For Mara's sake, please listen to me." Hearing Mara's name on his lips made me want to rip his throat out and drain him of every ounce of blood in his body. **Kill him. Kill him. *KILL HIM*.** The voice inside my head was so loud, so demanding. It took every ounce of my control not to fire off at him again. Something in my heart was stirring. Like slowly waking from a very long midday nap.

BONUS CHAPTER

The Dread was studying my face with a burning intensity that made me feel like he could see my soul. "There was no other way than to take Mara from the castle in Delinval. The history you've been taught is a lie. Your king began the Great War, stole our princess from us at the end of it all. He brought her to the castle and raised her under his wing, for reasons that are entirely his own."

Our princess. I could hear my pulse pounding in my ears. My hand twitched on my blade. **He thinks Mara is his. He is claiming what is ours, what has always been ours. Kill him. Rip him apart. Gut him while his village watches. Burn him alive-**

Something about his eyes. It was so familiar. Why was it so familiar?

The Dreads must all die. It is the only way to keep her safe. The only way to protect Mara. The only way to protect-

Was it the color? No, I'd never seen a shade of blue quite so white before. The shape? The look? There was nothing but truth in his eyes. I prided myself on reading people. On knowing when they were being honest.

Kill him. Kill him. Kill him. My head was throbbing. The noise within was deafening.

"For twenty years, we thought her dead," the Dread continued. "And when we found out otherwise, there were very few options as to how to proceed. But she was a prisoner under Grathiel's thumb, and she needed to be rescued."

He lies. He serves the Deceiver. He is a Dread. Kill him. Kill him. Kill him.

"You're lying," I said. I hadn't really intended to. It felt like the magick was taking the reins again, leading me. Guiding me. *Controlling me.* I hated the feeling.

"You know I'm not," he replied softly. "I know you can

BONUS CHAPTER

feel the magick coming off her, Adrian. Just as I know it is love that has driven you so blindly to this madness. Please, let us show you. Let us *help* you." He extended a hand towards me.

My heart felt oddly distant. Love. Yes, that was what had brought me here. Not my hatred for the Dreads. My love for Mara. What had spurned me to set the village ablaze before finding her? All I wanted was to find her. To know she was safe, and alive-

He is trying to trick you. He manipulates your heart. He sees your weakness for the princess. You must not lose her to him again. You must kill him. Kill him. *KILL HIM. KILL HIM. KILL HIM. KILL-*

"Then you have corrupted her!" I screamed at the man, raising my sword high again. How could I have ever let my guard falter to him? "I will rend the sickness from her body. I will burn away your hold on her, flay every piece you have touched from her figure, and she will be pure once more."

What was I saying? I could never hurt Mara. Never. I loved her no matter what. Even if she was forever enchanted, I would love her just the same. All I wanted, all I ever wanted, was to be by her side-

NO.

The Dread was bleeding. His magick was no match for mine, sparking feebly at his fingers like sparklers at a faire. This was it. The moment I had thought of for months was finally here. I was finally going to get revenge for all the lives lost in the Great War, for the time they stole from Mara and I, for whatever they did to my love while she was trapped here with them.

So then why did I feel so hollow?

Someone was rushing towards the Dread from the

BONUS CHAPTER

darkness beyond. No. No, anyone but you. Mara was running for him, looking at him....looking at him the way I look at her. I had never felt pain like I felt in seeing that. I couldn't stop the magick that shot from me. I could only stare on in horror as it rocketed towards the pair of them. The Dread raised his hand, and I was suddenly blinded.

There was shrieking in my head, a million voices screaming in tandem. I was thrown backwards through the air, the Dread's magick shredding through me as it went. It was so bright, I couldn't see. I couldn't hear above the screams. Zenoths please, make it stop, *make it stop.* I wasn't sure how I was still on my feet. It felt like I was being torn apart. Like something was clawing for freedom from within me. I was bleeding, pulling my hands from my face to see how much.

My palms were covered in black, sticky ooze. It was coming from inside of me, seeping from my wounds. *"I saved her from the corruption that now eats you!"* The Dread's words whispered through the haze of earsplitting screams. I was...corrupted? No...No, that can't be. That can't be right. And yet...

The Dread was running at me, golden lightning cracking from him like a whip as he attacked. But this time, I did not heed my magicks cry to defend myself. He struck me in the chest, crashing through my armor like it wasn't there at all. I staggered, dropping to the ground. The screams were so loud now, I felt my head might split.

The voices I had been hearing, the ones I thought were my own anger taking shape...It had been dark magick all along. And I think something, somewhere in me had known it since the very first moment. I had shoved that instinct, that *light*, down into my depths. And I would do it all again, if I thought it would have saved Mara. I turned to where she lay, unmoving. She had looked so scared,

BONUS CHAPTER

begging me to listen to her. And I could see now that it wasn't fear of the Dreads that made her look so. It had been fear of *me*. Fear that I may not love her, if I knew the truth.

But oh, my Mara. I would love you, even if you were the Deceiver himself. I would love you to the End of All. To the Beyonds and far past eternity. I would have stood at your side and fought anything that came against you. But this is a battle I fear I cannot conquer.

The Dread was descending upon me, golden magick raised in a final attack. I knew the look in his eyes well. He would die to protect Mara, just as I would. She would need someone to take my place. To be her shield against the darkness I had become lost in.

I reached for the Dread, feeling the magick inside of me fighting to retake control. "Do it." I was crying. I couldn't recall the last time I cried. "I cannot hold on any longer. I cannot fight it. Please. Please, while she's not awake to see. You have to do it." She'd never forget it, if she watched the life leave me. I'd already caused her so much anguish, seeing me this way. I couldn't bear the thought of causing any more. Even if all I wanted in the world at this moment was to look into her eyes. Just one last time.

The Dread's pale eyes were glistening. And I understood now. This was not just the love a subject had for his Queen, or the love a Knight has for his duty. No. This was everlasting. If I knew nothing else of this man, that would be enough. He knelt beside me, taking my hand. Warmth began to spread through me. Like being right next to a fire after a month of snow. There was a strange halo of gold brimming on the edge of my vision. It reminded me of the sun.

"There is no greater honor than laying down your life

BONUS CHAPTER

to protect those you love," the Dread said in a gentle voice. "You are truly as legendary a warrior as Mara told us."

My heart swelled with pride. They had spoken of me. That was why he knew my name. Because my Mara had told him of our adventures together. It felt like I was going to be suddenly, violently ill. I opened my mouth wide, and shadows billowed from within me. The sunlight in my veins chased all the darkness from every recess of my soul. I felt empty. Hollow. But the sunlight was filling me, replacing the evil with unending radiance.

I stared up at the Dread, and it suddenly hit me. The reason his eyes looked so familiar. There was a glimmer in their depths, a sparkle that I had only ever seen once before. In the eyes of my love. I sighed, gripping his hands as hard as I could. I felt like I was slipping away, the dawnlit magick inside gently ushering me on.

"Keep...our princess...safe..." I felt like I was speaking underwater, the liquid pooling in my mouth and choking me a little.

The Dread nodded, squeezing my hand reassuringly. It felt safe. Warm. "With all I am. Forever."

That's all I could ask for. That she be safe, always. That she be loved, the way she deserves, for eternity. The sounds around me were dimming, the Dread's thumb stroking slowly across the back of my hand. I was dying. I could feel it. But I wasn't afraid. I had a sudden memory of laying beside Mara in the grass outside the castle, staring up at clouds as gray as these. She was humming a tune that the court jester often frequented. A song about a lark and very silly hat. It felt like I was living it again. Like I was laying there with her right now.

"Do you ever think about it?" Mara said, rolling to prop herself on an elbow and stare down at me.

"Hmm, about how very difficult you can be?" I

BONUS CHAPTER

smirked at her. "Yes, actually, I think about it every moment, of every single day-"

She smacked my chest, winding me. "No, you prat. *Death*. The great *END OF ALL* and whatnot." She waved her hands dramatically. "If Lady Len and the ancient texts are to be believed, then there's a whole new world out there for us. Just waiting in the Beyonds."

"Oh? So confident you are that you won't wind up in the End of All Things then?" I laughed, watching her incredulous look.

"Zenoths fucking blood, Adrian. You are a spitfire today." She grimaced, rolling onto her back and staring up at the gathering clouds.

I sighed, turning to stare at the side of her face. She was so, so beautiful. "I think that it's silly to fear the inevitable."

"Well, I think it's perfectly healthy to be worried about the unknown." She turned to smile at me. I would have done anything to see her smile like that, for always. "But I suppose you're right. I've nothing to fear as long as you're waiting there for me." She crinkled her nose, a playful expression on her perfect face. "Guess that means I'll *have* to make sure I get into the End of All Things though, doesn't it? Seeing as that's *absolutely* where *you're* going…"

I launched at her with a mock roar of indignation, wrestling as we rolled through the grass. Her laughter was music in my head. The world was radiating with golden light, the images blurring. I was rising, but something was slowing me to a stop. The golden light waivered, the sound of Mara's laughter vanishing all together. I was thrown into darkness, cold and forever. Alone.

"Oh, I think not, my son. Destiny calls. And there is much work yet to be done."

CPSIA information can be obtained
at www.ICGtesting.com
Printed in the USA
LVHW091739150723
752491LV00036B/597